Rosie

Ted York

Matador
5 Weir Road
Kibworth Beauchamp
Leicester LE8 0LQ, UK
Tel: (+44) 116 279 2299
Fax: (+44) 116 279 2277
Email: books@troubador.co.uk
Web: www.troubador.co.uk/matador

This book is a work of fiction and, except in the case of historical fact,
any resemblance to actual persons, living or dead, is purely coincidental.

ISBN 978 1848 764 460

British Library Cataloguing in Publication Data.
A catalogue record for this book is available from the British Library.

Typeset in 10.5pt Palatino by Troubador Publishing Ltd, Leicester, UK

Matador is an imprint of Troubador Publishing Ltd

Printed in Great Britain by the MPG Books Group, Bodmin and King's Lynn

A massive thank you to June, Marie, James and Darren for their support.

"The web of our life is of a mingled yarn good and ill together"

William Shakespeare

Contents

Prelude

Cynthia (Rosie) Holder is Born 1877

It was a wet blustery October night, the wind blowing heavy rain, but Jack was in particularly good spirits. Initially he had been disappointed that the baby had not been a boy - the Holders had been working in the docks for over one hundred years and a boy would have continued the tradition - but as soon as he held the tiny figure and looked at her face, he fell in love.

As he walked through the mass of drinkers crowded into The Grapes, his local, the rowdy crowd burst into cries of congratulations. He made his way to the bar amidst much back patting; virtually all of the men and women in there knew Jack.

A dockers pub, it was like a second home, despite the dingy décor and smoky atmosphere. 'Fat Nelly' – one of a smattering of prostitutes by the bar – waved and stood up to embrace him in a bear-hug.

"How's our Molly?" she asked. Fat Nelly was in fact Jack's sister in law and had been forced to turn to the oldest trade after her husband had died in an accident on the docks five years before.

Jack looked at her, a surprised expression on his face.

"She seems to be doing well," he muttered, feeling embarrassed. It hadn't really occurred to him that she might not be, despite the high mortality rate of mothers at childbirth. Fat Nelly shook her head indulgently as Jack escaped to the bar, taking refuge with his mates who were already there swilling back pints of dark beer.

"Here he is lads, the proud father," said a burly docker, handing him a glass. "Here's to your daughter, Jack."

Word of the birth had reached the pub ahead of him courtesy of his brother Nelson, somewhat amusingly named in honour of the famous admiral.

"Well, I suppose Nelson's given you all the details?" grinned Jack, taking a gulp of the warm beer.

"What you gonna call her then?" asked Nelly. He had already been presented with several names by his wife, none of which he really felt comfortable with. But he loved her and would do anything for her.

"Er, Molly wants to call her Cynthia Rose," he muttered.

"Oh my gawd," a rather drunk man leaning against the bar waved his glass in the air in Jack's direction. "My, aren't we getting all la di da." Nelly clipped him around the ear.

"That's enough of that Jim Blighty. My Molly can call her baby anything she likes and don't you go and forget it."

And so it was Cynthia Rose Holder, known as Rosie by her dad and most of his friends, was introduced to the world and christened at the 'Grapes' in Bow, East London.

Back at their house, Jack's wife lay in bed with her new bundle wrapped tightly in her arms.

"Okay ducks, time to feed the 'ol man'." Dolly the 'midwife' came bustling into the room. A portly woman, she had ten children of her own and was considered the expert in the area, the first person to call when a baby was on the way.

"Don't forget to keep introducing her to the nipple and ask Jack to come and see me if you have any problems." Molly was absorbed with her baby and hardly noticed Dolly leaving. Gazing down into her daughter's blue eyes she talked quietly to her.

"What will life hold for you, my love?" she whispered, stroking her soft cheek.

Molly herself was quite a well known dancer at 'The Britannia', the music hall in Shoreditch. Occasionally acting in small parts, she needed the few extra shillings the work brought in and knew that next week she would have to return to dancing to feed her new daughter. Jack was a docker and work was dependant on the big schooners arriving at the East London Docks. It was irregular work, which he supplemented by labouring in the warehouses. Even so money was always tight. Molly glanced at the clock on the wall, conscious that her few hours rest were over and she needed to begin preparing the carrots and potatoes for their evening meal. With a small sigh, she set her baby down. Her musings were cast aside as she started work on the demands of the present, all thoughts of the future pushed to the back of her mind.

Chapter One

Rosie

As Cynthia – 'Rosie' to everyone, even to her mother – grew up she entered a world of poverty, sickness and often sadness. Her Aunt Nelly who had been so good to her had recently died of what she heard her father describe as a mixture of booze and the pox, which she did not understand. Her cousins, Nelly's four children, were virtually street urchins and the youngest three were taken to the workhouse – it was their only chance. The oldest, a boy of thirteen, was taken by Jack to the docks and managed to earn a meagre living running errands and general labouring.

In contrast to life on the docks, her trips with her mother to the Britannia were full of colour and excitement. With the surroundings of the theatre almost as familiar as her home, it was no surprise that Rosie made up her mind from an early age that she was going to follow Molly onto the stage. By the age of five, she had begun to appear as a child actor and support singer.

It was at this point that she also started receiving private tuition, along with her brothers and sister. Rosie wasn't old enough to realise that this was unusual and didn't think to wonder how her family could afford to pay for it. Despite her steadfast ambition to work in the theatre, Rosie studied everything Mr Trumphet, her tutor, threw at her, including English, Mathematics, History, French and Latin. She was an intelligent girl who read avidly, unlike her brothers who were not really interested in studying, although they did learn to read and write. It wasn't long before they were fed up with the lessons, though, and asked their father if they could work instead. While Freddie got a job at the docks with Jack, and Billy helped a street trader selling fish, Rosie and her sister, Alice, carried on with their tuition. Alice had already decided that she wanted to be a nurse, inspired by stories of Florence Nightingale, and the two sisters proved themselves to be good pupils.

Alongside their studies, they also enjoyed deportment lessons, conducted by the grey-haired Miss Emily Simmons, a retired school teacher whose remit was to teach them the rules of etiquette and how young ladies should behave. A somewhat serious lady, Miss Simmons was not amused by what she termed 'high jinks' in the classroom. On one occasion, the girls were attempting to balance books on their head, giggling uncontrollably and making faces at each other. Miss Simmons watched them exasperated and when the books fell off their heads simultaneously, causing them to laugh until they cried, she pursed her lips and with a grim expression headed to see their mother. She gave an ultimatum: either the girls took the lessons seriously or she would not continue the tuition. Despite their pranks, Rosie wanted to carry on with the lessons and she persuaded her sister that they should behave.

Their education continued with lessons on how young ladies behave in public, which included dressing for the occasion. Here again Rosie and her sister were lucky as their mother knew a girl called Gwen, who was the senior seamstress at a dressmaker in Cheapside. The girls were often given nearly new dresses which had been rejected by some rich woman who had ordered the latest fashion for her daughter.

So, they progressed with etiquette, deportment, how to dress 'properly' as Miss Simmons put it and, for Rosie, most importantly she had a steady stream of books. She read most of Charles Dickens' works and particularly liked David Copperfield, romantically imagining the subject of the book wooing her. Whilst she found some of William Shakespeare's plays interesting and even funny, she found others much too serious. When Miss Simmons insisted they studied Henry the Fifth she expected to hate every minute but was pleasantly surprised. Robert Louis Stevenson, Thomas Hardy, George Eliot, she enjoyed them all and was astonished to find out that George Eliot was a woman. Poetry was another matter. Mr Trumphet absolutely adored poetry and spent an hour each day reciting Keats or Shelley – or, worse still, acting out Chaucer's plays. Rosie was quite the romantic and liked some poetry but Alice just could not get on with it and fidgeted or coughed or tapped her pencil throughout the lesson. Mr Trumphet seemed oblivious and it was often Rosie who caught her sister's hand to stop her banging a hole in their old desks.

Mr Trumphet's house was a treasure trove for Rosie. Situated on the Mile End Road, Bethnal Green, it was a simple terraced house but once you got inside it was a veritable Aladdin's Cave. Mr Trumphet had taught at a public school in Brighton and also for a while in India working for the East India Company teaching the children of Company employees. Alice had heard her mother and father talking one night about his unfortunate liking for the demon drink and, whilst she didn't entirely know what they meant, when she repeated the conversation to her sister, Rosie explained. However, he behaved impeccably in front of the sisters and when her mother asked them 'how he was' they always gave him glowing reports.

Mr Trumphet had never married and his life was teaching. Watching these two young girls soak up knowledge was a good replacement for the alcohol that had nearly ruined him. He had got sent home by the East India Company after he had turned up at lessons completely drunk and not for the first time. With only a small pension from his previous school he had happily applied when he saw a position advertised in 'The Times':

"Tutor required for children from a poor background £10 per week."

He was interviewed by a gentleman at a club in Pall Mall. The gentleman explained he would be paying for the tuition, told him about the four children and swore him to secrecy. He was not under any circumstances to discuss his appointment with the children or their parents. If they were curious simply explain that they had been chosen by a philanthropic gentleman for free lessons. He knew the girls also went to see Miss Simmons, a lady he was not acquainted with, and when his curiosity got the better of him and he asked Rosie where she lived he went calling on her. Miss Simmons was not entirely pleased to see him, but when he explained how his appointment had come about she realised the same gentleman had interviewed them both. They didn't have the faintest idea who he was but why look a gift horse in the mouth, which was how Miss Simmons described their good fortune.

Life was preferential for the Holders' four children and this led to problems. Their cousins called them names and both brothers were often in fist fights with local boys who called them 'nobs', whatever that meant. During all this time Rosie, occasionally accompanied by Alice, went with her mother whenever possible to the Britannia theatre. When she got the chance she appeared on the stage singing with other children and despite the impressive education she was receiving what she actually wanted to do was perform on the stage. Molly, her mother, acutely aware of her daughter's ambition, didn't discourage her interest but insisted her lessons came first.

Miss Simmons wasn't acquainted with Rosie's brothers, although occasionally the older boy, Freddie, met the girls to walk them home. It was the early 1890s and a fearsome man they called Jack the Ripper was murdering girls rumoured to be prostitutes in the Whitechapel area and no woman felt safe. Miss Simmons insisted that they always wait for their mother, father or brother to accompany them home and then promptly locked her door for the night.

It was on such a day when Rosie had expected to be going with her mother to a new review at the Shoreditch Britannia that her brother did not turn up to meet the sisters, as arranged.

Alice and Rosie waited with Miss Simmons for over an hour, but when it began to get dark Rosie told Miss Simmons firmly they had to go. Miss Simmons was not as quick as the girls and they were gone out of the door before she could stop them.

"Oh dear, oh dear," she muttered to herself as she got her coat on to follow.

"Come on Alice, keep up," said Rosie, almost pulling her sister along.

"I can't walk any quicker" replied Alice moaning loudly. It was dark now and Rosie was starting for the first time to think should they go across the common or go the long way around? Stupidly she chose the common, her good sense overcome by her need to get home before her mother left for the theatre.

They held hands tightly, but as the moon came up they saw a shadow. Walking very fast they carried on. Rosie could hear a noise behind them, was someone following them? The girls quickened their step but the common was pitch black and it was only the lights in the distance that enabled them to head toward the road across the wet grass.

Miss Simmons had hurried as fast as her 62 year old frame would allow but lost them going into the dark common. She was very reluctant to follow and was pondering what to do next when a carriage pulled up alongside her.

"Miss Simmons," a voice called from the carriage. She walked towards it cautiously and was surprised to see the gentleman who had appointed her.

"Where are the two girls?" he asked. She explained how they had left before anyone had arrived and she was trying to catch them but had seen them go across the common.

"James," shouted the gentleman. "Run after those girls and discreetly follow making sure they get home." The footman on the back of the coach leapt down and ran at speed toward the common.

Rosie was very frightened as she was convinced now that she could hear someone running behind them.

"Come on Alice, let's run!" The girls reached the edge of the Old Bow Common and turned down their road. Banging frantically on the front door their young brother Billy opened the door and they bolted inside.

"Where's mother?" Alice cried.

"There's been some sort of accident down at the docks, Freddie and mum have gone down there to see if father is okay," replied Billy, looking at his sisters in confusion as they stood panting in the hall.

That explained a great deal but it meant no music hall tonight, Rosie thought as she caught her breath, her scare forgotten in her disappointment.

Meanwhile, James, the Footman, had seen the girls go into a dingy terraced house and reported back to a rather anxious Miss Simmons and his employer. Miss Simmons was given a lift back by the gentleman but before she got out he sternly told her that under no circumstances in future was she ever to let the children leave her house without an escort. She apologised profusely and considerably shaken up, went inside to take a small sherry, her nerves in pieces.

Molly approached the dock gates rather pensively; an accident at the docks meant one or more could be dead or seriously injured. The loads sometimes shifted or ropes broke and if there was anyone underneath it was often fatal. 'Old Dockside' was on the gate when she arrived. They called him that as no one knew his real name and, whilst he was often worse for a drop of gin, he did his job.

"It's alright Miss Molly," he said as she made her way towards him. "The dead man is one of the blacks, Solomon." Sometimes the employers took on the occasional black man; they were enormously strong and were cheap to hire. They usually came up from Bristol Docks seeking work. Some were grandsons of slaves brought to England many years ago and always seemed to Molly to be very shy. She hurried through the gate and quickly found Jack, hugging him tightly even though he tried to hold her away.

"Molly you should take the boy back home, I have some clearing up to do. Solomon was crushed under bales of cotton, the doctor's down there now," he said soberly.

Arriving home late, Jack heard about Alice and Rosie coming home on their own and was very angry.

"Don't you girls know there is a madman at large?" he shouted.

Rosie knew it was useless to answer back and lowering her head, just nodded. They were sent to bed; there was no going to the theatre tonight declared Molly.

Jack watched them wearily as they left the room. Up at 5am he worked a long day, but as foreman at the dock and a union representative he took his position seriously.

He explained to Molly that Solomon had been living with a black girl called Mary. They had two children and he had to go that night, to pay them a call and explain what had happened to poor Solomon. Molly squeezed his hand in wordless sympathy, for she knew that this would be a difficult job for her husband.

A short while later, Jack knocked quietly on the door of the address he had been given. The house in Wapping was in a particularly run down area and eventually he had to bang quite loudly to attract attention. A Negro came to the door.

"What you want?"

"I have come to see Mary. I am the foreman at the docks, Jack."

"Wait and I will get her," the man shut the door, not inviting Jack inside.

After a moment, the door opened again and a petite Negro woman stood there. Jack realised that she had been crying and must already know Solomon was dead. There were no benefits for the widow of a man killed working on the docks in those days and all he could do was give her the ten shillings he had collected from the men that afternoon. Not much for a man's life, he thought bitterly as he made his way back home to his family.

"Now, today you stay with Miss Simmons, who will bring you home if your brother doesn't call to collect you," Molly said, fixing Rosie and Alice with a stern gaze. They nodded solemnly back at her and she hurried them out of the front door to meet Miss Simmons. Arriving at their teacher's house, Molly sent them in with one final warning to be on their best behaviour. She watched them head inside and then turned to Miss Simmons to inform her of the new system: if someone didn't call to collect the girls; she was to accompany them back home.

"Well girls, how do you feel after yesterday's drama?" Miss Simmons shook her finger at the sisters. "You were most unwise to leave on your own and I cannot allow you to ever do so again." She looked at them seriously for a couple of seconds before allowing a small smile.

"Now, today we are going by cabbie to St Paul's Cathedral and then to a fashionable coffee shop at the Ritz Hotel." Rosie and Anne looked at each other and began talking excitedly about the day trip. This was a great treat for the girls and it was fun listening to the cabbie who chatted non-stop during the forty minute journey to St Paul's.

As they pulled up outside their destination, Miss Simmons instructed him to wait outside for them and led the sisters into the building for their first ever visit. Rosie stood at the door awestruck, gazing in wonder at her surroundings. Miss Simmons prodded her gently and they walked further into the interior, Miss Simmons keeping up a dialogue explaining who was buried in the Cathedral, whisking them around the edges to show the plaques and tombs where many of England's historical figures were buried.

"Make notes now girls as Mr Trumphet wants to discuss all the famous people buried here as part of the next history lesson," Miss Simmons said looking at the sisters. They nodded in unison and scribbled away, Rosie pausing every now and again to look up at the magnificent dome, arching above their heads.

After visiting St Paul's they went on to the coffee house at the Ritz Hotel. Tea was a very formal affair at the Ritz and the girls had been warned by Miss Simmons to be on their best behaviour. They had entered rather nervously but were soon enjoying the experience and the tea was going well until Alice dropped her plate on the floor. Blushing furiously, she proceeded to tread on the two cucumber sandwiches that had been on her plate. While the tea had ended somewhat embarrassingly, Miss Simmons congratulated the girls as they headed to Mr Trumphet's house for afternoon lessons. Their first introduction "to Society" as Miss Simmons put it had been a success.

That summer went quickly, with glorious weather occasionally punctuated by showers. Molly had become increasingly concerned about her sister's children, who were in the workhouse on the Bethnal Green Road. The gloomy building was a terrible place according to Nancy, her neighbour, so Molly decided to make an unannounced visit to see how the children were for herself.

Walking into the workhouse was a shock she would never forget. A large and dusty old building, it was crawling with humanity. As she made her way towards the door, an unkempt looking man came towards her.

"Yes, madam," he said, looking her up and down, "what do you want here?"

"I have come to see my sister's children," replied Molly. He stared at her for a second and then reluctantly led her towards the office.

"What are their names then?" he grunted. Molly obliged him with the details and he went off to find the children. After a long wait, Steffie, Alfred and Sammy shuffled into the room. Molly looked at them silently, shocked to see their thin frames and tattered, filthy clothes. Alfred sported bruises on his face, which later she found on his back and arms. Molly had seen enough. "Right, I am taking them out of here," she said decisively, moving towards them.

"Well that's up to you," the unkempt man muttered. "But don't think you can bring 'em back; once you go, you're out for good."

Molly raised her eyebrows at him, as if to imply that that was no bad thing and took them home with her. As soon as they got in the door, she starting heating water to fill the tin bath in the front room so that the children could have a wash, something they clearly hadn't had for a month or more. Molly had made them undress outside in the back garden, collecting their clothes for burning as they were heaving with lice and fleas. The bedding arrangements were a little more complicated as they would have to treble up in three rooms, with one of the boys sleeping downstairs. But they managed and, after Jack's initial shock at finding even more children in the house, he agreed they couldn't have been left at the workhouse. They found old clothes and scrounged others from neighbours and made sure the children were scrubbed until they were pink. "We may not be rich but we are clean," said Molly, as the children stood glowing in front of her.

Rosie had been looking forward to her fifteenth birthday for a long time. Today was the day her father had promised she would be allowed to sing solo at the music hall. She smiled to herself in anticipation as she set the table for dinner; it had felt like such a long time since she had last performed on stage.

By the time Rosie was ten she had been doing the occasional solo when one of the other artists was too drunk to appear on stage or had been beaten by their man. She was a very popular turn. In fact the bawdy audience at the Britannia loved her – the innocence of this beautiful child contrasted with the normal entertainers. Rosie loved going to the music hall and amongst this den of drunks, thieves, prostitutes and rich men looking for a good time she became a much loved part of the evening review, even if only as a stand in.

By the time she was twelve, though, crude catcalls had begun to replace the once innocent atmosphere and her mother noticed more and more of the men admiring her blossoming figure. They were now not so much listening to her beautiful voice as contemplating when they would see more of her developing figure. Finally her dad had put his foot down.

"No more luv," he said firmly, cutting off her protestations. "I can't have my daughter being the eye popper at the Britannia, it won't do. The boys are starting to talk at the docks and I had to give one of them a busted nose just yesterday. Maybe when you're older." Rosie had known it was useless to protest, the best she could do was to make him promise she could go back when she was fifteen if she still wanted to. So that was that, Rosie's budding career on the stage had come to an abrupt halt, although she vowed to herself that she would keep her dad to his promise.

But today was the day she had been waiting for. She was fifteen and allowed to decide for herself – and there was never any doubt what she was going to do.

"I know," said Molly, as her daughter hovered around her. "You want to join the review."

"Can I go today Mum, please?" replied Rosie eagerly.

"No, your dad wants to see you when he comes home." Rosie was impatient but knew better than to argue. Her father was a formidable man and what he wanted he got. She'd waited this long so a few more hours wouldn't make a difference.

Her father returned from work with her brother, absolutely exhausted as usual and a little bit tipsy.

"We couldn't walk past 'the Grapes' without saying hello to the lads," he said to Molly with a wink. After a special meal of meat and potatoes specially prepared by her mother for her birthday, Rosie cleared her throat and faced Jack squarely.

"Dad, you remember you said that I could go on the stage after my fifteenth birthday? Can I go down the Britannia and see the manager?"

Jack paused with his drink half way to his lips. He always knew that it was inevitable that his daughter would want to return to the revue, it was in her blood. He nodded his head reluctantly before gulping down the rest of his drink and the following day Molly and Rosie went to Shoreditch on the horse drawn bus.

It didn't take any persuasion. Stan, the manager at the Britannia, knew his patrons and saw a beautiful buxom girl standing in front of him who he already knew could sing like a nightingale.

"I'll pay you two shillings a week, starting next Monday," he said.

Most of the time Rosie played young men. Dressed up like a man with a stuck on moustache, she looked the part and the punters enjoyed her renditions of the singalong songs. She usually finished with 'A Nightingale Sang in Berkeley Square' which brought the house down. Although she loved being on stage, she couldn't help but be envious of some of the other performers. Elsie Fitzsimmons always had a flood of admirers at the stage door, with gentleman callers queuing to see her. It was even rumoured that the prince had asked to see her privately. A luscious redhead, her risqué songs and the top of her bust tightly popping out of her costume enraptured her audience and always earned her a standing ovation. Sharing a room with the chorus, Rosie knew that her figure and good looks matched any show girl's and yet she was performing as a boy. As she watched Elsie and the cheering audience for what seemed like the hundredth time, Rosie made up her mind: she had to convince Stan to stop giving her boy's parts and let her go on stage as a woman. While the crowd roared their appreciation for Elsie, Rosie set her mind to work devising a risky plan.

Stan didn't always remain backstage and on this particular night he was nowhere to be seen. The chorus girls had made Rosie up and she was dressed in a daring outfit lent to her by one of the girls, which accentuated her breasts. She had never worn such a low cut dress and felt a little uncomfortable in the tight bodice, but as she surveyed herself in the mirror she knew the effect was stunning. The stage hand called over to her: "Come on Rosie, you're on" and she emerged from the room she shared with the dancers looking radiant and feeling absolutely fabulous, a grown woman rather than a child dressed as a man.

The master of ceremonies liked to pontificate and provide a grand introduction for the girls, but that evening he failed miserably as he understated: "For your delectable enjoyment the delightful songbird Rosie."

The crowd fell silent as Rosie's willowy figure appeared from the wings. She walked slowly on stage to a growing cacophony of wolf whistles, with a small smile on her face as she realised the effect she was having. The pianist, momentarily stunned by her appearance, was a little late starting but quickly moved into Rosie's opening number 'Two lovely black eyes'. She had a voice like an angel and the combination of this and her new costume had the audience hooked. When she finished, the hall erupted and flowers flew onto the stage.

Stan had been in the audience at the start of the performance and moved backstage before she finished singing, intending to give her an earful for taking such a liberty. His anger soon evaporated, though, as he heard the reaction from the punters. "Well don't stand here Rosie, get back on, give 'em another," he said, giving her a gentle shove back towards the stage. The audience exploded with catcalls and wolf whistles, and the shrewd band leader broke into 'The Man Who Broke the Bank of Monte Carlo". After that Rosie had 'a turn' every night, much to the delight of the regulars at the Britannia.

The months went by and the pattern of their lives continued. By the time she was seventeen, Rosie was an outstanding success at the Britannia. Molly had been chaperoning her but Jack, her dad, got into several fist fights with amorous drunks trying to get on to the stage and he insisted men were employed to keep the rabble in check. Stan had increased her money to five shillings each week; she gave four shillings to her mother and kept the rest. However, as the takings at London's most popular music hall rose, it was obvious it was Rosie bringing in the 'toffs', who now paid at least five pounds for a box. Molly approached Stan and told him that several West End music halls were sniffing around. He needed little more persuasion to raise Rosie's money to £2 each week.

As she continued to blossom, she became used to the interest of men. They fell over themselves to send her flowers, boxes of chocolates and even poems declaring their undying love. While she loved the attention, on the advice of her mother she didn't let any get close. "Keep the mystery and you will keep the punters," Molly had told her and Rosie remembered the words even as she was swept along in the excitement of being adored. Even Stan was forever trying to touch her and get her on her own for a clinch. Fortunately for Rosie her mother remained close by and the chorus girls, feeling protective, banded together to keep an eye open.

Not all the girls were happy for Rosie's success, however. Dolores, one of the regular singers, had had her act reduced to accommodate Rosie with more songs. Furious, she began to threaten Rosie, persisting in making her life difficult until Molly stepped in and had a quiet word. Dolores left Rosie alone then, but continued giving her dark menacing looks. Rosie wasn't too concerned; her delicate looks belied a certain toughness in her personality that helped her to shrug off such incidents. She loved being on stage and her confidence was growing with every performance.

Rosie glanced impatiently up and down the street. There was no sign of her father, even though it was 10.30pm. She was an eighteen year old woman now, she thought crossly, shifting her weight from one foot to the other, and this chaperoning of her mother, father and brother was beginning to feel suffocating. For a start, it was preventing her from meeting one of the many handsome young men from the audience. It was true that there were those who greeted her act with bawdy cries, but there were also tender moments as they threw single roses onto the stage.

Queenie, one of the chorus girls, stopped in front of Rosie.

"You still here? I'm heading for the bus if you want to come along," she said, offering her arm. Rosie thought for a second. The late horsedrawn bus would drop her round the corner from her house and there was still no sign of her father. Smiling, she nodded at Queenie and set off home on her own for the first time. The two women had only a short walk to the bus stop and they laughed together about the frolics of the men, their footsteps echoing as they walked through the gaslit streets.

"Did you see him tonight?" Rosie asked, as their conversation veered onto the mysterious 'man in black' as they called him. He visited the theatre every night, sitting in the upper tier box, paying ridiculous amounts for its exclusive use.

"Yes," replied Queenie. "He was in his usual – he's a strange one, isn't he?"

He wasn't a young man and appeared always dressed in black with a sweeping black cape. Nor did he cheer and shout like the other men; he sat silently and unnervingly gazed downwards at the stage. Occasionally he raised binoculars to sweep the stage and always he wore a red rose in his lapel. There were various rumours circulating about him and it was a favourite pastime to imagine all sorts of scenarios to explain his shadowy presence, each one more exaggerated than the last. The girls giggled over the latest theory as they approached the bus stop, which was crowded with late revellers, most of whom had probably spilled out of the Britannia. Rosie became aware of a coach pulling up alongside them and a figure appeared at the window, the face shrouded in darkness.

"Can I give you ladies a lift?"

Queenie was always on the look out for what she called 'a rich toff' and looked up with her best smile lighting her face. "And who are you, ducks?" she asked flirtatiously. Rosie gasped as she suddenly realised that they were looking at the man in black. She pinched Queenie's arm, trying to signal who it was, and saw that the gentleman was opening the door.

"No thanks, here is our bus," she said, managing to pull Queenie away. There was no time to talk about what had happened as the girls immediately faced a barrage of whistles and catcalls from drunk or partially drunk men as they realised two show girls had got on the bus. They pestered them all the way to Bow Common, but Queenie dealt with them all, smiling sometimes, slapping a face from time to time and keeping the groping hands from their bodies. As they drew near to her stop, Queenie offered to stay on and see Rosie home.

"No, you go Queenie. I'll manage, they're harmless enough," said Rosie, laughing. And it's time I dealt with this sort of situation myself, she thought to herself.

"If you're sure," said Queenie, stepping off the bus with a number of her adoring passengers. Rosie was left alone, but was able to cope with the younger men making a nuisance of themselves. In some ways it was flattering and all part of the territory, she reflected as she reached her stop. She stepped into the darkness to walk the final ten minutes, feeling pleased with herself for handling the journey on her own.

"Can I walk you home, darling?" a drunken man leered in front of her, blocking her way.

"No thanks, please move," said Rosie as firmly as she could, hoping the quiver in her voice wasn't noticeable. The drunk moved menacingly toward her, the stink of his breath overwhelming as he tried to kiss her. Suddenly a man in a black cape appeared and grabbed the drunk, throwing him against a wall. Dazed, he tried to rise, pulling a dagger from his pocket. The gentleman responded by swiftly drawing a rapier from his walking stick and held the man at bay.

"Don't be a fool. Go home, sober up and leave the dagger behind," he said. The drunk slowly got up; feeling the point of the rapier, he backed away before finally dropping the knife and running as fast as he could. Rosie turned toward the dark stranger with relief.

"Thank you," she said. The man was about to reply when three men came rushing down the road shouting "Rosie!" It was her father, brother and Mickie O'Callaghan, a friend of her father.

"Who are you Sir?" asked the man in black, his hand on the hilt of his walking stick.

"Rosie here is my daughter," rasped Jack. "Mores to the point who are you?" He turned to Rosie. "Are you alright? Has this man been bothering you?"

"No dad, he just saved me from an awful man who was threatening me."

Jack turned and looked at the stranger. "Well sir, I am grateful to you. May I know who you are?"

"Just a friend," said the man in black. "And now I will say goodnight. Miss Rosie, Gentlemen," he nodded at them and left. Rosie stared after him.

"Rosie?" said Jack, interrupting her thoughts. "I'm cross with you, why did you leave on your own?"

"I did wait Dad but you didn't come. I am 18 now I ought to be able to come home on my own," Rosie replied calmly.

"We will talk later," said her father after a pause and that was how Rosie's new freedom began. She was never entirely alone: her mother often accompanied her back from Shoreditch on the horse drawn bus but if she did travel with one of the other girls, her father, her brother or cousin shadowed her, 'just keeping an eye that she is safe' as her mother put it. After all, they had never caught that "Jack", the murderer who had been killing prostitutes, and Molly shuddered as she thought about what might have happened if the man in black hadn't have come along when he did.

Chapter Two

1896

By 1896, life for the Holders was changing. The might of the Empire had brought prosperity to England. The rich of course got richer, but the poor also began to see their standard of living rising. New breeds were born: there were the 'toffs' as Rosie called them and those Jack termed the 'workers' as well as a middle order of teachers, doctors and professional people. Many were still scratching a living, but Jack and Molly found themselves doing very nicely. Jack was a union leader responsible for labour relations on the East India, Victoria and St Katharine Docks. The unions may not have had any real power but it made the men feel good to belong to something which in theory represented their interests. Jack was amidst a thriving part of the city of London and relished the activity. Ships came from the Dominions regularly, loaded with lamb and mutton from New Zealand and all sorts of exotic fruits and spices such as almonds, figs and oranges from the far reaches of the Empire. The arrival of the first frozen meat and butter up the Thames from Australia was an event he would never forget in 1880 and the time was coming when the London Docks would be a vital part of the food chain, once the railway was completed in 1900.

Away from the Docks, Rosie continued to make a name for herself singing at the Britannia Shoreditch and had branched out into acting at the Theatre Royal Drury Lane. The backers of the Theatre near the City of London were quick to realise they had discovered a real gem in Rosie. Not only did she have an amazing ability to memorise the lines but she really could act. From Countess to maid, she threw herself into the part, coming alive on the stage. She soon began to appear more and more regularly, leaving her days at the Britannia behind. Despite her fondness for the old place, the Theatre Royal Drury Lane did have the greater attraction for her. For a start it paid better money and secondly there were no drunken men cat calling or making lecherous comments. She loved her time on the stage there, particularly performing in Shakespeare plays, Romeo and Juliet being her favourite.

It was during her time playing Viola in Twelfth Night that she first noticed a young man sitting alone in a ground floor box, constantly smiling up at her.

He wore a red rose in his lapel and came to every performance. She couldn't help but blush when he gazed at her and, although she thought she should avoid his stare, she couldn't help risking sneaky looks in his direction and found herself feeling bitterly disappointed one day when he wasn't in his usual spot. She laughed to herself as she realised she had started to look forward to his presence. Then the flowers started arriving at the stage door – two dozen red roses after each performance. This was nothing new; Rosie had been receiving different quantities of roses since she was fifteen but not usually two dozen. After some time, this became two bunches of two dozen roses arriving with a card signed: "From your adoring servant who sits in box one, Stafford." As Rosie read the card with a slight quickening of her pulse, the doorman approached to deliver a message, handing her an envelope with a grin: "The young man is persistent Miss. He has been here every day for the past two weeks and would like to see you."

Rosie opened the envelope and looked at the card inside, blushing slightly as the doorman watched her with the grin still on his face.

"Please do me the honour of meeting with me, I will die if we don't talk soonest." It was signed: "Your Servant, Stafford". What could a girl do? Although she was used to male attention, Rosie couldn't help but feel a little flustered as she told the doorman to bring her admirer through. She shared a dressing room with two other girls, who beat a hasty withdrawal as the doorman knocked.

"Rosie, this is the gentleman," he announced.

In walked the most handsome man Rosie had ever seen. He was tall, yet full bodied with dark black hair and a clean-shaven face, except for long sideboards. He introduced himself as Stafford Mornington and, as she looked into his blue sparkling eyes, she realised that she was already entranced.

So began the first courtship of Rosie Holder.

It became the custom that Stafford would pick her up in his carriage and take her to Bow. By now her father had bought a small house just off the East India Dock Road.

Stafford was twenty one and the son of an eminent surgeon, Sir Charles Mornington. He lived in Harley Street and had inherited a tidy sum from his grandmother when she died, which had been kept in trust until he was of age. As part of his celebrations, he was escorting Rosie to the opera in Covent Garden. She was absolutely thrilled as she had always wanted to go but it had seemed the prerogative of the 'toffs' as her dad put it.

"You don't want to be bothering yourself with all that nonsense," he said to her as she sat waiting for Stafford to pick her up. "Your mum," – who was his oracle on all things – "tells me they sing in that Italian and you can't understand a word."

Rosie shook her head indulgently and then leaped out of her chair as she heard Stafford arrive. He was in his father's carriage which he had borrowed especially for the occasion. She felt her heart swell as he entered the house and shook hands with her father. He was charming, witty and, most importantly as far as her father was concerned, he was a man's man. The whole family liked him but Molly had some reservations. He had been calling on Rosie for four months now, but she had still not met his parents. It seemed odd to Molly; if a young man was keen surely he would proudly introduce his lady friend to his parents?

However, today was not the day for questions such as these and Jack and Molly waved their daughter goodbye, smiling. Dressed in her best full length dress of white and black plaid wool twill with puffed sleeves and frills at the collar and cuffs, she was looking extremely attractive. She had asked Stafford if she should wear a gown but he had advised against it. Her outfit was finished with a small grey checked straw hat with a black velvet ribbon, which set off her skin tone perfectly. With an excited flush on her cheeks, she looked absolutely striking and the effect was not lost on Stafford, who gave her admiring sideways glances as they travelled to Covent Garden.

The production was Bizet's Carmen, a very popular opera. Stafford had assured Rosie that people attending the matinee did not dress lavishly as they did in the evening but nevertheless she was surprised to see ladies in Japanese style gowns and one handsome woman had on a white silk padded satin evening coat embroidered with a white chrysanthemum pattern.

"I can see men don't know everything," thought Rosie wryly. "Women will always dress up for an occasion." She resolved not to let herself dwell on it, but it was a lesson she would not forget.

The opera was simply stunning. Rosie knew she would enjoy it but the whole thing was just magical. With magnificent jewel coloured costumes and beautiful singing, Rosie felt overwhelmed, shedding a tear when Carmen died. The afternoon went by too quickly.

"I want to savour every moment," Rosie said, smiling at Stafford.

He looked down at her, his blue eyes twinkling: "Ah, but we have not finished yet. I have agreed with your father that I can take you to dinner now."

Rosie gave an excited gasp. "Oh, how lovely. Where are we going?"

"That's a surprise," said a smiling Stafford.

In fact the journey was a short trip up the Strand. They turned off into Maiden Lane and stopped outside an eating house called 'Rules'. Rosie felt like clapping her hands in delight; she had never been taken to one of the new eating houses. They had sprung up all over London, many attached to hotels and replacing the traditional coffee houses.

Stafford was clearly well known to the maître d' who welcomed them warmly. The pair settled into a booth and Stafford ordered champagne. Rosie was not a great drinker; she disliked what it did to many of the men and women she had seen, so she sipped her glass slowly whilst Stafford cleared his almost at once. There followed a sumptuous meal of Oysters which Rosie found very strange slipping down her throat, roast beef with piles of vegetables and a sort of pie Stafford called Yorkshire Pudding. Rosie couldn't finish the vegetables and declined a delicious looking trifle, much to the disappointment of Stafford who felt it was only gentlemanly to do likewise.

Afterwards, they rode along The Strand and Rosie marvelled at the number of handsome cabs and coaches as well as the horse drawn buses and trams. London was alive but they seemed to be heading in the wrong direction.

"Where are we going?" Rosie asked, surprised.

"I am taking you to see my parents' house in Harley Street," said Stafford.

Rosie looked at him in alarm. "I am not sure I am ready to meet your parents."

"Don't worry, they are away at Uncle Albert's estate. It seemed a good time to show you where I live."

Rosie glanced at him but said nothing. She was not entirely silly – she knew that her father would not have agreed to her going alone with a young man, even a gentleman such as Stafford.

It was a long journey, down the Strand, around Trafalgar Square, down Piccadilly and into Old Bond Street and then Wigmore Street before finally they turned into Harley Street. Rosie had been around London before with her father in a handsome cab but it never ceased to excite her and, when she arrived at Staffords parent's house, she was flushed from spying so many sights and sounds on their journey. She was pleased to be greeted by a maid when they went inside; they were not entirely alone.

"Did Sir want tea?" enquired the maid.

"Yes please," nodded Stafford. "Come my dear, let's sit in the drawing room."

Rosie had practiced the etiquette of drinking tea with her mother and Miss Simmons many times. Molly had been a maid to a lawyer in Fleet Street for several years when she was younger and made sure Rosie knew what to expect and how to hold the tiny cups, what to eat or not as the case may be. After the tea was served, Stafford became quite serious.

"Rosie, there is something I must tell you. Now I am twenty one, I intend to sign up for officer training in the army. I have a place at Sandhurst – my Grandfather was Brigadier you know and I want to follow the family tradition."

Rosie felt taken aback but what could she say? Here was a fine young man who wanted to join the army to fight for King and Country – what right had she to argue against it? She tried to put it from her mind and they moved on to talk about the opera, with Rosie excitedly recounting the entire story to Stafford. As they started the long journey bac to East India Dock Road, Stafford held Rosie's hand and gazed into her eyes.

"Rosie, it would really make my birthday if you would allow me one kiss."

Rosie had been imagining what a kiss from Stafford would be like for sometime and, whilst she did not want to seem a forward girl, she agreed to one small kiss. She closed her eyes and leaned toward Stafford. As they embraced, Rosie found herself becoming increasingly passionate and had to breathlessly hold Stafford back.

"Stafford, this is not the time or the place, but one day I promise you I will be yours." She tried to compose herself and looked out of the coach window, recognising the start of the East India Dock Road. "Lucky," she thought, "I might not have been able to resist much longer."

Stafford had mixed emotions; firstly elation that she had said that one day she would be his, but then disappointment that it wasn't to be now. He was a gentleman, however, and would do anything she asked of him.

Arriving home at gone 10.30pm, her father looked vexed but her mother warmly welcomed Stafford and thanked him for bringing her home. The two women entered the house chattering excitedly about the events of the day and evening, but not before Rosie thanked Stafford for a wonderful day, with a chaste peck on the cheek.

"I will never forget today as long as I live," she told him. As he looked into her eyes, he knew he was falling deeply in love with her.

Stafford joined the Army and went to Sandhurst. They met whenever possible, Stafford once arranging for a handsome cab to take her all the way to Sandhurst and wait to take her home. Their meetings became increasingly romantic. Stafford showered her with gifts and expressed his undying love, finally asking her to marry him. Rosie had been expecting his proposal but was concerned. Her mother had reminded her that he had still not introduced her to his family – what if they were hostile? Despite her strong feelings, her practical nature felt that it would be best to wait and see how the romance developed, so she gently refused his offer of marriage.

"I will think very seriously about it my love," she promised.

Stafford was being fast tracked through Sandhurst and had received his commission as a 2nd Lieutenant in March 1897. As the months went by, their romance continued to blossom and Rosie found herself falling more and more in love. The summer ended and a cruel winter began. On a cold November day, Stafford arranged to see Rosie. He usually met Rosie in public tea houses, but today she was brought by his father's coach to a small cottage in the village of Chilham in Kent. Stafford greeted her at the doorway, ushering her inside out of the sweeping rain.

"My darling you look beautiful," he said, giving her his customary red rose.

"This is not where we usually meet, Stafford," queried Rosie, looking around the charming cottage.

"I know, but I have got some news I didn't want to share in a tea house," Stafford replied. "As you know, General Kitchener is to take an expedition into the Sudan to avenge General Gordon's death at Khartoum." Rosie nodded; the news had been front page in the papers for some time. Stafford paused and then quickly went on: "I and some of my fellow officers have received orders to join the steamship 'Leamington' at Southampton waters in three days."

Rosie was stunned by this news and found herself unable to speak. So little time and he was going to that place that she had read about. The dreadful dervish and what they had done to Gordon, an invincible hero to the British people. Stafford held her hand firmly.

"You know I love you, don't you?" Rosie nodded, biting her lip.

"I can't bear to go away without showing you my love," said Stafford. Rosie blushed. Young men had tried to romance her many times but not like this and not her adorable Stafford.

"My darling, I love you. Can I kiss you?" he said, moving his body towards hers.

She closed her eyes and their lips met, tentatively at first and then passionately. As they continued to kiss and caress each other, Rosie felt a sensation that she had never felt before and it seemed quite natural when his hand gently began rubbing her breasts.

She began to pant heavily and felt his hand moving down her skirts. Frantically he tried to part them and then suddenly he was touching her in the most intimate of places. No man had ever touched her so and yet she found herself yielding to his gentle probing. She moaned and he moved to undo her dress which slipped from her shoulders. She lifted her bottom as he pulled down her undergarment and finally he removed her elasticated knickers. Moving on top, he began to tug at his trouser buttons and suddenly his penis was free from his trousers and he was guiding himself to her entrance. She felt a sharp pain but as she clung on to him, the pain turned to ecstasy. He moved in and out of her and each time she felt the hardness and became aware of a sensation previously unknown to her. She held on to him and just then, he let out a groan and exploded into her. Afterwards, they lay in each other's arms until Rosie began to feel cold and then they dressed and just sat, not talking but looking adoringly at each other.

"Oh my darling, when I return from this campaign we will be married," Stafford said, kissing her once more.

Reluctantly she returned to London later that day feeling elated, but at the same time dreading saying goodbye and replaying in her mind the last few wonderful hours.

The following day a note arrived by hand. It was from Stafford.

"Sorry my darling, no chance to say goodbye – the orders have been brought forward. I am having to leave for Southampton straightaway. I love you more than anything in the whole world. I will be thinking of you constantly, you are my love. Yours in love, Stafford." A red rose fell from the envelope.

Rosie's eyes filled and warm tears trickled down her cheeks. Would he return? Would she ever see her love again? She sobbed uncontrollably until her mother came and found her. Molly put her arms around her sobbing daughter and held her tightly. Rosie had already told her Stafford was under orders to proceed abroad and Molly knew that Rosie was now facing the reality. She was heartbroken, but then two days later received another hand delivered letter.

"My darling Rosie,

I am about to board Her Majesty's ship of the line HMS Leamington. I cannot stop thinking about you my love and the wonderful times we had together. That day in Chilham was the most wonderful of my life. I love your nose, your face, your hands and your dainty feet. I adore your eyes; your voice is to me a nightingale. When I am apart from you I am nothing. I must bear this pain as I hope you do but we must look forward to our next meeting when our love will be for all the world to see.

I am your adoring and loving,

Stafford

PS If you think of me in this foreign land of barbarians remember I shall be always thinking of you and longing to kiss your lips and stroke your hair, my love I am desolate, I will write as soon as possible".

Rosie burst into tears and clutched the letter to herself, but after a few minutes brought herself under control. Her mother after all had always told her: "Life must go on" and she knew she had to leave for a performance at the Theatre Royal of 'Twelfth Night' shortly.

Fortunately, Rosie's life was always hectic. It was February 1898 and she appeared at the Theatre now every night acting in the Shakespeare play, 'Two Gentlemen of Verona' playing Julia a lady of Verona, beloved of Proteus. In two months they would be rehearsing for 'Much Ado About Nothing', a light and sparkling comedy – but one which had certainly got Rosie thinking of oppressive institutions run by men and women's rights. She was to play Beatrice, a niece of Leonato and immersed herself in the part.

'Much Ado About Nothing' was to run at the theatre for a month and then it was rumoured the play was being taken to Paris for a two week run. Everyone was excited, particularly John Adam and his friend, Peter, who was to play Leonato. It would give them the chance that had eluded them, to bed Rosie.

Rosie waited for a new letter from her love everyday, but it was three months before a rather dog eared letter arrived in Stafford's handwriting.

"My Darling,

I hope this letter arrives safely. There is much skulduggery here, you cannot trust anybody. I am in General Kitchener's advance guard and we are to shortly commence our march to retake Khartoum from the Dervish. I have met a new friend, a brave fellow called Winston Churchill. He is a tenacious fighter and a man I am pleased to have as a friend. We have had one or two run-ins with these devils already. They attack cannon riding horses and camels and suffer terrible losses before turning away. I find I am developing an admiration for their courage, if not they themselves.

Enough of the talk of war. I dream of you everyday and long to be back in England in a coach coming to meet you. I have the lock of your hair you gave me in my bible and how often I touch your golden locks and imagine you are here beside me. I hope you are not too sad. Our weeks, months apart will strengthen our love for each other until we can at last marry.

Longing to see you. I have written a poem, which does not do justice to my feelings for you.

Affectionately yours,

Stafford"

A further note fell out of the letter headed, 'A Poem to my Beautiful Rosie':

"What is life on this foreign shore?

Alone without you here to share,

I dream of you when I may return,

And once again kiss your tender lips.

I dream each day of your warm embrace,

Your lovely lips and beautiful face,

I would die today to once more be in your arms,

My heart is yours.

Sleep oh bring me sleep!

For in my dreams I find you,

I hold your hand and kiss your lips,

I feel your touch, see your smile,

My lovely Rosie, I will love you always

Signed your loving Stafford 1st January 1898"

Rosie knew that Stafford was no Bard, but read the poem with tears in her eyes. She did not hear from Stafford again and, when the proposed visit to Paris was postponed, she did not care. All she could think about was how Stafford was faring abroad. Then a letter arrived addressed to her in strange handwriting, dated February 1898.

"My Dear Rosie,

I hope you don't mind me calling you by your Christian name; I feel I know you well, Stafford having spent each night entrancing me with your looks and disposition.

There is no easy way to tell you this, so I will start from the beginning.

Stafford was asked to lead a scouting expedition down the Nile. Using a captured Dervish Dhow, he was to lead a company of Dragoon Guards to a tiny place called Wadji. Here he was to march inland to an oasis, which the General required him to hold at all costs. General Kitchener, including yours truly, was simultaneously bringing the main army overland toward the oasis. The General did not want the horses and camels smelling the waters of the Nile too soon. In any case he felt that the Dervish scouts would recognise the edge of the Nile as a perfect ambush point. A messenger arrived from Stafford confirming he had reached the oasis and was dug in.

I am sorry to say that when we reached the oasis with the main column there was no sign of anyone, only one battered battalion flag remained and rifle shell casings. There were no bodies, no horses and no sign of Stafford's patrol.

We pressed on toward Omdurman, where a great battle took place over which we triumphed. As you receive this letter Her Majesty's Government is likely to be announcing the huge victory that has broken the power of the Dervish.

I will keep searching for Stafford as long as I can but I fear you must steel yourself, as I believe he is lost.

I will call on you when I return home.

Yours in friendship,

Winston Churchill"

Rosie's hands were shaking as she read the letter and it dropped to the floor as her whole body began to tremble. Tears streamed down her face. Molly, fearing the worse, had allowed her time to read the letter before knocking on the door. Seeing her daughter in tears confirmed her awful suspicion. Molly knew her daughter well and had long suspected her relationship with Stafford was a loving one, although she had not passed her opinion to Jack for the fear of what he might do or say. Now she saw her daughter standing before her utterly inconsolable. All she could do was hold her tightly, stroking her long blond hair as she sobbed uncontrollably in her arms.

Rosie threw herself into her work to forget the pain. Her thoughts constantly imagined what had happened to Stafford, but she remained the ultimate professional. Only her best friend in the cast of players, Sylvie, knew about the tragedy that had overtaken her friend. Rosie appeared in 'Anthony and Cleopatra' later in 1898 to rave reviews and, following that, took the part of Lady Macbeth, which was to run for nine months in 1899. This demanding role absorbed much of her time and slowly she felt herself returning to some sense of normality. There was also much excitement for the actors at the theatre as the management announced that they were to travel to Paris in December 1899 to perform 'Much Ado About Nothing' at the Paris Metropole Theatre as British representatives at the 'Paris Exposition'. They were all thrilled at the prospect until Sidney, their director, told them that they had to play their parts in French, a daunting task.

In the meantime, Churchill was as good as his word. He searched for Stafford, asking informants and spies to seek out what had happened to the British soldiers captured at the Wadji Oasis. Then he heard the tragic news. A prisoner taken at Omdurman had been captured with a British Army pistol in his possession. After forceful questioning, he told the story of how he had bought the pistol from a warrior who had captured some British soldiers at Wadji Oasis. Churchill asked to see the gun and recognised a mark Stafford had made on the butt, "R". As soon as he got leave to return to England, Churchill headed for East London to meet Rosie. He had found her address amongst Stafford's personal effects, which he had agreed to deliver to Stafford's father.

He stood at the doorstep and knocked loudly. Molly answered and looked in surprise at the well-presented slightly balding gentleman standing in front of her.

"Hello my dear, my name is Winston, I was a friend of Stafford. Is Rosie here?"

"I am afraid Rosie is not here, she is at rehearsal at the Theatre Royal," replied Molly, inviting the gentleman inside. Winston thanked her and set off for the Theatre.

Rehearsals had started for the French version of 'Much Ado About Nothing' and simultaneously twice each week a professor from the London University came to help them with the French translation. He also spent one hour each day with each of the major actors. Amazed by Rosie's ability to memorise her translation and the accent she perfected, he began to teach her day to day conversational French. So Rosie became distracted; Stafford's memory was still ever present, but at least when she thought of him she did not feel tears well up in her eyes.

Then Mr Churchill came to the Theatre. He was a charming man but made it clear to her that he thought Stafford was dead. As he puffed on a rather large cigar, he explained about the discovery of Stafford's pistol and that in his view Stafford was lost. Rosie slumped in her chair, sobbing quietly as all her grief, kept tightly contained for so many months, spilled out of her now she finally heard the words she had dreaded. Churchill sat with her for a while then excused himself to go to a meeting at the House of Commons. As he left, he said:

"Stafford was a very brave man; our friend is dead but will never be forgotten."

Rosie nodded and sat quietly by herself for a while after Churchill had gone, remembering the man who had made her fall in love for the first time.

Chapter Three

1900

The months flew by and soon it was January 1900 and they were setting off for Paris.

Rosie travelled to Victoria Station with her mum and dad to board the train to Dover. They made their way to platform three and she said her goodbyes, promising to write. As the train slowly drew out of the station, the smell of smoke filling the air, Rosie leaned out of the window to wave goodbye until they were out of sight and then settled back into her seat with a contented sigh. She had never been on a train before and was fascinated as the landscape slipped by the window. While the other members of the cast chatted, she studied the landmarks. Row after row of houses backed onto the railway, many with washing hanging on the clothes line. Why, she thought, hang washing on the line with the smuts and smoke bellowing around from the trains? The train was soon chugging through the countryside of Kent and finally pulled into Dover Station, where the cast disembarked for the next leg of their journey. The train had pulled up right alongside Admiralty Pier where the steamer that was to cross the Channel sat waiting, although it took the stage hands a further sixty minutes to load their trunks and props.

As the steamer edged out of the harbour, the cast glanced at each other in a mixture of trepidation and excitement; none of them had been on a boat before. Rosie insisted on going up to the upper deck to get the best view, but only Sidney Stone and Peter Defries joined her. It soon became apparent that Peter was interested in more than the white cliffs of Dover as he slipped his arm around Rosie's waist. She removed his hand. "Now behave yourself Peter or you'll be taking a swim," she said firmly as Sidney laughed.

Rosie had never had such a great time in her life: first the train journey and now the sea crossing As she stood on the deck with the fresh wind blowing around her, she took in a deep lungful of the air. The expanse of grey blue water was like nothing she had ever seen. In the distance the busy shipping lines were full of masted ships and big steamers and she fleetingly wondered where they were all going or had come from.

The voyage passed quickly enough, even though Peter hardly left her side. She was more interested in the sea than his attempt to sweet talk her.

"Look at those birds, I wonder how far they can fly?" She knew Peter was keen on her and hadn't decided whether to encourage him or not. He was a leading actor who expected most young women to swoon at the mention of his name, but Rosie wasn't so easily won. She quite liked him. He was handsome in a boyish sort of way, with a short fashionable moustache and she did notice his blue penetrating eyes, which she frequently turned away from. Still it was nice having company on the journey. Poor Sylvie, her friend and confidante, had spent most of the crossing being sick. A pity it wasn't the venomous Edie, Rosie thought. Edie, however, had spent most of her time in the small salon laughing and joking with Sidney Stone, the director. Rosie had a vague thought that this was strange as she hadn't seemed to like Sidney much, preferring the amorous advances of Wilson Jones, a leading man. As she looked out at the land ahead, she forgot all about it; it was probably just the excitement of the sea crossing, she thought.

As they approached the harbour at Calais most of the actors and members of the orchestra had crowded onto the top deck, straining to get their first glimpse of France. The steamer gently struck the dockside and men scampered to tie up the ship.

"Right," said Sidney. "Collect your own personal belongings as they come ashore and take your bags and cases to the train. Members of the orchestra make sure you have your instrument." George, who was the senior stagehand, was instructed to arrange for porters to help transport the trunks and the stage props to the baggage compartment on the waiting train.

Rosie boarded the train only to be horrified to see that French trains had wooden seats.

"No, not that part of the train Rosie," said Peter, always in attendance. "We are travelling second class and this is the third class carriage." Thank goodness, thought Rosie, who did not fancy a three hour train journey sitting on wooden seats.

The steam train left Calais station and began the journey to Paris. Paris! How excited they all were. Rosie and Sylvie giggled as they discussed what the men would be like in Paris. Sylvie said she had heard they were very gallant and flattering.

Rosie smiled and looked out of the window at the passing countryside – it didn't seem much different to England, except the cattle and livestock were more apparent and the fields seemed to stretch on and on. She decided to go and have a word with Sidney, the director. As she neared his seat, she bumped into Edie. Did she imagine it or was there a look of triumph on Edie's face? She cast the thought aside as the train started its approach to the Gare du Nord.

About the same size as London's Victoria Station, it was buzzing with people. Sidney quickly found the transport for the players and the orchestra – they were to go by horse draw carriage to the hotel, taking with them their own belongings. Sidney had arranged for several large carriages to be loaded with their stage equipment and the trunks, but flapped around as the French drivers seemed to disappear at the crucial moment. Rosie and Sylvie left together and their coach headed toward the hotel. Trotting through unfamiliar streets, Rosie looked at the scenes around her. So this is Paris, she thought with a smile. People were milling about, the place was alive. Their hotel, the 'Formetle Marabeuf', was a thirty minute ride away, which gave Rosie plenty of time to absorb the unfamiliar territory. They twisted and turned down interesting 'rues' or 'boulevards', as she had learnt the French called their roads. Houses were grand, but some areas were rundown, as in London. She couldn't see any shops but perhaps they were travelling in the business part of Paris. Looking at what the ladies were wearing, they seemed similar to London but the ladies' hats were distinctly more flamboyant with grand feathers clustered around large brims.

Arriving at the hotel, they unloaded the baggage and a nice French man came to the carriage helping the girls on to the pavement saying "Bonjour avez-vous besoin d'aide pour vos bagages?" Sylvie looked at him non-plussed but Rosie, surprised that she had understood, answered, "Oui monsieur, merci." Sylvie grinned at her, "Ooh, look at you, speaking French." Rosie smiled back and they went inside to the reception.

"Bonjour, sont les acteurs de théâtre anglais," Rosie paused, as she did not know the right word for theatre. "Et nous avons une reservation," she finished.

"Ah, les anglais," replied an elegant young man on the reception desk. "We are pleased you are here," he said in heavily accented English. Rosie introduced Sylvie and herself and helped Sylvie complete the checking in form, making a mental note to study more French; she was struggling to understand the young man as he spoke so fast.

Fortunately help arrived in the form of Monsieur Devois, who had been engaged by Sidney as translator and French tutor while the players were in Paris. He looked at the girls solemnly. "Bonjour mademoiselles. I am Henri Devois, at your service," he said and kissed their hands. Sylvie giggled.

"Are we the first to arrive?" Rosie asked.

"Yes," replied Monsieur Devois. "I will make the arrangement for you to be shown to your room, you are together."

A bellboy was summoned, dressed in a smart uniform and pillbox hat. Gosh this was a grand hotel, thought Rosie as they accompanied the silent lad to their room on the first floor. Inside the room was no disappointment – a crystal chandelier lit up the room, which contained a huge double bed with a satin bedspread and an elegant dressing table. Rosie and Sylvie were taken aback by the sophistication of the room and forgot the bellboy, who left them.

"Oh dear," said Rosie. "It is traditional to tip. Next time we see him we will give him something."

Sidney had insisted that all the players, members of the orchestra and helpers had been paid partly in French Francs for their last performance in England.

"You must have some money of your own," he had explained. "And you will get used to paying for things in French Francs." Some of the lower paid had complained bitterly afterwards that whilst they were in France their loved ones would have a difficult enough time without them going home with less money now. One stagehand, Marcus, had told Sylvie that his wife was expecting their sixth child and his money was all they had to feed the children. On hearing this, Rosie had organised a small collection, which they gave to Marcus, who was clearly overcome with their kindness.

"It's only a few shillings," said Rosie.

"No Miss, it is bread for the next three weeks until I can send some money home."

After that, Sidney had promised to pay all the cast in Francs and pounds whilst they were in France, which was a relief to all of them except Edie, who had intended to buy French clothes whilst she was in Paris.

As the girls started to unpack their things, Sylvie spotted a note on the bedspread.

"Sidney wants us to go to a meeting at 6.00 in the main lounge," she said, glancing up at Rosie.

"Well, that gives us two hours to rest and get ready for dinner," said Rosie, glad to have some time to organise herself.

Shortly before 6pm, the girls found their way to the huge galleried lounge, lit up by another chandelier, even larger than the one in their room. The players, members of the orchestra and the support staff all gathered and Sidney arrived with Edie in tow.

"I want to talk to you all about our itinery whilst we are in Paris," he began. "We will be going to the theatre for rehearsals at 10am starting tomorrow, every day except Sunday for the next week. We will travel by carriage; there is a list of those who will travel together. You will stick together, don't be late or you will hold everybody up. Any questions?" He looked around the room as everyone shook their head or remained silent.

"Finally, during the evenings and on Sunday your time is your own, but do not go out alone, you do not know Paris or speak good enough French. Ladies do not get separated. Is that clear?" They all nodded.

Fortunately, the next day was a Sunday so they had the day for their leisure. Rosie arranged with Sylvie, Peter and the music director Edward Boyd to take a carriage to the Champs Elyses and the Eiffel Tower. The French had apparently built this huge tower a few years ago, which you could climb to the top.

As the coach clattered along the busy Paris streets, Rosie was fascinated by all she saw. They were running parallel to the magnificent French river, which dissected Paris, called 'the Seine'. She was reminded in some ways of when her father had taken her to Whitehall in 1897, which had been preparing for Queen Victoria's Diamond Jubilee Celebrations. Like London, the roads of Paris were festooned with flags and bunting. She thought about that coach ride with her father; they had passed the Banqueting House from which Queen Victoria's procession would commence, circled St Paul's Cathedral and headed down Fleet Street, where people were four and five deep on the pavement and coaches virtually went at a walking pace as there were so many people.

"Rosie…" She looked up, her thoughts interrupted. "What do they call a bridge?" asked Sylvie.

"Pont," replied Peter.

"Don't they have some funny names?" laughed Sylvie. They all smiled and soon the coach arrived at the Eiffel Tower. There were large crowds and they had to wait some time to climb what seemed like a thousand steps before they reached a platform and looked out over the city. What a sight awaited them. The wind whistled around them and the girls' hair was blown all around their heads, but no one could dissuade Rosie from taking in the magnificent view. She insisted they get their bearings and pointed to the Champs-Elysees where they were going next. "This is a sight I will always remember," she thought to herself, looking at the city spread out below her.

They made their way to the Champs-Elysees and enjoyed sitting at a traditional French café watching the Parisians going about their business. The French certainly enjoyed their wine, thought Rosie. Peter had insisted they try the traditional French coffee but Rosie and Sylvie had not been impressed.

The day went by all too quickly and they returned to the hotel for 5pm to get ready for dinner. Rosie loved the fabulous dining room with its glass ceiling and patterned tiles around the extravagantly decorated walls. The meal was not quite what they were used to and Sidney, Wilson and Mary Anne didn't finish the meat dish. When Peter announced it was 'cheval' or horse meat, Edie said she felt sick and rushed out of the room. Rosie, however, found that she enjoyed the French food and Sylvie enthusiastically wolfed it all down.

Breakfast the next day was equally strange to them all – a spread of black coffee, cakes and funny crescent shaped rolls. The jam was very pleasant but everyone expressed a wish for a cup of 'Rosy Lee'. Soon, they were all on their way to the theatre in the groups Sidney had designated. L'Hippodrome Theatre was a typically grand French affair. The billing outside showed the forthcoming production of 'Much Ado About Nothing' performed by 'Les Anglais de Shakespeare's Theatre Royal', which sent a ripple of excitement amongst the cast. It was really happening! The flush of excitement soon dulled as they began to rehearse strenuously, staying for eight to ten hours each day. Everyone was so tired that early nights were often the order of the day. After the evening dinner, which Rosie only struggled with if it was offal or sweetbreads, she sometimes studied some French books in the hotel library, contemplating what she had just eaten. However she rather enjoyed Foie Gras with toasted bread and of course the wine! Sometimes they played cards or chatted until the party broke up each evening on Sidney's orders by 10pm.

All too soon, it was only one day until the dress rehearsal and the cast felt a mixture of impatience to be on stage and nerves about the impending performances. Sidney had called a meeting and stood pompously, enjoying the power, as he coughed for attention.

"As you know several of you have been learning various parts as understudies," he said. "I want to now go through the players for the dress rehearsal. Listen everyone," he raised his voice as a buzz went around the room. "Peter will play Don Pedro, Wilson will play Don John, Herbie will play Claudio, Anthony will play Benedick," Sidney continued through the list of the male actors and then moved onto the female parts. "Edie will play Hero." There was a gasp, but he ignored it and carried on. "Mary Anne will play Beatrice and Rosie will play Margaret and Ursula."

There was a hush in the room. Rosie was not to play either of the main parts of Hero or Beatrice. This was incredible. How had Edie got the part of Hero – Rosie was a much better actress and spoke French fluently, compared to Edie who struggled desperately.

For a moment Rosie sat stunned, then she got up and left the room. Edie watched her go and whispered to Mary Anne, "It seems Rosie is a little upset." She smirked, clearly pleased with herself.

Rosie lay on her bed, her eyes welling up with tears. I will not cry she thought fiercely. She was angry with herself that she had reacted in front of the cast. Was Edie the right choice for the part? She began to question herself.

Downstairs the meeting broke up with excited babble, some of the actors happier than others. There were several who did not even have a part and were stand-ins and they looked dejected.

Peter made his way to Rosie's room and knocked on the door. When there was no answer, he knocked more loudly and heard movement inside. Rosie came to the door. "Oh Peter," she said as she burst into tears.

Peter held her tightly in his arms whilst she got the frustration out of her system. It was something he had been rather hoping to do for some time and he could feel himself getting excited as he pressed her close to him. "Not now, you idiot," he thought to himself, realising this wasn't the right time for that. Rosie broke away and they sat on the bed talking.

"Why did he do that?" Rosie said, wiping her eyes.

Peter looked at her, thinking how he could put it. "Rosie, Edie and Sidney are lovers, they have been for weeks."

Rosie shook her head. "Oh, so that's it. He gave his mistress the part she wanted."

"I am afraid so, but it's not the end of the world; you are still in the play."

Rosie took a deep breath and began to get herself under control. "Alright, I will play the parts of Margaret and Ursula like they have never been played before," she smiled defiantly. Peter sensed it was time to leave.

"You will be great, I will see you tomorrow bright and early." He squeezed her hand and walked to the door. After he had gone, Rosie crossed to the bathroom to wash her face. It was a disappointment but she was determined not to let it get the better of her.

Waking early the following morning Rosie washed and sat at the dressing table staring into space.

"What you doing Rosie?"

"Come on Sylvie, we are going to be late." Rosie went down to the dining room ignoring the looks from the other girls and sat with Peter sipping her coffee calmly.

"Right, come on," said Sidney. "Ten minutes and the coaches will arrive."

The owner of the Theatre Royal was rumoured to be arriving today to watch the dress rehearsals. Sidney had arranged for groups of school children to come in and enjoy a free performance so the stalls were full as Rosie peeked through the curtain. The hustle and bustle in the theatre was shared in the dressing room as the actors calmed their nerves with false laughter and the odd quip.

"Five minutes," shouted the stage manager. "To your places please."

The first half was effective without being sparkling. Sidney knew something wasn't working but was not sure what it could be. Despite the children cheering wildly, Rosie and the other actors knew it hadn't been their best performance.

In the box at the back of the theatre a figure had appeared at the beginning of the play. Rosie saw that there was a gentleman sitting there, but he was a distant figure and the lights were bright.

"Is that the owner in the upper box?" she asked Peter during the interval.

"I guess so, none of us have ever met him."

Unfortunately, the second half did not improve; in fact there were several prompts required which the young audience didn't notice but others did. At the end the children were ecstatic and cheered loudly until the actors came back for an extra curtain call.

As Sidney was watching the actors take their bows, he was approached by a messenger and given a note. He frowned as he read it and left quickly. The players went to their dressing rooms and cleaned off their make up, changing back into their day clothes. They were not buzzing like they usually were after a performance.

"Some of us are going to order a bottle of wine," said Peter when they were on their way back to the hotel. "Will you join me, Rosie?"

"No thanks. I feel tired, I think I'll have a rest before dinner."

Sylvie came up to the room a little worse for drinking several glasses of wine.

"Something's going on," she said.

"What do you mean?" Rosie sat up.

"Well, Sidney has left the hotel with his luggage. Micheal Crowe the conductor tried to talk to him but he just rushed out and got in a cab and left."

During dinner, the cast talked about the latest events. There was a mixture of bewilderment and curiosity amongst them. Sidney had been the director of the company for over two years; where had he gone?

The following day was a Sunday and some of the cast had arranged to go out for the day. Their first stop was the Musee d'Orsay, which had recently been built. What a wonderful place, Rosie thought to herself as she wandered around each gallery, marvelling at the paintings. She sat down in front of a painting in the Impressionist gallery, called 'Mademoiselle Isabelle Lemonnier'. As she gazed at it, a young man sat next to her.

"Have you seen the 'Monet Family in the Garden'?" he pointed down the gallery. She looked up and found herself staring into the face of a handsome young man, smartly dressed, clearly a gentleman.

"I like them all, but there is something about Monet," he said when she didn't reply. They sat together absorbed by their own personal thoughts, the gentleman occasionally glancing sideways at Rosie.

"May I introduce myself?" he said eventually. "Frederick de Courcy, at your service."

Rosie hesitated for a fraction before replying. "Rosie Holder," she said.

"It is really nice to meet you Miss Rosie Holder. It is Miss?" Rosie nodded.

"May I escort you to the next gallery featuring Manet? Manet is an extremely talented painter, have you seen his work?"

They spent the rest of the day together going from gallery to gallery. When it was time for Rosie to meet the other actors, she introduced Frederick and he suggested they had lunch at a nearby café. They readily accepted, hungry after their morning at the museum.

"And then you must all accompany me to my friend's gallery, the Musee Grevia," Frederick insisted.

They set out in horse drawn cabs, which drove alongside the Seine, crossing the bridge toward the Boulevard Montmartre, a lovely road lined with large lime trees. Arriving at the museum fifteen minutes later they all piled out of the carriages and Frederick went inside, reappearing after a couple of minutes with a smile.

"Come on everyone, I have spoken to my friend, Arthur, and we are most welcome."

As they entered the Musee Grevia, Rosie immediately noticed it was not as grand as the Musee d'Orsay, but it had a more intimate feel.

"Ladies and gentlemen, allow me to introduce my friend Arthur Meyer," said Frederick, with a small flourish. In the French tradition, Arthur kissed the ladies hands in an exaggerated way.

"Arthur won't tell you this but he opened the Musee with his friend Alfred Grevin. Alfred is a sculptor, costume designer and cartoonist and you will find a number of his exhibits as you go round the halls," Frederick explained, beaming with pleasure.

They began to walk around the gallery, with Frederick pointing out pieces to them all. "You are lucky to be in Paris at the moment, it is a very exciting time. There are celebrations for the centenary, the disposition and the metro opening shortly and they are hosting the Olympic Games."

"I didn't know the Olympic Games were being staged here," said Wilson quizzically.

"Oh yes, the opening ceremony was last week and some of the events are already under way," Arthur replied.

Sylvie who had been fairly quiet walking around the museums was looking at him in interest. "And the Metro, what is it?"

"Ah," said Arthur. "It is an amazing piece of French construction – an underground railway."

"The train travels underground?" asked a startled Rosie.

"Yes, the first stations are shortly to be opened between Porte de Vincennes to Ponte Maillot. Fulgence Bienvenue, a man we know, was the engineer in charge of construction and my friend Alfred knows Hector Guimard who was responsible for the art at the entrances." Arthur replied. Sylvie nudged Rosie with a smile. "He's got a lovely accent," she whispered dreamily.

The trip around the Musee Grevia was much shorter than the tour of the Musee d'Orsay but Rosie particularly liked the extravagant costumes designed by Alfred.

"He is a fine sculptor," said Frederick as they examined a classic bust of a French general. Rosie wondered if it was Bonaparte.

As they said their goodbyes, Frederick pulled Rosie to one side.

"You did not tell me where you are staying," he said. "Perhaps we can meet for dinner?" Rosie hesitated. "Sylvie, Wilson and any of your friends could join me tonight for dinner," he added quickly.

Rosie looked over at Wilson who had overheard the conversation. "Love to," he said with a nod.

"Well, that settles matters. I will arrange for two carriages at 8.00pm. What is the address of your hotel?"

Once they were settled in their cabs, Sylvie leaned over to Rosie confidentially.

"He really likes you Rosie, he has hardly taken his eyes off you and he offered you his arm several times," she smiled.

"He is certainly very gallant and handsome," said Rosie, looking out the window at the barges and the single masted boats battling to go downstream on the River Seine. Arriving at the hotel they'd only just entered the foyer when Edward Boyd, the conductor, appeared.

"Thank goodness, you've returned. The owner has asked us all to attend him in the lounge." Rosie and Sylvie looked at each other and made their way to the room. In swept two men, one a distinguished looking gentleman but the other appeared somewhat bohemian. His jacket and trousers did not match and he wore an open collared linen shirt and had a red beret on.

"I am Lord Berkeley, I own the Theatre Royal," said the gentleman. "And this gentleman is Monsieur Copeau who is your new director." There was a moment of silence and then ten people all tried to talk at once. Lord Berkeley held up his hand to silence them. "Sidney has been replaced and has gone back to England owing to certain... irregularities." Was he glaring at Edie? "I have asked Monsieur Copeau to do us the honour of directing our play." He held out his hand, welcoming the short colourful French man who stepped forward.

"Merci, thank you, your Lordship." Copeau was a small man but had a booming voice and a presence you couldn't help but pay attention.

"I have seen your dress rehearsal and there are improvements we must make. I will meet you all in the morning, at the theatre. Maintenent, for tonight, enjoy your dinner." The cast waited for Lord Berkeley to say something else, but he simply nodded. They all filed out slowly, somewhat taken aback by this new turn of events.

Rosie had been studying Lord Berkeley since his surprise introduction to them. "I have seen his lordship before," she thought with a small frown, but was soon distracted by the non-stop chatter as the cast discussed the scandal.

"Sidney sacked, well I never," said Sylvie, putting her arm through Rosie's.

They reached the bedroom and slumped on the bed, both tired after touring two museums. Rosie's eyes were heavy and she dozed dreaming of paintings, sculpture and Frederick.

Waking up with a start Rosie realised it had got dark. Looking at the timepiece a gentleman had sent her when she played Cleopatra at the Theatre Royal, Rosie jumped out of bed.

"Wake up Sylvie, Frederick is calling for us in 40 minutes."

The girls quickly bathed, dressed and did their hair minutes before the smartly dressed bellboy knocked for them.

"Excuse me Mademoiselle, Monsieur de Courcy is waiting for you in the foyer," he said in broken English.

The girls rushed downstairs joining Wilson who was in deep conversation with Frederick and Anthony.

"Ah the Mademoiselles Rosie and Sylvie," he said, kissing their hands. "Shall we go?"

They made their way out to a large carriage. "There is plenty of room, I have been assured this is the largest carriage in Paris," said Frederick as the doorman pulled the step down and helped the ladies inside.

The journey was wonderful and Frederick entertained them with the history of the place they were visiting.

"I mentioned to you what an exciting time it is to be in Paris now. The French are in a period they call 'the Belle Époque' or a golden time of beauty, innovation and peace," he said, gesturing at the streets outside. Everywhere they looked bunting and flags celebrated the Exposition.

"We shall be going to the Musette this evening, but will eat first at a nearby café."

"What is the Musette?" queried Sylvie.

"The Musette is where the French gather to listen to cabaret and music and sometimes there is dancing – in England you would call it a club. It will not be serious but great fun," Frederick laughed at the blank faces. "Paris is one big party and is the City of Lights, but first let us eat."

The carriage stopped outside 'Le Café Noir'. "The Black Café," thought Rosie "What a splendid name."

"Attendez," instructed Frederick to the coachman. "Nous reviendrons à dix heures."

As they entered the smart café they all looked astonished. The walls were completely black, with red lamps on the dining tables in booths along the walls and a large central chandelier, which seemed out of place but created a magical effect as the lights bounced off the moving crystals and struck the black walls.

"Bonjour Monsieur de Courcy et amies," said a smart man dressed in black with a white shirt. He seemed to know Frederick well and led the party to a booth.

"Votre table, síl vous plaît." The gentlemen let the ladies go in first, and Frederick deliberately sat next to Rosie and opposite the other three.

"Souhaitez - vous un apéritif?"

Frederick ordered five glasses of sweet white wine, which he called 'Muscat'. He explained that this was a pleasant sweet white wine, which he felt sure they would enjoy. The others smiled and nodded their agreement and all were taken with the wine when it was brought to them. As they talked, Rosie looked around the room, soaking in the wonderful ambiance of the sparkling light. They were all reluctant to leave at the end of the meal, but at Frederick's insistence rejoined the carriage, which was waiting outside.

"Now to the Musette," he beamed.

The chatter in the coach had increased in volume from their earlier journey as all were enveloped with the warmth of sumptuous food and a number of glasses of fine wine. After five minutes, they arrived at their destination and went into what appeared to be another café. The premises were huge and not very well decorated. Crowded with a bustling party atmosphere of Parisians enjoying themselves, it was cloudy with the smoke from cigarettes. Rosie had already noted that even French ladies smoked cigarettes, which was not yet the fashion in England.

Once again Frederick was recognised and a waiter showed them to a table marked 'reserve' close to the dance floor and a small stage. Frederick ordered a carafe of red wine and they sat back taking in the atmosphere and excitement generated. Parisians certainly knew how to enjoy themselves, thought Rosie.

Suddenly a spotlight lit the stage. A man appeared, speaking rapidly and they all looked at Frederick to translate.

"Tonight we are very fortunate one of the most famous Musette players is performing with his group of musicians."

A tall dark man accompanied by three other men came onto the stage. Pumping a device under his right arm, which Rosie later found out it was called a 'bellows' in English, he filled an airbag held in his left hand. After a few minutes, he began to play the pipe and it began to emit a strange wailing sound. The result was wonderful, like nothing they had heard before. The other musicians joined in, playing violins and one beat a long stick on a drum in time with the music until the most tremendous cacophony of sound filled the music hall. The audience buzzed in appreciation, with several people getting up to dance. Rosie watched as they performed a very provocative dance. It was unlike anything she had seen back home; perhaps something like a waltz but with a powerful sexual chemistry. The women wore short dresses, which ballooned up as their partners whirled them around the room.

"What is that dance called?" asked Rosie, unable to tear her eyes away from the display in front of her.

"Ah, that is the Tango," Frederick replied with a smile. "Would you like to learn it?" He offered her his arm.

"Oh no, not tonight Frederick I would be embarrassed. Perhaps you will show me and Sylvie how to dance another time."

"I would be delighted to."

Frederick went on to explain that they were in the famous 'Bal Musette Dourlans', one of the most renowned Musette dance halls. The atmosphere was electric but Frederick, knowing that the actors had to perform the next day, had arranged for a carriage to pick them up at midnight. Reluctantly they left the smoke filled room which was pulsing with a vibrant beat.

"May I call upon you after your performance at the theatre?" Frederick asked Rosie, as he escorted her to the hotel.

"I would love to see you, but I don't know if I can obtain a ticket at this late stage. I believe they are sold out."

"Don't worry, I have already acquired a ticket," said Frederick as they reached the door. "I am greatly looking forward to the performance and will call afterwards – perhaps we can go out to dinner?" Rosie nodded and they parted with Frederick kissing her hand. She realised that she had rather hoped he would kiss her on the lips, but it seemed the etiquette was different in France.

Waking early the next day, Rosie decided to take a bath. The French provided bathing rooms adjacent to your bedroom, which was a great novelty. Dressing, she woke up Sylvie, and went downstairs for breakfast. It was Monday and the day of the first performance.

Director Copeau sprung upon them when they arrived. He announced that there was to be a change in casting and Rosie would now be playing Hero, with Edie taking the parts of Margaret and Ursula. Edie gave Rosie a black look and stormed out of the room. The director shrugged and nominated one of the understudies to play the two roles. Rosie ate her breakfast quickly, feeling excited but apprehensive. She was to play a major role in French, but luckily she had been rehearsing the part of Hero as understudy.

The day flew by and soon Rosie was peeking at the audience through a crack in the curtain. The theatre was full that night and she searched the seats for Frederick.

"Right, come on everybody, positions please," shouted the stage manager. The orchestra began playing a short introductory piece and a hush settled backstage, the lights dimmed and the curtain opened.

The first performance was near perfect, even though one of the understudies bumped against some scenery at the beginning of the second act and almost caused a disaster. The cast were buzzing. Director Copeau was complimentary, but asked them all to come to a pre-performance meeting tomorrow – "Just to go through some small points," as he put it.

Rosie had stolen the show and received a standing ovation when she came to take her bow but with the footlights in her eyes and the large audience she could not spot Frederick. Glancing up she saw Lord Berkeley in his box but couldn't read his expression. Excited and buoyed by the audience reaction she returned to the dressing room she shared with a fellow cast member, Mary Anne. The stage doorman, Maurice – a small mousy man who pinched the girls' bottoms given a chance and constantly walked into changing rooms – appeared at the door.

"Hey, don't you knock?" said Mary Anne sharply, pulling a robe around her.

"Pardon," he leered at the girls. "There is a gentleman at the door who says he has arranged to meet Rosie. He's sent his card." He passed a card to Rosie, moving close to try and look at her bosom.

"Tell him I will be 30 minutes and to wait please Maurice," said Rosie, moving away slightly.

She arrived 45 minutes later at the door.

"Sorry for keeping you waiting," she smiled to Frederick. He smiled back and kissed her hand, escorting her to his carriage.

"Where are your friends?"

"They cannot come this evening," she lied as she settled on the seat. They began to discuss the performance.

"You must have been pleased with the audience reaction to the play," Frederick said. "And when you bowed, most of the young men went into raptures," he added laughing.

"Are you teasing me Frederick?" Rosie looked at him sternly.

"No not at all, I am enchanted by you." He took her hand.

"Where are we going?" Rosie asked, glancing out of the window.

"Ah, that's a surprise."

As the coach sped along Frederick pointed out all the landmarks until shortly they pulled up outside 'Le Grande', a hotel near the Champs-Elysees.

A smart looking doorman opened the carriage door and Frederick offered his arm to Rosie, sweeping her inside.

Gazing around the foyer, Rosie was enchanted by the wonderful wooden panelling and the smell of newly polished floors. A huge chandelier lit up the hall.

"This way, please Sir," said the bellboy summoned by the concierge. He led them into a large dining room. Rosie let out a small gasp as they entered the most spectacular room she had ever seen. Round mirrors adorned the walls, which were decorated with dark red wallpaper, and large chandeliers sparkled from the ceiling. The effect of the glass and light was captivating.

"I hope you like this restaurant, they specialise in traditional French fayre," said Frederick as they sat down. Rosie nodded, still looking around her in wonder. She smiled at him across the table.

"Now Rosie, at last I have you to myself," Frederick said, leaning forward intimately. "Tell me about yourself, your family." Rosie paused for a moment, considering what she should tell this man, before deciding to give him the truth.

She explained that she came from a poor part of London with two brothers and a sister. That her father worked on the docks and her mother was a seamstress in the theatre – omitting her mother's dancing career.

"Excuse my curiosity," Frederick said as she paused to take a sip of her water. "You are such a brilliant actress and speak French fluently; you must have worked really hard to learn the language."

"I was very fortunate. My brothers, sisters and I had private lessons.

When I was five we all started to go daily to two tutors, Miss Simmons in Shoreditch and Mr Trumphet in Whitechapel, to learn English, French, Latin, History, Maths and Geography. My brothers found it very difficult, as previously we had had elementary lessons at a local school, but my sister and I loved it." Rosie smiled. "Mr Trumphet lent me books to read and my sister and I stayed until I was fifteen. Then I went every Saturday on my own and had elocution and deportment lessons from Miss Simmons and studied French."

"But how was your father able to provide that level of education, private lessons must have been expensive?" Frederick wondered out loud, before putting his hand to his mouth in horror. "Oh, I am sorry, that is an indelicate question." Rosie shook her head.

"I never understood how he did it either, and when I asked mum once she just said 'we manage, don't you worry'."

"Well Mrs Simmons did an amazing job. Not only do you look wonderful, you are a delight to be with," said Frederick, raising his glass to her.

Rosie picked up the menu and pretended to read whilst studying the man opposite.

"My French may not extend to all these dishes," she said demurely.

"Well leave it to me, I will order for both of us."

The meal went quickly as they talked about London, her acting parts and his studies. As they chatted, Rosie enjoyed her meal immensely – Foie de Gras, with chicken or poulet as she learnt for a main course and a fruit compote, a delicious desert she had not tasted before. Time seemed to go so quickly in the company of this man and it was 11:30pm when he called for his coach and they went back to her hotel. She hadn't enjoyed an evening as much in her life and when he suggested meeting the next day to go to the Sacré-Coeur Basilica she was delighted.

She went up to her room with a dreamy smile on her face and spent an excited 30 minutes telling Sylvie about the evening. In the end sheer exhaustion set in and she fell asleep on her bed fully clothed. Sylvie gently took off her dress and covered her with a blanket.

"Sweet dreams, love," she said, turning off the light.

Rosie had a leisurely start, deciding not to go down for breakfast. Frederick arrived promptly and they enjoyed another wonderful day together exploring the city. When they were on their way back, he gave her a small box. Rosie looked at it for a moment in surprise.

"What is this?" she asked.

"Open it and see," Frederick smiled. She opened the box slowly and gasped. Nestling inside was a beautiful gold locket. She lifted it from the cushion and let it trail through her fingers, noticing its lustrous shine. Frederick took it from her and gently fastened it around her neck.

"It's beautiful," she said warmly. "But I cannot accept it."

"Rosie, this is just a small token of my esteem for you, you must take it, I insist."

"But it is so expensive."

"Rosie, it is an inexpensive gift. I will be honoured if you will accept it."

Rosie thought for a moment.

"Thank you," she said, leaning forward to kiss him on the cheek.

Frederick looked so pleased with himself he nearly forgot to tell the coachman to stop outside a café in Montmatre. They spent the next hour gazing into each other's eyes, but time moved on and Rosie had to return to get ready for the evening performance. Frederick kissed her hand.

"May I take you to dinner later?"

"Another day," she said regretfully. "I promised a group of the actors we would go out tonight."

"Oh." Frederick looked crestfallen.

"But what about lunch on Wednesday?"

"That would be perfect," he replied.

The week passed with amazing speed as Rosie met with Frederick every day for lunch and often dinner. She was completely swept off her feet, although she was a little disappointed he hadn't kissed her yet. She was waiting for him to take her in his arms but he was a true gentleman and merely kissed her hand when they said goodbye. Sylvie had told her that he was in love with her but she did not really believe it – after all, they had only met a week ago. But she had to admit to herself that her own feelings were growing stronger and she secretly hoped he would soon declare his undying love, imagining the romantic scene as she lay in bed each evening.

Saturday was a big day for the cast as they were going to the British Embassy for a reception, which included the British Olympic team who were participating in the Paris Olympic Games. Coaches arrived and they set off down the Rue De L'Elysee toward Rue D'Anjou. The British Embassy was a magnificent mansion with wonderful columns and ornate balconies. When they went inside Rosie was greeted by a young man who said he was an under secretary. Rosie had no idea what that meant but he was certainly very charming, the son of Sir Rupert Hershaw, vice chancellor of Oxford University. He explained his father had wanted him to follow an academic career but he preferred the Army – they compromised and he joined the foreign office. Rosie, reminded of her past love, asked him if he had ever met Stafford but he had not.

"May I introduce you to some of our athletes Miss Holder," he said. As they entered a grand room Rosie had to concentrate not to stare at the wonderful paintings.

"Miss Holder, this is James Eardley one of our long distance runners."

"Nice to meet you Miss Holder. May I introduce Miss Cooper." Rosie smiled and they shook hands.

"Charlotte, but everyone calls me Chattie," said the slim athletic girl.

"What is your sport?" asked Rosie

"I play tennis."

"How wonderful I have never played."

"Well perhaps when we return to England I will show you the basics. What part do you perform in the theatre?"

They spent a lively twenty minutes discussing sport and the theatre and instantly liked each other. Rosie was swept around the room, meeting athletes, boxers, swimmers, fencers and some very strong looking tug-a-war members.

As they said their goodbyes to the British Team and their hosts, Chattie hurried across to Rosie.

"You must come and see me in my final next Monday," she said. "Here are two tickets."

"Oh that will be wonderful, thank you," Rosie replied. "Good luck in the match."

As she travelled back to the hotel, Rosie reflected on her trip to Paris. She had been so lucky to meet many interesting people and enjoy such wonderful experiences.

The buzz of the reception soon seemed far away, though, as the cast prepared for their evening performance. Rosie felt more nervous than usual as the cast had heard the French Prime Minister and the British Ambassador were in Lord Berkeley's box. They suffered a minor drama when Edie's part had to be recast as she had developed a terrible cold and laryngitis. Despite this small hiccup, the performance went splendidly, bringing the house down. All the players had three curtain calls and then the leading man Wilson walked with Rosie to the front of the stage to rapturous cheering and a standing ovation. As she looked around at the smiling faces, Rosie felt overwhelmed and had to pinch herself to believe it was real.

When Frederick called for her she was still on a high and he had to wait an hour before she finally appeared, still flushed from her success.

"Rosie, that was the most superb thing I have ever seen," he said breathlessly. "You were truly magnificent."

Rosie chatted to him excitedly until they reached their destination. As they stepped down from the coach, she looked up at the large sign – 'Moulin Rouge'.

They were shown to their table near the stage. Red, white and blue spotlights lit the curtain and the huge room was nearly full, a hum of chatter and clinking glasses.

"We will eat first then watch the show," said Frederick as a waitress came to the table dressed in a rather low cut red blouse and a short black skirt. Frederick ordered steak for them both, which he assured Rosie was beef, accompanied by a selection of vegetables and a bottle of Moet Chandon

Champagne. They talked about the performance that evening and Rosie asked him about the Moulin Rouge, which Frederick answered with some humour.

After dinner the lights dimmed and brilliant white spotlights bombarded the stage. The curtain slowly opened and Rosie gasped. There on the stage were two groups of dancers in brilliant sequined costumes. The orchestra started playing and Rosie watched open mouthed as two further groups of girls filtered onto the stage – all showing their breasts. She turned to Frederick who was watching her reaction.

"Frederick de Courcy, what have you brought me to?"

Glancing back at the stage she laughed as she suddenly realised that some of the 'women' were men. As the audience clapped and cheered loudly, Rosie joined in, smiling at Frederick. The evening ended with a sparkling 'ballet' if you could call it that and Frederick suggested they go before the crowd started to leave.

"That was most unusual," Rosie teased as she sat in the coach.

"I do hope you enjoyed the show," Frederick replied, pleased that she was amused by the evening.

They arrived back at Rosie's hotel and once again Frederick kissed her hand and made a date for Monday. Rosie had invited him to accompany her to the Olympic Games Tennis Final to see her new friend Chattie play.

In 1900 Paris hosted the Summer Olympics, which rather competed for visitors to the World's Fair. The Olympics were reduced to a bit of a sideshow and the seating area was not full when they arrived. Chattie had already explained to Rosie that this was the first Olympics where women had been allowed to participate.

The match started with both players winning their early games. Then Chattie broke her opponent's service and went on to take the first set.

"Isn't she something?" said Rosie, cheering loudly.

"I am not enjoying the match quite as much as you," Frederick grimaced. The Swiss girl, Chattie's opponent, tried hard but in the end lost in two straight sets.

Frederick made out he was not pleased but when they went down to the exit door he warmly embraced Chattie as they congratulated her on her gold medal.

"Please come to my medal ceremony," she said to them both.

"We would love to," beamed Rosie.

As the national anthem was played by a French brass band missing a number of notes, Rosie's eyes filled. The ceremony was very moving as she discovered she had a nationalistic streak and clapped loudly as a local dignitary put the gold medal around Chattie's neck. When they played the national anthem again and as Chattie shed a tear so did Rosie.

That evening, the boulevards of Paris were alive as people enjoyed the excitement of the 'Exposition' with street artists and clowns. Once again, though, Rosie went to bed disappointed. Frederick seemed to want her but, always the gentleman, he had simply kissed her hand and departed. She discussed the problem with Sylvie, aware that her time in Paris was drawing to a close.

"Well there is always Peter," chirped Sylvie as they switched off the lights. "He is disconsolate that you are seeing Frederick and is always asking me if you are still seeing each other." They both giggled but sleep came slowly that night as Rosie thought about the tennis match, the wonderful meal, and Frederick. He was such a gentleman... maybe a little too much a gentleman for her liking, she thought in frustration.

The weather continued cold and dry. Rosie visited as much of Paris as possible, Frederick making his coach available even if he was unable to go along himself. All too soon, though, it was the day before the play was due to end its run. So much had been packed into their trip, but in truth many of the actors were pleased to be going home. Rosie was not – she was dreading saying goodbye to Frederick. Their developing romance seemed about to end and still he had not tried to kiss her. Rosie knew she would be unable to resist if he took her in his arms and wanted to make love. Sometimes she yearned for him to sweep her off her feet and bed her.

The final night was once again a resounding success, with no less than four curtain calls and the stage covered with a blanket of roses. A smiling Lord Berkeley gave a speech about 'entente cordial' which pleased the French audience.

As she sat in the coach Frederick seemed a little subdued and throughout dinner he was quiet and seemed to have something on his mind.

They returned to her hotel, the coach moving slowly along the river one last time. Frederick suddenly moved across the seat next to her. Holding her hand he took a small box from behind his back.

"Rosie I know we have only known each other a short while but you must know how much I adore you. I love you Rosie, I cannot live without you," he said fervently.

Rosie was stunned by his sudden intensity; this quiet, reserved man was showing a different side.

"Rosie, I will be coming to London later this year working at my father's bank and I would like you to accept this small gift as a token of my love for you." He handed her the box. Rosie knew by now it was useless protesting and slowly opened the lid. Inside lay a beautiful diamond pin in the shape of a heart, sparkling in the moonlight.

"Oh, Frederick it's absolutely lovely, I will treasure it always," she said, her eyes glistening.

At last they kissed. Frederick embraced her passionately and Rosie found herself responding to his love making, but knew not to lead him. She had perceived he had a notion of how to behave with a woman and it didn't include his lady love taking control. He broke away.

"Rosie, swear to me you will wait for me in London. I will write telling you when I am coming." Rosie agreed and they kissed again, Frederick holding her tightly to him.

"Can I drive you to the station tomorrow?" he asked, as he accompanied her into the hotel reception.

"I don't see why not. We are leaving at 10am, come to the foyer then."

"My darling Rosie I shall miss you so much." He kissed her hand and left.

In the morning all the players had an early breakfast, packed their personal belongings and left their rooms, which had been home for the past two weeks. Monsieur Copeau beamed as he shook hands with the men and kissed the women on each cheek. When he reached Rosie he hugged her.

"Rosie, you were magnifique, your performances have been truly… how you say…" and he kissed his fingers in appreciation. Rosie smiled and glanced around the lobby with a heavy heart. There was no Frederick. The groups began to board the coaches and she looked around her for the last time, sure that he would come striding in. Welling up Monsieur Copeau helped the ladies into the coaches and shook hands again with his actors.

"Bon voyage," he shouted and they moved off, a long stream of horse drawn coaches heading for the station. Rosie sat in her carriage and tried not to let any tears show. She could not believe that Frederick had not been there to say goodbye.

At the Gare du Nord they boarded their train, finding reserved seats in the second-class carriages. Rosie decided to enjoy the two hour journey to the coast. It was a lovely day and the sun was shining brilliantly. Despite herself, though, she couldn't stop wondering where had he been and why he hadn't come.

Reaching Calais they boarded the steamer and Rosie headed for the top deck, a breeze blowing her clothes around her.

"Rosie, Rosie!" She turned around, her heart in her mouth as she hardly dared to hope it was him. Looking down at the dockside, she felt butterflies in her stomach. There was Frederick. As she watched, he spoke to two men at the gangplank and rushed up the stairs, reaching Rosie and sweeping her into his arms.

"Frederick, I thought you had forgotten," she said as they embraced.

"My coach didn't arrive and I had to find a cab," he answered. "When I made it to the station, the train was pulling away."

"How did you get here?"

"I ran up the platform, jumped on the guard's van step and luckily he let me in. I bribed him to let me ride in his van but he made me wait until the train emptied before I could leave and find you."

A horn sounded loudly. Frederick looked at the lovely woman in front of him.

"I must go Rosie, please remember me and wait for me in London."

"I will," replied Rosie as they kissed and parted. The steamer slowly edged away from the dock and she waved down to Frederick. She felt a hand on her shoulders and turned to see Peter standing behind her.

"Peter please don't do that," she said crossly and pushed his hand away, moving down the rail to keep Frederick in sight. Peter followed her.

"There was a time when you welcomed my attention," he said.

"I am sorry Peter, I don't want to mislead you. I am in love with Frederick and will wait for him in London." She watched as Frederick got smaller and disappeared as the steamship headed out of the harbour. Her eyes filled with tears and she brushed them away quickly.

"He will follow you my dear," said a voice behind her. She turned to see Lord Berkeley.

"Forgive me my sadness, Lord Berkeley. My young man is still on the dockside."

"I know, but I think you can be certain he will follow you."

"Do you think so?"

"Oh I am as certain as can be," he said with a twinkle. "Don't be too sad." He patted her arm and walked away.

For Frederick the goodbye was very painful. In ten days he had formed a deep attachment for this beautiful girl who was witty and loved the things he did. When that actor Peter had stood alongside her on the deck, he had felt a mixture of anger and jealousy. He would have to persuade his father to bring forward his trip to London. As he journeyed back to Paris, he thought about what lay ahead. He knew that it would be difficult to persuade his father as his future was carefully mapped out. Finish studies at the Sorbonne, which in effect he already had, return to Zurich work in the bank for two years then go to the Paris or London branch of his fathers Merchant Bank. In his heart he knew he would not disobey his father, so everything depended on him creating a plausible story or at least a good reason to visit London.

The sea crossing was a pleasure for Rosie. Unlike most of the cast and stagehands she liked the sea and the gentle rocking from side to side did not affect her. Sylvie on the other hand began to look green after 30 minutes out of Calais and Rosie had to help her to the ladies room quickly. Eventually, Rosie managed to get her up into the fresh air and, as the White Cliffs loomed, Sylvie visibly improved.

The steamer pulled into the busy port and they all disembarked. Lord Berkeley was on hand to direct them to the train waiting nearby and they left Dover for London. The journey was uneventful save for another attempt by Peter to talk to Rosie, but she wasn't in the mood. As she watched the countryside flash by, she dwelt on her two liaisons. There was her dear Stafford, lost to her forever, and now, unexpectedly, Frederick, a charming and attractive man. He was much more serious, but enjoyed many of the things she did. Would she see him again?

Arriving in London 10 minutes late, the train slowly pulled into Victoria Station. Smoke bellowed all around making Rosie cough as she stepped down from the carriage.

"Rosie!" An excited mother and father forced their way through the crowd waiting on platform 2 and embraced Rosie. A barrage of questions followed the hugs and kisses. Her father picked up her valise.

"Come daughter, I have secured a cab for our journey home."

He arranged with a porter to load her trunk on a trolley and they moved away, but not before Rosie went around all the actors and the helpers saying goodbye and hugging Sylvie, Wilson and Mary Anne. She was careful to avoid hugging Peter as she didn't want him to get the wrong idea.

The streets were thronging with cabs, carriages, buses and trams. Rosie, who liked travel in any form, enjoyed the journey home. Her mother had an endless number of questions about her trip and even her father was interested in her meeting Chattie, especially when she told him she was the first woman to ever win a gold medal at the Olympics. Returning to Bow Common and her father's terraced house she suddenly realised that her glamorous life in Paris, her trips to restaurants, galleries and clubs was at an end. "Back to earth Rosie," she told herself as she made her way inside.

Once she had settled indoors, she suddenly remembered that Lord Berkeley had handed them all a sealed envelope which she had completely forgotten about. She slit open the handsome envelope and a single sheet of paper dropped out with two £5 notes.

"Dear Rosie,

Your performances in Paris were a pleasure to watch. You were truly the star of our show and great credit goes to you at our reception at the British Embassy in Paris. Such was the reputation of our play the houses were always full and I have given each of the actors, stagehands and helpers all a token of my appreciation. Spend it wisely!

I will be appointing a new director for the Theatre Royal shortly and he will send you a message to appear for rehearsals.

Yours sincerely,

Lord Berkeley"

Rosie was tickled pink – fancy Lord Berkeley writing her a note. She passed the letter to her mother to read.

"Are you alright Mum?"

Molly had turned ashen and quickly put the letter back in the envelope.

"It's alright dear, just the excitement of the day. I am feeling a little tired that's all."

"What will you do with the £10?" piped up her brother, Albert. Rosie smiled and handed the money to her mother.

"Put this away Mum for a rainy day."

"Oh Rosie, you are such a good girl." Her mother hugged her.

"Cor blimey," said Albert. "What I couldn't have done with that." His father playfully clipped him around the ear.

"Earn it son, it's the only way."

They all laughed and Rosie looked around her contentedly. It was good to be home. And then she thought of Frederick again – would he visit London as he had promised, she wondered?

Chapter Four

Summer In London

The summer of 1900 was very pleasant. Rosie enjoyed walks over the common and even took a bus to Fleet Street one day to visit St Paul's Cathedral and several other churches in the area. Two weeks passed and then a note arrived from 'The Right Honourable Peregrine Woolstenhome' inviting her to a meeting at the Theatre Royal.

Rosie was excited. She felt like she couldn't wait to find out what lay ahead for her at the Theatre. No letters had come from France and it seemed Frederick had quickly forgotten her. She was disappointed, but told herself that it didn't matter and was eager to throw herself back into her work.

The day arrived for her meeting. Travelling across London by bus and tram was not easy. The buses and trams were irregular and both were jammed full, with people even hanging off the back. Changing once, Rosie arrived at her stop near the embankment and took a short walk to the theatre.

The actors were all assembled when Lord Berkeley strolled in with two men, one a podgy looking young man who did not appear all that well. He held up his hands for silence.

"I would like to introduce you to The Right Honourable George Alexander, our musical director, and The Right Honourable Peregrine Woolstenhome, your new director." There was a ripple of applause.

"Thank you, Lord Berkeley," replied Peregrine. He turned to the actors. "I am sure you have come here today to find out what our first production is to be. I propose that we return to one of the most beloved of Shakespeare's plays, 'As You Like It'." There was a hubbub of noise as the actors discussed this latest news. Peregrine held up his hands to quieten them.

"We will commence rehearsals on Wednesday this week and open on Saturday 22nd August. Meanwhile I have made a list of the parts and if you are lucky enough to be acting in the play your name appears alongside your part in the play."

A list was passed around. Some looked glum, others whooped with joy and when the list reached Rosie she looked down for her name. Her face flushed with joy as she saw she was to play Rosalind, one of the leading parts.

"Those who are in the play, please wait behind to collect your scripts. For the rest of you there is an understudy list pinned over there." Peregrine pointed to the exit and a pile of scripts to learn. "We will begin reading tomorrow sharp at 9 am."

For over a week they rehearsed for twelve hours each day. Rosie was enjoying the challenge but it was also exhausting. She worked hard, though, and by the time of the first performance, was ready to take to the stage. She couldn't help feel nervous, which was unusual for her. Appearing at the Theatre Royal was the ambition of every actor in London and she had one of the major parts: the play centres around Rosalind, daughter of a Duke exiled to the Forest of Arden. When she is also expelled from her father's former dominium, she disguises herself as a boy and has great fun interrogating the various characters and exposing their absurdities. Rosie loved the part and was determined to do it justice. As she waited backstage, she took a deep breath and prepared herself for her entrance. The first words were spoken and she found herself in front of the crowd, all nerves suddenly forgotten.

The play went well and as Rosie returned to the stage for her final scene in Rosalind's female dress, she smiled at the audience and delivered her line: "I charge you, O women, for the love you bear to men, to like as much of this play as please you." This was well known to bring a cheer from the women in the audience and this performance was no exception. As the clapping broke out, the actors took a deserved bow. Rosie was led forward by Wilson and they both received rapturous applause and whistles.

The cast had decided to celebrate the opening by going to the 'Fox and Whistle' a nearby public house. There, amongst much back slapping and great joviality, Peregrine declared: "Well done my dears, let us be sure to keep this standard when we continue on Monday."

The party broke up after two hours. Peter offered to escort Rosie home, but fortunately Lord Berkeley's coachman arrived at that moment to drive her. As the coach trotted along Rosie looked out at the streets, seeing couples walking hand in hand and wondering about Frederick. Where was he now? What was he doing? Had he forgotten so quickly, their romance in Paris?

The following day there was a loud knock on the front door.

Molly opened it and was surprised to see a young man standing there, tall with dark hair and clearly a gentleman.

"Hello, are you Rosie's mother?" he asked. Molly nodded, her curiosity aroused.

"My name is Frederick de Courcy, I had the pleasure of meeting your daughter in Paris, is she at home?"

Molly looked at him for a moment.

"Ah, you're Frederick, please come in. I am afraid you have just missed Rosie, she has gone to the theatre for the evening performance. Can I offer you tea?"

"That is very kind of you but I will make my way to the theatre, my cab is waiting outside. Is she performing at the Theatre Royal?"

"Yes, are you familiar with the theatre?"

"No, but I am sure my cabbie will know the way." And he left after shaking hands.

"Well I never," thought Molly. "I hope I have done the right thing telling him where Rosie was."

It was early evening and the road was busy; to an impatient Frederick, it seemed to take forever for the cabbie to weave his way through London. Arriving at the theatre, he saw Rosie's name on a billboard starring in 'As You Like It', not a play he knew much about. Entering the foyer he went to a box office.

"May I buy a ticket for tonight's performance?"

"I am sorry young man," the woman at the box office laughed. "All the tickets were sold a week ago, there is not even any standing room."

Frederick turned away disappointed.

"Why, hello," a voice called across to him. Frederick looked around.

"Ah, good evening Lord Berkeley."

"I thought I recognised you, is there a problem?"

"I was hoping to purchase a ticket for tonight's play but unfortunately there are none available," said Frederick, looking downcast. Lord Berkeley stood silently thinking for a second.

"I tell you what, why don't you join me."

"Oh, I couldn't impose on you like that," said Frederick in surprise.

"Don't be silly," said Lord Berkeley. "It's a real pleasure to enjoy the play with someone else. Meet me here at 7pm."

"You are most kind," replied Frederick and they parted.

Rosie arrived at the theatre by cab – these days she was delighted that the director arranged for her to be picked up and taken home. "I can't have my star travelling on the bus," he had said.

"Hello Miss Rosie," beamed the stage doorman. Rosie smiled back at him and headed toward her changing room. She did not have to share these days and had her own dresser who helped with the make up and costume.

The performance went well; the production was thoroughly enjoyed both by London's elite and the theatre goers who paid less to stand at the back. The Theatre Royal taking out seats showed the performance 'in the round' with a barrier preventing those standing from reaching the actors.

Rosie made her way back to her dressing room and disappeared behind a screen to change her clothes. There was a knock on her dressing room door. "Get that will you Carol please," said Rosie to her dresser, her voice muffled.

Carol opened the door to see a gentleman standing there with a huge bunch of red roses from which he was peering behind.

"Is Miss Rosie here?"

Carol looked at him suspiciously. "How did you get past the doorman?"

"Oh, I am a very good friend," replied Frederick.

Rosie froze behind the screen, recognising the familiar voice.

"Frederick, is that you?" She poked her head around the screen to see him standing by the door. She rushed towards him. He kissed her on the hand and she could barely contain herself from hugging him.

"What are you doing here?"

"If you will allow me to escort you to dinner, I will explain everything," he replied with a smile.

An hour later they were sitting in Simpsons on the Strand. They had both chosen the roast beef, but barely noticed the courses arriving, thoroughly immersed in each other, catching up on their time apart. Frederick explained that he had persuaded his father to send him to London for a while to meet some important people and familiarise himself with the English banking system. Rosie nodded, taking a sip of her wine.

"I have a present for you," he said and handed her a beautifully wrapped box. Her face flushed with excitement as she opened the small package. It was a simple pearl necklace, the beads gleaming with a lustrous shine underneath the restaurant lights.

"Oh Frederick, it's wonderful," said Rosie as Frederick gently fastened the necklace around her neck.

"It is merely a small token for the most beautiful woman in London."

"Now you are in London you must meet my mother and father," said Rosie, looking across at him. She was slightly apprehensive about taking Frederick home as they came from such a different backgrounds. How would the immaculate mild mannered Frederick react to her working class parents? What would her father think? Everything could be spoilt by the wrong word – or by Frederick seeing her as she really was, a girl from the East End of London. Still risk or no risk, if they had any future then she must, as her grandmother used to say, 'take the bull by the horns'.

They arranged to meet the next day for lunch and then to visit Rosie's parents.

They had lunch in a small restaurant in Fleet Street frequented by workmen and lawyers. Rosie looked carefully for signs in his behaviour: how did he react to the London working men? She felt butterflies in her stomach as they set off for the East India Dock Road.

"What number, sir?" said the coachman, leaning down.

"Twenty seven," replied Rosie. The coach pulled up and they alighted, Frederick helping her down from the footplate.

The East India Dock Road was a row of brick built terraced houses built fifteen years ago. Consisting of three bedrooms, a front room and a living room with a small kitchen and outside toilet, the properties were a profound step up for the working man. To Frederick they appeared most unusual. He had never seen or been inside such a property, but he was an open-minded man.

They reached the front door and Rosie knocked, smiling somewhat nervously at him. Molly appeared in her best Sunday dress.

"Mother, this is Frederick," said Rosie.

Frederick gave a short bow and shook hands.

"We met before Mrs Holder," he said in his impeccable English.

"Please call me Molly, everyone does," Molly ushered them inside. "Come in, come in, my husband Charlie is not home yet but I am expecting him shortly."

She showed them into the front room and Frederick subtly glanced around him, taking everything in. A simple room, but clean and tidy with a homely feeling he never felt when he went to his own home. Before he could say anything, there was a sound of heavy footsteps outside and the front door closed with a bang. In walked a burly man in shirtsleeves.

"You must be Frederick," said Charlie, extending his hand towards Frederick confidently.

"Pleased to meet you, sir."

Charlie went over to Rosie and kissed her on the cheek. "My apologies for being late, but there has been another accident at the East India Dock, a man was killed today."

Rosie gasped. "Anyone we know?"

"No – his name was Billy Tardy, he was nineteen," Charlie replied sadly. "Still that's the risk, I am going to wash before tea and we will talk in a minute, young man." He nodded at Frederick as he left.

"Right," said Molly briskly. "Let's get some tea – you do take tea Frederick?"

The afternoon went well. Rosie felt herself relaxing as she noted Frederick's natural polite manner with her parents. He and Charlie spent some time discussing the workings of the docks and the import of goods and Rosie exchanged a smile with her mother.

"I like that young man," said Charlie approvingly as the coach drew away. Rosie hugged her father.

"Oh, thank you dad for making him feel so at home."

Rosie settled into a new routine of playing Rosalind in 'As You Like It' and frequent dinners with Frederick at either Simpsons or Rules. She was blissfully content: the show was still very well received and she was thoroughly enjoying her time with Frederick. As they said goodbye after another perfect evening out, he looked at her seriously.

"Let's meet for dinner tomorrow, I have something important I wish to discuss."

Rosie felt her heart flutter but kept her voice calm. "That sounds very formal Frederick, what is it?"

"Let's wait until tomorrow," he replied, before saying goodbye.

To Rosie tomorrow seemed like an eternity. She performed in the afternoon matinee and evening show somewhat mechanically, her mind elsewhere. What was Frederick going to say to her, was he leaving? The relationship was over? Frederick knocked on her dressing room door at 10pm as arranged and, for once, Rosie was ready and waiting. She glanced at him as they made their way to their restaurant, Rules, talking lightly about that evening's show. He didn't mention her slightly lacklustre performance. There was a buzz in the restaurant as they entered and Rosie was clapped to her table as diners recognised her.

The waiter popped the cork of the champagne Frederick had ordered and poured a quantity into the champagne flutes, leaving them to ponder the menu.

"A toast to the most beautiful woman in the world," Frederick raised his glass and clinked it against Rosie's. "No man can be as lucky as I, an angel appeared before me in a Paris art gallery and I have never been happier since."

Rosie didn't know what to say, but Frederick was in full flow.

"I often dreamed as a boy about this lovely girl Alice who had a magical adventure. I hoped I would meet my own Alice and I have."

"Alice in Wonderland?" asked Rosie, still not quite sure what all this meant.

"Yes, my dream turned me into her Prince Charming and I helped her and in the end we were married. That's what I want to talk to you about, Rosie. You know what I feel toward you, I cannot live another day without you. I think of you constantly, Rosie will you marry me?"

Rosie looked at him for a second, completely taken aback. She had never imagined Frederick was intending to propose marriage.

"I can see that you are surprised, but I know that there will never be a better time as father intends me to return to Zurich shortly and I would like to take you with me."

The waiter approached to take their order. Rosie shook her head, still trying to take Frederick's words in. He took charge, ordering the speciality of the restaurant, an oyster soup followed by chicken, and a bottle of claret. The waiter went away again and Frederick sat back in his chair. Rosie hadn't spoken since his proposal and he began to feel nervous.

"Well Rosie, what is your answer?"

"Oh Frederick you know I love you, but I must think about what you have said. We come from different backgrounds, what if your father does not like me?" she said anxiously.

"Don't be silly, he will be enchanted and he has been urging me to find a bride so he can be sure of having grandchildren to continue the line."

"So I am being considered for breeding purposes," Rosie said, her eyes twinkling.

Frederick look flustered. "Oh, I am putting this so badly," he muttered.

"I am only teasing Frederick, but I cannot give you my answer now. Please allow me time to think."

They turned their attention to the meal but it was not really enjoyed by either of them. Frederick was concerned he had botched the proposal while Rosie's mind was alive with thoughts. They agreed to meet the next day after the evening performance and Frederick sent her home in his carriage. Normally he would have accompanied her, but he ordered a cab, preoccupied by what had happened that evening. Why oh why did he not make a better job of the proposal?

Rosie arrived home to find her mother and father had gone to bed as it was after all 1:30 in the morning. She was bursting to tell them her news but knew her father had to get up at 5am to go to work.

She slept fitfully, seeing Frederick's face. She felt excited at the proposal, but something was not right. Waking at 7:30, she went downstairs and could hear her mother singing in the kitchen.

"Mum, can we sit down a moment?"

"What is it dear?" her mother looked concerned.

"Frederick proposed marriage to me last night," said Rosie seriously.

"Ah I see," Molly's face beamed at her daughter. "Well I am not surprised, it was quite clear the young man is smitten with you."

"But what should I do?" Rosie asked.

Molly frowned. "You should not need to ask me dear. Let you heart tell you."

"That's just it I am not sure. I do love Frederick but..." Rosie's voice trailed off as she tried to find the words to explain her confusion.

"When your father proposed to me in the Swan, a pub on the river, he went down on one knee in front of the whole place. I knew immediately I loved him and wanted to be his wife. If you don't feel that then you must say no."

Rosie nodded and went to get ready for the day ahead, leaving her mother concerned. Why had her daughter not reacted more positively to the proposal? Surely this meant she was not certain – perhaps it would be better to advise her to wait? Molly sighed to herself. She had to trust Rosie to make the right decision.

As usual Lord Berkeley woke at 7am. His servant Redding had laid out his clothes and run his bath and he quickly washed, dressed and went downstairs.

"Redding, can I have the kippers followed by scrambled egg and tea," he said, sitting down. He pondered for a moment the announcement he was to make later today. He had sold his interest in the Theatre Royal and simultaneously purchased another theatre in Drury Lane. Shakespeare would always have a place but he thought the mass audience were turning toward stage revues and plays.

Intending to meet Rosie and several other members of the cast before the matinee this afternoon, he set off for the theatre.

Rosie had been picked up as usual by the cab at noon. The journey to Cheapside to collect one of the other actors, Sebastian, was a blur to her, however, as she was lost in her private thoughts.

"Hello ducks how are you today?" said Sebastian, as he climbed into the cab. He looked at her closely, sensing she was subdued. "Is there something wrong Rosie?"

"Wrong – no nothing wrong, just something I need to work out," she replied hastily.

"Well it's a lovely day for working something out and you have worn just the right dress to do it."

Sebastian was a favourite with the actresses because he had such a good eye for an outfit and loved to talk about make-up and lipstick.

"Is it man problems luv?" asked Sebastian, when Rosie remained silent.

She nodded. "It's Frederick, he proposed to me last night."

Sebastian's face lit up.

"But that's wonderful! He's such a nice boy, did you say yes?"

"Well, that's what I need to work out. My heart wants to say yes but my head – that says there are obstacles," Rosie replied frowning.

Sebastian laughed and gave her hand a squeeze.

"Nonsense, go with your heart – I always do. Look he's rich, good looking… what more do you want?"

Rosie pondered on Sebastian's advice throughout the brief journey around St Paul's and down to the embankment toward the Theatre Royal. Sebastian was twittering away about a summer wedding – how wonderful and could he help her to prepare? Her thoughts were interrupted as they arrived at their destination.

"You're here miss," the cabbie called down. He always ignored Sebastian.

Rosie was surprised when she entered to learn that Lord Berkeley was waiting for her in the back office. Knocking on the door Rosie temporarily forgot her dilemma over the proposal: what did Lord Berkeley want?

"Come in my dear, sit down. I wanted you to be the first to know that I have sold the Theatre Royal and the company of actors will now be employed by the Honourable Alastair Stewart. I'm sure you have heard of him, a fellow thespian."

Rosie looked at him in shock, speechless at the news.

"However, I want you to come over to the Regency in Drury Lane and join my cast of actors there. I intend to put on a number of plays and some light revues and even some opera – would you be interested?"

Rosie broke into a smile. "Yes I would," she said without hesitation. "I have always wanted to do other things and I started my career in music hall at the Britannia Shoreditch."

"I know my dear. You will be earning a slightly higher weekly wage and will be head lined where the part is appropriate. The cabbie will always collect you and return you home."

Rosie left the room absolutely delighted at this turn of events. Then she stopped abruptly. "Oh," she thought. "Frederick wants me to accompany him to Zurich!"

How she managed to do the matinee and then the evening performance was a miracle, her mind was preoccupied turning over the startling information of the past twenty-four hours. Shortly after the evening performance Lord Berkeley called all the players back to the stage and announced his decision to sell the Theatre Royal. Everyone was stunned and immediately began wondering about their future. Rosie was oblivious to the announcement and did not even hear the snide comment made by one of the girls when Lord Berkeley announced Rosie would be joining him at the Regency as his principal lady. After the announcement, Rosie hurried back to the changing room. She was late, Frederick would be waiting.

Outside Frederick began to get very impatient. He got out of the carriage and paced up and down and finally walked toward the stage door. Suddenly he was confronted by two burly toughs.

"You Frederick?" one of them said.

Frederick nodded thinking it was something to do with the theatre when he was hit on the head. Falling, he attempted to shield himself as boots and blows hit his body. Mercifully he soon passed out. The coach driver who had been relieving himself came back to find Frederick unconscious outside the stage door.

"Can someone get a doctor," he shouted as he ran inside. "My fare has been beaten and is in the doorway."

The doorman, who knew who Frederick came to see, sent one of the stagehands to fetch the doctor and went to tell Rosie what had happened. She rushed to the stage door and gasped as she recognised her poor Frederick bloodied and lying unconscious.

"What happened?" she said, bending over him.

The doorman didn't know and the coach driver was no help. It seemed an eternity as Rosie cradled his head in her hands waiting for the doctor. When he finally arrived, the doctor decided that Frederick's injuries might be severe and they carried him to the coach to proceed at haste to Charing Cross Hospital. Rosie went with him, her face pale with shock and worry.

"Please wake up dear Frederick," she whispered, holding his hand tightly.

Frederick sat up in bed in the Eaton Square house. Everyone had been asking him questions about that night – the police, Rosie, the manager of the Bank. What had happened and why he had been targeted? He had given them all great cause for concern, remaining unconscious for twelve hours. With no known relatives in London, a message had been dispatched to the bank he worked at in the City of London. When he had eventually woken, the doctors declared he was out of danger, but he did have two broken ribs and severe bruising to his body. And then the questions had started. He didn't know what to tell them as it had all happened so quickly. Now his father had arrived from Switzerland and Frederick couldn't help but feel he would have to relive the moments all over again.

Baron Wilhelm de Courcy was a large man who dominated the room. As he walked into the bedroom the atmosphere immediately changed. Here was a man who was used to authority, who expected everyone to do his bidding and Frederick was his only son.

"Frederick what have you been doing?"

"Father," replied Frederick, suppressing a small sigh.

The two embraced, Frederick not at all surprised by his father's arrival; it was typical of the man.

"You must tell me all that has happened, I have spoken to your doctors so there is no need to discuss the injuries, but the police seem mystified as to your assailants."

Frederick settled back into the pillows.

"I am afraid my recollection is not good. I remember waiting in a cab for my friend and walking to the stage door – "

"Ah yes, the famous Rosie," interrupted his father. Frederick looked at him quizzically. What did his father know of Rosie?

"Well go on," the Baron sat on the edge of the bed.

"As I said, I walked across the street to the stage door. The next minute two ruffians appeared and attacked me."

"But why, they did not rob you, your gold watch was still in your waistcoat and they left your money?" said his father, shaking his head.

"I don't know father. Everyone has been asking me the same question and I simply don't know," said Frederick, with a frown.

"Well I have summoned one of London's finest detectives to investigate and I have stationed a man outside the front door of this house on guard until we get to the bottom of this."

"That seems a little drastic father," Frederick began. He had been staying for the past two weeks at their London house in Eaton Square and doubted a guard was needed on the door, but it was pointless arguing with his father.

"Now, how do you feel?" the Baron said, changing the subject.

"Other than very sore ribs and a slight difficultly breathing through my nose, I don't feel too bad."

"Well I will call back later and you can tell me all about this young lady Rosie." His father beamed at him as he got up to leave and Frederick sighed again to himself.

Leaving Eaton Square, the Baron went straight to the city where he interviewed George Knight, a private detective. George had been an inspector in the City of London police before his fondness of drink and prostitutes came to the attention of his superior.

"I wish you to investigate an attack on my son. Find the brigands and tell me who and where they are. I will pay a bonus of one hundred pounds and all your legitimate expenses for a result within the next week."

The Baron knew all about Knight's background and liked using men he had a hold on.

"That may be difficult, sir, as there is little evidence and no eye witnesses," replied Knight.

"Mr Knight you have been recommended as the best detective in London. I pay well for results not for failure, do you understand me?"

"Yes your Lordship I do."

"Go on then, get on with it. Go into the gutter and find out what you will and if you need to bribe people to find out who did this, do so," said the Baron, striding out of the room without waiting to hear Knight's answer.

Rosie had visited Frederick every day since the attack and on several occasions Molly accompanied her.

"The poor boy," Molly said. "No one to look after him in London."

Although she had only met Frederick three times, she liked him already. He was, in her words, 'a gentleman'.

They made their way across Eaton Square and were surprised when they arrived at the house to find a guard at the front door.

"What's your business here?" he asked.

"We have come to see Frederick," Rosie replied.

"Is he expecting you?"

"Well yes, I mean not exactly, but he will see us."

The burly guard looked at the two attractive women and decided they represented no threat, but his orders had been explicit: let no one in other than the doctors unless the Baron sent authorisation.

"I am sorry Miss, I have my orders, no one is to be admitted."

Rosie and her mother were taken aback, but didn't want to create a scene. Rosie scribbled a note and asked the guard to give it to a maid to pass to Frederick.

Frederick sat up in bed eating lunch of a clear soup and bread when the maid appeared.

"Excuse me sir, but two ladies left this note for you."

Frederick read the note and was furious. Getting out of bed he put on a dressing gown and went downstairs to the front door.

"You, come in here," he commanded. "Why have you stopped my friend and her mother visiting me?"

He was very angry and began to feel shaky. Suddenly he crashed to the floor. The guard reacted quickly, picking him up and carrying him back upstairs to the bed whilst the maid went looking for a nurse, who was being regaled by one of the footmen in the kitchen.

The Baron was summoned and arrived an hour later. Frederick, having recovered from his faint, was sat up in bed reading 'The Times'. He looked up as he his father walked in.

"Father," he said quietly. He looked tired. "Why did the guard prevent Rosie and her mother visiting me?"

"I would have thought that was obvious Frederick. You cannot walk to the door and I won't have anyone exciting you."

"But father that was Rosie, what will she think?"

"Alright, don't concern yourself," said the Baron calmly. "I will travel to the theatre where she works and explain."

Frederick thought quickly.

"I don't think that's necessary father, just allow me to send a note explaining and asking if she can come tomorrow."

"No. I will go myself," the Baron said firmly and left the room.

Frederick leaned his head against the pillow. He was concerned: his father was a formidable man and dominated most people. Then he frowned to himself. How did he know where to find Rosie in any case?

Chapter Five

The Baron

The Baron, being the man he was, had of course known where Rosie worked and who she was for sometime. Knight, the private detective, had sent him a full report on Frederick's activities in London together with photographs cut out from London newspapers showing this beautiful woman. The Baron knew about Rosie's family, her background and had told Knight to investigate whether she had had any previous lovers. He presumed his son was making love to this girl, but Knight had not been able to confirm any intimacy.

His carriage stopped outside the front entrance of the Theatre Royal and he walked to the box office.

"I wish to see Miss Rosie Holder. Here is my card, please tell her I am here," he commanded.

The girl called to the door attendant: "Jack, a message for Rosie. Tell her a gentleman is here to see her and pass this card."

A few minutes later Rosie appeared.

"Baron de Courcy?"

"Ah, you must be Rosie," he smiled. He could be a charming man when he had cause to be and he reached out and kissed her hand.

"Do you know who I am?" he asked.

"Yes, you must be Frederick's father."

"I am delighted to meet you, is there somewhere we can go to talk?"

"Yes, come with me."

She led him to her dressing room and closed the door.

"I visited Frederick today and was refused entry," she said, looking at him steadily. She was not a timid girl and refused to be easily dominated by any man.

"My apologies my dear, that was my fault," replied the Baron smoothly. "I left instructions that Frederick was not to be disturbed as he is still very weak from the terrible beating he took. He asked me to call and explain and would like to see you tomorrow."

Rosie relaxed and smiled.

"In that case, please tell him I shall be calling at noon."

"The thought occurs to me that we do not know each other and have got off to a bad start," the Baron went on. "May I arrange for lunch tomorrow at Eaton Square, after which you can visit Frederick?"

Rosie paused for a moment. What could she say to that?

"I look forward to it," she replied.

After making the necessary arrangements, the Baron returned to his carriage, instructed the driver and sat thinking. Opening his small black leather case he extracted two papers.

"Hmm," he muttered to himself.

The following day Rosie got up early to bathe and select an appropriate outfit. She chose a simple pale lace full length dress buttoned to the collar with a red silk belt and a flamboyant feather hat. Putting on the pearls Frederick had given her she looked at herself in the mirror. Yes, that was the effect she wished to convey – conservative with a dash of individuality. She tied up her hair and dabbed her body with lavender water. There was a knock on the front door and she head her mother call for her. The Baron had sent a cab to pick her up.

The Baron arrived early having arranged for caterers to set up a meal in the grand dining room. His personal butler would supervise two serving girls and leave them alone to talk at the appropriate time. He had chosen a light wine, a moselle, not to drink himself but to relax Rosie. He had a great number of questions he wanted to ask this young lady.

Rosie arrived and was shown into the library where the Baron joined her.

"Welcome, would you like an aperitif? Sherry or a chilled German Moselle?"

"No, thank you Baron, I never drink at lunch time as I have an afternoon matinee."

"Very commendable I am sure; come let us go through to the dining room."

The butler pulled her chair out and she sat at the lavish dining table, alongside the Baron who was at the head of the table. She felt slightly nervous but nonetheless curious. What did he want? Frederick hadn't exactly spoken fondly of his father, in fact he hadn't really spoken of him at all. The Baron smiled at her.

"How long have you known Frederick?" he asked.

"Since Paris, in January," replied Rosie.

"I wonder, my dear, what Frederick has told you about us, about our family?" The Baron nodded as a waiter placed a plate of cold meats in front of him. "I do hope you like cold meat, I tend to eat lightly for luncheon. It is a Bavarian habit I got into when I was a boy."

"Thank you. I also do not eat very much at this time of day and, in answer to your question, I know very little of you or your family."

"Ah, I see, well let me give you a brief history," the Baron said, taking a forkful of food. "The de Courcy's have had a residence in Zurich,

Switzerland's largest city, for over 400 years. Frederick went to Zurich University before he continued English studies at the Paris Sorbonne – ah, but you know that I am sure", he paused for a moment.

"The history of the de Courcy's is interesting. A distant relative was involved with the defeat of the Hapsburgs at Semach in 1386 and a Baronet was awarded to the de Courcy's. After two wives failed to produce a male heir, the title went to the son of his brother, my distant relative."

Rosie nodded and took a sip of water.

"The de Courcy's were a family of French decent and the Baron at that time was a leading figure, who helped create the Swiss League in an attempt to unify the country. This led to the rise of a military power and in 1477 another Baron de Courcy led the Swiss in victories over Charles the Bold of Burgundy and over Emperor Maximilian I. Switzerland was then granted virtual independence – I'm not boring you my dear I hope?" the Baron broke off suddenly.

"No, not at all. I am very interested," replied Rosie, who was trying to hold her concentration through the Baron's history lesson.

"Well, as you can imagine fortune favours the brave," he continued. "My Grandfather, many times removed, became very wealthy owning lands around Zurich and a large number of houses in the city. He also built the Chateau Esseu on Lake Geneva for the family to spend rest periods and holidays," he stopped again, collecting his thoughts. Rosie looked at him attentively, waiting for him to resume.

"By 1513 there were 13 Cantons – these are the regions of Switzerland – but unfortunately the French had ambitions on European domination and defeated the Swiss Army at Marignano in 1515. The then Baron de Courcy was killed in the battle and his son Roger became the Baron de Courcy of Esseu aged 16. Peace followed, which formed the basis of Swiss neutrality today, but as a nation we were not yet formed until the religious Civil War of 1531 when the Catholics defeated the Protestants."

Rosie accepted another helping of the cold meats and tried not to let her mind wander. She wasn't sure why the Baron was telling her all this, but he clearly felt it was important, so for Frederick's sake she tried to take it all in.

"After this relative peace my forbears gained even greater wealth and started a bank, Le Banc de Courcy, situated in Zurich in 1724. Zurich was a central banking region where large sums of money were deposited by European and worldwide investors, usually in gold. In the 18th Century Switzerland's wealth steadily increased, which also encouraged intellectual visitors and scholars. Then came a rather foolish move by some of the Cantons to oppose the French Revolution. I am pleased to say the then Baron, my grandfather, brokered the Act of Mediation in 1803, which partly restored the old federation," said the Baron proudly. "In 1815 the Pact of Restoration substantially established the old regime and then the armies of Napoleon were defeated. The de Courcys lost a great deal of money supporting the Napoleonic Wars neutrally you will understand, but my Grandfather was a shrewd businessman and quickly started a new political party called 'The Radical Party'. He favoured greater centralisation and, after a brief almost bloodless Civil War, at the age of 81 Grandfather saw his ambition fulfilled - the Confederation became a Federal State under a new constitution he had part written. Regrettably, he died six months later and my father inherited substantial wealth, a Merchant Bank and numerous properties."

Stopping to think for a second, he added: "National unity has been good for Switzerland and we are proud to retain our independence and neutrality. I am now President of the bank and a representative of the Zurich Canton. Regrettably I carry the burden alone, my wife died two years ago, but my son has always been groomed to take over when the occasion arises."

He looked at Rosie.

"It is for that reason, my dear, I cannot agree to your marriage to my only son."

Rosie was taken aback and blushed.

"What do you mean?" she asked, confused by this abrupt news.

"It is alright my dear, I know your plan: seduce my son and you will become a rich woman."

Rosie pushed her chair back and stood up, looking at him with distain.

"I have never been so insulted in my life. I am not staying any longer."

Before the Baron could respond, his butler approached.

"My apologies sir, a gentleman has called to see Frederick but on being told he cannot, has insisted on talking to you."

The Baron took the card handed to him.

"Show him in, Miss Rosie is just leaving."

Rosie shook her head and moved towards the door just as Lord Berkeley strode in.

"Ah Rosie, I wondered if you would be here," he said. He stopped as he saw the tears in her eyes. "What is it my dear, is something wrong?"

"I am sorry Lord Berkeley I cannot tell you, please excuse me." She rushed past him out of the room.

The Baron came to meet Lord Berkeley at the door, extended his hand and they shook.

"It is nice to meet you, Lord Berkeley. I have long admired your bank. Come through to the drawing room," he said.

"I also your various enterprises Baron," replied Lord Berkeley as he sat down in a sumptuous leather chair. "I had come to see Frederick, who I met through his acquaintance with my leading actress, Rosie, at the Theatre Royal many times but I have found my way blocked by some wretched fellow."

"A thousand apologies, my guard was simply carrying out my orders to avoid Frederick becoming over excited. He has had a difficult time and the doctors are still watching him closely for a delayed concussion."

"I understand," replied Lord Berkeley. "But why was Rosie in tears?"

"In tears, sir?" said the Baron, seemingly incredulously. "I did not notice any. There is no reason I can assure you."

"I think I should make something quite clear Baron. Rosie is a protégé of mine and I would not like her to be in any way hurt or unhappy."

"My dear Lord Berkeley, she is a charming and beautiful girl. I am pleased Frederick has such a friend."

"Well, I will take my leave," Lord Berkeley rose. "Please inform Frederick that I called. Perhaps when he is a little better you will let me know."

"Of course," said the Baron and called for his butler. "Please show Lord Berkeley out. " They nodded to each other, shook hands and Lord Berkeley left.

The Baron sat back down, pondering on this call. "Well, well, well," he thought. "The girl is a protégé of Lord Berkeley, what does that mean? Does he want her for himself? Hmm, I bet that's what it is, she is an extraordinary woman, very beautiful. I could be enchanted by her myself."

His thoughts were interrupted by his butler.

"Frederick would like to see you, sir."

The Baron entered Frederick's bedroom.

"Who was that father?"

"Just business. As you know we are on the verge of arranging a huge loan to Britain and I am negotiating the finer points."

"Father, I have not seen any of my friends, has a young lady called Rosie called?"

"Not to my knowledge my son," replied the Baron. "Now you need to get some rest so do not worry yourself with these matters."

As he left the room, a moment of doubt crept into his mind. He wondered if he had made a mistake warning off the girl. Time would tell.

Lord Berkeley was not happy. He had detected a problem concerning Rosie and he didn't like it. He suspected that the Baron had found out about her relationship with Frederick and objected. He considered how best to deal with the problem. As his coach passed through Fleet Street, an idea came to him.

Rosie had caught the cab waiting outside but, despite the driver's cheerful chat, had felt miserable. When she got back home she went straight to her room. Her family tried to console her and when her father found out about what Baron de Courcy had said, he was all for storming around to his house and giving him a piece of his mind (and much worse). Molly calmed the situation.

"Look, once Frederick finds out what his father has done you will find out how much he really loves you."

"Yes," her father commented. "We'll see if the lad has a backbone! It is no use tying yourself to a fop."

Rosie began to see the sense of what they were saying and quickly pulled herself together. "Dad is right," she thought. "Frederick's behaviour will tell me what I need to know."

Meanwhile Lord Berkeley visited his old chum Viscount Mornay, head of the Bank of England governors, in Threadneedle Street. They had been to both Eton and Oxford together and were lifelong friends.

"Charles, I need a favour," said Lord Berkeley after they had exchanged greetings. "Are you still negotiating the loan with the Swiss?"

The Viscount nodded.

"In that case, can you do something important for me?"

"My dear chap, just ask," replied his friend.

"Please don't ask me why, but will you arrange a dinner for the governors and, say, the Prime Minister, Chancellor and / or the Treasury Minister at the Mansion House, concerning the proposed loan being arranged – and invite the Swiss and particularly Baron de Courcy?"

Lord Berkeley looked at his friend who thought for a second.

"Shall we say this coming Friday dinner at 8.00pm?"

"Charles, I am very grateful. One day I will tell you why," said Lord Berkeley, relaxing a little.

"I am intrigued, but know you better than to pursue the matter. In any case, it will be extremely useful to meet over such a dinner and iron out any last minute detail. As you know the PM is keen to proceed with the loan to meet defence overspend, as the budget has escalated since the Indian difficulty and now we have trouble with the blessed Arabs which has caused us to send a standing Army to Egypt."

Lord Berkeley, who was also a Bank of England Governor, knew very well the reason for the loan; the Chancellor had miscalculated his budget and needed to borrow two hundred million pounds to balance the books. The Swiss were broking a deal using private funds and money from certain European countries and would themselves take a handsome turn on the interest rate.

"Thank you, Charles. May I ask one more favour?"

"I am in the mood dear boy, ask away."

"When arranging the seating, I would like to be next to Baron de Courcy with you sitting on his other side."

"Consider it done."

Lord Berkeley left the Bank of England planning his next move. He had five days: next stop the Bank of Chicago in Cheapside.

The Governor of the Bank of England was as good as his word. An embossed invitation arrived simultaneously to the Swiss Ambassador, the London Director of Credit Suisse and the Zurich Bank, together with the

Baron on behalf of the de Courcy's Bank. A few messages between the bankers established that this was indeed a meeting to discuss the major loan the British were seeking and present at the meeting would be the Chancellor, various Treasury officials and Bank of England Governors. The Baron was delighted: his trip to London would be very profitable yet. His London Director was not as effective as he could be and hadn't closed the deal. From Zurich he had led a consortium of Swiss Bankers, had raised the capital at particularly beneficial terms and was standing to make a considerable amount of money from the deal.

Lord Berkeley called Charles the following day.

"I am so grateful for your help, Charles. Have they all confirmed acceptance?"

"Yes, no problem old boy the Swiss are falling over themselves," Charles replied, laughing.

"By the way, is it true the PM has a meeting on the same day with the American Ambassador?" Lord Berkeley asked.

"Yes, it's a long standing invitation hence he was unable to break it."

"Thanks again Charles, I owe you."

Lord Berkeley smiled to himself. Well Baron, the bait is set, he thought. Now to spring the trap.

Chapter Six

Peter Reappears

Rosie had had a miserable week. She had not been working as there was a delay of a fortnight before the Regency Theatre was ready for them to begin an exciting new Gilbert and Sullivan musical play, called HMS Pinafore. Rehearsals started in ten days and she was learning her part. Lord Berkeley had also arranged for her to spend two hours every other day with a voice tutor in Chelsea, so she was not bored, just frustrated. She hoped that as soon as Frederick regained his strength he would seek her out, but she couldn't help thinking of the Baron's statement warning her off.

There was a sharp knock on the door, interrupting her thoughts. Rosie, glad to have a break from studying her part, stood up to answer it and was somewhat taken aback to find Peter standing there.

Somewhat inevitably, given the circles they moved in, gossip about Rosie had reached his ears. He hadn't seen her since that day on the boat coming from France, when she had made it quite clear that he had no chance. Still smarting from the rejection, as soon as he heard about the stalling romance with Frederick, he decided to try again. It was not often that a woman refused him and he was determined to reverse the situation.

"Hello Rosie," he said with a smile. "I heard you were a little low and thought I would call and cheer you up."

"You had better come in then," replied Rosie a little reluctantly, gesturing for him to enter. "Would you like tea?"

"That would be grand, Rosie."

Peter reverted to Irish when he wanted to soften an atmosphere. His mother had been born in Dublin and he knew how to be charming with the lilting accent. As Rosie disappeared to prepare the tea, he surveyed the room.

"So, tell me Rosie what are you working on at the moment?" he said, as she came back with a mug of tea. He already knew but feigned ignorance, watching her carefully.

"I have got a part in a new production at the Regency Theatre Drury Lane of HMS Pinafore," she replied.

"That's good," he said, taking the tea. "You not having one?"

"No, I don't really like tea that much."

"Well, here's to you," he raised the mug in a mock salute. There was an awkward pause. "Don't you want to know what I am doing?"

"Yes, sorry. I am miles away. What are you doing, are you working?"

"No, but I am hoping that the new owners of the Theatre Royal will cast me, I am trying out for a part in Macbeth."

"That's good, do you see any of the Paris cast?" said Rosie politely, wondering how long he intended to stay.

"No, I haven't seen anyone since the train home. When I did not get a part in 'As You Like It' my work dried up and I have had to live at home with my mother. "

Before she could reply, Peter put down his mug and moved closer to Rosie.

"Rosie, you know I fancy you like crazy and I hear that Frederick has gone, so how about you and me…" He slipped his arms around her waist and pulled her towards him. She struggled to break his hold, but he was strong.

"Now come on Rosie, what about a little kiss?" He tried to draw her closer, his hand on her head.

"You've been drinking," said Rosie in disgust, still struggling to free herself from his grip.

"Well what of it?" he snarled. "Come on, let's make up for lost time."

Rosie sensed things were getting out of hand and she began shouting at him as she pushed him away.

"Peter, what are you doing, let me go before I scream."

He clamped his hand over her mouth and pulled her to the floor. His body was on top of hers and very heavy but she struggled desperately to avoid his mouth, moving her head from one side to the other. She tried to scream again, but he struck her around the face. Feeling her cheek tingling, she thought furiously – she needed to get away from him.

"Shut up, you'll attract attention. Now come on, you know you want to," he said, panting now from the effort of holding her wriggling form down. She was completely trapped underneath him but managed to free one arm and simultaneously bit his lip and hit out with her right hand.

"Well, I knew you were a fiery one but this is even more exciting," Peter said, leering at her. He began to fiddle with his belt and lowered his trousers. Rosie knew it was getting very serious and, as he tried to raise her skirt with one hand, she brought up her knee sharply. She had wrestled with her brothers many times and this always seemed to work. Connecting with Peter's groin, he rolled off her holding his testicles.

"You bitch!" He grabbed her hand and pulled her back towards him, hitting her in the face hard. She tasted blood in her mouth. "Look why not enjoy it, you know you want to."

Suddenly all hell broke lose. Molly stood over him with a broom in her hand and was raining blows down on him. Her brother Billy was hitting him with slightly better effect using a poker he had picked up from the hearth.

"Stop Billy, you'll kill him!" shouted Rosie. He stepped away from him reluctantly, leaving Peter writhing in agony on the floor.

"You bastards, you've broken my leg," he groaned.

"That's the least you deserve," said Molly grimly. "Billy, run down the dockyard and fetch your father."

Rosie sat down shakily, the reality of what had just happened sinking in. By the time Jack rushed back, she had composed herself enough to tell her father about it, still holding a wet flannel to the side of her face where Peter had hit her.

"I could kill the bastard," Jack growled, clenching his fists, barely containing the rage that had built up inside him as he listened to Rosie.

"I need a doctor," muttered Peter, who had sobered up but not yet shown any remorse for his drunken actions. Jack looked at him in disgust for a moment and made up his mind.

"Right, Billy go and ask Bill if you can borrow his cart," he said.

Molly went over to Rosie and put her arms around her. Ten minutes later the cart arrived at the front door.

"Okay let's get him up on the back."

They picked up Peter, who screamed in agony, and placed him on the cart.

"Right we'll take him to the Whitechapel Hospital. You stay here and clean the place up," said Jack, hurrying out of the door. Rosie lifted her head and watched silently as they carried Peter out of the house.

A tense two hours went by for Molly and Rosie until they returned.

"Everything alright?" asked Molly, anxiously.

"Yes, it is all sorted out," said Jack grimly. "He won't be bothering our girl again."

Rosie had regained her presence and hugged her brother and father.

"If he comes near me again Dad, I swear I will swing for him."

"Don't worry luv, he won't," replied her father, going to get a drink.

Jack knew Peter wouldn't bother his daughter again because he and Billy had not taken him to the hospital. Instead they had walked the covered cart down to the docks, nodding to Old Sid on the gate as they went past. He was enjoying a nice bottle of rum at the time and waved them through. Jack was the top union man in the dock and he owed him a lot.

"So what if he's filching," thought Sid, taking another swig from the bottle. "Everybody does it a bit, no harm done."

In fact, Jack and Billy were wheeling an unconscious Peter in the cart, Jack having knocked him unconscious with a cosh as soon as they left the house. They made their way into a disused warehouse, tied him up and put a tarpaulin over him in the corner, before wheeling an empty cart back to their neighbour.

That night, Jack left the house at 9:30pm. He knew everyone would have gone home from the dock by now and that Sid would likely be asleep in the gatehouse, worse for wear. If not he would tell him he had forgotten to secure warehouse six where he had been working all that day.

Reaching the dock, Sid was indeed asleep and Jack unlocked the side gate and let himself in. As foreman, he had a number of privileges including being a key holder. It was a miserable night, rain tipping down and running off the brim of this cloth cap. He moved swiftly, reaching the warehouse where he had stashed Peter. Unlocking the door, he moved inside and flicked on the light switch, making his way towards the tarpaulin. He had already planned how he was going to drag Peter to the deep water terminal and weight his legs with cement and drop him in. No, he would not trouble Rosie anymore. He pulled the tarpaulin and blinked in shock – gone, he was gone. Suddenly he felt a blow to his head and fell. Seeing stars, he looked up. He could make out a figure, he assumed it was Peter, hauling himself through the warehouse door. Shakily he got to his feet. Blood was dripping down his face and he tried to walk slowly towards the door. He made it half way across the room before the walls and ground reeled around him and he collapsed.

When Jack didn't come home, Molly was not initially concerned. He had told her he had gone to 'the Grapes' and often was a little late. When it reached midnight, however, she became extremely worried and roused Freddie and Billy.

"Boys, your father has not come home."

Freddie had come back from the pub over an hour ago but hadn't thought to mention to his mother Jack wasn't there.

"I am worried, where could he be?" asked Molly.

"Billy and I will go and look for him, Mum. You wait here in case he comes back."

Billy knew exactly where to go and the pair rushed to the docks. Trying the gate they found it still unlocked. Billy headed to the warehouse where he had helped his father unload Peter and they stepped inside. It was completely dark, but they could hear a low moaning from in front of them. Billy struck a match. It was his father.

"Dad, what's happened?"

His father stirred and whispered: "Get me to Doctor Kline."

The boys, both six-foot strapping lads, had difficulty getting Jack up and half carried him, half dragged him staggering to the dock gates.

"Lock the door," Jack muttered and they stopped to find the key. It wasn't an easy journey but luckily it was a miserable wet night and no one was around. Knocking on Doctor Kline's door, they finally roused him. The doctor had a coat wrapped around his nightshirt.

"What is it, don't you know what time it is?" he said rather angrily.

"Sorry doc, our dad's had an accident, he's fallen in the dock and hurt his head," said Freddie. Doctor Kline knew the family well and had often had a bottle of his favourite tipple from Jack Holder.

"Alright bring him in."

As he opened the door, light flooded the street and for the first time the boys could see that their father had been bleeding heavily, his shirt and face were slicked red with liquid.

"Lay him down on the couch," said the Doctor quickly. He examined him and looked up seriously at the boys. "He's not good, we have to get him to hospital, that's a nasty head wound. Billy, run up to the Shoreditch Road and get a cab waiting for the music hall to turn out and hurry."

Billy managed to persuade a cab to help him; the driver was not best pleased as there were usually good takings from the gentlemen coming out of the music hall. They lay Jack down inside and all three crowded into seats on the other side of the cab. As they reached the Whitechapel Road, Freddie told Billy to keep the cab and go and get their mother.

As Jack lay in hospital that night he drifted in and out of consciousness. Deliriously he shouted warnings about a man, swearing profusely as he cried out. Molly was beside herself and when the doctor told her that his brain may be damaged and that a small piece of bone was lodged in his skull, she felt her knees buckling momentarily before controlling herself and facing her children.

"How's Dad?" said Rosie, as Molly approached them.

"Oh, he is still unconscious but the doctor thinks he is fine," Molly replied comfortingly, knowing this was far from the truth. She shut her eyes briefly, fearing the worse, before settling in for a long night of worrying and waiting.

Daylight arrived and suddenly Jack sat up in his bed.

"I am hungry, where am I?" he said, looking around him.

Molly woke in an instant and, half laughing, half sobbing, sent Billy to find a nurse. A rather pretty woman Billy would have had other designs upon, but for the circumstances, followed him down the ward to his father's bed.

"How are you feeling Mr Holder?" she said, taking his temperature, pulse and looked at his pupils.

"As right as nine pence, luv. Can you tell me what am I doing here?"

Lord Berkeley arrived at Mansion House and was shown in by the doorman. Two police officers stood by the front entrance, as many government ministers and important people were to dine there that night. Lord Berkeley, in conversation with the Chancellor about the cost of engaging the Arabs in Egypt, noticed the Baron arriving out of the corner of his eye, accompanied by the Swiss Ambassador. An usher, dressed in a handsome livery, escorted the Ambassador, Baron de Courcy and the Chancellor of the Exchequer.

"You have met the Governor of the Bank of England?" said an elegant man, apparently a treasury lord.

"Yes, hello Charles," said the Baron and Count Barle the Swiss Ambassador shaking hands.

"Ah Baron nice to meet you again and Count Barle. I trust you are enjoying the inclement English weather?" All three men laughed, as the wind howled around the building as they spoke.

"Let me show you to the table plan," said Charles. "Baron, you are next to me and Count Barle, you are seated next to the Chancellor and a treasury minister."

They both nodded as a waiter approached with a tray of champagne.

"May I give you a toast," said the Baron. "To English and Swiss harmony. I believe that is the word – harmony!"

"Quite right Baron, to harmony," responded Charles.

"Is that Lord Berkeley over there?" The Baron enquired.

"Yes, in fact you are sitting next to each other," replied Charles.

"How excellent, always good company," said the Baron, taking a sip of his champagne.

The guests and their hosts were called to dinner. An elegant menu, fitting to the occasion, had been selected of Oyster soup, a duck terrine, Beef Wellington – named after the illustrious General – followed by marvellous sweets and cakes, washed down by a charming Chablis and a wonderful claret. The guests settled into their seats and the evening was spent mainly discussing the proposal of the Swiss to lend the Bank of England £200,000,000 in gold. The Swiss would have preferred a mixture of currency and gold, but the Chancellor and treasury officials had been well briefed.

"As Governor of the Bank of England you must be awash with gold, surely paper or bonds will suffice?" the Baron commented to Charles, as the brandy, port and cigars were passed around.

"No I am afraid not old boy we want gold and that's it."

Lord Berkeley had sat quietly talking to a junior treasury minister on his right for much of the evening. Not taking part in the discussion on the loan was deliberate, even though he was on the treasury committee who decided such things and was an ex-Governor of the Bank of England.

"I don't suppose you have had time to see Clarence Carter?" he said casually. The Baron's ears pricked up.

"No," replied the tall distinguished looking Sir Martin Peters, the senior treasury official. "But I have arranged to meet tomorrow."

The Baron knew immediately who they referred to. Clarence Carter was the head of operations for the Chicago Bank, who he knew were tendering for the loan. He frowned slightly and sensing a lull in conversation, he turned to Lord Berkeley.

"How is that charming young lady, the friend of my son, Rosie I believe is her name?"

"She has been less than herself lately," Lord Berkeley replied.

"Oh why's that?"

"Well, first her good friend Frederick gets attacked and she has been unable to see him and now her father has had an accident on the dock where he works."

"What a great shame, give her my best wishes – oh, and by the way she is welcome to visit Frederick now, he has quite recovered from his injuries and is dying to see her," replied the Baron.

"Hmm. You do realise," said Lord Berkeley looking at the Baron, "that the two young people are very fond of each other. In fact, I did hear a rumour that Frederick had proposed marriage."

"You are remarkably well informed my dear Lord Berkeley, I believe it might be my son's intention to propose at some future date."

The Baron was quickly realising that Berkeley knew a great deal more than he thought.

"And what would be your reaction to such a union?" The Baron shook his head and went to speak, but Lord Berkeley interrupted. "Now before you answer that, let me tell you something in absolute confidence." He lowered his voice. "Do give me your word as a gentleman nothing I tell you will ever be discussed with anyone?"

The Baron nodded, intrigued, listening intently as Lord Berkeley whispered in his ear. When he had finished, he sat back in surprise, puffing his cigar thoughtfully.

"Well, that does change things considerably. I don't know what to say."

The Baron was speechless – what a mistake he had nearly made.

"I am wondering," said the Baron after a pause, "if the loan will proceed with our consortium of Swiss Banks?"

"Well, as a member of the Bank of England's bank committee, I feel that Rosie's happiness and the loan are almost inextricably linked," replied Lord Berkeley quietly.

"Ah, I see... Well, rest assured: should my son decide to propose to Rosie I will more than welcome the union," the Baron said softly.

"What are you two whispering about; a typical couple of bankers with their secrets," Charles said, winking at Lord Berkeley, who merely smiled.

Jack left hospital two days later with a large bandage around his head, but he could not remember anything prior to the attack. The doctor had told Molly that this was to be expected with his head injuries but that it was likely his memory would slowly return. The doctor's instructions were that he was not to work as complete rest was necessary for a full recovery. Jack stayed in bed as Molly fussed around and sung him his favourite songs from the music hall but in three days there had not been much change.

Jack sat up and looked around. He felt really hungry. Molly walked in the room.

"How long have I been here Molly?"

"Four days, how are you feeling?"

"Much better and I can remember I was down the docks and got hit on the head." Jack got out of bed staggering slightly.

"Now Jack Holder, get back into bed. You have had a nasty knock on the head and Dr Kline said you must get plenty of rest," Molly ordered.

"I've got work to do, I can't stay here," he protested, but seeing Molly's stern gaze he reluctantly climbed back into bed, sinking against the pillow.

"Can you remember what happened?" Molly asked.

Jack closed his eyes and thought for a moment. "Yes, I went down to the dock to see about that scum Peter. I walked into the warehouse where I had left him and… and then everything goes black. He must have hit me from behind, I don't remember anything else until I woke up in hospital."

"What were you going to do with him down the docks?" Molly said, looking concerned. She already knew from questioning Billy they had taken that lout Peter to the docks but wanted to hear for herself what Jack had been planning.

"Oh, just teaching him a lesson – rough him up a bit," replied Jack.

"Well, he's well clear now," said Molly. "Freddie's been trying to find him but other than tracing a man of his description to the Whitechapel Hospital two hours before you were admitted, there's been no sign of him."

"What about the Whitechapel Hospital, did Freddie say?"

"A man arrived and gave a false name. Freddie checked through an orderly he knew – he had a broken leg put in a splint, he left very quickly," said Molly, arranging the blankets around Jack.

"And you say there is no sign of him, where is Freddie now?"

"At work, he is on the early shift and will be back at 3. Now, that's enough of questions, get some rest," replied Molly firmly.

Later that evening, Jack and Freddie had a long chat about Peter.

"Put the word out through the lodge and the union that I am looking for this man – personal business," said Jack and Freddie nodded.

Jack had many friends and contacts, but a few days later, nothing had turned up. To their frustration, it seemed Peter had disappeared.

Lord Berkeley was feeling very pleased with himself. Rosie was back to her old self: smiling, singing like an angel and acting brilliantly. Dress rehearsals were in full swing and, other than the usual pre-performance hitches, everything was going well. Rosie had seen Frederick every day since his talk with the Baron and Lord Berkeley knew from her demeanour that she was very happy. But what of the marriage proposal? He didn't like to ask her, but was curious whether she had given an answer.

Rosie was expecting Frederick to call for her after the rehearsal as she had promised him an answer to the question he had now repeated three times. Despite having thought about it at least a hundred times, she still couldn't decide. She felt a confused mix of emotions. He had certainly swept her off her feet in Paris and she was very fond of him. But did she love him? Her distress when he had been attacked had made her think that she did, but there was a lingering uncertainty. She couldn't help but compare her feelings for Stafford. But perhaps that wasn't fair: he had been her first love after all. And so her thoughts went round in circles and she was no nearer to making a decision. Frederick, however, was expecting an answer and had made it clear that this was his last proposal. She sighed. Perhaps she was making this more complicated than it needed to be.

Frederick called at the stage door with considerable trepidation. If Rosie refused him, he knew he would have to give up. He had tried three times and his pride would prevent him continuing to ask her. In addition, his father had made it clear that if his amorous advances were not returned, it was time he returned to Zurich. The Baron had travelled back to Switzerland some weeks ago, after the British Government had agreed a massive loan brokered by the Swiss Bankers.

Rosie, looking particularly lovely, arrived at the stage door.

"Hello my darling, you are looking absolutely beautiful," Frederick said, kissing her hand. His coach took them to the Mayfair Hotel, a fine building near Park Lane, where Frederick had arranged for a private room to be festooned with roses. As they entered the room, Rosie gasped. The smell of roses was intoxicating and she had tears in her eyes as she looked around; it was so beautiful. The Maitre D held Rosie's chair and she sat down at the table for two. Frederick was not very confident but tried to cover up his apprehension by talking about the new motorcar he had seen yesterday.

"It was amazing Rosie, you steer it with a round wheel," said Frederick.

"But how does it move?" Rosie asked, although she already knew as she had studied the internal combustion engine and had followed with interest the advance of the steam railway, shipping, electric trams and now petrol driven automobiles, as transport at the turn of the century emerged.

"Come on Rosie, I know you realise how an automobile works, stop teasing me," Frederick replied seriously. Now was the time to find out. He took a sip of his wine. "Rosie, you haven't answered the question that has been burning in my heart since I first asked you. Will you marry me?" He took her hand. "Can I put this engagement ring on your finger? I love you Rosie, you are the most precious thing in my world, please say yes."

Rosie paused for a second, uncertainty still clouding her mind, and then, before she knew what was happening, said: "Yes Frederick, I will marry you."

Frederick virtually knocked the table over as he swept her into his arms.

"Rosie, that's wonderful, I will make you happy I promise."

They spent the rest of the evening holding hands, talking excitedly, planning their lives. Rosie felt exhilarated.

"We will have five children: two girls and three boys," said Frederick.

"It's nice to know you can control nature, Frederick," Rosie giggled.

Over the next week they planned their wedding. Frederick sent a message to his father while Rosie announced the good news to her family. Molly and Jack were delighted but a little concerned as to how their daughter would fit into the new world she was entering. The Baron seemed genuinely happy, which surprised Frederick somewhat as he had sensed that his father had not been greatly pleased by his attachment to Rosie previously. With the two of them caught up in a whirlwind of wedding excitement, however, he did not have much time to ponder his father's mysterious change of heart and concluded that the Baron must be as susceptible to her charms as any man might be.

Chapter Seven

The Wedding

The wedding was planned for December third that year. Frederick came from a Protestant family and the Baron had insisted on a traditional wedding. Rosie was not deeply religious, but she knew how important it was so was happy to agree.

Planning the wedding was like a military operation for the Baron. He knew that his son wouldn't have much of an idea what to do and he obviously could not leave the arrangements in the hands of Rosie and her parents given their social position. The Baron therefore sent his personal secretary George de Lapadou to pull together the truly spectacular occasion the Baron intended. He had attempted in vain to hold the wedding in Zurich but Rosie refused all overtures: she was a London girl, her family all lived in London, she was going to marry in London. The Baron's perceptive secretary soon realised that she would not be moved on the question. Luckily, he was able to use an old friend to introduce him to the Bishop of London at Westminster Abbey and he knew immediately that this would be the perfect venue. As for the Bishop, he was a shrewd man and recognised the opportunity that had presented itself: he had been looking for a rich benefactor to pay for some work on the roof of the Abbey.

So Rosie found herself in the Lady Chapel at Westminster Abbey with Frederick and her mother talking to the verger about dates and times. Molly was frankly overwhelmed but the self-confident Rosie, who was used to the adoration of audiences, had turned over the idea in her mind and knew that it was the best way to appease Frederick's father.

"It's fine Mum," she said, when Molly anxiously questioned the choice. "I would love to marry Frederick here – just look at it, what a stage!" Rosie waved her arms and smiled brightly. "Anyway, it's all done and dusted," she finished, borrowing her dad's phrase for describing the deals he got involved in at the docks. Molly nodded, still not fully convinced, but she knew what Rosie was like when she had made up her mind.

Rosie turned away, her smile fading. Despite her assurances, she remained a little concerned – how would her family stand up to the day, not only mingling with the upper class but coming to Westminster Abbey? And nagging at the back of her mind… had she made the right decision to marry Frederick?

Her doubts were swept away by the sheer magnitude of the preparations. There was an awful lot of planning to do and George, having secured the church, moved briskly on to the reception. His first thought had been Claridges, but as he reminded himself of the opulence he realised it would not do. He had to find somewhere that would be suitable for Rosie's family and guests. The Baron had not minced his words on the matter: "Don't expect the girl will accept any possible embarrassment to her family, so make sure the reception is luxurious but low key. After all we won't be filling the place with our guests."

As he dismissed venue after venue, privately George was at a loss why the Baron was even allowing the wedding to take place. The girl was certainly very beautiful and, he had to admit, absolutely delightful company – she even seemed well educated, but how could the Baron allow Frederick to marry so far below his class? Pulling up outside the Savoy, he surveyed the exterior deep in thought. No, too grand, he decided. During his time studying English at London University, George had been to many restaurants and as many were attached to hotels he was very familiar with the best places. Despite this, he began to feel like he was running out of choices.

Inspiration struck him: "What about the Peridot?" He instructed his driver and they soon arrived at Harrington Gardens. Not a bad journey from the Abbey to Kensington, he thought as he walked inside. It was, in essence, a restaurant – no less formal or less luxurious than many he had visited but he could hire the entire establishment. Named after a beautiful gemstone, the Peridot had an elegance based on Venetian décor, with delicate hues of greens and pastel yellows. The fixtures and fittings were tailor made and there was a sumptuous mosaic floor en route to a delightful seating area full of beautiful silk lined chairs. George walked around the venue, nodding his approval at each step. The overall effect was a tearoom style that oozed class and quality.

He enquired about the hire of the entire venue on the Saturday in December only to find that a group of merchants had hired the main salon for a dinner.

"However, we can seat 70 in the Alexander Room if that is suitable," said the manager. He showed George to the first floor room. It was enchanting, with long windows and a balcony. At the centre of the room, the banqueting floor which overlooked the charming chandeliered entrance hall, was a grand setting for speeches. The turquoise coloured Daniel Room could be used as a reception area and there was a wood panelled Cigar Divan Room with leather sofas for the men to retire. George nodded approvingly. The space worked well, but how would the Baron react to restricting guests to 70? Could he persuade the merchants to give up their reservation? He left to make enquiries and to write a message to the Baron indicating his progress to date.

That evening, Frederick and Rosie were dining out. They had begun to go out to dinner and shows with friends of Frederick's and on this occasion were with Francis Turnbury, son of Sir Oliver Turnbury, the chairman of Seymours Merchant Bank. He escorted Sarah Rowcastle, granddaughter of the Earl of Warwick. Sarah was a socialite who liked to mix in avant-garde circles. Amongst her many friends was Christabel, the daughter of Mrs Pankhurst, who was a fervent believer in votes for women.

Frederick enjoyed the company of Francis; they had met at Eton and were known as the twins as they were virtually inseparable. A skilled horseman and polo player, Francis was everything Frederick was not. He also played tennis, representing Britain in competition, and was a superb swordsman. His dashing lifestyle and daring was admired by Frederick to the point of hero worship. At that moment, Francis was enjoying once again being the centre of attention, describing a near death experience as he recounted a trip he made to climb Ben Nevis last year.

"Ralph, you remember Ralph Hinds, Frederick?" Frederick nodded. "Well, he slipped as he was crevassing and nearly brought us all down," laughed Francis.

"What happened?" asked Sarah.

"As he fell, I had to brace to hold his weight and pray to good my pitons held. Slowly, as he swung perilously over a ledge a good 1500 feet up, I hauled him back."

Sarah and Rosie looked spellbound, both privately imagining the brave Francis' muscles bulging as he saved his friend.

"Thank God for British steel," said Sarah always practical.

"It was a little more that than," smiled Frederick. "Francis was a hero."

"Nonsense," said Christabel impatiently. "He is just a silly man risking his life for no good reason."

Ignoring Christabel's comments, who he knew rarely had a good word to say about men, Frederick stared admiringly at his friend who was regaling further tales of daring do to the other ladies at the table.

"Are you still intending to enlist, Francis?" Sarah asked.

"Yes I am dashed keen to go to India, my father served there with the Dragoons and I have applied to join the regiment."

Frederick didn't like to think about his friend joining the army as he had vividly dreamed some time ago that Francis was killed in a battle. He changed the subject quickly.

"I do hope you are all going to join us on our happy day?"

"Yes of course," they all choroused.

"You must be getting excited Rosemary," said Sarah, who always called Rosie by what she considered her correct name. "Is it true Frederick's father's man is organising the wedding?"

"Well yes, the Baron has made his personal secretary available to help with the arrangements, but I would hardly say he was organising the whole wedding," Rosie replied calmly. She was, frankly, a little peeved: the Baron's man had at great speed arranged for the wedding at Westminster Abbey and now she had been told that the reception was to be at a place called 'the Peridot', a place she had never even seen. Still Frederick seemed content to let George get on with things and seemed impervious to Rosie's feelings on the matter, so there was little she could do. It certainly would be seen as terribly rebellious to disagree with any of the arrangements. After all, what girl from the East End of London would turn down getting married in Westminster Abbey?

The evening passed with great frivolity and excitement until the coaches arrived.

"Rosie," said Christabel. "Some ladies are meeting outside Downing Street on Monday to publicly demonstrate for my mother's 'votes for women' campaign. Will you join us?"

Rosie had never seen herself as a feminist but Christabel was a lovely girl and it all seemed harmless enough.

"Yes, I will," she replied, with a smile.

"Steady on old girl," said Frederick. "You know Mrs Pankhurst is quite the activist; there will be lots of angry ladies carrying boards and chanting. I went past a demonstration outside the House of Commons last week, it was pretty unpleasant."

Francis rejoined the group. "What's this, our Rosie is becoming a militant?"

"Not at all," replied Frederick. "She is just helping a friend."

That Monday, Rosie set off with her friend Fanny to join the other ladies in Downing Street. Rosie was somewhat taken aback when they arrived to find at least two dozen ladies faced by two rows of policemen and a crowd of people, mostly men, who were shouting abuse. The women were trying to push their way into Downing Street to deliver a petition signed by 10,000 people for 'votes for women'. Standing towards the rear of the baying group, Rosie was amazed by the anger around her. Many of the women carried placards and Rosie could sense this confrontation was beginning to get out of hand. Just as she contemplated the ugly nature of the crowd to her left and the rows of policemen in front, someone threw a stone. The policemen immediately began to change their tactics from blocking the women from entering Downing Street to physically manhandling them. Rosie saw Christabel at the front get hit by a truncheon and several of the women were carted away unceremoniously. Fanny was horrified as this was not at all what she had envisaged; she didn't even understand the issue and when a burly policeman approached them, she turned and ran. Rosie wasn't quite as lucky: before she could think about what to do for the best, the policeman picked her up and carried her kicking and screaming to a black carriage where another policeman told her to get in and keep quiet.

The whole thing was over in a few minutes and the coach headed off.

"Where are we going?" Rosie asked a policeman, trying to calm herself.

"You'll find out soon, luv," he replied.

As Rosie was directed out of the carriage, she saw that they had been taken to Bow Street Police Station. She was questioned before being dumped unceremoniously in a cell. Dark and dingy, the place reeked of stale urine and vomit. Rosie felt herself retch and sank down miserably onto a dirty mattress in the corner. She could not quite believe where she was and squeezed her eyes shut briefly to block out the sight. Taking several shaky breaths, she spoke to herself sternly, trying to control herself. Someone will be here soon, she thought, trying to forget the fact that nobody would know where she had been taken.

As Rosie waited in the police cell, Fanny, who had turned to see her friend struggling with the policeman, had made her way to Eaton Square to tell Frederick what had happened.

He listened incredulously.

"What – she's been arrested?"

"Yes, I am afraid so," replied Fanny tearfully.

"Where did they take her?"

"I don't know," and she began to cry.

"It's alright Fanny, you did well to come to me, now rest whilst I make some enquiries."

Frederick had recently installed one of the new telephones, much more reliable than the early version. He moved towards it, trying to make sense of what Fanny had told him.

"Could I speak to the Ambassador please, it's Frederick de Courcy."

Frederick was put through to the Swiss Ambassador, a distant relative on his mother's side of the family.

"Frederick, dear boy, to what do I owe this pleasure?"

Frederick explained what had happened.

"Now Frederick, you must understand that we have no immunity for Mademoiselle Rosie. She is English, they can deal with her how they wish," said the Ambassador, after a pause.

"I know that," Frederick responded, "but you do know the Home Office Minister. Can you contact him and at least find out where they have taken her?"

"I will try, I will telephone you."

Frederick replaced the receiver with a sigh. Thinking for a moment, he picked it up again to call Lord Berkeley; he had been a very good friend to Rosie, perhaps he could help.

Lord Berkeley was understandably shocked to learn that his leading lady had been arrested. He immediately made enquiries and soon discovered her whereabouts. He made his way to the police station and, after some negotiation and six tickets to the opening night, Rosie was released with a warning not to get involved with 'these extremists'. Rosie gave Lord Berkeley a hug.

"Does Frederick know?"

"Of course he does. Fanny went straight to him and he telephoned me. I suspect the Home Office are also searching for you as Frederick phoned the Swiss Ambassador and asked him to contact the minister."

"Oh lord," said Rosie, becoming increasingly concerned about what Frederick was going to say. She was not one to cry easily, but she looked crestfallen.

"Don't worry Rosie, it has all been sorted out now but do please try and keep away from these groups, they are only trouble," said Lord Berkeley as they made their way to Eaton Square. She nodded miserably.

Rosie did not go to a 'Votes for Women' rally for quite some time after that and was surprised how sympathetic Frederick had been as she vividly outlined her ordeal in the cell at Bow Street 'nick', as she called it.

Rosie was still rehearsing heavily and in seven days the show would open. Things had not gone particularly well. One of the principle characters, Little Buttercup, had fallen ill. Lord Berkeley had moved swiftly, though, and amazed the entire theatre world by obtaining the agreement of Lillie Langtree, the Jersey Lilly, to play the part for a short while. Nobody quite knew how he had done it, but he appeared on excellent terms with the celebrated artist. As soon as the word got around, the performances were booked for the next four weeks, which was unheard of with a new production.

Rosie liked Lillie immediately and spent a great deal of time chatting in her dressing room and listening to her anecdotes. She had a wink when she told Rosie that she had 'known' Prince Louis of Battenberg and she was delighted to recite a 'who's who' of men she had had as lovers and friends including Robert Peel, Oscar Wilde, Whistler the painter and countless other wealthy men. She regaled Rosie with her stories about her time in Northern California, where she owned a 4,200 acre winery in Northern California that manufactured claret. Rosie found her tales both unexpected and fascinating. Lillie had become an American Citizen and in 1899 she married Hugo Gerald de Bathe, who Rosie liked very much. Hugo was a much younger man than Lillie and hovered around her attentively, very well aware how attractive she still was. Men adored Lillie and she loved men. She had come back to England to see what was to happen to the Old Imperial Theatre. She had managed the theatre for a while before she left for America and was concerned as it was closing down.

"You cannot interrupt progress my dear," Lord Berkeley said to her. They clearly were very close friends and Rosie wondered if Lord Berkeley had been one of her string of lovers.

Lillie had told Rosie that this was to be her last performance in London as she was intending to go and live in France or Monte Carlo.

The production was finally ready to open and the first night, along with the performances over the next few months, were an overwhelming success. Lillie stayed on and was the star of the show. Rosie, although playing the leading lady, didn't mind at all that it was Lillie who, when she took her bow, brought the house to its feet. Lillie and Rosie often took a final bow together and the stage would be covered with Lillies and Roses which they swept up in their arms. Many gentlemen came back stage, mostly to see Lillie. Rosie was amazed that Lillie actually received many of them until Lillie told her that the most expensive gift she received that week had been a diamond brooch. Apparently she received gifts of jewellery, chocolates and even beautiful gowns. Men are so easy to please, thought Rosie wryly.

The other major production in Rosie's life was also drawing ever closer. The excitement was mounting: Rosie had been to Bond Street for a final fitting of her dress and her bridesmaids – her sister, Alice and cousin Steffie – had also had their final fittings, as indeed had Molly, her mother. Frederick had been extremely generous, paying for all the outfits. He also had a tailor make morning suits for her brothers, cousins and father, despite her brothers' adamant protests that they didn't want to 'dress up like toffs'. The worse thing for the men was that Molly made all of them have a bath before going for a fitting, including Jack.

"You can't turn a sow into a silk purse," he grumbled, but was amazed when his sons paraded in front of him. They really looked the part, young gentlemen all of them, even though Billy tugged at his collar.

Everything was falling into place. Frederick had arranged that they would honeymoon in Zurich, where they were going to spend one month at the lakeside house.

Rosie coped with the pressure of her impending wedding in her usual calm manner. Lord Berkeley couldn't help but admire her cool. Despite all the demands of the preparations, she had once again been the star of the show in his view. Lillie, of course, was Lillie – as usual magnificent. Rosie, though, was also a truly brilliant actress and singer. He had been invited to the wedding and reception and was contemplating what gift he could purchase them when a chance conversation at a dinner party gave him the idea. As he sat back in his seat, taking a sip of his drink, he overheard Frederick in conversation with one of his neighbours.

"I must, when we return from the honeymoon, get Rosie a pianoforte," said Frederick "Have you heard her play?" They discussed music for a short while, but Lord Berkeley had heard enough.

That's it, he thought. He would buy them a pianoforte. Rosie was an accomplished player; it was a perfect gift.

Frederick paced nervously as he waited for Rosie to arrive. His father, immaculately dressed as usual, had earlier engaged the Holders in an animated conversation, trying to calm their nerves. As he had suspected the sheer spectacle was too much for them – but if we get through the ceremony it's over, he thought to himself. As Molly glanced around her, she felt even more nervous than she looked. The guests on Frederick's side were like a 'who's who' of English and Swiss culture. Her sons looked terrific, she thought proudly, as did her aunt's children all decked out, but they only took up three rows, whereas Frederick's guests numbered at least ten times as many.

Lord Berkeley arrived and, stepping into the church, immediately perceived the imbalance. Walking with his niece, the Hon Jemima Waldecot, who was shortly to inherit her late father's estate in Norfolk, he nodded greetings to many of Frederick's guests and then, much to many people's surprise, took up his place on the bride's side. Then in came Lillie, in a fantastic red silk dress, a truly flamboyant hat and a beautiful brooch pinned to her breast. Some of Frederick's guests even applauded as she made her entrance and, accompanied by her husband, also sat on Rosie's side. A buzz went around the church. Then the cast of HMS Pinafore bustled into the church, filling up another three rows as Rosie's guests. Lord Berkeley smiled to himself. He had done his bit to spare the Holder's any awkwardness. Molly looked back, overwhelmed at the new arrivals. She caught Lord Berkeley's eye and gave a small smile as he nodded to her.

Outside in the coach, Jack was nervous. Of course, he would not have admitted that to anyone for the world – but this toff's shirt was pinching his neck and he felt trussed up 'like a dog's dinner'. They were late, but then Molly had said it was traditional for the bride to keep them waiting and not to worry.

Frederick chatted quietly to Francis, his best man, and then the Prime Minister arrived with his party, which signalled to Frederick that Rosie was outside. Why his father had insisted the PM came he did not know as there were already three government ministers, the Swiss and German Ambassadors, Lords and Ladies, rich bankers and countless relatives from home. He saw his Aunt Frances, his father's sister, take her seat. She had met Rosie the night before and declared her 'a beautiful and delightful girl' which he knew meant that she was accepted at a stroke. A small murmur rose from the guests as Frederick's father who had gone outside entered, escorting the Countess de Blois. An old flame, she was a striking woman. In her cream silk dress, with a red belt and a superb hat, she had every man's head turning as she entered. Then the organ started playing Mendelssohn's traditional wedding march and everyone stood.

Frederick longed to turn around, but resisted. Time seemed to slow down as he waited for Rosie to make her way down the aisle – and then suddenly a vision in white appeared beside him.

Rosie's silk dress was trimmed with exquisitely cut lace, with a thin pink silk belt. She wore the magnificent diamond necklace that the Baron had presented to her the night before and a wonderful hat, with white and pink feathers. She looked stunning. Francis looked into her blue grey eyes for a second and envied his friend for the first time since they had met at Eton when they were 4 years old. Molly gazed at her daughter with tears welling up in her eyes. Jack looked a right gent, but she knew he would fidget with his collar - it had taken the best part of this morning to persuade him to wear the necktie at all.

Rosie had picked a traditional service. The words of the ceremony echoed around the church and music floated around the congregation as a fine string quartet played Bach's Air on a G string and the organist Jesu Joy of Man's Desiring. And then it was all over: they were pronounced man and wife. Before she knew it, Rosie was walking back down the aisle – this time, as a married woman.

Outside Francis had organised a guard of honour of their old friends from Eton making a bridge with cricket bats. A crowd had gathered and they cheered as people began to exit: they didn't actually know who was getting married but they had seen the Prime Minister, the Marquis of Salisbury and Lillie Langtree going in, so knew it must be someone important.

There was time for a few photographs on the green outside the Abbey, with groupings of the bride and groom, with bridesmaids, page boy, ushers and then with the parents, followed by a photograph with everybody. Not all the guests were going on to the reception: a selection from Frederick's side and a handful of Rosie's closest friends. It had taken great diplomacy from Frederick, who had explained how uncomfortable they all would be. Frederick had also taken Rosie's father, brothers and cousins to the hotel under the guise of a rehearsal and gone through the whole meal. He had laid on somebody to demonstrate the appropriate etiquette and, when Jack had asked if he could avoid a speech, Frederick had promptly arranged for Lord Berkeley to step in.

Most of the guests were enjoying the contrast between their society and the lower class. Quiet comments followed a usually brief conversation between the two sides. It would have been dreadful if Lord Berkeley hadn't have been so magnificent. He drifted between both sets of guests – a conversation here, a little story there, laughter and anecdotes to keep everybody happy. And Lillie was also terrific. The upper class had always doted on her; she held an attraction for them that even she didn't understand, but they thronged around her, Lords and Ladies alike. The Baron moved amongst his guests, pausing for only a brief word with Rosie's parents. Soon it was time for them to sit down for the sumptuous wedding feast: oysters, a Vichyssoise soup, a cold table of roast meats including pheasant, duck, beef, quail and turkey, all washed down with a superb Chardonnay, imported specially from Switzerland, and a delightful French Claret. The Holders were not used to fine dining and didn't drink much wine so struggled throughout the meal. Rosie noticed that more than once one of her brothers disappeared for a lengthy period and knew they were nipping outside for a cigarette. As the formalities came to a close and the last of the guests left, Lord Berkeley summoned his coach, handing an envelope addressed to Frederick and Rosie. Rosie knew how hard he had worked and kissed him on the cheek impulsively – was that a tear in his eye?

The Holders gleefully boarded their three coaches and immediately the men tore off their shirt collars and lit up cigarettes.

"Did you see that lah di da bugger?" said Freddie. "He must have eaten an entire turkey on his own."

"And what about Lady Whatsername, the one with the big feather 'at. She said to our Alf 'And what do you do my man?'" said Samuel, copying her upper class accent. "When he replied he worked in a skinning factory, she nearly fainted."

The men all roared with laughter.

"Look what I've got," said Billy, showing a handful of cigars.

"You crafty bugger," replied Freddie.

"That's not all – I've got half a duck here," grinned Billy.

Luckily Molly and Jack were in the next coach; they would have felt a little disappointed that their sons and cousins had pinched everything that was not bolted down, including salt and pepper sets, knives and forks, food and cigars. One of them even had a bottle of claret, which he didn't even like. Frederick was to comment later to Lord Berkeley, much to his amusement: "You know that reception cost us nearly as much in missing knives and forks as the actual meal."

Rosie drove away to Victoria Station wondering where the day had gone. They were getting on a night train to cross the channel then the sleeper to Paris. She felt strangely deflated. She knew the occasion had been difficult for her family and friends as they simply did not move in the upper class circles. However, as far as she was aware, they had behaved impeccably. That was not the source of her disappointment. It all felt like an anti-climax, perhaps if she pinched herself she would wake from a dream.

"Well darling, we are married."

Frederick's voice interrupted her thoughts. Rosie felt her wedding ring and smiled at Frederick. He was such a sweet man, she reflected. When they had reached their reception hotel earlier in the day, Frederick had ushered her to an upstairs room where he had arranged for rose water and refreshments for her mother, bridesmaids and herself. It was typical of his thoughtful nature. During the ride from the Abbey he had held her hand not saying a great deal. Rosie thought he was overwhelmed. Fortunately he came back to life when Francis appeared and laughed gaily at the anecdotes about his childhood during the best man's speech.

Soon they would be in Paris where they met. They had planned a week there visiting some of the places they had so enjoyed on their previous visit, followed by a two day train journey to Venice. Frederick had indeed planned a wonderful honeymoon for them both.

On their first wedding night in Paris they consummated their union. It was rather a speedy affair. Rosie decided that clearly Frederick was not an experienced lover. Still there was lots of time, she would just have to show him. Lillie had once explained to her that most men are unable to restrain themselves for too long and sometimes a woman had to take the lead. Rosie sighed to herself and tried to shake off the sense of disappointment – the rest of their time in Paris was all it should have been and Frederick was his usual charming and attentive self. They loved each other's company, enjoying the same things, and the time passed quickly.

Rosie had thought her favourite city would always be Paris until she reached Venice. As the train had approached over a long bridge, she had gaspèd at a view so magnificent it would remain in her memory forever. They travelled by fast boat to their hotel, a beautiful 17th century building on the Grand Canal. The first week was spent visiting all the famous sites and winding their way across the intricate maze of canals.

Frederick had explained that Venice sits at the heart of a lagoon separated from the sea by a line of defensive sand bars. "The city has over 100 islands, 350 bridges and 170 canals, which the Venetians divide into six districts or sestieri," he said, pleased to have remembered the figures to tell her. Rosie felt that she could never get tired of gazing at the vista of the Grand Canal from the bridge of Accademia. The Piazzo San Marco was another favourite. They would sit there for an hour in a comfortable silence, sipping hot chocolate or coffee, watching the strolling Venetians.

That evening, Frederick and Rosie had been invited by an Italian Banker a friend of the Baron to join them for dinner. Senior Guiseppe Salvie was chairman of the Venetian Bank and had met the Baron on business numerous times. His house, like all those in the city, was on wooden piles sunk deep into the original lagoon. Rosie had been amazed when she first entered. From the street, the house appeared old and just a little shabby, but inside it was like a palace – high ceilings with ornate plasterwork, beautiful furniture in each room, magnificent paintings, sculpture and fine wall coverings in a dark red silk, thick full length curtains. Rosie listened fascinated as her host explained how Venice had been built on the water. In some places the walls were crumbling and the Venetian builders and architects were working hard to prevent the walls from deteriorating further.

Salvie's wife, Sophie, was a charming woman who spoke a little English and excellent French. Rosie spent some time discussing with her how the Italian masters compared to the French artists. Frederick and Giuseppe were talking in Italian about banking. Sophie was intrigued by Rosie's acting career: she had been in London last year with a girlfriend and had seen the 'As You Like It' production at the Theatre Royal. The men turned their attention toward the ladies.

"Frederick tells me your real name is Cynthia, a charming name," commented Giuseppe.

"Why do they call you Rosie?" queried Sophie. Rosie explained that Rose was her second name and that in England it sounded a more suitable name for an actress or stage performer than did Cynthia. They all looked interested but Frederick could sense that they clearly felt that Cynthia was a much more 'acceptable' name and he realised that this was true. He would have to talk to Rosie later.

"This is a wonderful house," said Rosie, looking around her contentedly.

"Ah, yes," replied Giuseppe. "The history of Venice is very colourful. This house has been owned by generations of my family for over 300 years and, before we had separate offices, the business of the bank was run from here."

"When did your forefathers first arrive in Venice?" asked Frederick.

"There were Salvie's in Venice at least 400 years ago," declared Giuseppe. "We came from Corsica and were initially money lenders."

Rosie knew that Giuseppe was a Jew, but she had read that it had been very difficult for the Jews in Venice.

"When did the bank start?" she asked.

"The bank was formally started in 1770, my great great grandfather being the first chairman. Come let me show you the original ledger."

Proudly Giuseppe led Rosie toward a magnificent cabinet. He opened the ledger and showed Rosie the original entries, explaining what they meant as she couldn't read Italian. Sophie moved to rescue Rosie.

"Come Rosie, let us go on to the balcony. I want to show you the gondoliers on the Grand Canal at night."

As they opened the doors to the balcony Rosie heard a baritone voice singing in the distance.

"He is singing to his lady that he loves her and wishes to kiss her passionately," explained Sophie. "Look at the gondoliers coming now."

There must have been a hundred or more, thought Rosie in surprise. They were all festooned with lamps, each competing to outdo the other.

"Even in winter, lovers wrapped up in furs liked to be serenaded on the canals with a gondolier singing love songs to them".

Rosie smiled, entranced by the sight of the lights bobbing on the water before her.

"Listen to that," said Sophie. "I will translate for you. 'Per la Gloria dadorarvi – for the love my heart doth prize'; 'Voglioa marvio, o lu-ci ca-re – O charmful eyes I would adore ye'."

"That's lovely," said Rosie softly.

"It's from the opera 'Griselda' by Giovanni Bononcini," replied Sophie.

"I just love opera – such beautiful music and poetry."

"Then we must go – I will make the arrangements, yes?"

"Oh, we will need to ask Frederick."

"Come on Rosie, let it be our surprise!"

Rosie giggled. "Yes, let's arrange it," she said conspiratorially.

"What are you two laughing about?" asked Frederick as the men stepped out onto the balcony to light their cigars.

"Just ladies talking, my darling," replied Rosie demurely.

The next day, they decided to take a walking tour so Rosie could explore one of the city's great charms further – the inter connecting canals and today they had decided to walk. Giovanni had insisted that they had an escort and one of his sons Marco, escorted them around the city.

"We will go to the Rialto today to see the market and the Ponte di Rialto, one of our famous bridges, which we will cross and then to the Santa Maria dei Miracoli," Marco said decisively.

Traders jostled with customers at the market stalls on the Fondamanta del Vin by the Rialto Bridge and they went onto the bridge for a better view. Marco was very insistent that they take no obvious signs of wealth. He explained that there are many sneak thieves and pickpockets and they must stay close to him. Rosie had a suspicion that close was not as close as Marco kept to her, constantly touching her arm or shoulder to point out some architecture or interesting gondolier. Frederick didn't seem to notice and was enchanted by Marco's relaxed commentary and easygoing manner.

"While the Ponte dell'Accademia has a wonderful view of the Grand Canal, this bridge gives a view of all the life in Venice," he said, as they looked down at the narrow stretch of canal below them, which was teaming with traders.

Crowds flocked on and around the bridge and boats in the water were selling vegetables and fruit. Suddenly Rosie felt a hand squeeze her bottom; she turned to confront the person and found a smiling Marco.

"Look Rosie," he said with a twinkle in his eye. "Those are – how you say in English – ladies of the night." He pointed to two women being crooned at by a rather handsome gondolier.

"Why do they ride in the gondola?" she asked ignoring his too-familiar squeeze.

"They are looking for a rich man who wants double the fun," laughed Marco.

"Double the trouble more like," said Frederick.

Marco looked at him quizzically, but moved them on pushing his way through the crowds. They walked chatting about the difference between the facades of the Venetian houses in the street compared to those on the canals. Then they reached the next stop, the delightful church 'the Santa Maria dei Miracoli'.

As they paused to look up at the exterior, Marco gave them a brief history lesson about the building: "This church was built to house an image of the Virgin, painted in 1409. It was common in those days to place a painting on the outside of a house. When a series of miracles was associated with the image in 1480, there was an avalanche of votive donations, which led to the authorities being able to afford to commission Pietro Lombardo, one of the leading architects of his day, to build a new church." He gestured towards the Santa Maria.

"Pietro created a building that relied for its effect almost entirely on colour – you can see he faced his church with a variety of marbles, porphyry crystal rock panels and serpentine inlays. Legend has it that the decorations consisted of leftovers from the Basilica."

Rosie thought the effect was beautiful and noticed that the small moat like canal in front of them was like a shimmering mirror for the coloured marbles.

"Come, let us go inside," said Frederick eagerly.

Rosie was even more delighted by the interior, if not a little awestruck. The striking ceiling was covered with paintings of saints and prophets. Marco explained that this was the work of Pier Penaachi in 1528 and pointed out the work adorning the high alter: Nicolo di Pietro's 'Madonna with Child', the miraculous image for which the church was built.

They left the church reluctantly to find a restaurant for lunch, retracing their steps to the Rialto and an appealing small restaurant near the fish market. Marco explained that this was one of the best fish restaurants in Venice.

They then spent the afternoon wandering around the city. At the colossal church of San Niccolo da Tolentino, a wedding was taking place. The square in front of the church and the huge pillars of the church were a breathtaking sight as the bride and groom emerged. People clapped and the dark haired bride laughed with her husband. Rosie glanced at Frederick, but he was engaged in an animated conversation with Marco at the time and they left the wedding party noisily celebrating behind them.

Marco was extremely good company and Rosie was sorry when he said goodbye outside their hotel. He kissed her tenderly on both cheeks and shook hands with Frederick, before making his way home.

They were tired after their long walk and Rosie retired to the bedroom for a rest – she knew there was to be a surprise tonight. Before she closed her eyes to sleep Rosie found herself day dreaming about Marco of all people. Had she imagined her bottom being pinched? He seemed such a nice man, so handsome and confident. He was an extrovert whereas her Frederick was much more reserved. Still Frederick was very kind to her and she did love him, didn't she?

"Wake up my dear," Frederick gently shook Rosies shoulder. "You said to wake you at 4pm." He kissed Rosie on the forehead. She blinked sleepily.

"Now Frederick," she said, sitting up. "We are to dress formally tonight. I am going to wear my black gown trimmed with fur and that beautiful hat with feathers."

"Where are we going? You already know?"

"I have been sworn to secrecy by Sophie. They will send a motor launch at 6:30pm," she replied. Frederick was intrigued.

"Come on Rosie where are we going?"

"You'll see," she laughed.

A little while later they were in the launch and Frederick still couldn't guess where they were going. They pulled up at their destination and were escorted by one of the boatmen. Frederick suddenly realised where they were.

"How wonderful, we are to see an opera at 'La Fenice'," he exclaimed, referring to Venice's famous opera house. Rosie laughed in excitement and they made their way inside to greet their hosts.

"What a wonderful surprise, I love the opera," said Frederick, as they shook hands.

"We shall be seeing 'L'elisir d'amore'," said Sophie. "Are you familiar with the work of Donizetti?"

"No, I have never seen it, have you Rosie?" enquired Frederick.

"No, please do tell us a synopsis," Rosie replied, looking at Sophie.

The auditorium was buzzing as they made their way to their seats.

"This is a comic opera about a young peasant man who is hopelessly in love with Adina a rich landowner," whispered Sophie, as they sat down. "Adina is pursued and proposed to by a Sergeant Belcore, who is a swaggering self-confident man. The shy young peasant called Nemorino tries to make his feelings known to Adina, but she says she considers him a kind and agreeable youth but is not in love with him. Appearing on the scene then is a Doctor, his name is Dulcamara. He is a rogue claiming to be able to cure gullible villagers' ills with his potions. Nemorino asks the Doctor if he has any potion he can take to influence Adina to love him. The crafty Doctor gives him a cheap bottle of red wine and tells him to drink it and his passion will be reciprocated. Well, of course it does not work and meanwhile Adina has accepted the proposal of marriage from Sergeant Belcore. Nemorino drinks too much of the potion and does not realise that Sergeant Belcore's regiment has been ordered to leave and the wedding has been brought forward to that evening. Luckily for him Adina is disturbed by the non-appearance of Nemorino and does not go through with the marriage."

"It sounds exciting," said Rosie. "What happens next?"

"Nemorino has gone to the Doctor again and obtained more potion, but has no money to pay for it. Nemorino earns the money for the elixir by agreeing to join Belcore's regiment in return for a cash payment."

Frederick leaned across to Rosie. "Well my dear have you found out evertything about the opera?"

"No, Sophie is just enlightening me, go on Sophie."

"Well, the village girls find out that, although he does not know it, Nemorino's wealthy uncle has died, leaving him a fortune."

"Oh, what intrigue," said Rosie laughing.

"Nemorino appears and all the girls crowd around him – he thinks it's the magic elixir. Seeing the village girls crowding around him Adina becomes jealous. Dulcanara, the Doctor, then boasts about the efficiency of his elixir and when Adina discovers that Nemorino has enlisted in order to pay for the magic potion to win her love, she begins to realise that she loves him too and goes off to buy back his enlistment papers from Sargeant Belcore. She returns and hands Nemorino the papers, telling him she has set him free. When she says nothing else to him, he rejects the papers telling her that if she does not love him, he may as well die in battle."

"Exactly as any man in love would do," piped up Giuseppe.

"Shush Giuseppe, let me finish the story. Then this at last brings a confession from Adina that she does love him. Belcore greets the changed situation philosophically and all join in praising a surprised Doctor Dulcamara and his magic elixir."

"Oh, how lovely and romantic," Rosie said. "How do you know this opera so well, Sophie?"

"I have been to see it at least ten times," Sophie laughed. "It is my favourite opera of the light hearted type. Next week, when unfortunately you will be gone, they are putting on one of Monteverdi's operas. He was a maestro di cappella at the basilica of St Mark – here in Venice, we regard him as a true Venezian."

"No, I have not seen his work, but I have read about him. My music teacher loved opera and was always playing different gramophone records."

"L'Orfeo is a deep opera, not much fun unlike this one," remarked Sophie, returning to a whisper as the conductor and leader of the orchestra took their places to a round of polite applause. Rosie settled back into her seat to savour the spectacle in front of her. As a performer herself, she thoroughly enjoyed watching this production and found herself completely caught up in it; laughing as the Doctor gave Nemorino his magic potion, feeling tears in her eyes when the lovers finally were together.

After a fine evening, they returned with Sophie and Giuseppe to their house for supper. Marco and another young man, Simone, were also there.

"Will you play and sing for us, Rosie?" asked her new friend Sophie. A chorus of agreement followed from the men and Rosie had little choice than to agree. She played part of a Beethoven Piano Concerto and then sang one of her favourite songs, Mozart's 'Laudate Dominum'.

When she finished they all stood spell bound and then broke into a spontaneous applause.

"My dear that was absolutely enchanting, where did you learn to sing like that?" asked Giovanni, kissing her hand.

"I was fortunate," replied Rosie. "I was sent to music lessons and my tutor encouraged me to sing. He then introduced me to a lady called Beatrice Ross, who was a voice coach to the divas at the Royal Opera in London. I haven't really sung opera although I would like to."

"Well," said Marco. "You are so talented and with such good looks, you must pursue a career in the opera." Frederick coughed.

"Oh, sorry Frederick are we monopolising your wife?" said Sophie. "Come on now gentlemen, leave Rosie alone, let's have supper."

Later that evening, after they had returned to the hotel, Rosie lay in bed with Frederick snoring lightly beside her. What an evening: the fantastic opera and then the compliments on her singing and suggestion she became and opera singer. She must not be swept along by it all, though, she thought to herself. Frederick didn't seem at all keen and when they had returned to their hotel, they did not even make love. He seemed distant and had apologised when Rosie asked if anything was wrong.

"No," he replied. "I have a slight headache, that's all."

Rosie thought of the past few weeks. Yes, Frederick had taken his conjugal rights – but that was exactly what it felt like. There was no finesse, no build up of anticipation, just straight in and quickly finishing. He then just said that he loved her, rolled off and usually went straight to sleep. It was not what she had dreamed of. Indeed her previous lover Stafford had been far more skilled. She began to quietly fantasise to herself about Stafford, tender and passionate at the same time, and found herself getting aroused. She moved her hand to touch herself, with Frederick oblivious next to her in a deep sleep. Afterwards, she lay there with a small frown. Was she doing something wrong? Perhaps she was not alluring enough – perhaps he was regretting the marriage? Many thoughts went through her head before sleep came that night.

The following day Frederick was bright and cheerful, complimenting her on her marvellous singing and suggesting that she ought to consider an audition for the Royal Opera house. He felt sure they could find someone who knew someone. His melancholic mood had swung again.

That day they were visiting the Gallerie dell'Accademia with Marco. As they walked around the many rooms, Frederick and Marcus were deep in conversation and Rosie found herself becoming slightly jealous. What is it about men, once they start talking nothing else seemed to matter. Rosie wandered on her own, studying the canvases. Finding the Accademia's most famous painting – Giorgione's mysterious 'Tempest' – she sat to study it in more detail. A stranger sat next to her and suddenly lunged, pulling her handbag away from her before running off. Rosie was stunned. A woman rushed toward her.

"Are you hurt?" she asked in Italian. Rosie told her she was English and then Frederick and Marcus arrived.

"What has happened?" asked Frederick.

Rosie explained that she had been studying the painting when a man snatched her purse. "Where were you both? I have walked around this gallery virtually on my own!" she said angrily, feeling tearful.

"We apologise profusely Rosie, we were looking at the paintings," replied Marcus.

Rosie was shaken by the incident and asked to go back to the hotel. Once there, a policeman arrived and Rosie recounted the story again before wearily making her way to their room. She had a blinding headache so shut all the drapes and lay down on the bed. Frederick had said that he and Marco were going to a shop Marco knew to buy her a new purse. Rosie didn't care. The snatched purse had been given to her by Stafford and now it was probably gone forever. Exhausted, she slept for an hour, waking to find herself alone, the events of the afternoon still fresh in her mind. There was a knock at the door. A bellboy stood at the door with a huge bouquet of flowers, red roses. Rosie tipped the boy and looked at the card attached: 'We are so sorry that your purse was stolen and will call at 7:00 to take you and Frederick to dinner' signed Sophie and Giuseppe.

That evening they went to a Venetian restaurant that specialised in traditional fish recipes and, whilst Rosie was not in a happy mood, they worked hard to take her mind off the theft. By the end of the evening she felt much better.

The following day, as some normality began to return, a note arrived for Frederick. He read it quickly.

"I am sorry my dear, father has asked me to go to meet the Vatican banker in Rome. Would you like to come or wait for me here?"

"I will come, I have always wanted to see Rome," said Rosie.

They journeyed by train to Rome, alighting at the Stazione Centrale, and then by coach to the Vittorio Emmanuelle Hotel. Tired after the journey, they had dinner at the hotel and retired early. The following day, Frederick went to the Vatican while Rosie spent the time visiting the sights of Rome, accompanied by Gino, a hotel employee.

Frederick met Cardinal Carducci the head of the Vatican Bank and after the formalities, discovered that the cardinal intended for two million dollars to be deposited in their bank in Zurich. The reason was a little vague, but Frederick did not delve deeply: he knew his father would be delighted with the deposited funds. The Cardinal was a charming man and knew of Frederick's recent wedding.

"Bring your wife to the Vatican tomorrow I will show you around the Pope's personal quarters and also the Vatican Museum."

Rosie could not believe that she would be visiting the Vatican. They had a late breakfast and made their way there in great excitement. Introducing Rosie to the Cardinal, they went in his company to the Pope's quarters. There they had an extraordinary surprise. The Pope was in residence and had agreed to a brief meeting. Rosie was stunned and almost froze as Cardinal Carducci introduced her. Frederick was very gallant and quickly engaged the Pope in Italian. Rosie followed some of the conversation; the Baron had apparently met the Pope when he was with a Cardinal in France and the Pope was reminiscing about the week he spent at their house on Lake Geneva.

The meeting went very quickly, with Rosie tongue tied for perhaps the first time in her life. Cardinal Carducci then took them to the Vatican museum and once again Rosie was spell-bound. The crowds which normally flocked around the museum had left an hour before, so they had a private tour. Rosie was transfixed by the Michaelangelo painting on the ceiling of the Sistine Chapel.

"Michaelangelo worked on the ceiling for four years," explained the Cardinal. "He single-handedly painted this wonder while lying flat on his back. If you look at each scene you will see the Creation of Adam, the Creation of the Sun and Moon and the original Sin panels and between the scenes the writhing athletic males known as ignudi as they were naked. In the lunettes about the windows he depicted the Forerunners of Christ and in between those the Sibyls and Prophets."

Rosie had seen pictures of the ceiling, but the actual thing was awe-inspiring and took her breath away.

Rosie and Frederick fell into bed that evening absolutely exhausted, but excitedly discussed their meeting with the Pope and his blessing of their marriage, which would delight Frederick's father. They promised each other that they would have to return to Rome one day and Rosie fell asleep with a small smile on her face.

Chapter Eight

Switzerland

Rosie looked around her. They had arrived exhausted at Zurich station an hour ago, after travelling over the Italian border into Switzerland, a one day journey across some truly breathtaking terrain. As the train had huffed and puffed up the steep gradients, Rosie had felt certain they were not going to make it. The snow in Switzerland was a magnificent sight that had hurt Rosie's eyes as the sun shone on the blanket of white. Now she was in a charming room, with a four-poster bed and a superb Mural on the wall of the Last Supper. As she refreshed herself with rose water, she reflected on their journey from London. It had been wonderful, of course: Paris, then Venice and Rome – that beautiful frescoed ceiling she would never forget. But as her thoughts strayed she suddenly felt sad. Her intimacy with Frederick had not been as she had expected. He was not an experienced lover and she found her thoughts turning to Stafford, dear Stafford, as they had done increasingly often over the past weeks, although she would not admit that even to herself. Suddenly feeling shattered, she laid down on the bed and fell asleep. Frederick came into the room and found her there, still fully clothed. He looked at her for a second and gently placed a divan over her, leaving her to rest.

The Baron had been very pleased with the business that Frederick had concluded with the Vatican Bank. For many years he had courted the Cardinals who controlled the Vatican's finances, arguing that with world uncertainty they should deposit heavily in Switzerland, who were neutral. His thoughts turned to Rosie. What of this girl? He had determined that he would endeavour to get to know her better while she was here; after all, he hoped she would be the mother of his grandchildren, producing the heirs to the bank and his fortune.

The following day Frederick went out to see some old friend and Rosie, who still felt quite tired after their journey, stayed behind. The Baron chose this opportunity to engage her in conversation.

"Tell me Rosie – may I call you Cynthia, it is a name I much prefer?"

"Certainly Baron," replied Rosie calmly. "But few people will know who you are talking about."

"We will change that! From now on you will be known as Cynthia de Courcy. I like the sound of it," chuckled the Baron. Rosie merely raised an eyebrow, but decided to let the matter drop.

"Now let us talk," he continued. "It is important that you understand us and our history and, at the risk of boring you, I am going to give you a history lesson."

Rosie suppressed a sigh. Another of the Baron's history lessons. Feeling an urge to giggle, she controlled herself and sat back to listen to what he had to say.

"How much do you know of Switzerland? Our city of Zurich is the largest city, although Bern is actually the capital. The country is made up of Cantons and half Cantons, which is an area like your county in England. Zurich, where we are now, is a Canton," the Baron paused and Rosie nodded. She knew all of this as he had told her before, but let him continue.

"The adoption of the Swiss Federal Constitution greatly involved the de Courcy family. Adopted in 1848 and later revised in 1874, there has been a de Courcy involved as President of the Zurich Canton or involved with the armed forces for over 500 years.

"Having successfully defeated the Hapsburgs at Sempach in 1386 a Baronet was awarded to my ancestor, Juin de Courcy, a brave knight. His grandson, the Baron Phillip de Courcy, was an important part of a group who created the Swiss League, which rose in the 15th Century as the military power. In 1477, he led the Swiss in victories over Charles the Bold of Burgundy and over Emperor Maximilion I and in 1499, shortly before he died, Switzerland was granted virtual independence."

Rosie sipped her sherry. The de Courcy's heritage was obviously important to the Baron. As he talked on, she reflected that it would also become her heritage now and the heritage of her children. She thought she understood a little better why the Baron wanted her to know about it and looked at him attentively.

"By 1513 there were 13 Cantons, but war came and the French army defeated us at Marignano in 1515. My ancestor was killed in the battle. His son, Roger, inherited and then followed peace and neutrality, which became the basis of our national policy. Religious differences led to the Catholics defeating the Protestants in battle in, let me see, 1531. Our family were then Catholics. There then followed over 200 years of peace when the de Courcy's prospered. We started our Bank in 1705, principally in the Canton of Zurich, but steadily our influence spread until we were the largest bank in Switzerland," the Baron went on, a hint of pride in his voice. "In the 18th century Switzerland's wealth steadily increased as the country became a money and intellectual centre of Europe." He sighed. "Unfortunately, the Swiss leadership strongly opposed the French Revolution and this led to the French invasion. Afterwards the French established a Helvetic Republic in 1798 and a year later clashed with the Austrians and Russians – " he broke off. "Am I boring you my dear?"

"No, not at all," said Rosie quickly. "It's fascinating."

"The de Courcy's were not the military leaders they had once been, preferring to build the bank, and our influence spread throughout Switzerland. We began taking instructions from abroad. Then came Napoleon and his Act of Mediation – let me see – early in 1803, which partly restored the old confederation. The Baron Philippe de Courcy played his part and helped set up the Pact of Restoration, substantially re-establishing the old regime."

Rosie nodded, her mind wandering despite her best intentions. She could appreciate how important the family history was to the Baron, but couldn't help wonder how often she would hear this story in the future.

The Baron took a sip of his drink.

"A most important development, Swiss neutrality was guaranteed by the Treaty of Paris in 1815. My grandfather, despite being in his 80th year, started the Radical Party which favoured greater centralization and, after a brief and almost bloodless civil war in 1847, the victorious radicals, including my father, transformed the confederation into the Federal State under a new constitution."

He smiled.

"As you can imagine the name de Courcy is widely respected for our part in the Swiss Federation and for our bank, which is still the largest and most influential in Switzerland. Ah, and National Unity has helped Switzerland prosper. We keep neutral and avoid any conflict even close to our borders. We maintain an elite army, some of which guard the Pope in Rome. This seems odd to many people and still stranger when you consider how many Swiss are Protestant, including the de Courcy's who became Protestants in 1748 which was owing to my great, great grandfather changing our religion when he pursued the German, Dutch and English bankers."

The Baron looked at Rosie carefully.

"So, there you have it, a small history; but it is important that you understand our position… There must be no more protests from women in London. You must refrain from politics. Frederick and I will discuss your stage career later this week, but my first indication is that you must stop."

Rosie sat bolt upright, a sudden flush of anger spreading across her cheeks. So that was the reason behind the history lesson; she should have guessed, the Baron always chose his words carefully. She looked at him defiantly.

"I'm sorry – you really expect me to stop being an actress and pursuing my ambitions – to stop being my own person?" she said heatedly.

The Baron was momentarily taken back; people didn't usually talk to him like that.

"Calm down, Cynthia. You must understand our position. You are the future Baroness de Courcy. Frederick will be Chairman one day and the major shareholder of the bank. We cannot have an actress making us a talking point, if not a laughing stock."

Rosie stared at him, too angry to speak. She got up and stormed out of the room. She had never been treated so much like a child in all her life.

'Who does he think he is?' she thought stormily. She would do what she liked, when she liked. Where was Frederick? What did he have to say? Was he in cahoots with his father?

Frederick was in fact in an entirely different place. Oblivious to his father's talk with Rosie, he lay in the arms of his beloved Pierre. He had missed him terribly, only taking solace with 'friends' a handful of times in London and once in Venice.

Pierre was the male lead in the Zurich Ballet Company and had been his lover for 2 years. They had met at the Paris Ballet, having been introduced by a mutual friend. Frederick had known he had feelings for men since his early days at Eton and sometimes he had succumbed to his desires. His father had caught him in bed with a rather attractive footman when he was 17 and since then he had been more careful.

Pierre massaged his brow and leaned over to kiss him. The table was arranged by Pierre for afternoon tea and they sat chatting animatedly. Frederick loved his smile, his wit, but most of all he loved him.

"Why is it? You are married Frederick, I am very hurt."

"Pierre, you know I love you but I must produce a male heir for father or risk being disinherited."

"I understand, but what of this girl, do you make love?"

"Yes, we do, but it is nothing like us," replied Frederick seriously.

"I am jealous," Pierre feigned a pout, teasing Frederick.

"Don't be stupid, Pierre, you know I will always love you. But speaking of Rosie, I must go, she will be wondering what happened to me."

They kissed as they parted. Frederick signalled to his coach driver to pick him up, having left the apartment first. He had maintained the elegant apartment in the Rue de Strasburg since shortly after meeting Pierre and conveniently it was only a short coach journey to his father's house.

Arriving at the house he walked in to be confronted by his aunt, father's sister.

"Your father has been rather foolish Frederick," she said.

"What is it Aunt?"

"He insisted on taking the opportunity to enlighten Cynthia of the family history and her future responsibilities."

"Oh, lord, what happened?"

"Well, he just got carried away, as you know he can. He told Cynthia, in no uncertain terms, that she was to give up her career on the stage and concentrate on being your wife."

"That's disastrous," replied Frederick, who knew Rosie well enough to know that her free spirit would not have taken such instructions lying down. "What did she do?"

"Luckily, she just stormed off, but the Baron is very annoyed that she left without a word. But leave your father to me," replied his aunt.

Frederick went upstairs. His father could be insensitive and sometimes a bully, but he would explain that her career was her decision, after all he really did not care one way or the other. He found Rosie sitting on the bed thinking. She was not going to give up her career.

"It doesn't matter what Frederick's father says," she thought to herself. "How dare he order her? Did Frederick know his father intended to talk to her?"

The door opened and Frederick walked in looking concerned.

"My darling, I have heard from my Aunt Greta that Father has been rather heavy handed."

"Is that how you describe your father ordering me to give up my career and change the name everyone has called me for over 20 years?" Rosie replied hotly.

"He can be a little presumptuous, but don't worry Aunt Greta and I will talk to him."

"I should hope so, Frederick. I am not giving up my career. I love acting and singing."

"I know precious," said Frederick. He put his arm around Rosie and she began to snuggle into his shoulder.

"Do you know it's our 6 week anniversary tomorrow?" she said, rubbing his leg.

"Oh dear," thought Frederick. "There's no hope there, I am all loved out. Three times already today, I cannot rise to the occasion again." He smiled to himself at his pun.

Rosie continued to caress Frederick's leg, but there was no reaction. She sighed to herself. Would he ever change, she wondered. Moving away gently, Frederick said: "I am just going to see father, you rest dear and I will soon sort out this misunderstanding."

Frederick's aunt had already spoken to the Baron, who was not used to people disobeying him and walking out during a conversation.

"I know you are married Frederick, but you cannot allow your wife to dictate this matter. People will talk behind your back even more now."

"What do you mean father?"

"Don't you think rumours abound that your wife, an actress, has not taken her first lover?"

"Father!" exclaimed Frederick.

"Well, you must be realistic, people will forget what she was, but not if she continues in the public eye. You will have gossip and ridicule behind your back. What do you think actors and actresses are?"

"I don't believe Rosie's like that at all," replied Frederick.

"Did you know about her affair?"

"What do you mean?"

"Before you, she had been seeing a young Englishman and I have it on good authority that they were lovers," said the Baron.

"You have been checking her background?" Frederick shook his head. He shouldn't be surprised at the lengths his father would go to.

"Frederick, we have a good name to maintain," said the Baron calmly. "People only do business with us because our reputation is unblemished. I had to check out her history – she was joining our family and is likely to produce an heir for the business."

"Father you are impossible, the only thing you ever think about is business," replied Frederick, although he couldn't help be secretly glad his father had checked her out and found out so little. Admittedly, she wasn't a virgin, but he didn't care. All he had to do was make her pregnant and he could return to his previous life and lovers.

"Alright father, leave her to me, but I can tell you she will never react well to instructions. Let me persuade her, she loves me and will do what I want."

As he returned to the bedroom, he wondered how much his father knew about his son's life. He wouldn't put it past him to have checked him out as well.

He found Rosie asleep. As he gazed at her, his thoughts turned to Pierre. What a pity he couldn't have remained single. She was a complication and Pierre was terribly jealous. He had to make love to her, he had to delude her into thinking they could be happy together. It hadn't been too difficult so far, but he suddenly felt the reality of the life he had created.

The Baron sat in his library smoking a cigar and pondering the future. He had known for ten years that his son had homosexual tendencies and had already paid off, unknown to Frederick, one boy in Paris who had endeavoured to blackmail the Swiss Ambassador. He had had letters from Frederick expressing his undying love, which the boy, a student at the Sorbonne, thought he could use to blackmail the Swiss government.

One night, the boy returned from an evening with Frederick to his modest lodgings, when two men accosted him, beat him badly and made sure he understood what would happen to him if he tried to blackmail the Baron again. They left him badly hurt with 100 Francs for his trouble and a warning which he heeded, dropping Frederick like a hot brick.

That had stopped Frederick for a while, until he met the ballet dancer. The Baron had a private detective constantly monitoring Frederick's activities and reporting back weekly via the diplomatic pouch at the embassy. His uncle was the Ambassador and understood the problem, not sympathising, but more worried about being linked to a scandal and being recalled - and he had shares in the bank. They had not intervened, as the ballet dancer was a member of the Swiss National Ballet Company and any meeting would almost certainly have meant his son would realise he knew his secret.

The Baron pondered the current problems. He knew Frederick was still seeing the ballet dancer and it would be a disaster if his daughter-in-law discovered his lover before she conceived. He had encouraged Frederick's relationship with her after the talk with Lord Berkeley, who had made it very clear that the transaction with the Bank of England was dependent on his goodwill – which had relied at that moment on Rosie's happiness. He knew his son liked the girl and when he had proposed, the Baron had decided that he could accept her as part of his family: she was attractive, reassuringly intelligent and had impressed with her language skills. He needed his son to have a wife for several reasons, not only the obvious progression, but also as a front for Frederick's rather unsavoury behaviour. Whilst he knew many homosexuals, the subject was unspoken and you certainly did not flaunt your sexuality in public.

He put down his cigar and moved across the room to pour himself a drink. He might have to deal with this ballet boy yet, but would wait and see how events unfolded. In the meantime, he ought to build bridges with the girl. He had made a mistake asking her to give up her career, he could see that now, and she had reacted badly. He decided to take them both to the Grand Hotel tonight, where he had arranged a private dining room with a string quartet to entertain.

The evening went well. Rosie had made an effort to forget the earlier scene with the Baron, who was charm itself with her and his guest, the Countess. What an attractive woman, thought Rosie. She had liked her from the moment they met in London, so glamorous and yet charming and easy to talk to.

"A toast," said the Baron, raising his glass. They all stopped talking and looked at him attentively. "To our lovely ladies."

Frederick and his father saluted the ladies as the Countess, Frederick's Aunt Greta and Rosie smiled at the men. The Baron meant his toast. Rosie and the Countess both looked ravishing in low cut silk gowns, which seemed to accentuate their ample bosoms and curvaceous figures. He wondered what was going through Frederick's mind; did he even notice the wondrous sight in front of him.

The Countess was a striking woman the Baron had been pursuing for several years. She was married to Count de Blois, but he was 75 years old and quite poorly so the Baron had every hope he would die shortly. He smiled to himself as he watched her talking to Rosie. The last time the Countess and he had shared adjoining rooms at the Savoy Hotel in London, they had spent most of the night wrapped in each others arms. He couldn't help but imagine her beautiful body as he sat across from her – and then his thoughts wandered as he pondered his son's affair. At first he had been so angry when the detective's report had been sent to him. He had thought his son's activities at Eton had been boys experimenting with sex and hadn't taken any notice when the headmaster casually mentioned that Frederick had been caught with two others buggering a junior. The head apologised for mentioning "the little problem" but unfortunately the lad's mother had complained and the governors were concerned that the incident wasn't a one off. The Baron had told the head that he should ignore the situation before he had to expel half of the school and presented the school with a handsome donation to help rebuild the sports hall. The Baron had then managed to avoid any further controversy until the bastard who tried to blackmail the family, but he soon had him dealt with.

"What are you thinking about over there, you look very serious," said the Countess gaily, interrupting his reverie. The Baron discarded his thoughts and smoothly diverted the conversation onto other topics.

The evening ended with the Baron kissing Cynthia's hand, as he still insisted on calling her. The Countess and Aunt Greta were staying at the Baron's house and also retired. Rosie suspected the Countess and her father-in-law would be meeting again before long.

Frederick joined her in the bedroom.

"Only three days until Christmas," he said as he undressed. "Father is planning a big dinner party."

He sat on the edge of the bed and put on his nightshirt before climbing in beside Rosie, who was reading a French book, 'The Count of Monte Cristo'.

"Do you think my father will ask the Countess to marry him when her husband dies?"

"Oh, Frederick. I don't think we should speculate; the poor man is apparently in agony," Rosie replied, putting down her book.

"I know and I don't mean to speak out of turn, but father is clearly very fond of her."

"Yes, but how do you know the Count won't live another 5 years?"

"I don't think so," replied Frederick. "Once you have rested after the New Year's eve dinner we will be catching the overnight train to Paris for a few days and then on to London."

He turned the wick down on the gas lamp and the room darkened.

"Frederick?"

"Yes Rosie – or should I say Cynthia?" he laughed. She rolled towards him and began rubbing the outside of his leg with her foot. He ignored her for as long as possible before saying: "I am sorry Rosie, I am feeling very tired". Rosie stopped rubbing his leg immediately and lay still, feeling the familiar disappointment as Frederick rolled over and went quickly to sleep.

As she contemplated her husband's back, Rosie began to think that he must have a very low sex drive. Lillie Langtry had told her one night about a Duke she once knew, who pursued her relentlessly, but when finally she agreed to meet him, rather than becoming lovers, as she had expected, they talked, joked and had fun, but he never did bed her. Lillie had called it a 'low sex drive' – perhaps this was the same as her husband. After all, they had only made love six times since they married.

'Yes,' she thought to herself bitterly. 'I have counted the times.'

When they did make love, it was over very quickly and Frederick didn't really seem to enjoy the experience. She thought about her affair with Stafford and how different that had been. He had been caring and considerate, taking time to bring her to the peak of expectation. When they had finished making love they often remained locked together afterwards as he kissed her neck and face expressing his undying love. Frederick, on the other hand, always rolled straight over. Perhaps he was just very inexperienced. She would have to coax him. Lillie had told her that many men needed to be led to understand a woman's needs.

Over the next few days, they visited a number of Frederick's relatives in Zurich who had not come to the wedding and met his godmother, a rather elderly, pompous woman who was married to the Chairman of Credit Zurich Bank, a long standing rival of the family. It was typical of the Baron to choose a rival as a god parent, thought Rosie. Frederick had promised Rosie a visit to a prominent haute couture establishment in Paris to select some new gowns and Rosie amused herself by thinking about this as the woman spoke to Frederick, mostly in German or a strange Swiss dialect that she later learned was Rumantsch. Anyone else would have found Frederick's godmother rude, but Rosie simply smiled and let her mind wander. Finally they got away.

"I hope that is the end of visiting for today," said Rosie.

"Yes, I need to go to meet someone on business; the carriage will drop me off and take you back to the house."

Frederick alighted the coach and headed towards his assignation with Pierre at the flat rented in Gessnertrucke. A blissfully unaware Rosie headed back to the Baron's house in Bahnhofqual. Fortunately Aunt Greta was at the house and suggested that they go out. The streets were covered in snow and a steady fall of fresh snow made it slow going, but eventually the carriage arrived at a house in Hirchengraben.

"What are we doing here?" asked Rosie.

"The woman who lives here makes all my gowns," replied Aunt Greta. "I thought we would spend the afternoon looking at her latest creations."

Rosie laughed in delight and spent a happy afternoon with Greta. Madame Seganti was a very talented dress designer, who produced handmade dresses for ladies who could pay. She was Italian, but had worked in Paris for one of the leading designers, Minerva, but had left to seek her own fortune. This year, she explained, many designers were copying Japanese fashions and she showed them drawings of enchanting evening coats and dresses. Rosie did not need much persuasion to choose two stunning evening gowns in red silk. Aunt Greta and Rosie then went to the popular St Clair hotel for afternoon tea and, as they sat chatting, a young woman came over.

"This is Cecille Defries, an old friend of Frederick's," said Aunt Greta.

"Nice to meet you," said Rosie.

"Moi aussi," replied Cecille.

"Please join us," said Aunt Greta. The two Swiss ladies got chatting and looked pleasantly surprised when Rosie easily held her own talking in French. Cecille seemed rather taken aback that Frederick had got married. She had been friends with him since childhood and glanced at Rosie more than once. Rosie could sense Cecille's curiosity but could not understand what the young woman was finding amusing.

That evening at dinner, Rosie mentioned to Frederick that they had met Cecille earlier in the day. He looked at her strangely.

"Oh, really, how nice. She is a charming young woman."

Rosie was puzzled. He had seemed distant when he came home and Rosie was finding his behaviour since their arrival in Zurich to be more and more inexplicable.

The Baron was watching his son and daughter-in-law. Did he detect his son was entering one of his black moods? If so, Rosie would soon realise that all was not as she thought.

"It's Christmas day in three days Cynthia," the Baron said, persisting in calling Rosie by her first name. "What has Frederick bought you?"

"I don't know," Rosie replied and turned to Frederick. "Well, have you bought me a surprise?" she teased, smiling at him tantalisingly.

"Ah, that's my secret," replied Frederick, somewhat listlessly.

Frederick's Aunt was laughing. "Did you tell Frederick how much we spent today?"

"I don't mind," he said. "Nothing is too much for Rosie."

"Now then you two, you're making me feel we are interlopers," said the Baron. "And please – can't you humour an old man and stick to the name Cynthia. I do think it is really a very nice name."

"Come now," said Greta. "Leave the young woman alone. If she prefers Rosie let it be so."

"Oh, I don't mind Cynthia. I'll get used to it," said Rosie rather seriously.

The waiters arrived with their feast, including to Rosie's surprise a boar's head on a plate. The wine flowed freely, but Frederick's mood did not pick up. Everyone noticed how quiet, almost morose, he was. Rosie tried hard to bring him into the conversation, even delving into, what was for her, the mysterious world of international banking.

"The papers are talking about Germany building up their army," she said to him.

"I wouldn't worry about that," he replied, putting a forkful of food in his mouth and chewing carefully, signalling the end of the conversation.

Rosie was not deterred. "It is snowing really hard," she said, glancing outside. She had not seen such snow before; how quickly it could build up. There must have been drifts of four feet outside the house. She had ventured out for a walk when she and Greta had returned from their shopping expedition, but had only gone one hundred yards before deciding it was too difficult to walk on, even though a team of workers were cleaning the pavements.

Frederick didn't reply and Rosie looked at him with a frown. The Baron stared hard at his son across the table.

"Oh, sorry my love, I was day dreaming," said Frederick.

The Baron pursed his lips. 'Yes, I bet I know of what – or should that be who,' he thought to himself.

"Shall we retire to the library for a cigar," he said to Frederick pointedly, deciding it would be better to get him away from Rosie while he was in this frame of mind.

The days passed with no improvement in Frederick's mood. Rosie spent more time with his Aunt Greta than she did with Frederick. At night he was pleasant enough, but always seemed preoccupied. She had approached the subject once or twice, but he always laughed off her enquiry.

Most of Frederick's thoughts were concerned with Pierre. He was becoming desperate as his lover was returning to Paris shortly after Christmas. He knew Pierre was becoming increasingly friendly with a boy in his cast, called Jacques. The two of them were in the same hotel, they danced together and frequently were in each other's company – what was he to think? And what of Rosie? She was a dear, sweet girl. They had a great deal in common and he certainly did not want to hurt her. For what felt like the hundredth time, he considered the position he found himself in: he loved Pierre but was married to Rosie. Jacques was on hand and flirting with his lover and shortly they were leaving together for Paris. He meanwhile had two further weeks of honeymoon to be spent staying at his father's chalet near Lake Lucerne. Christmas was fast approaching and he had not yet bought Rosie a present, although he had made sure Pierre had 2000 Swiss Francs to buy himself a small present.

To make matters worse, Rosie was increasingly questioning him to as his mood and he knew he was becoming depressed and had to pull out of it. He had also noticed his father staring at him once or twice and it was not a friendly look on his face.

He put his head in his hands. How wretched he felt. All he could do was hope his lover was faithful and go ahead with the honeymoon, covering up his feelings and loss as Pierre returned to Paris. He then had to manoeuvre himself into a position where his father would let him visit Paris or attract Pierre to come to London.

With all these thoughts swimming around in his head, he went to Pierre's hotel. He knocked on the door of Pierre's room; no answer. He knocked again and it was then he heard movement inside. Quietly he knocked again and called out: "Pierre, are you there?"

An elderly woman walked past him in the corridor. Just as he was about to knock again, the door opened. Pierre stood in front of him in the rather fetching silk dressing gown Frederick had given him in Paris.

"Frederick, I was not expecting you."

"I know, but I had to see you."

"Well, I am resting for tonight's performance and really can't see you now," said Pierre, his hand on the door.

Just then a voice called out from the room.

"If that's room service Pierre, can I have some champagne?"

Frederick pushed past and entered the room, walking swiftly into the bedroom. He knew Jacques was in the room, but the sight that greeted him made him stop in his tracks. On the bed was Jacques and another boy dressed as a page boy. Jacques was completely naked and smiled knowingly as Frederick's anger welled up. Pierre moved towards Frederick.

"Don't touch me," Frederick cried and struck him across the face.

"Please don't hurt me Freddie," Pierre shrieked.

Complete blackness overtook Frederick and he picked up a poker leaning on the hearth, striking Pierre with it on the shoulder. There was a loud crack and Pierre screaming in pain. The two boys cowered in the corner as Frederick turned and advanced towards them. There was a knock on the door and a gruff male voice called out: "Is there anything wrong? What's going on in there?"

Frederick came to his senses. The black mist cleared and he surveyed Pierre clutching his shoulder and crying in pain. Frederick instructed the two boys to keep out of sight and went to the door.

"My friend has fallen in the bath and hurt his shoulder, please will you call a doctor?"

A flurry of activity followed, with Frederick ushering Pierre's playmates out of the hotel room just as the hotel manager appeared.

"I hear you need some assistance," he said. "My name is Monsieur Dupont. I am the hotel manager."

"Thank you, my friend has fallen in the bath and injured his shoulder," said Frederick. The manager looked at the two boys sheepishly passing him in the corridor and then at Frederick; certainly he was dressed as a gentleman.

"We have called a doctor but he will be some while in this weather."

Pierre continued to sob uncontrollably and the manager suggested he lie down on the bed while he went for some ice.

Frederick was glad to be left alone with Pierre who winced as he stepped towards him.

"Please don't hit me again Freddie. I am sorry, it was a foolish temptation. Those boys mean nothing to me, you know I love you."

"Don't talk Pierre, just listen," said Frederick quickly. "You slipped in the bath and hit your shoulder as you fell. Your companions and I were waiting for you to bathe and dress and heard the fall. After investigating we called for the doctor."

There was a knock on the door.

"Have you got that?" Frederick glared at Pierre.

"Yes Freddie, it's just as you said."

Frederick opened the door and a portly woman entered, accompanied by a small balding man. Frederick showed them in and then watched as the doctor gently manoeuvred Pierre's arm and shoulder. The doctor, who had been tending Madam Dupont's worsening gout, looked at his patient and his injury quizzically.

"You are very lucky, young man. There is a nasty swelling but no broken bones."

"Thank goodness," said Frederick. "Pierre is a ballet dancer appearing at the theatre."

Pierre said nothing as the doctor gently put his arm in a sling, placing an ice pack on the shoulder.

"Keep that pressed against your shoulder for two hours, then make sure you rest completely. I am afraid that you won't be dancing for at least two weeks."

As the doctor's words sunk in, Pierre starting sobbing again. "But if I don't dance, I will lose the part."

"I am sorry young man, if you exercise in any way you may permanently damage the ligaments in your shoulder."

"Don't worry Pierre, I will explain the situation to the Manager of the troupe. I am sure he will understand," said Frederick.

Madame Dupont and the doctor left the room, having settled Pierre in a chair by the fire, wrapped in a blanket.

Pierre looked at Frederick with fear in his eyes. Seeing Frederick's grim expression, he began to sob quietly to himself.

"Oh, stop it Pierre, you were stupid and I haven't yet forgiven you, but there is no need to cry, I won't hurt you again," said Frederick, realising that he was enjoying this new dominant role. "Will the manager be at the theatre now?"

"Yes," whimpered Pierre.

"Very well. I will go and explain matters. I am sure everything will be fine."

Pierre flinched as he kissed him on the head.

"Oh for goodness sake, if you carry on like this I will break your arm," said Frederick and he left the room.

In the end it was simple. The Manager of the theatre was well known to Frederick and he explained that Pierre had fallen in the bath. He gave him 500 Swiss Francs "for his inconvenience" and the manager immediately mellowed.

"Oh the poor boy, I will go and see him."

"He is resting; perhaps you should wait until tomorrow."

Frederick returned and explained to Pierre the successful outcome of his meeting and was pleased that Pierre had stopped over-reacting to his touch, but he could still see in his eyes the fear he had observed earlier and he discovered he rather liked it.

"I must go now. Rosie will wonder what has kept me, but I will return tomorrow with a present for you."

Pierre's whole demeanour picked up. "A present, what is it?"

"Just be patient," Frederick laughed and left.

Rosie had been unable to leave the house due to the weather, except for a brief trip in a horse drawn sleigh. Even though she had been wrapped in layers of furs, her face had been frozen, colder than anything she had ever experienced. She didn't venture out again. A servant was sent to collect the gifts she had purchased for Frederick and her father-in-law and she had already purchased an exquisite pair of gloves in Venice for Aunt Greta. Today had been a good day, though; the garments she had ordered had arrived for a final fitting which had been perfect. The magnificent Japanese style evening coat, known as a theatre coat, was made in white padded satin and embroidered with a red flower pattern while the gown had kimono sleeves and was a Mandarin robe, a style made in Japan by the designer, Takashimaya. Rosie had been assured that this coat was one of the first to be exported and as she tried it on, she saw that it was magnificent.

She had found herself in the company of the Baron for each of the last few days. Surprisingly, she thought, he had been very attentive, discussing many interesting topics, including the history of Swiss banking, which he had gone into in some detail. She now knew how their family bank had evolved from minor money lending institution to a major European bank over the past two hundred years. Somewhat to her astonishment she had found the subject fascinating and, as she questioned the Baron, she could tell he had also been taken aback by her interest.

The Baron had kindly arranged for two tutors to visit her, one to teach her German and an Italian gentleman, Senior Lambessco, who was a skilled pianist. With these new lessons, she had been kept extremely busy and it was just as well, as she had hardly seen Frederick for days. When she casually asked him where he had been, he always answered that he was busy at the bank, but her father-in-law had given her the impression the bank was virtually closed for yuletide. Rosie thought it was strange, yet his mood had changed and he seemed happy enough, so she didn't question him any further.

The Baron was sitting in the library studying a series of documents. The German government had approached him confidentially to raise a loan of 50 million Swiss Frances, an extremely large sum. Looking at the papers he noted that the Germans were proposing some very substantial investment in armament factories. Discretion had always been a byword at the bank, but this information could be of massive use. If the Germans were re-equipping factories producing armaments, then there must be a reason. Europe had been a hotbed of rumour and counterrumour for some time, but surely this was the posturing of countries? There was a knock at the door.

"Come in," said the Baron, putting away the papers.

"Father," Frederick stood in the door. "Can I discuss a banking matter?"

"Yes, come in. Shall we have some coffee? Do sit down."

The Baron rang the bell and ordered morning coffee. He was intrigued; Frederick did not often want to talk to him 'one to one'.

"Well, is there something I can help you with?"

"I was wondering if you could spare a few minutes, Father. I wish to discuss an idea I have," replied Frederick, somewhat uncertainly.

The coffee arrived and the Baron sat back in his favourite winged leather chair and looked at his son.

"I wanted to discuss with you, well, that is to say we… er, Cynthia and I… wanted to discuss whether we could be based in Paris?"

His father lit a cigar.

"And why would you want that?"

He blew out a cloud of smoke and puffed a few times to keep the large cigar ignited.

Frederick started to stammer. He always seemed to do that when he was feeling pressurised and talking to his father.

"W-we feel that it is the place to be… as a centre where b-banking business is beginning to take over from London…" He inwardly cursed himself; there was so much more he meant to say.

His father sat impassively and let out a great stream of cigar smoke.

"I don't see that Frederick, and neither would the operations director. If you are to live in Europe then it must be London."

He leaned forward.

"You have hardly met any of the key players yet. Paris is about fashion and we are in the money business. London is where we need you to be."

Frederick knew it was useless to argue and made a feeble excuse about having to explain to Rosie, who would be very disappointed, before leaving his father puffing his cigar. 'Now what was that all about?' thought the Baron. He couldn't imagine it was anything to do with the bank's affairs.

Frederick met Rosie in the hall heading towards the drawing room for her piano practice. She smiled, but Frederick virtually ignored her.

"Frederick what's wrong?" she said, her smile fading.

"Oh, nothing, I have just had a meeting with father and he did not agree with my view on something. Can you excuse me, I have to go out?"

He left Rosie standing there pondering her husband's behaviour. It was another example of his strange moods, which had become all too frequent since they had been in Zurich.

The piano tutor, kindly arranged by her father-in-law, was a flamboyant Italian. They had been practicing for her to play at the Christmas party her father-in-law had arranged. The de Courcy Christmas day concert and the dinner that followed was the event of the year in the household and this year would be no exception. Tomorrow guests would arrive for the concert, followed by a Christmas dinner held in the huge dining room. Senior Lambesco had explained to Rosie that she should conclude the concert with a traditional Christmas carol, but she would also play Beethoven's Moonlight Sonata and sing. In addition, she would perform a duet with the Countess, who was also a trained singer. They had been practising for a week with the small stringed orchestra who would entertain with various favourites. In truth, Rosie had enjoyed the practice sessions, but was a little nervous. She didn't even know many of the people who would be attending, except Frederick's Aunt, the Countess and her godson, who was staying with her. There would be a number of important business contacts, politicians and friends of her father-in-law, who would be coming with their wives. Despite being used to performing in front of strangers, she couldn't help feeling slightly apprehensive about the Baron's grand Christmas plans.

She missed her own family dreadfully; this was to be the first Christmas not spent in their small terraced house in East London. She wondered how they all were and hoped they had received her letters and the parcel she had sent from Venice. She also thought about her dear benefactor, Lord Berkeley; had he recast her part?

The Countess and Rosie had been meeting at her house to practice their duet. Rosie liked the Countess; she was stunningly beautiful and yet had a pleasant manner which belied her status and position. They enjoyed the rehearsals and laughed a great deal together, as you would with a best friend or sister. During the time they spent together, Rosie learnt a great deal about the Countess' life and family history, which she found fascinating. She had explained to Rosie that her mother, an English girl from a small Norfolk village, had been travelling in Paris when she met Count Rosini, then a young man studying at the Sorbonne. They had married secretly and, when the Count's father had found out, he had disinherited his son and changed his will to benefit his younger brother. It was then that fate took a hand. His brother had been killed in a sailing accident off Corsica and his father had no choice, if there was to be a succession, than to recognise his other son. In fact, in the years that followed he had come to find his daughter-in-law a delightful girl and a talented artist. When she gave birth to a baby daughter, Sophie, the new grandfather doted on the child. Sadly there were no more children and following the stillbirth of a son, her mother became reclusive and depressed. When both her parents had died, Sophie had become the Countess Rosini, inheriting a substantial estate and fortune as the only child.

Rosie knew that the Countess still had many men who hoped to become her suitor, but was surprised to learn that the true love of her life had always been the Baron. She had first met him at a house party held by her father when she was 15 and fell madly in love. He was a brash, handsome young man destined for great things. Even when he had married and broke her heart, he continued to see her; he had explained that his marriage was a business agreement, designed to merge two great banks and he had to go along with it. She was entirely under his spell. The Countess had married Count de Blois ten years ago, even though she had enjoyed the company of many men, seducing crown princes and members of the Italian, German and Dutch royal families. Many marriage proposals had followed, but she had chosen Count de Blois because he was a kind and very rich man. Despite her respect for her husband, she had been unable to break the hold the Baron held on her heart. When his wife died a year ago, the Countess had resumed a full relationship with him. Now they were together and her husband was dying, but the Baron had not suggested marriage and she had come to be glad she still retained her independence.

Today the two women were meeting at the Baron's house. The Baron had gone out, so the two ladies were able to rehearse without being disturbed. They had wanted to maintain the element of surprise for their performance.

As they enjoyed a short break, reassured that their duet was going well, the Countess asked if Rosie intended to return to the stage. She could see that the young Mrs de Courcy was delighted to be singing again.

"Oh yes," said Rosie, without any hesitation.

"You have a wonderful soprano voice," the Countess said. "Have you ever thought about having classical training?"

Rosie had explained that she had some classical training from her music tutor, who had insisted she learn scales, to read music and had taught her breathing techniques. The Countess nodded. It was obvious to her that Rosie had a natural talent and potentially a future on the classical stage. However, she knew it would be difficult for the girl to continue her career – the de Courcy's usually expected their women to keep house, entertain and certainly not work in such a public arena. Certain charitable work was, of course, fine but singing would be a different matter.

Their rehearsal was interrupted by the arrival of the Countess's godson. Phillipe Von Styner was the son of Sophie's oldest friend Marianne.

Marianne's husband, a major in the Swiss army, was visiting the Countess's husband, the Count de Blois, who was a distant cousin, in his chateau on Lake Lucerne. The Countess knew he was being kind, but regrettably the Major would find her husband had deteriorated to the point that he probably would not recognise him. He no longer knew who she was, which she had found difficult to begin with. Preferring to remember the charming Count as he was before he became ill, she had left for Zurich and the arms of her lover. Some might call her behaviour callous, but she knew her husband was in good hands and so was she. Her friend, Marianne, knew all about Sophie's love for the Baron and understood entirely why she was spending Christmas at her Zurich house. Indeed it had been very convenient, as it meant her son could spend Christmas with his godmother.

"Bonjour Phillipe."

The young man kissed the Countess on both cheeks.

"Bonjour Sophie, comment allez-vous?"

"Parlez vous anglaise Phillipe. This is Madame de Courcy, Frederick's wife," replied the Countess, switching to English.

"Bonjour Madame." Phillipe kissed Rosie on both cheeks and a spark of static electricity gave them both a minor shock. They both laughed and parted.

"You are electric," Phillipe smiled, surveying the beautiful woman in front of him.

"Please call me Rosie," replied Rosie, feeling herself flushing slightly.

"Well Phillipe, are you staying for lunch or dashing off again?"

The Countess motioned for Phillipe to sit. Rosie looked at the handsome young man.

"I would be delighted to stay for lunch in such attractive company," he replied, glancing at Rosie.

"Now, now Phillipe you know your charm is lost on me."

The Countess pulled the cord by the door and Dawson the English butler appeared.

"You rang Madam?"

"Yes, Dawson can you bring tea for us?"

"Certainly Madam." The butler left to find the housekeeper. Rosie studied Phillipe with more than a passing interest as he regaled them both with his stories of skiing off piste and had them laughing with his tales of his friends' antics.

The morning passed without the women rehearsing at all and the Countess had to send Phillipe gently on his way to her house at midday, otherwise the whole day would have been lost.

Concluding the day with her piano tutor, Rosie practiced her solo and, feeling exhausted after her long day, ordered a bath to be filled. As she soaked herself, she reflected that she hadn't seen Frederick since he left that morning, what on earth was he doing on Christmas Eve? Phillipe's face drifted into her mind and she laughed to herself as she thought of the gaiety of the young man, so happy and full of life. By contrast Frederick was so morose lately. If she was honest with herself, he seemed unhappy – was it her fault? She made up her mind to confront him on the subject when he returned.

When Frederick arrived he was, in fact, in a very good mood and laughed at a rather serious Rosie who had been curled up by the fire in the bedroom.

"I have bought your Christmas present," he said, taking his wife's hand.

Rosie looked at him with a smile.

"What is it, tell me!"

"No, it's a surprise," he said and kissed her on the brow. "Time to get ready for dinner".

Christmas Eve in the de Courcy household was a splendid affair. The cook had surpassed herself with a superb meal of pate de fois gras and soup to start followed by duck and a fish course, with Swiss cheese, crepe suzette and chocolate to round off. The food and drink flowed until 1 am when everyone headed wearily for bed. Frederick was not in any mood for a chat, having consumed copious amounts of port, and started snoring as soon as his head hit the pillow.

Rosie woke as the servant knocked on the door the next day.

"Morning tea Madam. May I wish you a Merry Christmas?"

"Thank you Genevieve"

"May I pull the curtains Madam?"

Rosie glanced at Frederick who lay comatose and nodded. She drank her tea and quickly dressed and went down to the dining room.

"Happy Christmas my dear."

The Baron got up and kissed Rosie on the cheek.

"I have a small gift for you."

He handed her a small velvet box.

"Thank you," said Rosie, opening the lid. She gasped as a ring sparkled and glinted in the winter sunshine.

"This is wonderful, thank you so much," she said, removing it from the box and kissing him on the cheek.

"The ring belonged to my mother. I have had it changed to fit your finger – allow me."

He slipped the ring on the third finger of her right hand. As she gazed at the huge diamond and sapphire ring, the Countess, who had spent the night, came into the dining room.

"Ah, Rosie, I see Manfred has given you the ring," she said, with a smile. "Isn't it wonderful?"

"It's beautiful," replied Rosie, holding her hand up to show the Countess how it looked.

Frederick didn't appear for breakfast, remaining oblivious to the buzz of the household as preparations were made for the evening. It was nearly lunchtime when he appeared. He beckoned Rosie into their room where he presented her with a large, flat parcel.

"What's this?" said Rosie.

"Happy Christmas." Frederick kissed her on the cheek. "Open your present."

Rosie carefully opened the box and was astounded to find a magnificent painting of two girls at a piano. She shouted with joy.

"I thought you would like it, it's called 'Girls at the Piano' and was painted by Renoir in 1892," Frederick said, with something of his old smile as he saw the radiance on her face.

"It's gorgeous," said Rosie, studying the painting. "I love the girls looking at the music."

"It so reminded me of you playing the piano." He lit a cigarette.

"Shut your eyes," said Rosie.

"What?"

"Come on Frederick, close your eyes."

Rosie tiptoed to her bedside table and opened the draw, taking out a small, carefully wrapped box.

"Happy Christmas." Rosie gave the box to Frederick, who looked surprised.

"What is it?"

"Open it and see."

Frederick tore the paper and opened the box. Nestling inside was an ornate tie pin with a diamond tip.

"Oh, Rosie, where did you find it?" said Frederick, looking up at her.

"I got it in Venice, do you like it?"

"I love it," he said, kissing her. "Happy Christmas, darling."

The guests began arriving, but Rosie had already decided on a late entrance. Countess de Blois and her godson, Phillipe, were warmly greeted by the Baron and a constant stream of guests were shown into the drawing room, including members of the Zurich Canton, Swiss bankers and the British Ambassador,

This was the moment Rosie decided to make her grand entrance. All eyes turned toward the double doors as she appeared, looking stunning dressed in a magnificent peach silk gown.

"Ah my dear, you look lovely," said the Baron approvingly.

"What a pity there is no dancing, I would love to whirl you around showing off," joined in Frederick.

The dinner was a sumptuous affair lasting more than two hours, but Rosie was relieved when the time came to perform. The Baron and his guests were ushered into the drawing room, which had been transformed by the servants, with seats laid out in rows. A string quartet played in the corner of the room. The Baron stood up.

"Dear guests and friends, my daughter-in-law, Cynthia, and the Countess are now going to beguile you with a recital," he said to a small ripple of applause as Rosie got up and took her place at the piano.

She began to play Beethoven's Moonlight Sonata and the guests soon realised that she was in fact a talented pianist. Warm applause – and a bravo from young Phillipe – greeted the end of her performance.

The Baron joined in the applause.

"That was absolutely spellbinding; a magical performance," he kissed both ladies. "Now Cynthia is going to treat us with her rendition of 'Vissi d'arte' from Tosca."

The guests clapped enthusiastically. Rosie took up her position and began to sing, enchanting them all. The Countess followed, playing Borodin on the piano, after which the orchestra started playing "Grieg". Once again the guests were enthralled and applauded with cries of "bravo" and "more" ringing out.

The noise died down as the quartet played the opening bars to 'Silent Night' and Rosie and the Countess led the guests, singing the popular Christmas carol in German.

"What a treat," said one guest as they began to leave. Everyone made sure they approached Rosie to congratulate her and she was warmly embraced by many – and had some difficulty extracting herself from a group of male admirers.

"That was great fun Cynthia," said the Countess, holding her hands. "They all seemed to really enjoy the evening."

The Baron approached them.

"Ah ladies, you were magnificent. Even Countess Defrie, who is virtually tone deaf, told me she enjoyed your performances."

They all laughed.

As the rest of the guests left, Frederick excused himself to smoke a cigar with his father in the smoking room and Rosie and the Countess retired to their bedrooms with the praise still ringing in their ears.

Rosie felt heady from the champagne she had drunk, which had flowed liberally. Frederick joined her in the chamber and was, it seemed, back to his old self. Full of compliments and slightly the worse for wine and champagne they made love for the first time in days.

Afterwards, Rosie lay thinking about the events of the evening. She had enjoyed the singing and playing the piano and the duet with the Countess had been great fun. Phillipe, the Countess's godson, had been in attendance all night and she had been flattered by the attention most of the men had given her. Frederick had complimented her on her singing, but on occasions had seemed far away. As the events of the evening replayed in her mind, she fell into a deep sleep, but woke with a start a short while later, having had a troubled dream. She had been running along the dock at St Katherine's in London and had slipped, falling into the Thames. Horrified she tried to swim, but there was a weight around her legs. She looked down and saw a young man hanging onto her legs.

Frederick stirred sleepily. "What is it my dear?"

"Oh nothing, just a dream," she said, as she settled herself down again.

Waking at first light, she washed her face in the bowl provided and cleaned her teeth, rinsing her mouth several times to clear the stale tartar from last night.

Shortly after breakfast a message arrived. The butler handed the Baron a note. He glanced at it and passed it onto Rosie. "A message for you from our London office."

Curious, she opened the sealed note.

"My dear Rosie, your mother has asked me to write to you as the bearer of sad news. There is no easy way for me to tell you this and regrettably I must advise you that your father has died."

Rosie dropped the note. She staggered to one side and was caught by the Baron.

"What is it my dear?" asked the Countess anxiously.

Rosie sat on a chair and shook her head mutely.

"Fetch smelling salts Freda," the Baron instructed a servant. He picked up the note. "May I?"

Rosie nodded. He read the note and looked up at the Countess. "Cynthia's father has died in London."

"Oh, you poor dear," she said, kneeling beside her and holding her trembling hands.

Rosie took a deep breath and asked to see the letter again. There was a further paragraph which she hadn't noticed in her shock.

"I am sorry to send this sad news by messenger. Your mother asked me to tell you that the funeral will be on Friday 6th January. If you can at all speed back to England, do so, but if not she will understand. My deepest condolences."

The letter was signed from Lord Berkeley.

"We must make immediate arrangements for you to return to England," said the Baron kindly. Rosie nodded numbly. She couldn't take the news in – her father dead? She stared around her and tears started seeping from her eyes as the reality of the message hit her.

Arriving at Dover, Rosie was relieved to set foot on dry land. She was generally a good sailor, but the sea had been very rough and she had been sick for a great deal of the channel crossing. But then so had all the passengers and many of the crew. The Captain, a short stocky Scotsman, had informed them on embarking in Calais that there was a gale in the channel and that the ladies would be wise to stay in their cabins. In fact, Rosie found it was marginally better to be topside, even though the smell of sick was everywhere. She pointed her face into the wind and stared blankly at the white horses as the ship rolled over the waves.

The fast train to London left Dover Harbour station and, as they settled themselves in a first class carriage, the compartment door opened and there was Lord Berkeley. Rosie stood up and fell into his arms. He held her tightly as the tears flooded down her face.

"It's alright, cry my dear. I fear there are more tears to come."

He had had his manservant prepare a picnic box with a cold breakfast and a flask of tea, which he offered to her once her tears had subsided. She sipped the tea but couldn't eat. Frederick sat holding her hand as Lord Berkeley explained what had happened to her father.

Rosie listened as he recounted how Jack had collapsed at the docks and been taken to East London Hospital. He had regained consciousness briefly, but lapsed into a coma before her mother had arrived with her brothers. The doctors declared that nothing could be done, which is when Molly sent Billy with a message to Lord Berkeley, who had arrived at the hospital as quickly as possible. Consulting with the doctors, he had regrettably advised the Holders that the prognosis wasn't good: they feared he had a brain tumour and there was little they could do, except wait.

Lord Berkeley held Rosie's other hand. "Your father was in no pain – he slipped away shortly after midnight on the day before Christmas Eve," he said quietly.

Tears rolled down Rosie's cheeks as she sat in silence, flanked by Frederick and Lord Berkeley, each holding her hand tightly.

Chapter Nine

Revelations

Jack Holder was buried in the graveyard of St Anne's Church, Shoreditch on the 6th January 1901. He had not been a churchgoing man, but Molly had asked the priest to arrange it. Folks in the area would always remember the day, saying he had the best turnout for the funeral that anybody could remember round those parts – "A good old East End funeral" as one of Jack's mates put it. The horse drawn carriage was followed by crowds of men, women and children who came to say their goodbyes, and many others lined the streets as the funeral cortège passed, first through Hackney, then Shoreditch. The Holders felt a sense of pride through their grief as they saw how much respect their friends and neighbours had held for Jack. Even the docks were closed for the day, much to the consternation of the owners.

Three months later, Rosie called on her mother as she had some good news. Molly had been quietly withdrawn since the death of Jack, but always perked up when her daughter called on one of her regular visits.

"Come in Rosie, I'll put the kettle on."

Molly led the way to the front room. After the funeral, Rosie had offered to come back home for a while, but her mother had refused. "I have the three great lumps here, I am not alone," she had said, referring to Rosie's brothers. "You must stay in your wonderful house with your husband." However, Frederick was now away on business in Paris and had been for over a month. Rosie felt lonely in the big house in Eaton Square, despite the bustle of the servants. She had not sought to return to the stage in the end and her trips to the East End benefited her as much as her family.

Molly prepared some tea and brought in a cake she had made.

"Oh mother, you should not waste your money on making cakes for me," Rosie said. She could guess how little money would now be coming into the house, but in truth she did not know her mother's financial situation.

Molly brushed off her remark and poured the tea.

"Tell me what news there is with you," she said, handing Rosie a cup.

Rosie beamed. "I have been to the doctor and he has confirmed I am expecting a baby."

Molly stopped with her cup halfway to her mouth and tears came to her eyes.

"Oh Rosie, that's wonderful news," she said as she hugged her daughter. "Does Frederick know?"

"No, I have sent a message through the bank's courier service and also to the Baron," replied Rosie, laughing at her mother's excitement.

They spent the next couple of hours talking about babies and only once did the conversation stray to talk about Jack. Molly knew Rosie had grieved the hardest of all her children.

"If we have a son, I would like to call him Charles, after dad," said Rosie quietly. Molly looked at her for a moment, seeming to make up her mind about something.

"There is something I must tell you," she said seriously.

"What is it mum?"

"I don't know how to start…" she began, holding Rosie's hand.

"Mum, what is it? You're frightening me," said Rosie, noticing the worried expression on her mother's face. Molly took a deep breath.

"When I was sixteen, I worked below stairs in a grand house in Belgrave Square. The life was tough, but the butler and cook were fair. I was a ladies maid to a beautiful lady, who was very kind. His Lordship was often away but his son, who was two years older than me, came back from his studies in the summer of 1876. He was such a handsome man. He talked to me about his plans and showed me an atlas of the world. He read stories from Dickens and I was smitten with him. Of course, I maintained my station but he kept holding my hand and telling me how pretty I was and I liked him. I liked him a lot."

Molly broke off, fiddling with the edge of the tablecloth.

"Well – what happened, who was he?" asked Rosie, her full attention on her mother.

"He went back to school and I didn't see him again until the Christmas of 1876. It was my seventeenth birthday and when I told him, he bought me a present, which he slipped quietly to me one afternoon – it was a hand mirror. I still have it. I knew it was silly and could never be, but I really liked him. He had wonderful brown eyes and would hold my hand – only when his mother had gone visiting or shopping, of course. One day – I remember it well – a Saturday, the butler had given me the day off. He met me in secret and we went to London Zoo. I was fascinated by the animals, the strange creatures I had only seen in books. I was wearing my best dress and he took me to a Lyons Corner House for tea. I felt like a real lady. When we got back to the house, it seemed very quiet. Mrs Moggs, the cook was nowhere to be seen and I knew Smithson, the butler, had gone to watch some new sport, called football. I had had daydreams about how this young man would sweep me up in his arms, carry me to a bedroom and kiss me. He had begun telling me about a piece of bone from an old creature that he had in his room and asked me if I wanted to take a look. I did not worry and went straight with him. He showed me what he described as a fossil and then a drawing he had made of a… raptor… an animal from thousands of years ago. We sat close together on his bed…"

Rosie noticed her mother had gone into an almost dreamlike state. "Well, what happened?"

"We kissed. The first time I had ever kissed a man, other than that silly Jack – your dad."

Molly paused.

"Go on mum."

"Well, one thing led to another and we did it." Molly blushed.

"Did it?"

"Yes… you know…"

Rosie was astonished.

"Mum, you made love with this man? Who was he?"

Molly looked at Rosie for a second.

"He was, is, your true father."

"What? What do you mean? I don't understand." Rosie shook her head, unable to believe what her mother was saying to her.

"I kept it a secret for ages, but I knew I was up the plum duff. Mistress noticed me one morning – I had been sick and was not feeling well that day – and I let my guard down. Her Ladyship was such a lovely lady. I told her, it was stupid, but I did it."

"What did she say?"

"Nothing, absolutely nothing. She summoned Mrs Moggs and when she came, sent me to my room. After that things happened quickly. I was sent back home to Wapping with £5 and told not to repeat a single word of the lies I told my mistress."

"My god, that's dreadful," said Rosie, imagining the situation her mother had found herself in.

"Worse was to come. My mother was furious, threatening to turn me out on the street. Only my dad saved me."

"Then what happened?"

"The most wonderful man arrived at the door," Molly said with a sob.

"Who, the son?"

"No, your dad, Jack Holder. He proposed to me. He explained that my dad had told him about my situation. He said he would bring up my child as his own. How could I resist? I married your dad and have never looked back and he has always kept his word. He treated you like his own –" Molly broke off again as a tear rolled down her face. Rosie pulled her mother towards her.

"Now, now mum, please don't cry." They remained silent for several minutes.

"Rosie, I must tell you who your real father is," Molly said eventually. Rosie quailed inside – did she want to know about this? It was too late to stop her mother's confession now though, so she waited, unconsciously holding her breath.

"There is a man who found out he had a daughter when his own mother was on her death bed. She confessed she had sent away a servant girl rather than risk that he would recognise the child as his out of a sense of honour." Molly took a gulp of air. "Rosie, that man was Lord Berkeley of Eastleigh."

Rosie sat still for second feeling like the wind had been knocked out of her. She thought about Lord Berkeley and how he had come into her life.

"My god, it makes sense now – the time he met me – the help he gave to establish my career – the kindness he always bestowed on me – " she stopped, unable to go on.

"Ah well, you don't know the half of it," her mother replied. "When you were young, he paid for you and your brothers to have lessons and when he saw you had a musical talent, he also paid for special tuition. If ever I wanted anything for you I only had to send him a note, any time for any purpose. I did not ask for much, though, and never very often."

"But what about Dad? Did he know?"

"Yes, of course he knew. When Lord Berkeley heard the death bed confession from his mother, he sent his man to see us with a letter." Molly stood up and left the room, returning a few seconds later with an old dog eared letter. She handed it to Rosie.

Dear Molly and Jack,

Forgive me for the bluntness of this letter but I have just found out that Rosie is in fact my daughter. My mother, on her death bed, admitted she had sent Molly away as soon as the pregnancy was discovered. I searched for you the following Spring when I came back from University, but I had no real idea where you lived and to my shame I eventually gave up. I would not have stopped looking for you had I known you were with child. My mother thought she was acting in the family's best interest – she was not. I understand you have been married these last three years and I have no wish to distort your lives, but I would like to help my daughter, whenever possible. Can I arrange to meet you – and possibly see her – to discuss how best I can help? I give you my word that I am not going to interfere with you or yours or attempt to establish paternity over the child.

Yours in honour,

Edmund Berkeley

Rosie finished reading and folded the letter, her hands shaking a little. "He came to see me when I was young?"

"Oh yes, he came several times and I know he watched over you when he could. Once he followed you and your sister back, when you rather foolishly tried to walk home from your tutor's house."

"I remember that," exclaimed Rosie. "A man gave us a lift in his coach, that was him?"

"Yes and on other occasions I know he watched you. I used to see him at the theatre in the shadowed upper tier box at the Shoreditch Music Hall. He

120

also sent me money for your clothes and food. We used it for the whole family as he was very generous."

"But what did dad think?"

"At first he didn't like him, but when he realised he was an honourable man, he warmed towards him. Once he even shook him by the hand and said 'God bless you Sir', which for your dad was quite a thing." Molly reached out for Rosie's hand. "Your dad also told me to tell you the truth when he died. He did not want you to be confused when he was alive, but felt that if he passed away you should be told. I have been waiting for the right moment."

Rosie sat silently for several minutes.

"I am sorry to give you this news so soon after your dad has died, but the birth of your child means it is also his grandchild and I think we must tell him, he would want to know about it."

Rosie was thinking of the many times Lord Berkeley had helped her. The train journey from Dover, when he held her hand all the way to London. The theatre in Paris, when the producer was so awful to her. Her wedding to Frederick, when he had helped her Mum and Dad. She shook her head – Dad, Lord Berkeley is my real Dad, how I am going to react when I see him, she thought to herself.

"Penny for them?" said Molly tentatively.

"I was thinking how strange it will be when I first see him. I don't know how I will be," said Rosie, blinking away tears. The enormity of her mother's revelation had not sunk in properly, but she knew she would be coming into contact with Lord Berkeley at some point.

"Leave that to me," said Molly. "I will tell him you know and arrange a private meeting between you both."

Rosie nodded slowly, fingering the corner of the letter. "Alright, thanks Mum," she said, contemplating to herself that she had a lot of thinking to do between now and then.

Molly was as good as her word and two days later a coach pulled up outside Eaton Square and Lord Berkeley's coachman opened the door.

Lord Berkeley stepped down form his coach. He was looking forward to the meeting, but was also apprehensive. How would his daughter react? Would she hate him? He lifted the large brass knocker and almost instantly the door was opened by Rosie. They looked at each other and then Rosie stepped forward, kissed him on the cheek and said: "Come in Father, let's talk." His face broke into a smile as he greeted Rosie as his daughter for the first time.

Rosie showed him through to the elegant drawing room, where she had laid tea.

"I have sent the butler and servants out until lunch time," she said.

"Good idea," replied Lord Berkeley.

"Please sit and make yourself comfortable," she added, reverting to her East End background.

"Thank you, my dear."

There was a pause.

"I can imagine this must be very difficult for you," Lord Berkeley said. "So I will talk and then perhaps you can tell me how you feel."

He explained the circumstances of her birth – how he had truly loved her mother, how he was prevented from knowing of her birth and only when his mother was on her death bed did she confess what she had done. He said that his father was remote from the family and he doubted he even knew he had a granddaughter.

"When I found out about your birth, I was mortified; how could my mother cast aside my daughter?" said Lord Berkeley, looking down. "I set about finding you both. I hired a private detective, an ex-policeman, who eventually traced Molly and of course this led me to you. Rosie, when I found out Molly was happily married, I knew there was no future for us, but I was determined to play a part in your upbringing. Your mother told you I know of the way in which I tried to help. You are my daughter, truly precious to me, and I want you to know that had I been aware of your mother's circumstances, I would have given up everything to marry her – I loved her."

He stopped as a tear fell down Rosie's cheek.

"Now, my dear I have no wish to upset you, but there are things I must tell you. I hope you will come to regard me as your best friend and I can only hope that one day, I may be your father. I know you loved your dad and Jack was, to my certain knowledge, a fine man. I will never try to take his place, but perhaps, one day, you will see that having two fathers is a very good thing."

He smiled and Rosie noticed for the first time how alike they were. His brown eyes mirrored her own. He had high cheek bones and a handsome face. It was strange she had never noticed their likeness before.

She settled down to a comfortable conversation about her mother, Jack, her brothers, and life in general, finding that she really enjoyed talking with him like this.

"I must tell you some good news," she said.

Lord Berkeley's face softened.

"Good news, what is it my dear?"

"I am expecting a child." Lord Berkeley sat back with a jolt. His fact lit up. "That's just wonderful, does Frederick know?"

"I have sent him a note, but it will be several days before he comes from Paris."

"Who is your doctor? I can arrange for you to see my physician in Harley Street."

"No it's alright, I have seen the family doctor and he seems very good," replied Rosie.

"Nevertheless, you must allow me to arrange for Dr Thornton to examine you. He is an old friend and one of the most qualified doctors in London," insisted Lord Berkeley.

"Very well, I will see him," Rosie said with a small smile.

They parted shortly before lunch, Lord Berkley inviting her to come to his house the next day. Rosie sat on her own for a while, feeling a mixture of elation and confusion. She was also slightly sick, but her mother had warned her that, as she had had a wretched time with sickness, she was also likely to suffer with it.

Frederick returned from Paris on the night train the following day. Suddenly he had changed back to the happy, charming man she had married – he was over the moon. He wanted to wrap her in cotton wool, but she managed to meet her father, Lord Berkeley, every second or third day, to talk. There was so much to find out about him and his family. She learnt that he had attended Cambridge University, just like his father and his father's father before joining the Army as an officer cadet. His training took place at Sandhurst and he passed out as a 2nd Lieutenant and was posted to North Africa. He distinguished himself in the field and was promoted to Captain after he rescued a platoon of guards cut off by the dervish, in an ugly skirmish early in 1885. He told Rosie that the dervish were skilled Arab warriors who were brave and often reckless, but were also vicious and treated British prisoners appallingly. His own father, her grandfather, had died in 1886 and he had to resign his commission and return to England to manage the Berkeley Merchant Bank, at age 25. He was unskilled in banking, but his father had built up a number of trusted employees, including Sir Edgar Mountfield who was a director of the bank. Slowly he took the helm and when Sir Edgar retired at age 70, he was a respected and proficient banker and chairman of the family bank. Rosie told him briefly of her friendship with Stafford, a young lieutenant who had been lost at the advance on Khartoum – he nodded sympathetically at the loss of a brave young man.

Rosie was feeling very content, spending time getting to know her father and seeing Molly twice a week. Her days were filled with her family and also lessons with Herr Grundwig, a senior employee of the Baron's bank in London, who was instructing her on banking and particularly lending money. When the Baron had asked her if she was willing to learn banking, she had readily agreed and Herr Grundwig sent back encouraging reports on her enthusiasm, curiosity and photographic memory.

As promised she visited Lord Berkeley's physician in Harley Street and after the consultation with the elderly Sir Philip Morrison, she had a shock.

"Madam de Courcy, you are indeed expecting a baby, but in my view you are to give birth to twins."

What a surprise and how excited everyone was. Rosie was glowing, but becoming increasingly frustrated as the over-protective de Courcy's tried to keep her to the house. Fortunately, Molly was an old hand and frequently told young Frederick that nature would take care of Rosie, even if the Baron thought nature should be assisted by no less than two personal servants.

Chapter Ten

Twins

Nine months had passed by quickly, with Rosie planning for her babies' arrival. She continued with her usual busy life. Lord Berkeley and Frederick (and, on occasions, the Baron) had encouraged her to accompany them to various dinner parties and functions, which often included dinners with the Governor of the Bank of England and the Prime Minister.

One such occasion took place on 17th September 1900 and, despite her advanced condition and against the advice of her mother, Rosie agreed to attend a prestigious dinner with Frederick, with the Lord Mayor of London at Mansion House in London and presided over by Prince Edward. Rosie looked radiant in a magnificent peach silk kimono style gown, which amply disguised her pregnancy. She looked attentive as the Prince stood to address the assembly – then suddenly felt her waters break. As she registered what had happened, she calmly leaned towards Lord Berkeley and whispered in his ear. Equally calmly, Lord Berkeley promptly and with hardly any disturbance, helped her to Frederick's waiting carriage. He had had the foresight to engage a physician to stand by and sent his man to summon the good doctor and a midwife, to meet them at Eaton Square urgently. He had also arranged for Molly to sit in an ante room at the Mansion House and the pair of them tried to settle Rosie as comfortably as they could as the coach set off at speed. Nobody knew whether it was the coach ride, or the excitement of the occasion, but before they were half way back, Rosie began to give birth in the rear of the coach. Lord Berkeley was unperturbed, rolling up his sleeves and working with Molly to deliver a baby girl on the seat, just before they reached Eaton Square.

Frederick, on the other hand, was in a state of shock. They dispatched him immediately to fetch the doctor and midwife, as the other twin pushed to enter the world. Molly had laughingly warned Rosie that, if she was anything like her mother, the birth would be like 'shelling peas' and Rosie couldn't help but remember her words as, exhausted and happy, she held both her babies for the first time.

They helped Rosie up to her bedroom and Molly and one of the wet nurses, carried the two babies to the nursery for a thorough examination by the doctor, both babies exercising their maximum lung power at the time. Lord Berkeley sat Frederick down in the library and sent the butler for some whisky to toast the birth of George and Anne de Courcy.

Later that week in 'The Times' a wag reporter said: "The presence of the Prince of Wales encourages Cynthia de Courcy, twins are born, mother and babies are all well."

Rosie received a visit from the Prince of Wales' batman, who brought two dozen roses and a note which she always cherished: "Congratulations on missing my speech, I am delighted all is well. Edward."

The twins were delightful and, despite the unusual circumstances of the births, Rosie quickly recovered her strength and took on the mantle of managing the household and the nursery. One of the upstairs bedrooms had previously been converted into a large nursery, where one of the wet nurses slept all night. Rosie would creep in at night to check the twins herself and stand for ages gazing at the sleeping infants. They were good babies.

"But by God," said Frederick. "George knows how to cry, perhaps because he emerged last." They laughed at the joke together. This was in fact the happiest period for both, as even Frederick found he enjoyed being a father. A steady stream of visitors admired the twins and Molly and Lord Berkeley often "baby sat" whilst Frederick escorted Rosie to an Opera, or play, or to a dinner party. Frederick regaled some of his friends, discussing the births in the coach. Not in great detail, of course – as he explained, he was not looking most of the time. A letter and gift had arrived from the Baron, congratulating them and enquiring as to when and where they would be baptised, as he needed to make plans. The gift he sent with his note, of a painting by Renoir of St Mark's Square, Venice, was to remain one of Rosie's favourite paintings and hung permanently in the dining room.

Frederick had gone to the City early that morning and a coach had been sent to fetch Molly. Molly had descended into a period of depression after Jack died, but the birth of the twins and her involvement had changed all that. She adored the twins and took over, much to the consternation of the nanny, Juliet, when she visited Eaton Place. Rosie was content to let her mother fuss over her and the babies. She had been concerned for her mother's well being, but now she was a changed person.

"Mother," said Rosie, looking up from her chair. Her mother turned, holding a contented twin in each arm. "We are discussing the christening and are planning the 15th October, which is a Friday."

"Whatever you say dear," her mother said, gazing adoringly at the twins.

"Lord Berkeley," – she did not call him father in front of her mother – "and Frederick would like to arrange the christening at Westminster Abbey."

Molly looked uncertain.

"I don't know dear, your brothers and I found it very grand last time."

"Don't worry mother, it will be a very private affair, only immediate family and very close friends."

Molly reluctantly agreed and an announcement appeared in 'The Times'.

The Countess was to be godmother for both twins and, despite some resistance form the Baron, Rosie's brothers, Billy and Freddie, were to be godfathers. The compromise had been that Lord Berkeley's cousin, Viscount Swinbourne, would also be a godfather to George and the Baron's sister, Aunt Greta, a godmother to Anne. Rosie's brothers took some persuading; they had not enjoyed their first visit to Westminster Abbey and it was only when Molly reminded them that Jack would have wanted them to do it that they both agreed.

The Baron and the Countess had travelled with Aunt Greta, arriving before the snow started in early October. All of them, including the Baron, fell instantly in love with the twins who displayed 'a calm temperament' as the Baron put it.

Rosie and Molly had spent the past weeks happily planning the day and the dressmaker Ethel Swan had been commissioned to produce new dresses for the occasion. Frederick greeted mother and daughter at the bottom of the stairs and had to admit that they looked fantastic. Dressed in a pale blue silk dress, Rosie had on a darker blue hat, with a fashionable imitation bird attached and Molly was similarly dressed but in lilac. The twins arrived from the nursery in white lace baptism gowns, one brought from Switzerland having been used by the de Courcy's for three generations, the other a beautiful Belgium white lace, passed down by Lord Berkeley's family.

The day went well; George objected strongly to the wetting of his head, but Anne just looked quizzically at the congregation and they all laughed. Afterwards they went to Lord Berkeley's house in Belgravia, which was bigger than Eaton Square, and where a sumptuous feast had been prepared.

The Baron and Lord Berkeley had excused themselves after a decent interval and sat in the library on leather winged chairs, each with a glass of champagne on the table.

"You wanted to talk to me Baron?" said Lord Berkeley.

"Yes, I feel it is important that you and I are of the same mind," the Baron smiled.

Lord Berkeley looked at the Baron enquiringly. He knew him to be a shrewd and, frankly, a devious man.

"What shall we be agreeing then Baron?" he asked.

"Well, there is the education of the twins to consider," the Baron replied, taking a sip of champagne. He leaned slightly forward in his chair. "Frederick's son should follow in his father's footsteps. I propose he goes to a residential school in Switzerland, then to the Sorbonne in Paris."

The atmosphere in the library had changed subtly; both men knew a negotiation was taking place.

"Baron, you know my daughter, if she doesn't like the idea, then that will not happen," said Lord Berkeley steadily.

"Ever since our talk before Frederick and Cynthia were married I have realised where her spirit comes from. But things of this nature must follow tradition and the view of a woman is… incidental."

"I agree George should attend a boarding school in Switzerland, but I can get him a place at Cambridge and you have much more of a chance of success with that compromise," said Lord Berkeley.

The Baron thought for a moment. It was just as he had suspected: if he suggested the Sorbonne, Lord Berkeley would prefer Oxford or Cambridge and suggest a compromise. He raised his glass slowly to his lips and took a sip.

"So, if we settle on the Swiss boarding school and Cambridge, you think you can obtain agreement?"

The Baron went to continue but Lord Berkeley held up his hand.

"I also value the importance of education and tradition and I would hope my grandson will, one day, be head of not one, but two great banks – you get my drift?"

"I also see great possibilities, so we are agreed?"

Lord Berkeley nodded.

"Now to other matters," continued the Baron. "I have presented my son, Frederick, with a Directorship in honour of the birth of his son."

Lord Berkeley noticed no mention was made of Frederick's daughter.

"For reasons best known only to me, I do not expect Frederick to succeed me as chairman."

Lord Berkeley sat forward in his chair. "Go on."

"Frederick is, you understand, first and foremost a de Courcy, but he is not a strong minded man, he prefers the arts and ballet," the Baron said, looking somewhat disgusted. "I have to consider how he would manage the bank's affairs – you understand? 400 years in my family cannot be risked."

Lord Berkeley wondered where the Baron was leading.

"I would, therefore, propose that we agree a course of action which I think would be of mutual benefit."

"I am listening," said Lord Berkeley, now very intrigued.

"In the event of my son having another male child, we will talk again, but if things remain as they are, then we will educate George to eventually succeed and inherit both our banks." He held up his hands as Lord Berkeley went to speak. "No, let me finish. In the meantime, I have noted you are schooling Cynthia in the ways of the banking world. I also recognise her talents; she is already an excellent linguist speaking fluent French, Latin and learning German. When she has mastered German, I propose she learn Canton, the Swiss dialect and perhaps, Italian or Russian. You continue to formally introduce her to many aspects of banking and then, in say, two, maybe three years we involve her more formally in our mutual banking affairs."

The Baron paused. Lord Berkeley sat back in his chair. He had been listening carefully to this shrewd man, very well aware that it was questionable how much he could trust him. He intended keeping most of his cards close to his chest.

"So," said Lord Berkeley. "You have noticed that my daughter has the potential to be quite a remarkable woman – she is of course very gifted and has inherited her grandmother's determination and brains. Couple this with her upbringing, an education in itself – "

"Yes," interrupted the Baron. "I think she will be an asset to both of us." He raised his glass. They finished their drinks and the Baron excused himself whilst Lord Berkeley set off for the smoking room, he needed a cigar.

Frederick had never felt so proud as he did that day. Never in his wildest dreams had he expected to be a father of not one, but two children. The compliments were flying. When a bouquet of roses arrived with a card attached which read: "Warmest congratulations, HRH Prince Edward" the entire party was excited as they thought of the interest the Prince was showing in the family. That morning his father had shook his hand, something he hadn't done for a very long time and then he told him he was to be a director of the bank, with special responsibilities for London and Paris. He was overjoyed. Rosie looked so beautiful, he almost started to believe he was in love with her, but then, as always, his thoughts turned to Pierre.

Chapter Eleven

Missing

It was a chill winter day and Rosie insisted that Nanny Roberts put an extra blanket in the perambulator. Rosie had been feeling a little under the weather so Nanny was to wheel the perambulator across the square on her own. The twins were becoming quite characters and held the centre stage at Eaton Square. Anne was more forward than her brother and Nanny Roberts said she was trying to stand in her cot – no one believed her, of course. How could a baby less than six months old be trying to stand?

Rosie kissed the twins at the door, helped tuck them in and then the butler, Simmons and Nanny Roberts lifted the heavy transporter onto the pavement in Eaton Square.

"Don't wait in the door Madam," Roberts said cheerily, heading off on her usual route around the square: two circuits, then head for the small green park in the centre to rest for ten minutes and "get the air". As Nanny Roberts caught her breath, she looked at the babies contentedly. Anne was gurgling and smiling, whilst George was trying to turn himself over.

"Now my dears, be good babies for nanny."

She began to hum a tune she had heard at the music hall. She had just got out her flask of tea when a gentlemen and lady approached.

"Are those the twins of Frederick and Rosie?" asked the man.

Nanny looked at him suspiciously. He was very well wrapped up, with a scarf obscuring his face. It wasn't that cold, she thought to herself.

"Yes," she replied starting to stand, sensing something was wrong. Too late she started to scream as a hand clamped around her mouth, and then she felt a sharp pain in her side, then darkness.

Rosie was looking forward to lunch as her mother was coming over. She tapped her fingers impatiently. Where was that girl with the babies? She glanced out of the window and frowned. Was that a man standing by Roberts? She froze as she saw another figure reach inside the perambulator and lift out one of her babies. She screamed – the man turned – she knew that face. She hurtled toward the door.

"Madam, what is it?" said Simmons, the butler, but she pushed past him, taking the steps two by two. She fell heavily, but immediately picked herself up, racing to the centre of the square. The blood hummed in her ears. She reached the perambulator and looked down – my god, one baby was missing. Her legs buckled. A low groan made her look down and she saw Roberts lying on the ground, blood on the side of her coat. Before she could say anything, Simmons reached the scene followed by Nanny Gordon, who began to scream uncontrollably.

"Control yourself Nanny," said Simmons sharply.

Rosie grabbed his arm. "Quickly Simmons, run and see if you can follow a man and a woman, they have one of the babies," she said urgently.

Other people began to approach, including Major General Collins, a retired army officer.

"What's happened my dear?" he said.

"One of my babies has been taken and nanny Roberts injured," Rosie said wringing her hands, her eyes scanning the roads around the square as she frantically thought about what she could do next. She lifted Anne out of the perambulator and held her close.

"By gawd – leave this to me." He rushed across the square to his house, summoned his batman and sent him for the police. He then brought out a sheet and proceeded to tear it into strips. Turning towards Nanny Roberts, he looked for the cause of so much blood; loosening her coat, he saw the wound and placed the torn strips of sheet tightly against her side. He felt for a pulse. Nothing. He tried the neck. Nothing. "This lady's dead, I am afraid," he said soberly and Nanny Gordon fainted.

Rosie stood in the centre of the square, clutching onto Anne tightly, trying to clear the fog in her mind – where had they taken her baby?

Two policemen arrived at the house at the same time as Molly.

"What is it, what's happened?" she said anxiously.

"We don't know yet Madam. Are you visiting or walking here?"

"My daughter lives here."

They knocked and were immediately let in by Simmons. Rosie recited the story, her face completely pale but her voice steady as she told the policeman what she knew as quickly as possible. One of the constables was sent immediately to mount a search of the area.

Simmons had run around Eaton Square hoping to see the man with a baby, but there was no sign. He had returned just as the Major had announced Nanny Roberts was dead. He had helped Rosie carry the other baby back to the house, whilst a servant, who came out of a house from across the square, fanned the fainted Nanny Gordon.

Molly listened as her daughter stood in the room, firing off instructions.

"Send for Frederick and my father, Lord Berkeley, immediately," she told the butler and he scurried away.

She paced around the room like a caged lioness.

"It's alright, Rosie, the police will find who did this," said her mother.

"I know that face, what I saw of it – who was it?" She continued to walk up and down restlessly.

"Best thing is to go and have a lie down luv," said the policeman.

Rosie stopped pacing and turned to face the policeman.

"Lie down? Lie down," she screamed. "My baby's been stolen. I won't lie down."

"Alright dear, at least sit," said Molly, who hadn't stopped shaking since she walked in the door.

Another policeman arrived, this time a Superintendent, and Frederick arrived at the door.

"What's happened?"

"Baby George has been kidnapped and Nanny Roberts murdered," replied Simmons unsteadily.

"Oh my God." Frederick gripped the stand in the hall. Lord Berkeley rushed into the room, having made a frantic dash in his coach from his office in Leadenhall Street. Rosie ran towards him and he put his arms around her, feeling her trembling all over.

"Which baby is missing?" he asked as he gently held his daughter.

"It's George," she replied.

"And who are you sir?"

Lord Berkeley approached the Superintendent, introduced himself and asked what action had been taken. For the moment satisfied, Lord Berkeley turned his attention to Rosie.

"You really ought to go and rest, with a sedative, to help you relax," he began.

"I'm not going anywhere until they find my baby," said Rosie numbly, her red eyes fixed on the door.

"Molly and Frederick, help me persuade Rosie to go upstairs and rest. She is in a state of shock," Lord Berkeley said and they managed to usher Rosie out of the room.

The Superintendent collected statements from all the staff and sent his men knocking on all the doors around the square, looking for witnesses. One scullery maid came forward. She had been to the market to buy vegetables and had been dawdling back to Eaton Square, when a man with a hood on his head and a woman with red hair rushed by her, nearly knocking her and her shopping bags over. They appeared to be carrying something, but she couldn't see what. A hansome cab driver was dropping off a gentleman in Ebury Street when he noticed a man with a woman hurrying along carrying a baby. The woman had red hair; they were headed down the street and turned the corner. There the trail turned cold with no further sightings.

Frederick sat in the library at Eaton Square, staring blankly at the walls around him. He did not know what to do. For once, his father was not here to put things right. All his life, whenever there had been a problem, his father had sorted it out. He decided he had to send a note to the Baron straight away – he would be able to tell him what to do next.

The Home Office Minister, Lord Cadbury, had heard of the kidnapping and murder and sent a card to Lord Berkeley inviting him to Scotland Yard for a meeting with the Police Commissioner, Sir Edward Noble. Lord Berkeley entered and introduced himself to a Sergeant sitting at a desk on the ground floor.

"Ah yes, my Lord, the Commissioner is expecting you. Please go to the second floor, an officer will show you to his room."

Lord Berkeley was greeted by a grey haired man with a small moustache who shook hands and invited him to sit down. There was a knock at the door and Superintendent Day stepped in, who was leading the hunt for the kidnappers.

"I thought it might help if we went through what we know and what we expect to happen," the Commissioner said, motioning to Superintendent Day to take out his notebook.

"Well Sir, at 11 am on the 26th November two persons identified as a man 5'10" – 5'11", tall with no distinguishing facial hair and a woman 5'4" – 5'6" tall, with vivid red hair, kidnapped the baby George de Courcy and using a thin knife, one of the kidnappers, we suggest the male, killed the nanny Miss Edith Roberts, who died at approximately 11.15 am without recovering consciousness."

Lord Berkeley remained passive, listening intently. The Superintendent continued.

"We have two witnesses who saw the kidnappers and were able to give the descriptions."

Lord Berkeley had had enough.

"That's all very well man, but have you made any progress finding the kidnappers?"

"Ah'm, this is a very difficult case, as the witnesses did not recognise either kidnapper. The knife is probably a thin stiletto, commonly available and there has been no contact made by the kidnappers," said the Superintendent.

"In other words, you have not got anywhere."

"Well, I wouldn't say that. We are conducting searches at the houses of known villains and have issued statements to all Metropolitan police officers with descriptions of the criminals."

"I know it is difficult," said the Commissioner. "But in our experience with kidnapping cases, you have to wait for the initial contact; they often give themselves away, or make a mistake collecting the ransom."

"You think they will demand a ransom then?"

"Almost certainly, these criminals will attempt to extract money from the family."

"Do you think the baby is safe?" asked Lord Berkeley.

"At the moment I do, there would be no reason to harm an infant," replied the Commissioner.

Lord Berkeley extracted a promise that they would keep him informed and agreed that the family would turn over the ransom demand as soon as it appeared.

The kidnappers contacted them on the third day. Simmons found a package addressed to Rosie on the doormat, presumably having been put through the letterbox overnight. Lord Berkeley had asked Frederick and Rosie not to open any ransom demand until he arrived and so a message was dispatched straight away. At the same time Rosie summoned Molly and her brother, Freddie. Her brother Billy had been using all his contacts in the docks in an attempt to find the perpetrators, but nothing had turned up.

Lord Berkeley arrived and immediately put on a pair of gloves – the police, he explained, were perfecting a way of using a person's fingerprints to trace them and he didn't want to impact on this – and opened the package. Inside was a newspaper folded into a tight square. Carefully Lord Berkeley loosened the paper and then he saw blood.

"My God, what is this?" he said, continuing to loosen the pages. A small object was wrapped inside.

"What is it?" asked Rosie.

Lord Berkeley picked it up and immediately felt his legs go. Even with all his combat experience, he was not ready to see the tip of one of his grandson's forefingers.

Rosie put her hand to her mouth, all the colour draining from her face before she fainted. Frederick stood completely still for a moment, unable to comprehend what Lord Berkeley was holding. Suddenly, he rushed out of the room and vomited in the hall.

Molly was shaking but bent over her daughter with smelling salts. Lord Berkeley and Rosie's brother examined the newspaper closely. There was no message, nothing to indicate the kidnappers' demands.

"Should we tell the bobbies?" asked Molly.

"Yes," said Lord Berkeley. "We must not withhold any information even if we think it cannot help solve the crime."

Rosie had recovered and was sitting shivering violently in the chair.

"Those people, have cut off the finger of my baby, why?"

Molly held her daughter tightly.

The doctor was called to give a sedative to Frederick. He stood in the doorway, weeping openly, unable to take in this atrocity.

"Poor Frederick," said Molly. "His perfect world has just been destroyed." She turned to Freddie. "Right, put out the word what they have done to mine and Jack's grandson. Lord Berkeley has said to offer a reward of £10,000 for information leading to the return of the baby. Call in every favour. Find these people, Freddie, find them. The red head is your best bet."

Her son nodded and left the house to find Billy and spread the word.

Little did he know, when he stepped down onto the pavement, he was less than one hundred yards from the man who held all the answers. The kidnapper sat in the hansome cab, anonymously surveying the scene, watching the comings and goings at Eaton Square. He still hadn't made up his mind how much to ask for. Ginger, his girlfriend, was becoming quite attached to the baby; perhaps they'd keep it – that would settle old scores.

"Alright driver, move on."

He left the square as unobtrusively as he had arrived. As the coach trundled along, he thought about what he had done and smiled. He had used a cigar cutter to snip off the tip of the finger and then sutured the wound with a red hot poker. The baby had cried all night; luckily nobody cared about baby's crying in that part of London, where he had lodgings. Ginger had got very upset and begged him not to hurt the baby anymore, but he just gave her a back hand and laughed. Still he had better be careful. They must be looking for him and certainly looking for Ginger. It's a pity he had to use her, but there was no one else who could have helped and a man with a baby would have been too obvious. When he was ready he knew he would have to dispose of her too.

He left it a week until he made contact again. He knew nerves would be frayed and there was more chance they'd pay big. Ginger was getting careless, though. She had taken the baby outside yesterday.

"He needs some fresh air," she had pleaded. Christ, is she stupid or what!

That morning, he had calmly walked across the square and put a letter through the coach window of that Lord Berkeley. The driver had not seen him as he retraced his steps and headed back to his lodgings.

As Lord Berkeley sat down in his coach he noticed the sheet of paper and quickly snatched it up.

> YOUR GRANDSON HAS ONE FINGER TIP MISSING
> IF YOU WANT TO SEE THE BABY ALIVE
> LEAVE £50,000 IN MIXED NOTES IN A
> PARCEL ON THE TOW PATH OF REGENTS CANAL
> UNDER THE BRIDGE AT PARKWAY TOMORROW AT 9 AM
> NO SECOND CHANCE, NO POLICE OR THE BABY DIES.
> I WILL BE WATCHING

He looked around and then quizzed his coachman.

"Lawrence did you see anyone around the coach?"

"No, your Lordship, I didn't see anyone."

Lord Berkeley surveyed the square and saw no-one except a street trader and a chimney sweep with a boy. He strode across to them to ask if they had seen anybody hanging around, but they gave the same answer as the coachman.

Returning to the house, he knocked and was met by the butler, who showed him into the drawing room. Frederick had gone to the City that day, it had been the first day he felt able to leave the house, and Rosie had a visitor. Her friend, Sylvie from the theatre, had heard what had happened and called to see her. The two girls had fallen into each other's arms. Sylvie had cried and Rosie had consoled her friend.

Lord Berkeley asked if he could see Rosie privately. Sylvie offered to leave, but Rosie asked her friend to wait in the library and showed her along the hall. She returned, steeling herself for whatever news Lord Berkeley had to tell her.

He handed her the note.

"Now we must act," he said. "I will get the money together, but we must decide whether to inform the police."

At that moment there was a knock at the door. It seemed fate had made the decision for them as Superintendent Day was shown into the drawing room.

"We have just received a note demanding money for the boy's release."

The Superintendent read the note. "At last, the vermin comes out from under the rock," he said.

"We are willing to pay the ransom, but what assurances do we have that the kidnappers will return the child?" asked Lord Berkeley.

"And," interrupted Rosie, "is this from the legitimate kidnappers? Could it be someone else trying to extract money?"

The Superintendent paused. "On the last point, it must be genuine: the note mentions the finger, but we have not released that information publicly. Concerning the release of your son, there is no guarantee that even if you pay the money, you will ever see him again."

There was a moment's silence as his words sunk in.

"Oh," Rosie said and sank down into her chair.

"As I see it," continued the Superintendent. "We must catch the kidnapper and persuade him or her to lead us to the child."

"That is a risky strategy," said Lord Berkeley, shaking his head. "If the kidnapper sees any of your men, the note makes it quite clear what the outcome will be."

"Come, Lord Berkeley, my men are professional officers. They will conceal themselves well. I will go to the drop point now and see how we are going to trap the person who collects the ransom. Can you get that much money together in time?"

Lord Berkeley looked at his daughter.

"Rosie, it's up to you as to whether we do this or not and perhaps we ought to consult Frederick, even though he has not been well."

"My husband Frederick has been on a light sedative since our son's finger tip was delivered," Rosie explained to the Superintendent. She thought for a moment. "The Baron is due here at midday. I wish to consult him."

"Good idea, meanwhile I will arrange to draw the money," said Lord Berkeley, kissing his daughter as he left.

"Would you like me to return this afternoon?" asked the Superintendent.

"Yes, my father-in-law will be here and together we will decide what to do."

"Very well. I will go to Regent's Park, Miss, and report back on the lie of the land when I return."

Rosie nodded. After everybody had left, she sat for a while before going to Sylvie, trying to control the shaking in her legs. So the ransom demand had finally come – surely now she would get her son back?

The Baron had decided to travel to London. His grandson had been missing for long enough and it seemed Frederick was not handling the situation well. He could not help but feel a new respect for his daughter in law. What a woman she was: with her husband a blubbering wreck, she was dealing admirably with the matter for both of them. Two days travelling had given him plenty of time to think. Realistically he knew the chance of recovering the baby was low; the criminals would attempt to extract money and then… Why give the baby back? But why not? He thought about the quandary they would be in. Wanted for murder, they would hang if they were caught. Would they keep their side of the bargain? He doubted it. In which case Frederick must produce another male heir – why hadn't the idiots taken the girl?

The Baron arrived at Eaton Square shortly before midday – he was tired and had not slept well during a rough crossing of the channel.

Greeting Rosie respectfully, he was shown to the drawing room.

"You must be tired after your long journey. Your room is made up, but before you rest, we need to talk."

Rosie moved to the writing bureau in the corner and lifted the lid. She clicked open the central compartment and removed the ransom demand. Handing it to the Baron he read it in silence.

"So the wolves came out of hiding? Who else has seen the note?" he asked.

"Lord Berkeley and Superintendent Day who is leading the investigation."

"Ah, I see and their proposal is?"

"Lord Berkeley is obtaining the money. The Superintendent proposes that we go along with the demand, but that he hides his men in the area and they capture the person who picks up the money," said Rosie calmly, hiding the fear she was feeling.

"And then what? Torture him to tell where the child is? This is not a simple situation." The Baron sat quietly for a moment. "Could I talk to your brother, Freddie, as soon as possible?"

"Yes, of course, I will ask him to call. What do you have in mind?" asked Rosie.

"We need two plans, Rosie, in case the police bungle things. For our reserve plan we will need help."

The agreed day and time arrived. Regent's Park was staked out by policemen dressed as keepers, traders, pedestrians, ice cream sellers and dockers, while Freddie had his men covering the policemen and the exit points. The package was placed, as directed, under the bridge. It was dark under there, so nobody would actually be able to see the person who picked up the package until they moved into the light.

Peter was not stupid and at 3 am that night he had climbed the fence and gone into the park. Choosing a position about one hundred yards from the bridge on high ground he had dug a hole about four feet deep. He dropped down into it, covering the top with a green water proof sheet he had purchased from a market trader in Brixton, who sold fruit and vegetables. He wasn't exactly invisible, but it was pretty good. If they were watching the pick up point, he would see them through the telescope he had bought second hand in a tavern in Rotherhithe.

The hours ticked by. He was very cold and was having trouble stopping his teeth from chattering. Scanning the area, he could see no sign of police, but there was certainly more activity than he would have expected in November. A man approached the drop point and looking around placed a package on the floor. So near: £50,000, he could almost touch it. But he told himself go slow, don't move. He noticed a street trader pushing a container – ice cream in November? The police are here, he thought, and they were laying a trap. He shook his head at their stupidity. Then his attention turned to the package, did they really pay the ransom? To dispose of the baby now with no money would be foolish. Another idea occurred to him and he settled in to watch for a while longer.

The police waited two hours before the package was picked up by one of them in a grey raincoat and they aborted. Thoroughly frozen, Peter rubbed his limbs to bring back circulation, climbed out of his hide and retrieved the small shovel. Extracting the thermos flask, what an invention they were, he finished the still warm tea and proceeded to bury the waterproof cloth in the hole. Satisfied, he straightened his clothes and came out from the bushes where he had hid. Checking he had the thermos and telescope, he relieved himself, then walked down to the canal and threw the shovel in. He looked like a London down and out, so nobody troubled him as he walked to the bus stop. Everyone gave him a wide birth as he sat thinking. He got off at London Bridge and walked down Borough High Street, turned into Market Street where he had cheap lodgings. He had decided what to do.

She was waiting with the brat in her arms, crying as usual.

"Well did you get it?"

"No," he said, his face contorted with anger. She had seen his periods of anger before and retreated back into the bed-sit. "Make me a cup of tea and put the brat down, he ain't going anywhere."

"He's been crying again," she said.

"He'll be doing more than that soon," said Peter grimly.

"What do you mean?"

"Mind your own business." She flinched as he moved to strike her. "You're not worth the effort and didn't I tell you to die your bloody hair?" She turned to face him, satisfied that the moment had passed, and then the baby started to cry, again.

"After I've washed and rested, I'm going out. Now keep that brat quiet or else I will."

She handed him a cup of steaming tea and picked up the baby and began to rock him gently, singing a lullaby her mother had sung to her. She watched Peter sit at the table and write.

"What you doin?"

"Just shut up and mind your own business." Satisfied, he thought how best to deliver the package. Let's give our Frederick de Courcy a shock, he smiled to himself.

"Bring the brat here."

"What for? What are you going to do?" she said, holding the baby close.

"Come here, or it will be worse for you ..." Reluctantly she drew nearer. "Come here!" He was angry now. He snatched the baby who started to cry. "Shut up you brat," he shouted, producing the cigar cutter.

"Don't hurt him! No, please not again," she pleaded, trying to snatch the baby back.

Peter swiped her away and got hold of the baby's hand. Positioning the cutters over his left forefinger, he snipped the tip off. The baby screamed out as he took the hot poker and sutured the wound.

"You bastard," said Ginger, sobbing. "Give 'im to me."

He roughly passed the baby over to her. "Just shut it up and get out of my sight." He wrapped the bloodied finger in newspaper as he had done before. Then spreading blood over the paper he had written, he put it inside, making up a parcel using plain brown paper he had bought from a man in Borough market.

"I'm going out," he snorted and slammed the door behind him.

He had addressed the package to: 'The Hon Frederick de Courcy – HIS

EYES ONLY'. Travelling by bus he reached Threadneedle Street and looked for the office of the de Courcy Merchant Bank. A doorman stood by the revolving door.

"This is an urgent package for Frederick de Courcy, from the governor of the Bank of England," Peter said. The doorman looked at him, he looked smart enough.

"Do you require a receipt sir?"

He nearly burst out laughing. "No thank you, just make sure he gets it straight away." He gave the doorman half a crown.

"Thank you sir." He tipped his hat and went inside.

Frederick was sitting at his desk when his secretary knocked and appeared carrying what appeared to be a package.

"I'm sorry to disturb you Sir, but this package has just been delivered. The doorman said it came from the Bank of England."

"Bank of England?" Frederick looked at the secretary quizzically as he took the package from her. It didn't look like an official document. Frederick put it down on his desk and after a few minutes studying the address, he took out a small pocket knife and cut the string. Slowly he unwrapped the brown paper. What was this? A newspaper. He took out the inner paper and suddenly noticed some blood. Before he could register it, he had started to open the paper and a small object fell out on his desk. For a second he didn't know what it was and then, with horror, he did. He retched violently and was sick over the desktop.

His secretary watched in shock. "What is it sir, are you alright?"

Frederick roused himself.

"Send a message to Lord Berkeley; ask him to come here urgently. Also send for my father, he is at Eaton Square."

The secretary left, unaware of what had caused the esteemed Mr Frederick to vomit on his desktop.

Frederick sat back in a daze, then after some minutes he walked to his sideboard and poured a large brandy into one of the crystal goblets. Downing the drink in one, he winced as the liquor burned his throat on its way down to his stomach.

"What sort of animal are we dealing with?" he said to himself. He looked at his hand, it was shaking.

Mercifully Lord Berkeley was in his office and rushed straight to Frederick's office.

"What is it my boy?"

Frederick looked ashen and pointed to the brown paper and newspaper on his desk.

"They have sent me another finger."

"Oh God," said Lord Berkeley. "Show me."

Frederick parted the newspaper with distaste and for the first time noticed another piece of paper.

Lord Berkeley took a pencil and moved the object, the tip of a baby's finger. He picked up the note and laid it down on the desktop. The acrid smell of vomit hung in the office, but he prevented himself from retching. He read the note carefully.

I SAID NO POLICE. YOU TRIED TO TRICK ME. THIS IS THE LAST CHANCE OR THE BOY DIES. THE PRICE HAS GONE UP TO £60,000 IN MIXED NOTES. SEND ROSIE WITH THE MONEY TOMORROW NIGHT. SHE IS TO LEAVE THE MONEY IN THE CENTRE OF LONDON BRIDGE, EAST SIDE AT HALF PAST MIDNIGHT. SHE MUST COME "ALONE" AND WALK TOWARD THE STATION. ANY TRICKS AND YOU WILL NEVER SEE THE BOY AGAIN BUT YOU WILL GET THE REST OF HIS FINGERS.

Lord Berkeley was not one for profanities but this was too much – another finger tip and now Rosie must risk her life to deliver the ransom.

Frederick started to regain his colour, probably the brandy taking effect and leaned over to read the note.

"No, no that's out of the question; I won't allow her to go," he said.

But Lord Berkeley shook his head, knowing what his daughter's response would be. "Come Frederick, she is a very bold woman, there is no other way."

An hour later, after both men had discussed the request, looking at all possibilities, the Baron arrived. He heard the story and read the note.

"I don't see that we have any choice, do you?" Lord Berkeley said. The Baron thought for a moment, any risk was worth getting the boy back.

"No, but no police this time, we will handle this ourselves."

"I agree," said Lord Berkeley. "But we will need more men. I propose we ask Rosie's brothers to assist. They seem to have some tough friends."

"Alright, let's go to Eaton Square," said the Baron.

"I must go to my office and arrange for a further £10,000 first," replied said Lord Berkeley.

"No, leave that to me," said the Baron. "I will pay the ransom."

It was a grim November night, dark skies and drizzling rain, which suited the man. At half past ten, he took up his position in the bell tower of Southwick Cathedral, on the South side of London Bridge, and trained his telescope on the bridge and surroundings. He knew that the gas lighter would come at midnight and extinguish the lamps on the bridge. In pitch blackness he would not be able to see much – but neither would they. He doubted Rosie would come alone.

At 11.25am Rosie came onto the bridge on the north side. With the lamps out, Lord Berkeley was glad that he had insisted she wore white so that they still had the possibility of seeing her. He was dressed in black along with Rosie's brothers and a dozen other men, who were secreted all around the north and south side of the bridge. They planned to allow the man to slip by them and then follow him – a risky strategy, but they had the hound and had carefully impregnated the package with meat, placing his favourite chops inside with the money from the Baron.

Rosie walked slowly. Her heart was thumping and she thought she might have trouble breathing. Placing the package in what seemed like the middle, she continued walking towards London Bridge station. As she reached the end of the bridge a voice called out to her: "Come over here". She walked towards it. Suddenly a hand clamped over her mouth and another held her in a vice like grip around her upper body. A man, with bad breath, was whispering in her ear. "If this is a trick Rosie you are dead, so start praying."

At that moment a boy darted onto the bridge, dressed in the clothes of a street urchin. He nearly passed by unnoticed, but not by Lord Berkeley who had manoeuvred himself opposite the package on the other side of the bridge. Dressed head to toe in dark clothes and with his face blackened with soot, he was camouflaged well. He breathed lightly and, as the boy picked up the package, followed ten yards behind.

The man still had Rosie in a firm grip. The cloud cover was a bonus to him, but also gave his enemies an advantage. Had he seen something moving? He whispered in Rosie's ear: "Soon you will be reunited with your baby." On hearing those words, Rosie pushed back with all her might and the man staggered and released his hold. The boy reached them and was suddenly unsure; the man had given him a Florin to pick up a package in the middle of London Bridge and was due to give him another when he brought it to him. However, he hadn't survived on the streets without having his wits about him and, as soon as he saw the lady struggling with the man, he threw the package in their direction and ran.

The man drew out his stiletto: "Say goodbye to Peter, Rosie."

Rosie's eyes widened as she suddenly realised why she had recognised the man. His hold on her had momentarily slackened and she struggled to reach the derringer in her pocket. It was a useful weapon for a lady and could easily be concealed about the body. Desperately, she gripped the handle tightly and tried to overbalance Peter.

"If only you had chosen me and not that fop Frederick, now you will join your baby," he snarled, lunging at her throat.

A shot rang out. Peter slumped and let go of Rosie. He could feel an excruciating pain in his side. Looking down, he saw the package at their feet, picked it up and hauled himself across to the wall, feeling for the rope he had placed there. He had planned this exit carefully, but hanging onto the rope and dropping down to the underside of the bridge while keeping hold of the package was tricky enough without the painful throbbing in his side.

"He's gone under the bridge."

Peter could hear men's voices.

"No I think he's jumped in."

Lord Berkeley reached Rosie. He had had to make a very speculative shot; luckily the cloud had parted at the right moment and he got a clear sight of Rosie struggling with a man. There was a knife to her throat and Lord Berkeley had not hesitated to fire at the man.

"Rosie, are you hurt?"

"No father," said Rosie quickly. "Go after him – it's Peter who used to be in the Company in Paris and London."

Lord Berkeley grunted and set off in pursuit. Rosie's brothers looked startled when she said: "Go and help my father." The dog began to bark and pull toward the north side of the bridge.

"He's under the bridge!"

Peter hurried as best he could; he knew if they reached the other side of the bridge first he would be trapped and he did not want to get into the water unless he had to. He manoeuvred himself along the underside of the bridge. He slipped and instinctively used both hands to keep himself from falling, but was unable to hold onto the package containing his £60,000. It dropped into the Thames, with a faint splash. He screeched in anger, but knew it was lost. It was over: now he would kill the boy and Ginger.

Lord Berkeley hadn't seen any of this, he was being very cautious as he did not know the structure. Under the bridge was a narrow shelf, barely wide enough for a person to walk – in the dark it was precarious. He heard men shouting and thought he heard a splash but he continued on.

Exhausted, Peter reached the other side. He jumped down onto the shingle beach and reached for the rowing boat he had left there. His luck was holding, when the cloud broke again. A shot rang out and a bullet whizzed over his head.

"Stand away from the boat." A figure all in black faced him. "Put your hands in the air."

"Alright, don't shoot, you've got me," said Peter, holding up his hands.

Lord Berkeley was a menacing figure all blacked up and with cold hatred in his eyes as he moved closer. He fired his gun, hitting Peter's knee, making him scream in pain.

"I suggest you tell me exactly where my grandson is or I will shoot the other knee and then each of your arms. I promise you, you will die in absolute agony," he said through gritted teeth.

Rosie's brother Billy, arrived with his mate Tony.

"Leave this to me," said Lord Berkeley. There was no response from Peter and he shook his head, shooting him again in the other knee. Peter screamed and lay sobbing.

"I can continue this as long as I like," said Lord Berkeley. "It's up to you. Where is my grandson?" He leant closer.

"Alright, alright," whimpered Peter. "The baby is with Ginger in the basement of 49 Market Street, just off Borough High Street."

"He had better be."

Lord Berkeley asked the two men if they knew where the address was. "Take me to it please."

"And me." Rosie had reached the scene.

"Billy, you and Tony take this scum to the warehouse. Try and keep him alive in case he's lying," ordered Lord Berkeley and the rest of them started running towards Borough High Street.

They reached Market Street and cautiously counted the numbers. Frustratingly, not every house had a number fixed on the door but by a process of elimination they approached the basement of No. 49.

"Stand back," said Freddie, as he charged the door. It was old with an equally old lock and gave away after several kicks. Rosie scrambled inside and frantically searched the small bed-sit, her heart beating furiously in her chest. She found an old crib and identified a blanket from her son's perambulator – but there was no baby, the place was empty.

"Oh God, please help us, he is not here," she sobbed, sinking down into a chair. This had been their best bet; she had been so sure she was going to find her son there. She looked around her as the others pulled the place apart. Where was he? She had kept herself together in the hope they would find her son. Now she slumped down further in the dirty chair, absolutely devastated.

"Come Rosie, let's not give up, we will go to the dock where your brothers are holding the rogue and question him further," said Lord Berkeley, gently leading her out of the house.

They reached the deserted St Katherine's shortly after 1 am. There was no guard and the gate was unlocked.

"Do you know where they will be holding him?" asked Lord Berkeley.

"No, we will have to rely on our signal," said Rosie, and at that she put both fingers in her mouth and whistled loudly.

They walked past large warehouses, barely able to see a few feet, when suddenly a figure loomed out of the darkness – it was Rosie's brother Billy.

"I thought it must be you Rosie. Did you find your baby?"

"No."

"Where is he?" said Lord Berkeley.

"Over here, but it will do you no good – he's a goner."

They went through a small side door, closing it quickly as the oil lamps inside illuminated the warehouse. There, propped against a table, was the inert figure of Peter, lying in a pool of blood.

"He's a goner," repeated Billy. Seeing the pool of blood, Rosie suddenly felt sick.

"Did he say anything?" asked Lord Berkeley.

"No, he just laughed and then passed away."

"Curse the fellow, how do you intend to dispose of him?"

"Oh, you leave that to us," said Freddie and they dragged the body of Peter to a tarpaulin, then wrapped him up and slung him onto a cart.

Lord Berkeley looked across to where Rosie was standing in a shaft of moonlight. Her hair and clothes were dishevelled from her struggle with Peter and their frantic run to Market Street. She looked pale and her eyes locked with her father's. There were no tears, just an empty look of despair.

"Come Rosie, let's go back to Eaton Square," said Lord Berkeley softly. He held Rosie's arm and escorted her back to the dock gates in silence.

Earlier that evening, Ginger had sat on the bed thinking. She had decided that Peter intended to kill the child and she couldn't be part of that. He was obsessed with the mother, Rosie. He kept saying: "She should have chosen me. This brat should be my baby." Ginger thought he wasn't quite right in the head.

After he had left the house, she had hurriedly put together her meagre possessions, wrapped the baby in one of her shawls and headed for London Bridge station. She wanted to get as far away as possible and had stolen two pounds from Peter's wallet when he was asleep. At the ticket office at London Bridge, she noticed a poster describing Brighton: "Frequented by the King and the Royal Family". It had a lovely picture of a huge domed building on it.

"How much to Brighton?" she asked the ticket clerk.

"Single or return luv?" he asked wearily.

"Single please and I have my baby."

"No charge for the baby luv. That will be 2 shillings. Change at East Croydon. Hurry now, there is a train leaving shortly on platform one."

Ginger had never been on a train before and had to ask where to go. A kindly, elderly lady was going to East Croydon and showed her the way. She had insisted on sitting with Ginger all the way to East Croydon, chatting non-stop about her children and her husband, who it seemed was away, somewhere, she didn't blame him. She had to deflect very few questions about the baby, as the woman only seemed interested in herself. Arriving at East Croydon, the woman pointed Ginger in the right direction: "You will need to ask the porter over there dear, what time the next train to Brighton is coming." Five minutes later, Ginger boarded the Brighton train.

Arriving at the station, she allowed herself to get caught in the general flow of the crowd. The pavements were not very good in Brighton and a few carriages clattered along the road. She came to a turning on her left; what prompted her to take it, she did not know. She was getting anxious now and when she saw a light on in a window, with a sign 'Room to Let', she decided to knock. A middle aged woman wearing spectacles answered the door.

"Sorry to disturb m'am, I am looking for somewhere to stay, just having come down from London."

The woman looked at her in the dim light and noticed the baby.

"Well you've chosen the right place, dear. I don't usually take people in so late but ... as you have a baby come in. That will be one shilling per night payable in advance. How many nights are you going to stay?"

The kindly landlady made her a cup of tea. Ginger had sensibly brought the two bottles and some nappies, so the landlady also heated a bottle of milk for the baby.

"You'll have to have the baby in bed luv, I've no crib."

And so Ginger settled down for the night hungry, tired, but knowing she had done the right thing.

In the morning, Ginger woke early as the baby started crying. She changed his nappy and took him downstairs with a bottle in her other hand.

The landlady was called Mrs Robinson, although she insisted Ginger call her Enid. She was a widow, her husband had been killed in North Africa and the house had been inherited from her parents. She eked out an income by letting rooms and had a small war widows' pension.

"Has the baby hurt its hand ducks?" she asked, looking at the dirty cloth tied around the baby's hand.

"Oh, an accident," replied Ginger, looking alarmed.

"Perhaps we should take a look at it?"

Ginger jumped and pulled the baby away.

"No, I just have. But thank you."

Mrs Robinson looked at her.

"I am just going to cook some bacon and eggs. You look famished, can I make you something?"

Ginger was very hungry and tucked into breakfast while Mrs Robinson fed the baby. She felt content in Mrs Robinson's warm house, but knew she could not stay. As she ate, she thought about what she should do with the baby? She was realistic enough to realise she could not keep it. She only had the money she had stolen and for all she knew, he was looking for her. She had to move on.

Mrs Robinson had no other lodgers and that evening, as she stoked up the coal fire, she began to talk about her sister. It seemed her sister was a good deal younger than her. "She had a lovely little baby herself, but we lost him to pneumonia," said Mrs Robinson sadly. Unfortunately her sister's husband had chosen that moment to 'go away', as she put it, and her sister was suffering terribly with the loss. Ginger listened, thinking how kindly Mrs Robinson was. An idea came to her and she planned her exit. Early in the morning she would sneak out of the house and leave the baby in the room, hopefully asleep. Mrs Robinson would surely find a home for the child, maybe even with her sister who had lost her own baby.

She left a note, but as she looked at the baby for the last time, tears streamed down her face. Then Ginger slipped quietly away, back towards the station.

In the morning Mrs Robinson woke as usual at 8am and went into the front room, raked the dead embers from last nights fire and shivered. It was a cold morning but she would wait a little while before lighting a fire in here, better to get the one going in the back room first, the girl and baby could have breakfast in there. She could hear that the little one was already awake. He's got a good pair of lungs on him, she thought indulgently. At 8.30am she began to wonder why the baby had been crying for quite some time. She tiptoed upstairs.

"Hello? Dear, are you alright?" There was no answer as she rapped on the door. She tapped harder. "Are you there dear?"

She opened the door and looked in. The baby was crying and there was no sign of the girl. She picked up the baby.

"There, there mama must have popped out."

Carrying the infant downstairs, she carefully poured boiling water in the baby's bottle and then warmed some milk which she tested with her finger. This is all very odd, she thought. The milkman called for his week's money and still no girl. She was getting panicky now. At midday she went to find Joan, her best friend at No.28, to ask her advice.

"Well, no wonder the bairn is crying," said Joan, looking at the baby's hands.

Maggie knocked loudly on her sister's door.

"Come in quickly," said Enid Robinson, beckoning her inside.

Her sister was acting very oddly – she had sent the young Tagg boy, one of her neighbour's children to meet her with the message: "Come quick, important news."

"What is it, why the mystery?" Maggie said.

Enid led her sister to the kitchen and went to a box, which was sitting on the table and lifted out a baby. A baby! Maggie couldn't believe her eyes.

"Christ, where did …" She stopped in mid stream. The baby opened its eyes and looked at her. She put her finger in its hand and suddenly noticed. "My god, what happened to its fingers?"

Enid sat with the baby in her arms rocking gently as she explained the events of last night and this morning.

"She's gone?" said Maggie, bewildered. "Maybe she's just gone out."

"No, she left this note."

Maggie picked up the small piece of paper and read: "I'm leavin baby in your hands, can't keep him anymore. I loved him dearly but its no good; please take care of him."

Maggie sat back in her chair.

"Why don't you hold him, Maggie?" Her sister passed over the baby, who gazed up at her with deep brown eyes.

"Is it a boy or a girl?"

"A boy," replied her sister.

"What shall we do?" said Maggie, smiling down on the baby and stroking his hand.

"What do you want to do?"

"What do you mean?"

"Well it seems to me, God has given us this child for a purpose – maybe to help you with your loss of William, after He took him last year."

"You mean we keep the baby?" said Maggie incredulously.

"Yes dear, you keep the baby – it was meant to be." Maggie went to protest, but looked down as the baby gurgled in her arms. Tears came to her eyes. She looked at her sister and nodded. And that's how Alfred, or Alfie as he was known, became the only son of Maggie Horsfield and was loved by his Aunt Enid. If people ever wondered where he came from, they never said anything and everyone who met him adored the little chap.

Chapter Twelve

Journey

Rosie screamed and a voice said: "Come on duck, it won't be long now, I can see the head."

A midwife held her hand as a doctor and another midwife coaxed the baby. Rosie cursed.

"That's it dear, push, push!"

One final push and the baby emerged.

"Is it a boy, is it alright?" Rosie was immediately sitting up.

"Yes dear, it's a boy." And, as the doctor smacked the boy's bottom, a cry let rip from the bundle of joy. "He's very well indeed."

Frederick was ushered into the room and moved towards the bed.

"Well done Rosie, it's a boy," he beamed.

Rosie smiled as she held her son. This time, she thought fiercely, I won't let my son out of my sight. They had already decided on names and Frederick Henry George took his place in the household, the heir to two great banking empires.

Frederick had returned to Paris and Rosie was a little bored. She often entertained Lord Berkeley's and the Barons' friends and business contacts in London, hosting lavish dinner parties. Once they had even entertained the Prince of Wales, who hinted that a dalliance with Rosie would be more than welcome, but she had pretended not to understand his obvious advances.

She had continued her learning and was fluent in French and German and could speak passable Swiss and Italian. She had attended board meetings of both banks and been involved in negotiations by businessmen and the finance minister of governments negotiating to borrow money. She was highly regarded by both her father and the Baron, yet she was bored.

The Baron had asked her to meet him at his offices in Threadneedle Street and both her father-in-law and father were present in the oak panelled office as she sat herself down.

"We've brought you here, Cynthia, to discuss a joint business venture." The Baron had persisted in calling her by her formal name over the years and she was used to it now.

"We are intending to send Frederick on a most important visit to America," said Lord Berkeley. "And we would like you to accompany him and be jointly involved with some of the detailed negotiations."

Rosie sat in the sumptuous leather chair and listened.

"In December, a ship leaves Liverpool bound for New York. The voyage should take approximately nine days. On your arrival in New York, you will stay at the Waldolf Hotel and spend two or three months on the business we have in mind," said the Baron.

Rosie smiled to herself, the two were like a double act and she felt sure they had carefully worked out the script.

"Naturally you will leave the children in our care; the family will move in to Lord Berkeley's house, with both nannies and your servants to assist the household," continued the Baron. "I myself will remain in London over Christmas, so the children will have a festive time."

The pair had tried to think of everything and both wondered, as they looked at Rosie, whether they had succeeded. She was, after all, an important part of their plan, as both agreed Frederick was not capable of arranging this business on his own and neither of the men wanted a lengthy stay out of Europe themselves. "A war is looming," the Baron had said of the activities of the Germans. "It's simply a matter of when."

Rosie sat silently waiting for the two men to finish.

"Well, what do you think?" asked the Baron.

"Why can't I take Anne and Frederick Junior with me?"

The two men had anticipated this question.

"Come, come dear," said the Baron. "It's a long sea journey and Anne will miss the start of her nursery school. It is better to leave the infants with Lord Berkeley and I, is it not? And you will be back barely before they notice you have gone."

Rosie was a loving mother and had barely let young Frederick Junior out of her sight since his birth, but she could not help feeling tempted by the offer. Two months in New York – and an important part of business negotiations on behalf of the banks. Her theatre career had fizzled out as she had settled into the role of dutiful wife and daughter in law and she missed the sensation of throwing herself into a project. She had flirted with the women's cause in England, frequently hosting dinner parties to muster support for her friends, but she knew her abilities were not being stretched by any means. And now here was her chance to prove her worth to the businesses. She realised that she was also excited at the prospect of spending such a long time with Frederick; he had only been at home for a few weeks in the past three months. With these thoughts in her mind, it didn't take the men long to persuade Rosie to go.

RMS Luciana was one of the most modern of the transatlantic passenger ships. Frederick and Rosie embarked from Liverpool and, as the huge liner inched away from the dock, they leaned over the rail waving to Lord Berkeley, who was holding up their daughter, Anne.

Their first class cabins were spacious, but Rosie soon found it demanding living with Frederick for any length of time. He wasn't in a good mood leaving England on Christmas Eve and she had known that he had argued with his father about going at all. During the day, Rosie enjoyed strolling around the deck and annoyed Frederick by visiting third class steerage to talk to the many passengers emigrating.

For the first few days, the Captain and First Officer wined and dined extravagantly and Rosie and Frederick were always their guests on the Captain's table, which was followed by cards in the lounge most evenings. A young ship's doctor, Alan Rees, had been called to see Frederick, who was suffering from sea sickness and as they chatted, Frederick visibly seemed to pick up. After that, the doctor and Frederick talked a great deal and spent much of the doctor's free time together, talking about the arts and particularly ballet. Rosie, meanwhile, attracted the attention of most of the men on board. The First Officer, a rather dashing Scot, with dark hair and deep blue eyes, which seemed to look right through you, was particularly attentive. He often seemed to brush her hand when passing something at the table, even once or twice escorting her around the deck, gently holding her arm "in case the ship was caught in a swell."

On the second day out when the sea was particularly rough, Rosie left Frederick in the cabin and went to the upper deck for a breath of fresh air. She had her sea legs and didn't find travelling by ship unpleasant.

"Out walking again Cynthia?" Rosie had been introduced as Cynthia by Frederick and hadn't bothered to correct him. She turned to find the First Officer looking at her. Suddenly, a particularly violent pitch lurched Rosie off balance. First Officer Kilbrade caught her in his arms and, as she gazed into his eyes, she found herself kissing him. Quickly she broke the embrace.

"I am sorry, that shouldn't have happened. I don't know what came over me," she said, blushing slightly. How embarrassing, she thought, what is wrong with me.

"Not at all, I rather enjoyed it; perhaps we can do it again sometime?" Kilbrade said, not minding at all Rosie's impulsive embrace.

Rosie smiled.

"The weather seems to be worsening."

"Yes I suggest I accompany you to your room. The Captain has asked passengers not to walk the deck tonight, as the storm is expected to intensify."

Holding her arm, Kilbrade escorted her down one flight of stairs. Rosie felt a tingle along her spine and was sorry when they parted at her cabin door.

The weather did worsen over the next day as they headed into a fierce Atlantic storm.

"Up to force 8 the Captain says." The cabin boy set the breakfast tray on the table. "Shall I draw back the blinds madam?"

"Yes please."

Frederick was still in bed suffering terribly and had already indicated he was not going to have breakfast.

"The Captain says it should calm down later today, Madam."

"Good, I would like to get out of this cabin."

That night, dining alone at the Captain's table, Rosie was not short of male admirers. Lt Colonel Mayhew was drinking steadily, much to the disgust of his wife and Rosie had to remove his hand from hers once or twice. Finally Captain McKay insisted that Rosie change places with him, as he wanted to talk to the Colonel. Rosie was now sitting next to First Office Kilbrade.

"You will be able to take a stroll around the deck later," he said. "May I accompany you?"

"We will see." Rosie shivered, remembering the kiss on the deck yesterday.

As they left the warmth of the ship, Rosie wrapped her mink stole around her against the night air. Kilbrade offered his arm and they set off around the deck. Reaching the bow rail they stopped and looked up. The sky was clear and an array of stars twinkled.

"What a lovely evening. Tell me First Officer Kilbrade, what is that constellation?" Rosie asked, although she knew very well what the group of stars was.

"Please call me Magnus. That constellation is the Milky Way." Rosie nodded. "Look up there," he gestured. "A shooting star."

As Rosie looked up he moved closer, slipped his arm around her waist and before she could stop him, kissed her, hard and passionately. She forced herself from his hold.

"Now come on Cynthia, you know you enjoyed that," he said with a smile.

"How dare you! I shall report you to the Captain!" And with that she turned and rushed off.

As she sat on her bed in the cabin, watching a distressed Frederick, she put her fingers to her lips. In truth, although she didn't like to admit it to herself, she had quite enjoyed the sensation of a man kissing her again, even if that man was not her husband, and decided she would not make a fuss. What would be the point anyway: he would naturally deny it and she would get involved in controversy and she knew what that meant – the Baron. The one thing her father-in-law always stressed was to protect the good name of the bank. She could hear his voice: "It is imperative never to expose the bank to ANY," he repeated. "ANY scandal." And so she did nothing.

They had a sumptuous banquet for the Christmas Eve dinner and, as usual,

Rosie and Frederick were on the Captain's table. Lady Maudsley-Wright got slightly tipsy and her husband, the venerable Lord Maudsley-Wright, struggled to keep her under control. Frederick didn't approve of women drinking excessively, but Rosie found the whole dinner great fun, particularly as the First Officer spent most of his time trying to play footsie with her. The grandfather clock in the atrium signalled it was midnight and everybody, except for those a little worse for wear, exchanged greetings. Frederick and Doctor Rees had spent a great deal of the meal talking animatedly, discussing the arts and particularly the opera and ballet. Rosie hardly got a look in.

Christmas Day the next day was a bit of an anticlimax. Away from home and her beloved children, and her mother, brothers and sisters, she was homesick. Frederick was in a good mood for a change and, as the sea was relatively calm, he had ventured on deck. He had brought some exquisitely wrapped gifts from the Baron and Lord Berkeley with him, secreted in his trunk. She opened the beautiful gold wrapped present from her father-in-law to find a small silver pen with a nib which screwed in and Lord Berkeley had sent her a book, which she was astonished to find was a first edition of a book of poems by Alfred Lord Tennyson. Frederick had given her a small box, wrapped in silk, which she excitedly opened to reveal an exquisite silver perfume holder, with space for two bottles, to which he had added a delightful lavender fragrance. She had presented Frederick with a small flat parcel, which he opened with curiosity. She had found a miniature of a scene from the Sleeping Beauty ballet, painted by an unknown Parisian artist. She had snapped it up on visiting a shop in Bond Street earlier in the year and hidden it, intending a Christmas surprise. It was a success and Frederick thought it was fabulous.

The following day was relatively calm, a welcome respite from the earlier storms. As Rosie walked the deck alone, as usual, she nodded to passing sailors, stopping for a brief chat every now and then with other first class passengers. She spied a familiar figure coming down the portside staircase – First Officer Kilbrade. She had done nothing about their previous encounter. When she lay in bed alone, she found herself fantasising about Kilbrade making love to her and became very aroused.

"May I accompany you on your walk Cynthia?" He smiled that smile and she nodded, thinking where was the harm in it? He held out his arm, which she took to steady herself as the ship was rolling a little this afternoon. They spent a few minutes in idle chat, when suddenly he led her under a staircase, which she knew led to the upper deck.

First Officer Kilbrade was a handsome man and had an eye for the ladies. Every single woman on the Lucania admired him and many a married woman shook hands and held his grip a little too long. Rosie felt her heart beating, as First Officer Kilbrade leaned toward her. She knew he was going to kiss her again and part of her wanted more than anything else for him to take her in his arms and make love to her. Frederick had been distant since the birth of their son. He had changed after the kidnapper had been killed and there seemed no prospect of finding George. It was almost as though he blamed her for their loss, even though he had agreed it was not the fault of poor Nanny Roberts, who had paid with her life. What was it about Frederick? He could be charming, good company and attentive, but for a long time now he seemed preoccupied and did not give her the attention she craved for. And here was a handsome ship's officer about to kiss her. At the last moment, she turned her head and he kissed her cheek.

"Come on Cynthia. You know you want to kiss me. Are you worried we are out in the open, shall we go to my cabin?"

"First Officer Kilbrade, you forget I am a married woman. Now please escort me to my cabin," Rosie replied indignantly.

"Very well."

They walked silently to the cabin. Magnus Kilbrade left her alone after that. They exchanged a quiet nod and polite conversation at the dinner table, but that was all; he had turned his attention to Mrs McCaully, a widow travelling to meet her brother in Washington.

Rosie was often lonely and bored on the journey to New York, but at least enjoyed her regular visits to the third class section of the boat. There were all manner of people travelling to America, mostly Irish emigrating, but she recognised her own cockney Londoners, who were seeking a new life. She was regarded by these people as a gentlewoman with a kind heart. She moved amongst them distributing food and sometimes drugs, if a child was ill and they couldn't afford to buy medicine. She became very fond of one family in particular, the O'Driscalls. Bonny, a Scottish woman, was travelling with five children, aged between five and twelve. The oldest, Danny, was a typical streetwise boy, sailing close to the wind on occasions. It was on one of her visits to the steerage section of the ship, handing out the food parcels she had prepared, that she felt a slight tug on her pocket. Instinctively and with incredible speed, she grabbed the hand as it withdrew from the pocket of her tunic. She gripped it tightly and turned to find the oldest O'Driscall boy.

"If you're going to be a sneak thief and pickpocket Danny, you had better practise a lot, because if they catch you in America, you will be flogged and sent to prison for a very long time," she said severely.

He looked at her with fear in his eyes. "Don't tell me ma!" he pleaded.

"What should I do with a boy who steals from someone who is helping his family?" Rosie stared at the boy.

He looked at her with his piercing black eyes. "Ma's desperate, lady. Little Jack is ill and we don't have any money. I was only trying to help."

"Don't try and fool me. Let's go talk to your mother, shall we?" She marched him off and, even though he was a big boy, he knew when to do as he was told.

Bonny shared a cabin with two other women, who all took turns in letting their children sleep on the bunk beds. Today, Jack, her youngest was in bed asleep. Bonny looked up and motioned Rosie to follow her out of the cabin to talk outside.

"Excuse me Miss for asking you to come outside. Jack has been awake all night with the fever and I have only just got him off.

"Has the doctor seen him?" asked Rosie.

"We can't afford no doctor Miss," said Bonny, shaking her head slightly.

"Don't worry about that, I will arrange it. Perhaps Danny will accompany me to first class."

"Go with the lady Danny," instructed his mother.

As they moved away from the cabin door, Rosie looked at Danny. "Now don't think you have been let off," she warned. "You will meet me everyday at noon and carry my parcels until we dock." Danny smiled. "And don't think you can simply not turn up, because my next step will be to visit the Captain, who takes a dim view of stealing on his ship."

"I'll be there," muttered Danny, running off.

The partnership proved most successful with Danny carrying an increasingly large number of food parcels. For the next few days Rosie distributed as much food as she could. A handsome tip to the ship's cook by Frederick and a nod from the Captain, enabled her to take food to the third class passengers, mainly bread, cheese, water and some cold meats. She had to limit the food parcels, though, as the Captain had quietly reminded Rosie one evening: "We have another two days sailing yet Mrs de Courcy and you are stripping me bare." He was a kindly man, yet knew the owners would not approve of feeding the third class passengers; after all they only paid a minimum fare.

Frederick had spent much of the first part of the journey feeling ill. He didn't travel by ship very well and had found himself unable to leave the cabin for the past two days and had even been taking his meals there. What little he could force himself to eat was supplemented by sherry and whisky. He figured that if he was to be comatose it might as well be due to alcohol. Then Rosie had become alarmed by his sickness and had called the doctor. At that point his whole journey had changed. The gorgeous Dr Rees was about his age and had the softest touch. As soon as their eyes met he knew they were destined to be good friends. It turned out that Dr Rees had left London in somewhat of a hurry and was working his passage to America. He had no plans and relied upon the Americans needing qualified doctors, an assumption that would prove to be true. As the doctor examined him he found himself gaining an erection. Feeling rather embarrassed he tried to think of other things.

"I see you are rather tense," the doctor had said, touching him. From then onwards the doctor visited his cabin when Rosie was at dinner or he visited the doctor's cabin during the day. They soon were keen lovers and he found himself forgetting his beloved Pierre who he had left behind in Paris.

Christmas had come and gone and they were due to reach New York soon.

"What will you do when we reach New York, Alan?" asked Frederick. They lay naked in each others' arms, rocked gently by the swell of the sea.

"I shall seek a position at one of the hospitals and then try and move into private practice," he replied.

Frederick looked at his handsome lover. "Well, I shall assist you in any way I can." Alan smiled at him and they kissed passionately.

They were two days away from New York when Danny knocked on the door of Rosie's cabin.

"Hello Danny, you're early today."

"Can you come quickly Mrs, Jack is much worse."

Rosie, who was already dressed, donned her jacket and followed the boy, who was almost running. Entering the cabin, Rosie could smell sickness in the air. She had lived in the East End long enough to recognise the scent of disease.

"Has the doctor been?"

"Not for a few days, we can't afford him."

"Danny," said Rosie. "Go and fetch Dr Rees and tell him it's for me."

The boy ran off. Rosie sat down next to the boy Jack and felt his head; he was burning up.

The doctor arrived and began examining the boy.

"He's got a high temperature and his breathing is shallow, the next 24 hours will be crucial," he said, glancing at Rosie.

"Is he going to be alright doctor?" asked Bonny tentatively. Like most poor people, she was in awe of anybody in the medical profession. Firstly they only tended to see you when someone was dying and secondly they cost money you usually didn't have.

"He is very unwell, I think he has pneumonia," replied Doctor Rees. "You will need to keep him as cool as possible. Place this cold compress on his brow and make sure it is changed regularly."

The doctor left and Rosie looked across at the family. "Stay with your brother, Danny. Bonny, I need to talk to you."

Rosie and Bonny stepped outside the cabin. "Bonny you are going to have to keep a watch on Jack for the next twenty-four hours. I will come back later and help you."

"Oh miss, you have been so kind," said Bonny. Rosie squeezed her hand and left her to resume her vigil.

That night whilst Bonny dozed, Rosie watched the boy and began to think of her lost son. He would be walking now perhaps. Would he have said any words yet? Suddenly, young Jack let out a sigh and Rosie looked down and realised he had stopped breathing.

"Danny, wake up," she said urgently to the boy, who was asleep on the floor of the cabin. "Go and fetch the doctor quickly."

Bonny roused. "What is it?"

"I am so sorry Bonny; I think Jack has just passed away."

Bonny rushed to her son. "Come on Jack. Wake up, come on Jack don't go. Please don't go," she sobbed.

Rosie was unable to prevent a tear trickle down her cheek as she watched this desperate woman try and revive her son.

The doctor arrived and swiftly examined the child.

"I am sorry madam, your son is dead," he said. "I will make arrangements for his body to be placed in cold storage until we reach New York tomorrow."

Bonny burst into tears. Rosie held her close and silently wept. She realised that she was weeping as much for herself as for Bonny. All the drama of her own loss had resurfaced and she wondered where her little boy was and if he was safe.

Frederick watched the two tugs as they helped manoeuvre the huge ship into position as they came into dock in New York. He was thinking about the time he had spent with Alan; his new friend had helped him to forget his troubles and he had begun to laugh again, for what felt like the first time in months. He glanced at Rosie, who stood alongside him. Her eyes scanned the people crowding to leave the ship and he knew she was looking for the family she had befriended in third class. Alan had told him about the death of the boy. Although Frederick was aware she had taken it badly, they had hardly discussed the matter at all. They were moving apart and he admitted to himself at least that it was his fault. He couldn't help it: he did not love her. He liked her and she was the mother of his children, but that was as far as he could go. He realised that he was the envy of many men. Look at the few times he had accompanied her to dinner on the ship. It was quite clear that half the men around the dining table were flirting with her and one man, the First Officer, was really too much! If he had cared for her in that way, he would have complained, but once he met the doctor he had left her to her own devices.

Frederick sighed and shifted position. If he was honest with himself, he sometimes felt jealous of his gifted young wife: she had an amazing memory and spoke languages better than he did. The Baron and Lord Berkeley had been schooling her in the ways of their respective banks and he knew that her father had given her a specific mandate to negotiate the purchase of an

American bank while on the trip. Everyone adored her – and that was his problem. He was Mr Invisible. No one even acknowledged him whenever she was around.

He caught sight of a group of children running around excitedly on the deck below and looked away. He rarely thought about his children; it hurt too much. The loss of his son had affected him more than he would have thought possible. He had felt so useless. The Baron and Lord Berkeley had taken over all arrangements and Frederick had been given no role. Even Rosie had played her part, as capable as ever despite her grief. And when George's little fingertips had been delivered… Frederick shuddered at the memory. He was angry with himself for not being able to deal with that situation; he felt like the fops he had seen in Paris, at the 'Club Angelique', dressed as women.

Now everything had changed. Alan was his new love and had given him a renewed energy, but he realised that he had to make more of an effort with Rosie. He knew she was a headstrong woman and secretly feared a confrontation over his sexuality. It was likely that there would be boys in New York who would tempt him, but after he had beaten that boy in Paris, he knew he had to be more careful. Hitting the boy had excited him – he had replayed the scene in his mind a dozen times and had realised that it was the control he liked. For once, he had felt in control, a man. The ship nudged the dock as it came to rest and the gangplanks were secured. Well, this trip would be his chance to take control of his life again. Frederick drank in the scene before him and took a deep breath, savouring the moment.

Rosie stood next to her husband, lost in thought. The dockside was covered in people and she searched the crowd for Bonny and her children. She had said her goodbyes last night and had been embarrassed when dozens of the passengers had reached to shake her hand.

"Take my lucky shamrock miss." A woman had thrust a small wooden shape in her hand. At the same time, she had felt a tug in her pocket and, putting her hand inside, drew out a piece of paper.

"Thank you miss for helping my family. I won't forget you. Bonny."

Rosie had smiled and blinked away a tear. Now she strained her eyes for her adopted family.

"Come Rosie, there's our man," said Frederick, interrupting her thoughts.

Reluctantly Rosie joined him and he escorted her down the gangplank to a fanfare and ticker tape welcome. A band played an Irish song.

"Mr and Mrs de Courcy?" A young man, not much older than Frederick, introduced himself as Malcolm Middleton, the de Courcy Bank's representative in New York.

As their coach took them away from the melee at the dock, Rosie took one last look at the crowds, but was unable to see Bonny or her children. She sighed and stared blankly out of the window as they journeyed to their hotel.

New York was like London: a cosmopolitan city, teaming with all humanity. Horse drawn coaches and the occasional automobile crowded the streets. The backfire of one automobile caused several horses to rear up. There was an atmosphere Frederick recognised as typical of a bustling city and he couldn't help but smile. He was going to like it here.

They arrived at their hotel, the Waldorf, which had been recommended by the Baron.

"It is civilised," he had said. "If not a touch over the top."

His words proved true as they were shown to their room: with ornate decorations in gold and blue, it certainly looked expensive but slightly gaudy.

They had a busy time planned. Middleton had arranged for a number of prominent American bankers to call to introduce themselves. Separately, Frederick knew his wife was to meet Sir Philip Haversham at the British Embassy. Sir Philip, an old Etonian friend of her father, was to act as the go-between for the possible purchase of the Bank of Manhattan. Frederick was going to meet Alan at his lodgings, but was waiting for a note of his address, which he had promised to send him when he settled in.

The next day, Rosie dressed carefully for her meeting at the Embassy, choosing a smartly cut, blue day dress. She took her top coat out of the wardrobe along with her hat and went with Frederick to the foyer, where Middleton was waiting.

"Good day Middleton," said Frederick.

"Happy new year sir. It is bitterly cold, I am afraid," Middleton replied, shaking hands with Frederick and Rosie. "Are you ready to leave?"

Rosie nodded. She kissed Frederick on the cheek and was escorted by Middleton to the waiting coach.

"I have taken the liberty of placing two rugs on the seat Mrs de Courcy and suggest you wrap one around you."

The journey was short, but for Rosie significant. Looking out of the window, she noticed the number of poor people. London's East End had a cosmopolitan population and many people were poor and lived on the streets, but few sights saddened her as much as the one she saw that day: men and women around braziers with coal and wood burning brightly, the people looking sullen as they huddled together for warmth. There were groups of black men, Chinese and many poor white men, mostly badly dressed for this freezing weather. She very nearly stopped the coach to give away her rugs.

"We have many poor people in New York, but don't be fooled," said Middleton, seeing her staring at the roadside. "They can be very dangerous and, if I may advise you, don't get out of your coach in these areas and don't feel too sorry for these wretched people, America is a land of opportunity after all."

Rosie wondered what sort of opportunity these people would find while around a brazier, but let the comment pass.

The journey to the Embassy offices took over forty minutes and Rosie was thankful for the rugs as she pulled them around her against the cold. She found herself observing the young man Middleton, or Malcolm as he insisted she call him. He had been in New York for just over a year and represented her father-in-law's bank in America. He was British, but spoke perfect French and they had some fun speaking French for a few minutes as he pointed out various interesting sights during the journey. He delighted in explaining that he had attended Eton then Oxford University and then went to work at the Bank of England, where his family connections had quickly advanced his career. He had been persuaded by the Baron to represent the de Courcy Bank in New York and he had soon become a regular at many upper class New York parties and he was on some very influential people's guest lists. When the American Government wanted to explore obtaining an international loan to aid their mounting expenditure on the army, they consulted him amongst others. The Zurich Bank had subsequently loaned the equivalent of $5 million, a great coup for a young man of 31 years. Rosie smiled as he told her about the achievement in a matter of fact way, but not quite able to conceal his pride. He looked across at her. He had never married, despite a number of tempting entanglements, and here he was escorting one of the most beautiful women he had ever seen – how his friends at Oxford would envy him now. Still, concentrate on the task at hand old man, he thought.

"We will be arriving in a few minutes, Cynthia."

Once again, the Baron had used Rosie's official christian name in the letter he had sent to Middleton who, of course, had duly arranged meetings for Cynthia de Courcy, having no idea she preferred Rosie.

Rosie's first meeting was with the British Ambassador, Sir Philip Haversham, who had travelled from the British Embassy in Washington to meet with her at their New York offices. Sir Philip was a natural choice to effect introductions for his old friend Lord Berkeley. They had spent many a happy hour in the hostelries of Oxford and found their first loves together when they dated two of the new nurses at the university.

Middleton had met the British Ambassador on several occasions and, after a brief wait in the outer office, they were ushered into a spacious and light room.

"Sir Philip, may I introduce Mrs Cynthia de Courcy?"

Rosie took a few steps towards Sir Philip, a distinguished looking man in his fifties with greying temples. She shook hands with him and he looked at her admiringly. When his old friend had written he had been curious to meet his daughter, but had no idea she would be such a stunning woman. Apparently she also had brains, an unusual combination in the diplomatic and business world he moved in.

"It is a delight to meet you my dear and how is your father?"

"He was very well when we left in December."

Rosie smiled and the whole room lit up. How enchanting, thought Sir Philip, no wonder Berkeley had sent her; she would entrance most of the men he knew she was going to meet.

"Tell me, how was the journey?" Sir Philip asked, as he rang a bell for tea.

"I enjoyed it very much, but my husband – who sends his apologies by the way; he has a meeting with the Swiss Ambassador – is not a good traveller," replied Rosie.

"Sounds like myself, more at home on the old terra firma, eh Middleton!"

"Yes Sir Philip," replied Malcolm.

"Now to business," said the Ambassador, as a young woman entered to serve their tea. "I have arranged a number of meetings for you. Shall we sit around the fire?" He motioned towards the dark leather chairs grouped around the huge stone fireplace. He glanced at his notes. "Let's see, firstly a light lunch tomorrow at the Waldorf. I have invited the head of The Corn Exchange Bank. I am not sure that they would be interested in your proposition, but they are expantionist and very ambitious. In the evening I thought we would dine at an Italian restaurant I like, near where you are staying and I have invited Johnson Drury, the Chairman of the Continental Trust Company of New York, who I believe is looking for a strategic partner and Morgan Renton, of the Chemical Bank, one of the oldest bank's here in New York."

Sir Philip went on to explain that he had 'padded out' the dinner by also inviting several other diplomats who were in New York shopping with their wives, and Lady Haversham.

"I have arranged a private room. Middleton do you have an escort?"

"Yes, Sir Philip, may I bring Guelma Baker, a young lady of my acquaintance?"

"Certainly. Well that's settled then, more tea?" He rang a hand bell and his secretary appeared.

They left Sir Philip at midday and Rosie was feeling very pleased with the outcome of her first official meeting.

"What a charming man," she said as Malcolm helped her into the coach.

"Lunch?" he suggested.

"Yes, do you have somewhere in mind?"

"I thought we could go to the New York Hotel, which is nearby."

Malcolm then spent the next hour totally engrossed in the life and times of Rosie de Courcy. Sensing her grief was still near the surface, he let her talk about the kidnapping, but moved the subject on when he could. After lunch, they headed back to the Waldorf so that Rosie could change for some sightseeing that afternoon.

As he waited for her in the foyer, Malcolm hummed a military march to himself. He was very much taken by the beautiful Mrs de Courcy and knew he was going to enjoy this assignment. He leapt up to greet her as she stepped out of the lift and they made their way to the front door. As they walked down the steps, a man came towards them.

"Excuse me Mam, are you Mrs Cynthia de Courcy?"

Rosie looked at the man, he was much taller than her, at least six feet tall, and he had steely blue eyes and was wearing a dark full length overcoat and a hat that covered most of his face.

"And who might you be sir?" said Middleton, positioning himself between the man and Rosie.

"Ah, my apologies. My name is Victorio Nia Tore, my friends call me Tore. Are you Mrs de Courcy?"

"What do you want?" said Rosie.

"My boss wants to meet you."

"Then he should make an appointment at the desk," Rosie replied briskly. "Now please, excuse me."

At that they quickly made their way into the coach, comforted by the presence of the driver, who had stood nearby and the doorman who had begun to walk down the steps.

Tore Corino stared after the coach as it moved off. He will not be happy, he thought. He glared at the doorman and signalled across the street. A black coach pulled up with three men inside. Getting in, he opened a flap in the ceiling. "Follow their coach Georgio and don't lose them."

Rosie and Middleton discussed the tall stranger. Who was he? What did he want? Middleton repeated the dangers of New York, which he seemed to think lurked around every corner. Arriving at the Metropolitan Art Gallery, they looked around before going inside but did not see the man. Relieved, they decided to begin by visiting the French Gallery. Middleton had promised her a surprising number of impressionist paintings, the new craze sweeping Europe. Rosie was thrilled, because she had begun collecting Renoir when Frederick and her father had both presented her with gifts in London of Renoir paintings. Middleton was astonished when he heard she owned 'The Swing', a charming painting of a young girl on a swing, with who appeared to be her father, husband and daughter watching. She also possessed 'Le Moulin de la Galette', a wonderful depiction of Parisian life in the 1870s. As they walked into the gallery, Rosie immediately spotted a lovely portrait painting by Edouard Manet called 'Mademoiselle Isabelle Lemonnier'. Reading the programme, she discovered that the painting was on loan from a distinguished collector and had probably been painted in 1879 or 1880 when Manet was staying at Bellevue, near Paris. Mademoiselle Lemonnier had spent her summer holiday at a nearby villa and Manet frequently sent her letters, charmingly decorated with watercolour sketches.

"She must have been a striking woman," said Middleton, as they gazed at the painting.

"Oh yes, I would love to meet her," replied Rosie.

"Do you think she is still alive?"

"I would have thought so. Say she was in her late twenties when he painted her portrait, she would be about fifty now."

"This is a very new painting Cynthia," said Middleton, who was standing in front of a painting by Camille Pissarro. Rosie went over to him and consulted her notes.

"Ah yes. 'Rue de l'Epicerie, Rouen', an oil on canvas. The cathedral in Rouen towers is a natural part of an urban lively scene," she quoted, looking up at the piece in front of her. She stood enchanted for several minutes. Eventually, she glanced around her to discuss the picture with Middleton and found he was not there. Instead the same man who had approached her at the Waldorf stood by her.

"The compliments of Don Corino, Mrs de Courcy, he still wishes to meet with you now," he said. The word 'now' was rather menacing. Rosie looked around, where was Middleton? She thought about screaming, but then he smiled.

"Mam it is safe, we mean you no harm. My boss wishes to talk a little business." He smiled again and proffered his arm.

"Firstly, where is my friend?" asked Rosie.

"He is coming with two friends of mine, he is quite safe."

The man 'Tore' held her elbow firmly and escorted her to a black coach standing at the entrance. Rosie was intrigued, but part of her worried about the sense in going with this man.

"My boss thought you might be frightened. Don't be – here, read this note."

Rosie opened the envelope. She knew that there could be danger here but still... She read the note, which was written in poor handwriting.

'Please excuse this intrusion, it is difficult to meet you. I understand you represent the Swiss bank, owned by Baron de Courcy. I would like to have a meeting now, to discuss placing a substantial deposit of $1 million dollars with your bank. Two hundred dollars is in this envelope for your time. Please accompany the man who gave you this note, I am expecting you shortly.'

The sweeping signature at the end of the note was indecipherable. Rosie thought for a second, a hand still gripping her elbow, before making her mind up.

"I will go with you, but first I will write down where we are going, the name of your boss and your full name and hand this note to the man in the box office at the gallery," she said firmly.

"Very well."

Tore reeled off the details in his charming Italian accent.

"We are going to 'La Sicilia', a restaurant downtown to meet Don Corino, my name is Tore Corino."

Rosie pulled out a small silver pencil and wrote down the information, walked back inside and handed the note to a startled looking man at the box office.

"Please send this note to my husband at the Waldorf Hotel." She handed the man the note and extracted five dollars from the envelope Tore had given her. "Here, this is for your trouble. Do it now please."

The man looked at Tore, then at Rosie. "Yes, Miss."

As they were leaving the gallery, Rosie, again held in an almost vice-like grip, saw that a policeman was standing talking to the coach driver, swinging his stick as he laughed.

"Excuse me officer." Rosie broke free from Tore's hold. "I am going to see a Mr Don Corino at the 'La Sicilia' restaurant, can you notify my husband at the Waldorf Hotel. His name is Frederick de Courcy?"

The policeman looked faintly quizzical, then he burst our laughing.

"Si, prego Senorita, I will deliver your message."

Rosie knew immediately that he was acquainted with these men and would certainly not deliver her message. It was then she realised how futile the note at the gallery had been. She summoned up all her courage. She was representing the Bank of de Courcy and here was a potential business transaction, she would not loose the opportunity out of fear.

"What is your name officer?" she asked.

"I am Officer Michael Vasperato of the 52nd Precinct." He winked at Tore, who smiled.

The officer saluted as she got in the coach. Tore playfully punched him on the shoulder and speaking in Italian said: "Take care Michael. The Don will be pleased." Of course they did not realise Rosie understood every word.

Rosie sat in the coach. She could feel her heart beating a little faster; what was she doing? She did not speak further and avoided eye contact with the man sitting opposite. After travelling for what felt like ages, they eventually arrived at their destination and Rosie was helped out of the coach and ushered towards a rather dowdy looking restaurant. The sign hang loosely from the wall: 'La Sicilia'. A light trickle of snow fell, swept along by a strong wind. It felt slippery underfoot and the man, Tore, offered Rosie his arm. She paused for a moment and then took it, holding her hat in her other hand. They entered the restaurant and she blinked in the warm, smoky atmosphere, her eyes adjusting to the dark interior. A man behind the bar looked up as they walked into the room and she could see another figure seated at a table in the centre of the restaurant, with two rather sinister looking men sitting nearby. Rosie composed herself as Tore guided her towards the table.

"This is Mrs de Courcy."

The man, putting down his fork, looked up and gestured to Rosie to sit opposite.

"Would you like a drink?" he asked, his English broken by an Italian accent.

"No, thank you."

He looked at her for a minute, eyeing her up and down.

"Are you sure you are Cynthia de Courcy?"

"Yes, of course I am. If you come with me to my hotel, I will introduce you to my husband Frederick," Rosie replied steadily.

He picked up his fork and twisted spaghetti around it absent-mindedly.

"No, that won't be necessary," he said, putting the fork to his mouth. Rosie had seen spaghetti before in Venice, but still found herself intrigued, despite her situation. She looked at the man carefully. She guessed he was in his fifties, his dark black hair slightly greying at the temples. He was rugged looking, with black piercing eyes and a small scar on his cheek. She shivered as he looked up.

"I wish to discuss a business transaction with your father-in-law's bank," he said, picking at his teeth with a wooden toothpick. "You will carry this note to your Baron and also a trunk, which Tore will give you when you sail for England. Tore will accompany the trunk to London, at which time your Baron will be responsible for the contents. Is that understood?"

Rosie found herself feeling quite unnerved as he stared at her.

He flicked his fingers and the man behind the bar came over.

"Yes, Don?"

"Coffee… do you want coffee, lady?"

"No, thank you," replied Rosie. She just wanted to get out of there.

"Are you sure she is the dame, married to the Swiss bank guy?" The man directed his question at Tore.

"Sure, no question."

The man they called the Don nodded and whistled through his teeth.

"Sure getting better looking bankers."

All the men laughed, but he did not join in.

"Alright, take her back to her hotel."

Rosie stood up swiftly, eager to get away. The man didn't look up again and she left quickly with Tore. She spent the journey back to the Waldorf calming her nerves, with Tore sat silently next to her. Arriving at the hotel, Rosie breathed a small sigh of relief and made a move to leave the coach. Tore put a hand on her arm.

"Now, don't frig the Don about – do as he says and everything will be fine. I will come and see you just before you are leaving New York."

He helped her out of the coach and she walked towards the hotel entrance, fighting an impulse to run.

Frederick walked into Paninni's Italian restaurant. He had finished his meeting with Claude Rivette, the Swiss Ambassador, with plenty of time to return to the hotel to change his clothes before meeting his friend Alan from the ship. He looked around the restaurant and smiled. There was Alan, as handsome as he remembered. They shook hands discretely.

"This looks very pleasant," said Frederick. "I wanted to try a typical New York restaurant and the bell boy assured me this was the place. As you see, they have these delightful private booths."

The pair smiled at each other as the waiter hovered, asking them if they would like an aperitif. Frederick nodded, ordering a gin for himself and a Alan a glass of white wine.

"I am really looking forward to after lunch." Frederick leaned over and briefly held Alan's hand. "Where have you decided we should go?"

"I thought back to my apartment, I don't know of any hotels yet," replied Alan.

The waiter returned with their drinks and they picked up their menus. Frederick positively oozed charm. He recounted stories to Alan of his many trips and described, in detail, his friend in the French National Ballet and their visits to the clubs in Paris. Alan giggled and sat enraptured by Frederick's experiences.

They enjoyed an excellent red wine, a Chianti, much to Frederick's surprise, and an excellent meal of traditional meatballs and spaghetti and a superb fruit cup for dessert. Feeling very satisfied with himself, Frederick paid the bill and they left the restaurant. The cab driver, who had been waiting outside, opened the door.

"Where to sir?"

Frederick had paid the driver ten dollars more than he would earn in four days and promised him another ten if he waited outside Alan's apartment.

Frederick and Alan were new lovers and the excitement of their coming together was intense. Afterwards, they lay locked in each other's arms. Frederick had fallen asleep and woke with a start. Alan was gazing fondly at him.

"What's the matter?" Frederick said.

"Oh, nothing. I was just thinking you will be leaving soon and I doubt I will see you again."

Frederick put his arms around Alan.

"Don't be silly, I shall visit New York regularly. We are arranging a deal here to purchase a major bank and I will probably be seconded to run the bank for some time to come."

They kissed and Frederick felt himself harden again, but glancing at his pocket watch on the bedside table, realised he had to leave.

"I must dress and return to the Waldorf, otherwise my wife will wonder what I have been up to."

The men shared a knowing smile.

A blanket of snow lay on the ground outside and the cabbie was sheltering from the snow flurries in his cab.

"Is the snow going to cause any difficulty getting back to my hotel?"

"No sir, it's not that bad."

They set off, Frederick covering himself in fur rugs and gazing contentedly out of the window at the smattering of snow flakes that still floated past.

Arriving at the Waldorf, Frederick was confronted by a clearly agitated Middleton.

"Frederick, thank god you've returned. Cynthia – she has been gone ages – with several very unsavoury men – "

"What on earth do you mean," said Frederick in bewilderment. "Calm down Middleton and start again."

Middleton explained that he and Rosie had been touring the art gallery when he found himself being frog-marched away from her by a couple of burly men. He had seen another man, one he recognised as having spoken to them earlier at the hotel, engaging Rosie in conversation. Alarmed, he had broken free and rushed back towards her, only to see her going out of the front door.

"A man then jabbed what I perceived to be a gun in my ribs and told me, in no uncertain terms, what would happen to me if I uttered a word. I think he was Italian. They then took me to their own carriage and kept me there for what I estimated to be approximately half an hour, before bringing me back here. They told me Cynthia would be brought back at 5.00 pm," Middleton finished shakily.

Frederick looked at his pocket watch: four forty-five.

"Didn't they say anything else? Have you no idea who they were?"

Middleton shook his head and was about to reply when he caught sight of Rosie coming through the front door, escorted by a rather large individual, who said something to her and left. Frederick and Middleton jumped up.

"Rosie, thank god! Are you alright?" Frederick said, glancing at the man who was going out the door.

"I am fine Frederick, it was nothing to be concerned about," said Rosie calmly. "Let's go to the room and I will explain."

They made their way to the room, Middleton bursting to ask who the strange men were and whether they should call the police. Closing the door behind them, Rosie then recounted the circumstances of her abduction. She didn't hide the fact that she had been a little frightened but once it became obvious that the leader wanted to talk about a business transaction, she admitted to quite enjoying the excitement.

"Did they hurt you?" said Middleton, looking concerned.

"Not at all, they were very gentlemanly."

As Frederick and Middleton discussed the events, Rosie let her mind wander. Despite herself, she couldn't help a little smile. She could get quite excited thinking about that man Tore…

Paul Kelly was easily able to move through the different levels of society in New York. Today he had arranged to join the lunch hosted by a Swiss banker, but this morning he was instructing two of his thugs to apprehend and give a serious lesson to an Irishman, Patrick O'Reilly, who had had the audacity to refuse to pay his protection money when he had taken over a bar off Broadway.

Born in Italy, Kelly had immigrated with his family to New York City in 1892 and quickly established himself firstly as a professional boxer and then as a leader of a gang. He was a quiet, well dressed man, softly spoken and well educated. He considered himself above the thugs he employed and tried to behave as a gentleman even though he was a cold-hearted and ruthless man. The chief of the 'Five Pointers', he controlled 1500 'soldiers' and they earned their money from prostitution, protection and political control – the three p's as Paul liked to think of his earners.

His thoughts turned to his schedule for the day. He was going to enjoy this lunch; he liked mixing with the rich and had earned his kudos. Most of the men present would have been to his Dance Hall, a flashy place on Great Jones Street, and many had received 'favours' in the form of the prettiest prostitutes or boys. He had investigated this banker Frederick de Courcy in preparation for the lunch and as he thought about his findings, he smiled to himself.

"Boss," a burly man with almost no hair came into the room, interrupting his thoughts.

"What is it Frankie?"

"I followed the broad as you said, boss."

"And?"

"The Sicilians grabbed her at an art gallery. I was waiting outside and out they came, it was the Don's son Tore and a couple of others."

"Carry on…" Paul was getting impatient, why did he have to deal with these brainless idiots?

"They took her to that Italian restaurant 'La Sillysomething'."

Paul winced. "Go on, go on."

"I waited outside and they came out with her and took her back to the Waldorf Hotel," which sounded as though he said Wallorf Hotel.

"It's Waldorf Frankie, not Wallorf."

"Oh yeah boss, that's the place."

"Alright, get Tiny and Nick to accompany me, I am going out," said Paul, gesturing for Frankie to leave. He sat for a while reflecting on the information he had received. So they had taken the girl to meet the Don – why? It didn't make much sense, he would have to put out some feelers. You had to keep up with the opposition, especially a strong gang like the Sicilians.

Standing up, he went to the washroom and looked at his appearance in the mirror. He wasn't a flashy dresser and looking at himself, decided a conservative stripped suit was sufficient for the occasion. He had a lot to think about. He was considering moving his operation in Broadway to Harlem and Brooklyn to gain control of the docks. This would be a bold step and involve a running war with his main adversary, Monk Eastman. Eastman had around 1200 'warriors' under his banner and they 'ran' the territory near the bowery. Paul knew Eastman had more politicians in his pocket, but Paul had more moneymen. Eastman claimed domain over an area from Monroe to Fourteenth Street and from the Bowery to the East River. Paul considered his Five Pointers had jurisdiction in the Bowery and there was constant feuding. The Sicilians would keep out of it: they ran booze, prostitutes, protection and pick-pocketing and didn't much bother with the politicians – a mistake thought Paul. He had an uneasy truce with the Don. He was after all, Italian by birth and could speak Italian fluently. Taking a final look at his appearance he set off for the Waldorf for his lunch with the bankers.

Malcolm Middleton arrived as arranged to meet Rosie and Frederick for a briefing, thirty minutes before their lunch. Frederick explained that their role in New York was to determine if one of the large New York entrepreneur bankers was prepared to sell a controlling interest to a combined bid by the Baron and Lord Berkeley, each acquiring at least 26% of the equity.

"The Baron and Lord Berkeley do not expect us to negotiate a deal, simply determine if one of the bankers is prepared to talk," finished Rosie.

"It is the Baron's understanding that several of the banks in New York are stretched and Lord Berkeley concurs," said Frederick. In addition he and Rosie had been briefed to travel to Washington with the Swiss Ambassador to meet the President concerning an undisclosed matter.

They took the lift to the foyer with Middleton and Frederick escorting Rosie, who was looking elegant in a pink silk day dress. The lunch had been arranged in a private room at the Waldorf, which had an adjacent lounge where they were due to meet their guests. The first to arrive was Sir Philip and then the Swiss Ambassador arrived with a clutch of bankers following. Rosie and Frederick were introduced to a nondescript man Paul Kelly. Frederick noticed he seemed to be held in a certain kind of awe by several of their guests and wondered who he was.

Lunch was served in the Rose Room and was a traditional New York light lunch of soup, steak and a cake for dessert. Rosie was sat next to the Swiss Ambassador, who spent most of the lunch talking about the Baron, a man he clearly admired. On her left was a Jewish banker, Abraham Aaronovitch, head of the Merchant City Bank of New York. As she talked politely, she ate sparingly, as they were due to meet Sir Philip, the British Ambassador, for dinner later that evening at an Italian restaurant. Sir Philip had more or less indicated that this lunch was a waste of time with 'second rate' bankers and corrupt politicians, but the Swiss Ambassador and Sir Philip chatted amiably, introducing the guests to Frederick and Rosie.

Rosie sensed the strange man, Paul, elicited a degree of unease from some of the guests. Yet he seemed so quiet, she puzzled, staring at him. He caught her gaze across the table.

"I am sorry Mrs de Courcy, I have not had the opportunity to speak. Do you have children?"

"That's interesting," thought Rosie. "Do I detect an Italian accent?" She smiled at him as she replied. "Yes I have," she paused momentarily. "Three children, two boys and a girl."

"How charming. I have been blessed with two boys," he replied. Small talk came easily to Rosie and she noted that this man seemed remarkably briefed on her life. He knew of her stage career, her deceased father's position in the docks and her real father. She was intrigued and wanted to find out more about him, but didn't get the chance as the lunch broke up for the men to smoke a cigar. Rosie and the Ambassadors' wives left for coffee in a room off the main dining room.

"Such a sweet man," commented Lady Haversham, smiling at Rosie.

"Who's that Lady Haversham?" Rosie asked, although she had a feeling she knew.

"That man, Paul something, sitting next to me."

"Ah yes, a man of mystery. Tell me, what did you find out about him?" asked Rosie conspiratorially.

"Very little, I am afraid, but I sense there is a great deal more to him than meets the eye."

Monk Eastman was in a very bad mood. He was never an easy man to deal with, but today everyone kept out of his way. The cause of his anger was a low life politician, Sydney Fine, who had reneged on an agreement to propose Monk as Deputy Chief of Police. In fact, what had happened was that the man's miserable interference had resulted in the post being abolished and Bill Devery, the chief of Police and a hated enemy, had been made Deputy Commissioner. Monk had seen Bill Devery just that morning boasting about his new office. A dangerous and formidable man, Monk – who frequently carried with him a large club and was always armed to the teeth with a blackjack, tucked into his belt and a set of brass knuckles on each hand – was so angry that he wanted to kill someone and not even 'Kid' Twist, his chief lieutenant would go near him.

"Kid," Monk hollered.

Reluctantly, Kid went into the seedy room in the club on Chrystine Street, near the Bowery, and blinked in the smoky atmosphere.

"Yes boss?"

"Tell me again about that bastard Paul Kelly, who did he meet for lunch?"

"We can't be certain."

"Course we can be certain, we own the bloody doorman."

"Well Ned told us that Paul Kelly and some of his boys were at the Waldorf and Kelly had lunch with a load of suits, including some British people and an attractive woman."

"More, is there more?"

"The waiter, Ned's cousin, said that Kelly was sitting next to some grand lady and opposite a doll and it seemed he was on his best behaviour."

"Christ, is that all I get. Why do I pay these shits. Go back to that fucking hotel and get hold of that Ned and tell him the sun ain't gonner shine any more, unless I get a complete breakdown of who those people were, particularly who that fucker was sitting next to – got it? Bring that fucker Ned here when he gets the gen."

"Sure boss." Kid backed out of the room, happy to leave; he didn't want to remain within reach until Eastman cooled down, which was likely to be later when he smoked some of the Chinese stuff.

Frederick had really been very bored over lunch; he disliked his life as a banker. His father had forced him down a path he hated. He had yearned to paint and write poetry, instead he had to make small talk with a load of boring bankers and politicians. Rosie did it all so much better anyway; she seemed to be able to charm men or women and actually seemed to enjoy talking about deals and trivia. He knew that in previous years his father would have sent him alone, but the loss of their son had changed everything. Rosie had recovered far better than he had. At least he had curtailed the drinking, partly with the help of Alan. Frederick smiled as he thought about him. What a lovely man he was. He knew he was falling in love with Alan and now had to scheme a way of staying longer in New York. Rosie and he, together with the two Ambassadors and their wives, were due to travel to Washington in two days to meet President Roosevelt, at the Executive House. He knew Rosie was not party to the reason for the meeting with the Americans and wouldn't be involved in the meeting, which was a pity – she was a very good negotiator. He reflected on how lucky he had been to find her: innocent, yet tough, beautiful and talented, and from what he could tell, loyal. He did not know of any affairs, even though he had not made love to her for over six months. Thinking of love, his thoughts turned back to Alan and he realised it was time for him to go.

"Rosie I am going out, see you later," he called out as he left. Yes, such a sweet girl, he mused. She never questioned him, but she surely must suspect something?

Rosie lay on the bed feeling quite tired after a long lunch. She seemed to do all the socialising, whilst Frederick was stuck to one spot like glue. As she heard him leave, she smothered a sigh. "Oh Frederick, what has happened to you?" she thought to herself. In a few short years, he had changed from lover to nothing and she knew her feelings for him were evaporating at every passing day. How long could their false life go on? No touching, no love making, no caring, she couldn't take much more. She needed the arms of a man who wanted her. She missed the closeness. As she lay there thinking, there was a knock on the door in the outer chamber. Her maid Margaret answered the door.

"It is the hotel manager Madam, he would like to see you."

Rosie checked herself in the dressing table mirror, put on her best smile and went into the main lounge area. The man, who she had met only briefly, introduced himself.

"My name is James Santori. I am the under Manager at the hotel."

"Hello, I am Mrs de Courcy," Rosie replied, gesturing for him to sit. "What can I do for you?"

The man paused and looked sheepish, almost embarrassed.

"I am sorry to disturb you, but I am in trouble."

"Oh?" said Rosie in surprise.

"Let me explain. It is the policy of the hotel to list all the guests on luncheons, like the one you had today, in order to send them a bouquet of flowers and an invitation to come and dine with us again."

"How nice," Rosie smiled.

"Yes well, unfortunately there has been a monumental mess up, the head waiter forgot to ask your husband for a list of guests and so I am, to be blunt, in a lot of trouble."

Rosie looked at this young man in front of her, not much older than Frederick, with brown wavy hair and a nice face.

"Well, I am sure we can do something to help. Do you have a pen and paper?"

James's face lit up.

And so it was that a list of attendees at the dinner reached Monk Eastman later that afternoon.

Rosie and Frederick were getting ready for the business dinner that evening at 'Mondini's', a favoured Italian restaurant on Broadway, a most popular area of New York.

Rosie liked the hustle and bustle of New York, but she didn't like the snow. It wasn't like Switzerland, it was dirty and many people huddled in doorways and hid in alleys around braziers trying to keep warm. Like London, she thought, the poor are always exposed in the winter and at that moment she felt homesick.

"Frederick, I am glad we are going home soon," she said suddenly.

Frederick was dressing in the dressing room and mumbled back at her, "Sorry dear, I didn't hear you."

"I said I was feeling homesick and glad to be going home soon."

"I know, but there is still the trip to Washington – and I may have to stay behind in New York for a while," he added quietly.

Rosie stopped in her tracks.

"But Frederick, I thought you were travelling back with me?"

"Change of plan old thing," Frederick replied in an offhand way. "Father needs me to try and bring a deal to the table, with one of these New York fellows."

Rosie sat whilst her maid brushed her hair and pondered on what Frederick had said. She felt disappointed that she was to travel back without him, but then again Frederick had hardly spent any time with her in the past six months. Frederick had changed and she was falling out of love. She was increasingly finding herself daydreaming about other lovers and flattered by the attention she received from men of all ages.

"Rosie, Rosie you are miles away," Frederick interrupted her thoughts.

"Sorry dear, what did you say?"

"Are you ready m'dear. We are expected in thirty minutes and it's still snowing."

New York had been suffering from one of its worst winters for many years. The sidewalks and alleys were full of starving wretches, whose roughly prepared fires were often dangerously close to the buildings. As Rosie donned her luxurious fur coat she felt a familiar twinge of guilt. She had such a lot, perhaps she would do more for the poor people.

'Mondini's' was a typical Italian restaurant, frequented by the wealthy, middle and upper classes of New York. From the outside it was fairly nondescript, but inside sumptuous blues, paintings of Venice and a huge wooden gondola hung from the ceiling, transforming the place and creating a piece of atmospheric Venice for the client. Rosie loved it, but then she did have the fondest memories of Venice.

Sitting next to a slightly balding banker from New York, who was an immigrant from Tuscany in Italy, and Johnson Drury, Chairman of Continental Trust, on the other side, was hard work for Rosie, mainly because Johnson had started to touch her foot with his and was so overly attentive that she was glad when the meal was over and the ladies left the men to their customary cigars, port or brandy.

Frederick was finding the meal equally as hard, but for different reasons. Banking was such a boring world, he mused, full of boring people who droned on about interest rates, world economics, the potential for wars affecting global trading and other pathetic subjects he wasn't remotely interested in. Still, he needed to beef up his story for his father, so he made an effort to work around the table making appointments in two, three or four weeks time for further meetings. Occasionally he looked over at Rosie and could see that she was enjoying herself with a rather outgoing, gregarious man whose name he could not remember.

The head waiter barely spoke English but Frederick, Rosie and the Swiss Ambassador and his wife spoke Italian which delighted him.

"The storm has passed," he announced as the group were saying their goodbyes and coaches began to line up at the door of the restaurant.

Johnson Drury held Rosie's hand for what seemed an eternity.

"It's been an absolute delight," he said, gazing into her eyes. "I hope you will call me and I believe we could have lots to discuss." He kissed her hand. Finally he let go and she said her goodbyes to the remaining guests before leaving in the last coach with Frederick and Middleton.

Middleton seemed uneasy and Rosie began to pay attention to the gangs of men that she could see roaming the sidewalk. They were on both sides of the road and it was rather menacing. Middleton, who had lived in New York for a little while, knew that coaches had sometimes been forcibly stopped and the occupants robbed. He had therefore taken the precaution of hiring an armed guard, but one man now seemed very little when Rosie nervously looked at the gangs on both sides of the sidewalks. Suddenly the coach slowed and the driver spoke down through the connecting hatch.

"There is an obstruction ahead, would you like me to turn round sir?"

Middleton stood and peered into the gloom and made a decision.

"Yes, is there another way?"

The coach slowed and started to turn but the road was not wide enough for one manoeuvre and right at the moment when they were half way in a three point turn, two men jumped on the running boards, one each side of the coach and peered in. They stank of alcohol and Rosie shrank back in her seat. A shot rang out.

"Get off the coach!" a voice instructed.

Both of the reptilian looking men got down from the running boards and another group of men seemed to usher them away. Suddenly another face appeared at the doorway – it was Paul Kelly.

"May I enter the coach?"

"Yes, of course," said Frederick. He and Middleton were looking decisively peaky. "Paul, you are most welcome," said Frederick somewhat shakily.

"You must forgive my impertinence but you were in grave danger. Monk Eastman and his Five Pointers gang blocked the road and those were two of the gang members who jumped on your coach."

"Who is this Monk Eastman?" said Frederick.

Paul smiled, "A notorious gang leader with a particular vicious gang of followers who they call the Five Pointers."

"What do they want?" Middleton had regained his composure.

"They were going to charge you for your carriage to pass through their blockade," replied Paul.

"It seems we owe you our thanks then," said Frederick.

"Not at all. Some of my men and I will accompany you back to your hotel. May I?" He tapped on the hatch to speak to the driver. "Driver, go back the way you came and take the shortest route."

Suddenly two men jumped on the running boards. Middleton looked startled.

"Don't worry," Paul said. "These are my men."

Rosie couldn't see their faces but felt reassured by Paul riding in their coach as their escort. Their journey back was uneventful and they chatted to Paul about the gangs in New York. It seemed that large parts of New York were ruled by roaming gangs of thugs and that sometimes even police officers were in the pay of the gangs. Rosie shook her head, finding herself again feeling homesick for London.

The coach pulled in front of the Waldorf and Frederick turned to Paul.

"Will you take a night-cap sir, we cannot thank you enough."

"No, not tonight thank you, but I know you have one more day before travelling to Washington. Please be my guests and come to my dance hall."

He handed Frederick a card with the 'New Brighton Dance Hall' emblazoned across it. It showed an address in Great Jones Street.

"Will you come tomorrow night?" he asked. Frederick glanced at Rosie. She nodded, thinking to herself that this might be something interesting and Paul seemed such a pleasant gentleman.

"I will send my carriage for you at 9pm. Meanwhile I must go. Can I ask your driver to drop me off?"

"Yes, of course, that's the least we can do," said Frederick.

Monk Eastman was furious. He had staged a roadblock to capture these Swiss bankers and that bastard Kelly had interfered. He swung his club and landed a telling blow on the head of the retch in front of him.

"Chuck him in the river," he instructed and a long haired, dirty looking man was dragged out. Both of the men who had given up so easily when Kelly rescued the coach occupants had paid with their lives. 'Kid Twist' his Chief Lieutenant was wary of him and knew it was wise to keep quiet when he was in this mood.

The following day the snow had stopped and Rosie decided to join Lady

Haversham for a tour of the city. Frederick had declined saying that he had business to attend, his usual excuse these days. Once Rosie had left, Frederick headed towards Stuyvesant Avenue and Alan's apartment. He had been obliged to call a cab as Rosie needed the coach. Frederick thought that giving the cab driver a handsome tip would guarantee his return at 3pm.

Frederick gazed fondly at Alan as he brought in two steaming cups of black coffee. Both men preferred their coffee with nothing added except perhaps a little sugar.

"I have good news, Frederick."

Frederick glanced towards his friend, taking a sip of his coffee.

"I have applied for the job at St Peters Hospital and I have been accepted."

"Oh, that's wonderful news," Frederick smiled. "When do you start?"

"Next Monday I am due to meet the resident physician. Whilst I have some limited surgical experience he was willing to train me to act as his deputy – it's very exciting."

"I'm so pleased for you, but it means we will not be able to meet as regularly. I am off tomorrow to Washington for two days but I have sent my father a letter saying I intend to stay on in America for two more months as I am close to securing a preferential purchase of a New York bank."

"Will he allow you to stay?"

"Oh yes, if he thinks there is a deal in the making."

The small talk finished as they urgently fell into each other's arms, delighted to hear each other's good news.

Rosie had spent an interesting day touring New York City. Thank goodness the snow had abated, enabling Lady Haversham, Middleton and their two maids to be driven around. The boardwalks, as they called the pavements by the side of the roads, were now a dark squelching mess. There were few people walking about, but there were some gentlemen escorting ladies to the many shops.

Firstly they went down a wonderful tree-lined road which was called Broadway, to view Trinity Church. The church was in the Gothic style and had a wonderful stained glass window above its alter. Lady Haversham had wanted to see Alexander Hamilton's grave, as the President of the United States had told her to visit the church and of particular interest was Hamilton's grave. A brilliant aide to George Washington during the War of Independence, Hamilton had founded the country's first central bank. The President had been teasing Lady Haversham, but nevertheless she dutifully went to the churchyard. Rosie and Lady Haversham had both sensibly worn boots but the bottom of their day dresses were still getting a little wet from the undisturbed snow in the grave yard. Outside on the boardwalk some of the more enterprising shopkeepers had cleared the pavements outside their premises and after the visit to the church both ladies decided to visit a store which had a coffee lounge. This was of great interest to them both as there were no such places in England. Most coffee lounges were still a male domain and ladies simply would not be seen in one.

After coffee they resumed their tour of the city, admiring the magnificent new building in Park Road which was called 'the Potter building'. They passed City Hall, the central municipal building, which had quite extensive grounds in front of the building. There were more people walking about now as the sun came out and the temperatures rose slightly. The snow was melting and the atmosphere in the streets was changing.

"The Americans are building a new underground railway and they are calling it a sub-way," said Middleton, as they gazed out of the window at the building activity adjacent to City Hall.

"I presume it will be similar to the Metro in Paris or London's proposed underground," replied Rosie and Middleton nodded.

The coach ambled on to Fifth Avenue where they stopped to observe a construction which had recently been completed. It was a huge and most unusually shaped building.

"That's the Flatiron Building, ma'am," said the driver.

The building dwarfed all the others and was like a wedge of cheese running along side Wall Street on a triangular plot.

"I don't think these Americans will build any higher. Do you dear?" asked Lady Haversham.

"They have such a large country, you would have thought cities would extend outwards not upwards," replied Rosie.

They stopped outside the Bank of New York in Madison Avenue where the ladies were to meet Sir Phillip for a light lunch in the boardroom. Rosie had already been briefed by Middleton that the Bank of New York was one of the oldest banks in the city and was in fact considered the financial heart of the city. Alexander Hamilton whose grave they had visited earlier, had helped shape the economy of America as Secretary of the Treasury in George Washington's first cabinet. As New York City and Hamilton's economic ideas took shape so did the Bank of New York. The bank had helped set up the New York stock exchange and been a principal backer of the railways and other transport projects, but it was a discreet sign that greeted them next to the doorway.

After a most enjoyable lunch, they went to the Metropolitan Museum of Art on 5th Avenue, where Rosie and Middleton were able to continue their tour of the gallery, this time without interruption. Lady Haversham was accompanied by a young curator of the gallery.

"The museum was founded in 1870 by a group of citizens as a museum to bring art and art education to the American people," explained the young man. Rosie had moved on to view a Van Dyck painting, but remained in the company of Middleton who had proved as attentive as usual. The tour ended with all of them admiring the few French impressionist paintings and Rosie making a mental note to persuade Frederick to invest in further paintings as she had a feeling they would turn out to be an excellent investment. The trouble of course was that men who dealt in money found it hard to accept that other investments could be even more profitable.

After a full day, the coach dropped Lady Haversham and her maid at her apartments and Middleton escorted Rosie back to the Waldorf, before heading back to his own apartment with a cheery wave. Rosie liked Middleton, he would receive a favourable report when she saw her father and the Baron.

Frederick left Alan at 3pm feeling very pleased with himself and delighted to find that the cab was waiting outside the apartment block.

Getting in, he instructed the cabbie to take him to the Waldorf.

"The weather is improving," he thought to himself. "A trip to Washington might after all be quite pleasant".

Frederick's head began to drop. He felt rather sleepy with the motion of the coach. He tugged his watch out of his waistcoat pocket: 3.35 pm. We must be nearly there, he thought.

The coach pulled up abruptly at the roadside and the door was yanked open. A tall, uncouth looking man with a mop of unkempt black hair stood in the doorway with a smile on his face.

"This is your stop, your Lordship," he grinned, showing several teeth missing. Frederick looked at the man and glancing over his shoulder and saw no sign of the Waldorf Hotel.

Shouting up to the driver he said, "Driver you've taken me to the wrong place." There was no answer. Dammit, where was the man?

"Come on, out yer get," said the uncouth man roughly. He seemed to be getting angry and Frederick began to panic. He was not the world's bravest man. He had been taught to fence and shoot but he didn't like either activity.

"Who are you?" he asked, remaining rooted inside the coach. The door opened on the other side and a tall, wiry, emancipated looking man entered the carriage.

"We've asked you nicely, now get out or I'll cut you."

Frederick gasped as the man waved a cut throat razor inches from his face. He edged along the seat, got up and left the coach, glancing up to see no sign of his driver. Pushed roughly from behind Frederick found himself entering a dingy looking door. He was truly frightened now. Middleton's words about New York crime and the close shave last night all suddenly came rushing back. What did they want with him?

He staggered slightly as a heavy hand shoved him forward.

"Up the stairs, fairy boy."

The two men laughed and Frederick was pushed through doors at the top of the stairs into another room. It was dark and dingy with a table and a chair set in the centre of the room.

"Sit down!" came an instruction from behind and Frederick did as he was told.

The two men hovered around making smalltalk and laughing. Frederick was thinking frantically, realising only Alan knew where he had been and he would not miss him for three days as he told him he was going to Washington tomorrow. Rosie was out visiting the sights of New York and shopping all afternoon and it would be hours before she would begin to wonder where he was.

The door opened and another man came in. Walking straight over to Frederick, he got hold of his arms and pinned them behind his back, taking off his overcoat and tying his wrists together – it hurt. A hood was placed over his head. God, what did they want? He began to protest and felt a blow on his back. His hands were going numb and sweat was falling down his face and the inside of his clothing. He hated being in the dark. Ever since an over-enthusiastic head boy at Eton had locked him in a small dark cupboard at the age of six, he had an aversion for darkness if he knew he couldn't get out. He tried to take a couple of deep breaths to calm down, feeling his whole body shaking. He heard the door open again and then further voices. Another man had come into the room.

"Take the hood off. I want him to see this."

Frederick blinked as the hood was yanked off of his head. As his eyes accustomed to the light, he found standing in front of him a man he hadn't seen before. He had a pigeon sitting on his shoulder. Frederick stared, but suddenly the man slapped him around his face, which sent the bird souring towards the rafters.

"Now you won't get hurt if you tell me what I want to know," the man said.

"But I don't know you," began Frederick.

The man laughed. "Who I am doesn't matter; it's what you know that does."

He hit him again and Frederick tasted a trickle of blood that had run from his nose down into his mouth.

"Bring him in," said the man. Frederick waited, wondering what was going to happen next. Two men entered the room, carrying between them a poor wretch whose face was covered in blood. Frederick looked at the man. Who was he? What on earth did it have to do with him?

"I want to demonstrate what happens to people who try and trick me and don't tell me everything I want to know. Bring him to the table. Hold out his hand."

The man that had been brought in to the room was virtually unconscious but sensed what was going to happen and started to scream and struggle to get free from his captives. The two men holding him forced his arm to be laid out on the table. The man began screaming.

"Now watch mister," said the pigeon man, as Frederick had christened him in his mind. As Frederick looked on in horror the pigeon man, whose face he would remember for the rest of his life, picked up a large club, took careful aim and then crashed it down on the poor wretch's hand. The man screamed in agony and passed out. Frederick looked at the mess on the table and was unable to identify any part of the hand left there. His legs buckled.

"Take him away and kill him!"

As the limp body of the man was removed, Frederick's mind whirled. In his panic, he could feel himself on the verge of passing out. Had he been captured by madmen? Did they think he was someone else? What could he do to survive this?

"Now pretty boy, listen closely," said the pigeon man, leaning towards him. "Because I am going to ask you questions, but only once. If you don't answer or I think you are lying I will use the enforcer." He lifted up the club and smiled.

"Nod, if you understand."

Frederick felt the bile rising in his throat but nodded.

"Right, you lovely boy. You had a meeting at your hotel, The Waldorf, yesterday. Tell me who was present?"

The meeting at the Waldorf yesterday? Frederick wracked his brains, trying to clear the fog of panic that was threatening to engulf him.

"Do you mean the luncheon?" he said, hesitantly.

"Now don't start bandying around stupid words, fancy boy."

The men all laughed and Frederick flinched slightly in confusion.

"Lunch, meeting, who cares what you call it – stop pissing me off! Who was at the bloody meeting?" He picked up his club. Frederick gulped for air and spat out some bile.

"Al-alright, give me a minute to think," he said shakily and began to reel off as many of the guests' names as he could remember.

"Sounds a la-di-dah group of bastards," muttered one of the men.

"Shut up!" said the pigeon man in front of Frederick as he thumped the club on the table. "You are missing people. Think pretty boy, think or by God you will lose your hand."

Frederick gulped and forced himself to go round the table in his mind.

"Ah yes, there was also a Mr Kelly, whom I did not know."

The men laughed again.

"Mr Kelly, is it? What did you talk to him about?"

Frederick received another slap round the face, harder than the others and momentarily saw stars.

"Nothing, nothing. I hardly spoke to him at all."

Another blow landed round his face.

"Wrong answer, lovely boy! What was he doing there?"

Frederick thought hard. "He was brought along by one of the bankers. He mostly asked questions," said Frederick.

"I'm listening…"

Frederick tried to think back on the conversations he had been part of.

"He seemed interested in a meeting my wife had had with a man," Frederick paused, straining to remember more details.

"A man? What man?" said the pigeon man.

"Yes, that's it. He was interested in a meeting with a man called Don Corino."

The man put the club down on the table.

"You sure it was Don Corino?"

"Yes, that's it. My wife was taken forcibly to a restaurant. She thought by a man they called Tore."

"Now we are getting somewhere. What did they discuss?"

Frederick finally felt on firmer ground; he wasn't going to hold back now. It seemed his only way of escaping the fate of the other man was to talk.

"He wanted to know about investing a sum of money in our bank."

Pigeon man smiled and muttered, "Did he now? Did he now? And how was he planning to invest the money, and how much?"

"They talked about a million dollars," Frederick replied. One of the men behind Frederick whistled.

"Shut up!" said pigeon man. He picked up the club again and twirled it in his hand. Suddenly he put the club down, unbuttoned his fly and pulled out his penis. Frederick was horrified.

"You like these, don't you lovely boy?"

He waved his penis in front of Frederick, who slumped further into his chair in disgust and terror. The pigeon man indicated to the men to pull Frederick up to an upright position and, before Frederick could move again, the pigeon man began to urinate over him. All the men laughed, quickly following suit. Frederick fought a wave of revulsion that mingled with his terror. He was soaked. His face and nose hurt and he stank of urine. Any control he had been able to keep during his 'interview' evaporated rapidly and he began to sob, his body shaking as his tears mingled with the blood and urine covering him.

"Now listen, lovely boy," said pigeon man. "You will tell me every move those bastards make. That means everything. If they as much fart I want to know, got it?" He hit Frederick again. "Say yes lovely boy, say yes."

Frederick spat out blood from his mouth. "Yes, yes, I will do anything you say," he managed to reply. He could smell the odour from his clothes, but managed to stop sobbing.

"If you don't," said pigeon man, "I will pick you up again or I might chose your fancy boy doctor or your wife – yes," he smiled, "I might choose your wife. I hear she's a bit of a looker. Every day you send me a note. One of my men will be waiting in the hotel foyer at nine every morning. You see him here?" He pointed towards one of his unkempt thugs. "You got it?"

Frederick looked at him blankly for a second, nearly at the end of his tether. He tasted blood in his mouth as he was struck again. "Yes," he muttered quickly.

"And pretty boy, I will know if you tell the police. Now remember, you fell over in the street and banged your head. Keep to that story and you and your friend will keep safe."

Pigeon man picked up his club and whistled. The pigeon flew down from the rafters and settled on his shoulder. He took something out of his pocket and held it out to the pigeon and then, to Frederick's relief, he left.

Before he could say anything, Frederick was bodily manhandled back outside and then thrown head first inside the coach.

"Take him back to his hotel and chuck him in the alley next door."

Frederick lay on the floor of the coach, his body shaking and his teeth chattering in the cold air. One of the men had kept his overcoat and he was freezing. After what seemed like an eternity, the coach stopped and the door opened. A man slid him along the floor and then yanked him out, dropping him on the road. He cut the rope tying his wrists behind his back and got back on the coach and left.

Frederick lay still for a few seconds, not daring to move, but then realising he was free, looked to see where he was. He was in an alley alongside the Waldorf. His body was still shaking, but he managed to get up gingerly and limped towards the hotel. The doorman, resplendent in a red and black outer coat, saw him but initially thought he was a local bum, after all he stank and was filthy.

"Help me," said Frederick weakly. "I have a room here. I've fallen over."

The doorman was not going to take this bum seriously and was about to tell him to move on when suddenly he recognised Frederick as the man with the beautiful wife. Shocked, he went to help him and then smelt the terrible odour and shrank away calling the bellboy. Frederick would later remember entering the hotel as the most embarrassing moment of his life. Everybody looked as he was helped into the lift and up to his room. A doctor was called, but Frederick managed to get his clothing off to be thrown away and shower before he arrived. As he was questioned, he stuck to his story, although he was obviously incredibly shaken up: he had slipped alighting from a coach and banged his head.

Rosie arrived back from her afternoon with Lady Haversham, horrified to find Frederick in bed with a bruised face and a steadily blackening eye. She listened to his story but was not convinced. He was shaking like a leaf and asked her to send a message to Alan, the doctor they had met on the boat. He wanted to talk to someone he knew.

Alan arrived an hour later and gave his friend a thorough examination. Like Rosie, Alan was not convinced that Frederick had simply fallen over in the snow but he gave him a sedative and a pat on the arm. He needed to get some sleep. He had clearly had a tremendous shock and his nerves were on edge.

That evening, Middleton arrived to take Rosie for dinner at the hotel restaurant.

"I don't see how Frederick is going to be able to travel tomorrow," said Rosie. She had left her husband asleep murmuring pitifully.

"Whatever happened, and I'm not convinced about his story that he simply fell over, he cannot travel tomorrow," said Rosie firmly.

"I don't see how we can cancel a meeting with the President of the United States," replied Middleton with a frown. "These things take a great deal of organising and whatever Frederick was to discuss with him this may be the one and only opportunity."

Middleton was first and foremost a banker. He had, after all, acted as the broker setting up the meeting through the Swiss Ambassador and knew the Baron would expect the meeting to go ahead, whatever the state of Frederick's health.

"Then if he is not in any danger, I shall go and you will accompany me," replied Rosie.

"But we don't know what the meeting was arranged to discuss," said Middleton.

"No, but Frederick does. He will have to brief me," replied Rosie.

The next morning Frederick woke early at 6.30am. He began to think that it had all been a very bad dream until he got out of bed and looked in the mirror. His face was covered in bruises and he had a black eye. He had never had a black eye before and looked pitifully at himself.

Rosie had already taken a light breakfast in her room and she came quickly to the point. Surprisingly Frederick was not at all difficult but insisted that he speak to the manager and arrange for two bodyguards to accompany her and Middleton. Frederick winced as he sat down at a bureau in the room and wrote a letter of introduction to the President and handed Rosie a file of briefing notes. Opening the file, Rosie saw the mark of The de Courcy Bank of Zurich and started reading.

Middleton arrived at 8am and two burly men joined him in the foyer five minutes later. Middleton was briefed by Rosie as far as she could and they set off for Grand Central Station. Scheduled to be rebuilt, Grand Central Station was a hub of activity but looked dilapidated. Rosie was glad they had secured two first class carriages to themselves. On another day she would have enjoyed the journey to Washington, but it was difficult to get out of her head the state that Frederick had been in the day before. She looked out of the window, puzzling over what could have happened to him. She did not believe his story about falling over for one minute.

Arriving in Washington, Rosie could see out of the window that there was little to view as everything was covered in a blanket of snow. They were met at the station by a representative of the Swiss Embassy, who had brought a large carriage. They were staying in the George Washington Hotel, close to the Executive House. Keen to rest before their meeting with the President tomorrow they had a light meal and went to their rooms. One of the bodyguards was positioned outside Rosie's door and a maid slept in an ante-room. Rosie used the time to write letters to her mother and Lord Berkeley to be couriered back to London through the Swiss Embassy and retired to bed early.

Back in New York, Frederick lay having his pulse taken by Alan who was looking suitably concerned. Frederick had taken the opportunity to recount his alarming kidnapping. He had shaken as he visualised the poor wretch's hand being flattened and the sickening thud. He had no idea who had inflicted this terrible ordeal on him but he implored Alan not to talk to the police and told him that he had to be in the foyer at 9am every morning as he had been that very morning – and for what? He had handed the thug a note saying nothing other than he would write again tomorrow as there were no further developments.

"It's no good Alan. After my ordeal with the kidnapping of my child and now to be manhandled myself, my nerves are a wreck. I have made my mind up; I am returning to London and will accompany my wife when we sail in three days time." Alan looked at him and realised there was little point trying to persuade him to stay. He could see that he was on the verge of a nervous breakdown. Instead he prescribed him a mild sedative and left him to sleep.

Elsewhere in the city, Paul Kelly sat smoking a cheroot as he pondered the situation. He had received a note from Cynthia de Courcy, the rather attractive wife of the fop Frederick, regretting that her husband was "indisposed" and they would be unable to join him at his theatre that evening. Kelly had not been able to find out what was wrong with the pathetic man but the doorman, a cousin of one of his henchmen, had said that he had looked as though he had been beaten up and stank, he thought, of urine. He had sent his spies out and hoped for some more news soon.

Rosie awoke with a start at the knocking at the door. Realising where she was, she sat up in bed. Today she would meet the President of the United States!

"Come in," she said.

"Good morning, ma'am. Would you like breakfast?"

It was her maid, a chirpy young girl who had accompanied her from England. Rosie nodded and forced herself to eat a light breakfast, concerned to feel at her best when she met the President. She already had butterflies in her stomach, but she rehearsed in her head what she was going to say over and over again as she dressed carefully, choosing a two piece blue suit. The skirt was a fashionable length to her ankle and she donned small boots in case she had to walk in the snow. The meeting was scheduled at 11am. A coach had called from the Executive House to collect them and they were being transported towards the grand house Rosie had seen in the distance. They were stopped twice as they approached the Executive House to check their identity and the two bodyguards, hired by Frederick, had to wait by the coach when they stopped at the West Gate. It's not surprising they have extensive security, thought Rosie, after all it was less than a year since President McKinley had been assassinated.

Having once again gone through the process of identification, they were shown into a passageway and eventually into a charming oval office with a huge desk near the window and a seating area in the centre of the room. A man came in and introduced himself as Leslie M Shaw, Secretary to the Treasury, and a few minutes later the President came into the room.

Rosie felt her nerves flutter as the introductions were made. Theodore Roosevelt had a slight southern accent but was a charming host. Quickly he set Rosie at her ease and, as they sat having tea, he drew a verbal picture of his family. It seemed to Rosie that she was talking to a kindly uncle but then noted how his mood changed as several other men entered. They were introduced as the Secretary of State, John Haye, and the Treasurer of the US, Ellis H Roberts. Together, with the Secretary of the Treasury, Rosie realised that she had the most important men in America sitting having tea with her. She had asked for Middleton to be present during the discussion but Frederick had overruled her, saying that he was not senior enough to be party to the discussions which were to take place. Alone with the four men, she knew that she had to overcome a degree of natural resistance regarding her station. She was here to conduct important business.

President Roosevelt seemed to sense the shift in her mood.

"Now my dear, despite your charming company, we must get down to business. Do you have a letter for me?"

Rosie passed the President the sealed envelope which he tore open. Firstly, he read the letter penned by Frederick, and then he opened a large envelope by cutting the seal. Silence engulfed the room and Rosie shifted in her seat. In the presence of these powerful men she didn't feel overawed, but she admitted to herself that she wasn't completely at ease, despite her usual self-assured nature. The President passed Frederick's letter and the other letter to John Haye, who read through the document carefully. The process was repeated several other times as the other members of the group looked at the correspondence.

"We will consider the proposal from your father-in-law, the Baron, and deliver our reply to be taken back to Europe and given into his hand only," said the President. He stood and they all did likewise.

"Charmed to meet you Cynthia de Courcy, I hope you are going to enjoy the rest of your visit to our wonderful country."

They shook hands and Rosie, escorted by John Haye, rejoined Middleton in the outer office. A security man then walked with Rosie and Middleton through the many corridors back to the West Gate.

As they walked along Middleton whispered to her, "How did it go?" He had sat frustrated for an hour not to be part of the meeting.

"I did what Frederick asked. There was no discussion," Rosie replied. "The President is a nice man, but I didn't take to one of his aides who seemed very rude, but perhaps that was just his manner."

Ah, thought Middleton, Rosie was always able to make allowances. He could imagine the reaction of a mid western senior official to being confronted by this attractive young woman with her air of self-assurance.

Returning to their Washington hotel they had a light lunch and, as it began snowing, Rosie decided to retire to her room to write some letters to Lady Haversham and the Swiss Ambassador's wife thanking them for their kindness during her stay in America.

Later that afternoon a messenger arrived from the Executive House bearing a sealed package and separately a letter addressed to her. Rosie opened the letter and was surprised to read that Edith Roosevelt had invited her to dinner at the Executive House that evening. Rosie knocked on Middleton's hotel door.

"Did you just receive an invitation for dinner at the Executive House?" she asked.

"Yes, I presume you did as well?"

"How exciting," Rosie said smiling. "I should go and get ready." She sped out of the room, running her wardrobe through her head as she went, leaving Middleton wondering, not for the first time, why it took women three hours to "get ready", before shrugging to himself and returning to paperwork.

Stepping out to the coach, Rosie felt the icy temperature on her face and not for the first time appreciated her warm fur coat. Arriving at the West Gate, they were ushered through the maze of corridors and were shown into a delightful room of pastel shades and luxurious silk curtains. They were the first to arrive, although to Rosie's delight Lady Haversham and Sir Philip entered shortly afterwards. Rosie was glowing in a Paris creation; a lovely gown of lace and taffeta trimmed with blue silk. Sir Philip was not slow to compliment her and Lady Haversham playfully smacked his arm.

"Come on now Philip," she said laughingly. "You are too much an old dog for Cynthia."

Men did gravitate around Rosie and tonight was no exception. She was introduced to several diplomats and their wives, but it was a group of three or four men who surrounded her when the door opened.

"Ladies and Gentlemen," a voice bellowed. "The President of the United States and his wife."

In swept Theodore with a woman Rosie estimated to be in her mid fifties on his arm. The guests were introduced in a line and when they reached Rosie, the President beamed at her.

"Edith, my dear, can I introduce this charming lady from England, Cynthia de Courcy?"

The two women shook hands before the introductions continued. A gong sounded and an orderly withdrawal took place to a room next door, equally as opulent. Set in the centre of the room was a magnificent dining room table and the guests walked around looking for their name on a place card. Rosie was disappointed to find herself sitting next to Leslie M Shaw, the man who had clearly regarded her as a pretty messenger when they had met in the Oval Office earlier. However, as luck would have it, she had a charming Italian diplomat on her left, Count Don Francesco, who regaled her with stories of his youth and several military campaigns. Rosie's laughter was infectious. Even Leslie smiled as the ladies around him responded to the Italian. As the meal came to an end, Rosie had wanted to break the tradition and join the men for a cigar. She had heard that Cuban cigars were the best in the world, but alas she was shepherded off with the ladies for coffee in an ante-room. She did, however, have a five minute conversation with Edith Roosevelt and discovered that the President was about to change the name of the Executive Mansion to the 'White House', an accurate description of the large mansion painted all white. Edith was also keen to show the ladies how the electric chandeliers worked and demonstrated the working telephone.

The evening ended with Theodore and Edith excusing themselves

"We always take an early night – pressures of State," explained Theodore to his guests.

Hands were shaken and the Italian offered to accompany Rosie back to her hotel which she politely declined, although he insisted in escorting her to the coach and kissed her hand elaborately, helping her on board.

Back at the hotel, Middleton escorted her to her room and they parted for the evening, Rosie agreeing that dinner with the President and his wife was certainly a highlight of her trip so far. Smiling to herself, Rosie entered her room. Suddenly a hand gripped her round the mouth and a thickly accented voice sounded in her ear.

"Where is the package?"

Rosie struggled and suddenly felt something sharp against her neck.

"I have a knife at your throat and will not hesitate to kill you. Now where is the package?"

The man released the hand from around her mouth and Rosie could see that her room had been torn apart.

"Where is my maid?" she said, catching her breath and looking around the wreck of her room.

"She's tied and gagged in the bathroom."

Trying to collect her thoughts, Rosie took a breath. "What package are you talking about?"

The man took her wrist and twisted it, making Rosie grimace in pain.

"Now don't make me hurt you..."

She could see him now in the huge mirror on the wall. He was dressed as a bellboy, was about six feet tall and with a dark complexion. Her mind raced.

"Come on," he seemed anxious. "Tell me where the package you brought back from the President is or I will kill you now."

Rosie held up her hand, which shook a little, and nodded slowly.

"I have it locked away. I will give you my key."

The man released her as she picked up her clasp bag. She opened it and in one swift movement fired her Derringer point blank. The man looked down at his chest with surprise on his face, went to move forward and dropped to the floor face downwards. Rosie heard him gurgling but running round him rushed out of the room and began loudly knocking on Middleton's door down the passage. Middleton came to the door in a dressing gown, shocked to see a distraught Rosie standing there. She quickly recounted what had happened and they ran downstairs to reception, where Middleton explained, gesticulating franticly, that Mrs de Courcy had been accosted by a man in her room and they needed the police and a doctor quickly. A stocky looking man walked over.

"Is there a problem?" he showed Middleton an identification card.

"Rosie, this is Agent Hawkins of the American Secret Service."

Rosie explained what had happened and Hawkins used the hotel telephone to summon assistance. Hawkins asked where the package was now and much to his surprise Rosie said that she had placed it in the flush of the toilet suitably wrapped in a waterproof bag. She also remembered her poor maid who was tied up in the bathroom.

"Please look after Margaret," she said anxiously.

"Wait here please," he said and left them to go up to Rosie's hotel room. After what seemed like a long wait, the police arrived and Agent Hawkins returned with the package, which was dripping water.

"Do you have a hotel safe?" he asked the night manager, who led him to a room behind the reception desk and he made arrangements to lock the package in the safe, but insisted that he keep the key, much to the disquiet of the manager.

Agent Hawkins returned to Middleton and Rosie.

"Well, you are a good shot lady, the man is dead."

Rosie had seen death before and was familiar with the rough house of the concert hall and the streets of London, but still she wobbled at the news. She had killed a man! The police were briefed by Agent Hawkins and, whilst they insisted on a further statement, Rosie was thankful that the agent was nearby as she suspected she would have been arrested otherwise. She was unable to discuss the reason for the man breaking into her room as the Secret Service agent had reminded her that this must be kept secret from the local police. In the end it was a combination of Agent Hawkins and another man who arrived later, who was introduced as the Chief of Police, who finally escorted Rosie to her room to endeavour to get some sleep. She insisted that her maid slept in the same hotel suite and Agent Hawkins reassured her that he would be outside her door in the foyer all night with two policemen who would stand guard.

Still it was hard for Rosie to drift into sleep that night. She kept seeing the man's hand around her mouth and the slight cut on her neck itched, a reminder of how frighteningly close she'd been to danger. As she went over the events in her mind, she realised that there was a part of her that had relished the drama, even while feeling scared. She told herself off repeatedly, but couldn't ignore the fact that she had had a sense of enjoyment with the adrenaline rush.

The following day, shortly after breakfast, the Secretary of State, John Haye, arrived. The news of the previous night had reached him.

"My dear, on behalf of the President, can I say how sorry we are that you were subjected to this attack on your person. We have appointed four agents to provide protection for you round the clock and they will accompany you back to New York and to your ship until departure."

"Who was that man?" asked Rosie.

"We don't know, probably just a thief who thought there was money in the package."

The man had taken a great deal of risk for what he thought might be money in the package, thought Rosie, but she bit her tongue and smiled up at the Secretary of State politely, keeping her musings to herself.

Chapter Thirteen

Return To England

Rosie waved to Middleton as the ship edged clear of the dock. She would miss his company. Lord and Lady Haversham had also accompanied them to the ship but Frederick had disappeared just as they had arrived aboard. Rosie didn't realise that he had been sitting in Alan's coach saying a fond farewell. As the ship was manoeuvred up the channel by two robust tugs Frederick joined Rosie at the rail.

"Good to see the back of that place," he said, staring at the disappearing dock.

Rosie turned around and looked at him. He had been behaving very strangely since his 'fall' – another incident she didn't believe. He had stunk of urine. She knew the smell from the drunks outside the music halls and she sensed he was frightened, very frightened of something or someone.

"I enjoyed the visit, but not the incident in Washington." She touched her neck.

"Yes, it must have been most unpleasant," said Frederick absent mindedly.

Rosie stared at him. Unpleasant? It's as though he doesn't really care, she thought. Was that it?

"Mr & Mrs de Courcy?"

Rosie turned as First Officer Kilbrade moved alongside of them.

"The Captain sends his compliments and asks you to join him for dinner this evening," he smirked and tipped his cap.

"We will be delighted," muttered Frederick.

Rosie thought to herself that delighted he might be, but it was most unlikely that Frederick would join them for dinner. Had he forgotten how bad a sailor he was? However, she would go. It was always interesting talking to the Captain's guests.

Earlier, Rosie had seen Tore coming up the gangplank with two burly looking men and knew that the case they held contained a considerable amount of money. Then she had been surprised to see Randolph Churchill. She knew him from various social functions but where was Lady Churchill? The next few days should prove to be very interesting. She was looking forward to going home.

Rosie made a special effort for dinner that evening dressing in a striking, low cut, red silk dress underneath her wrap. Frederick had indeed succumbed to seasickness shortly after they left the harbour and remained in the cabin. The ship was lurching from side to side as Rosie took her seat at the Captain's table. The seating plan had been changed, taking into account Frederick's indisposition, and Rosie found herself sitting next to Jennie Churchill. She liked Jennie; she was very beautiful even though she was at least fifty. The gentleman on her right was an American who the Captain introduced as Morgan Rydell. He seemed familiar, but barely spoke two words. This was not the normal effect she had on men, so Rosie was intrigued and endeavoured to engage him in conversation.

The Captain apologised for the 'tricky dining conditions' as he called them. They had sailed into a force seven gale.

"Still not too bad," he said cheerfully as the boat rocked with the swell.

Looking around the sumptuous dining room, Rosie spied Tore across the room. Briefly their gaze met and he smiled. She found herself looking away – why did she do that? Thank goodness First Officer Kilbrade was not on the table. After his attempt to kiss her on the outward journey she had felt a strange thrill to see him again, yet she had a reluctance to be alone with him.

Jennie Churchill inched closer to Rosie.

"Have you seen Edward recently?" she asked quietly. Rosie knew she meant the king – Edward VII.

"I had the honour of meeting him at the Lord Mayor's ordination, at Mansion House in November," replied Rosie.

"Ah yes. No, I meant socially." Lady Churchill smiled at her.

Rosie paused – Jennie was searching for something, what was it?

"He attended a production of "As you Like It" at the Old Vic theatre shortly before Christmas. I was in the next box and he was kind enough to ask my father and I to join him," replied Rosie.

Jennie Churchill picked up her napkin and dabbed her mouth.

"And was he with anyone?" she asked.

Rosie knew now where the conversation was going. The king had a string of mistresses and it was rumoured Jennie was one of them. Gossip said the Queen knew about his dalliances and turned a blind eye. Rosie was not immune to the King's gaze. He had indicated, on more than one occasion, that he would like a private meeting. It had not come about because she knew he was having an affair with Lily Langtree, her friend, and she would not do anything to upset her. She thought back to that night at the theatre.

Jenny whispered, "And who did you say he was with?" Rosie saw no reason for secrecy.

"He was dining with Alice Keppel," she replied.

"Alice Keppel. She's a recent friend of the King?"

"I only met her that night. I didn't know her before then. Were you in New York on business?" Rosie asked, changing the subject.

"Randolph was, and I met my aunt," replied Jennie. Suddenly the table lurched wildly but fortunately dinner was over.

"I suggest, Ladies and Gentlemen, you adjourn to the card room. I must apologise, but I must attend the bridge," said the Captain. Everyone stood as he left.

"Do you play cards Cynthia?" asked Randolph.

"Poorly, I'm afraid."

"Come now, join Jennie and I for a game of bridge."

Reluctantly Rosie made up a four with the Churchills and another guest. She didn't talk much during bridge as she found she needed all her wits about her to remember the game and follow the bidding. Luckily she didn't have to play a game herself as Randolph, who partnered her, was a very skilful player, so much so that they won by two rubbers to one before Jennie declared she felt tired and wanted to retire to her cabin. Lord Randolph offered to escort Rosie to her cabin but she declined saying that she wanted a breath of fresh air on the deck.

Opening the outside door, Rosie realised she wouldn't be outside very long. The ship continued to sway alarmingly and the howling of the wind was incredible.

Suddenly she felt someone hold her arm.

"I think you would be wise to retire to your cabin."

She looked round to see who had hold of her and was concerned to see Kilbrade, the First Officer.

"Oh, don't worry I won't accost you," he laughed as he saw her expression.

Gently, but firmly he escorted Rosie to her cabin and saluting, he smiled and wished her a good evening.

As she settled in her cabin for the night, her thoughts skipped ahead to home. She had only been away three weeks but missed her daughter's delightful smile and incessant chatter. How was her baby, she wondered. She had been surprised how easily she had enjoyed herself away from her children and was somewhat disappointed in what she thought must be a lack of maternal feelings. She had thought often about her children, but not with a sense of loss, all except for the hurt she felt when she thought about her missing son, George. She loved her children, but knew that she also loved her independent life. Her mother had chided her once or twice about leaving the children so often in the "care of others". But she liked her exciting lifestyle. The Baron had been very keen to extend her business acumen. Her father had positively encouraged her to continue her education and even now she was learning Italian and Spanish. She knew she had an amazing memory and preferred to learn languages using a tutor as they practiced the spoken word and she did not have to pour over books of verbs. She thrived on a busy schedule, but was unsure how that reflected on her as a mother. She sighed and decided not to puzzle the matter any further for that evening; after all, soon she would be home and in the company of her family once more.

The rest of the crossing was uneventful. Frederick remained closeted in the cabin looking very peaky. He seemed to survive on soup and water, but rarely ventured out of the cabin to get any fresh air, but Rosie was able to walk the first class deck often with the Churchills.

She had another brief encounter with Kilbrade, who made it more than obvious that he needed only the slightest hint to make an advance, but she walked away. Tore kept out of her way, travelling steerage. He could not enter the first class lounge, but she saw him from a distance. He didn't seem to see her and once he was laughing loudly with a redhead who was clinging to his arm.

Morton Rydell, the man she had met on the first night, was always closely in attendance and Rosie continued to rack her mind as to where she had seen him – and then it came to her. She had seen him at the Executive House, or the White House as the President had renamed his residence. She frowned to herself. What was he doing here?

Docking at Liverpool they journeyed to London by train. She didn't see the Churchills again but Mr Rydell and Tore, with his two companions, got on the London train and she saw them in the first class compartment.

Frederick improved almost the moment his feet touched dry land and was actually laughing and joking with the conductor and enjoying a sandwich shortly after the train left Liverpool mainline station. By the time they reached London, he was completely recovered. Rosie was reflecting on one evening aboard the ship when she overheard Captain McKie telling Randolph Churchill that someone had attempted to break into the safe in the Purser's office. The Purser had caught the person in the act and had been hit over the head and was apparently in the infirmary. It turned out that the Purser's assailant had been wearing a mask but he thought his hands suggested he was, as he put it, "a dusky gentleman". She had noticed at the time that Mr Rydell suddenly sat bolt upright showing interest and he asked a question.

"Have you searched the ship for the thief?"

"Yes," replied Captain McKie, "but to no avail. We did not have a good description and there are dozens of men on board who are, shall we say, of overseas origin."

"Have you put a guard in the purser's office?"

The Captain shifted in his seat becoming a little perturbed by Rydell's questioning.

"Well, no," he replied.

"Captain, can I see you privately for a moment?" said Rydell.

Rydell and the Captain moved off and when they returned there was no further talk of the attempted theft. Rosie had thought that strange at the time and mentioned the conversation to Frederick, as they had deposited jewellery and the President's letter in the Purser's safe. Frederick, suffering from his sickness, was not really interested in safes or theft and Rosie was not able to have a serious conversation with him about anything. He had continually moaned that death would be a welcome relief to his suffering and Rosie had decided that he was quite a wimp at sea. It was during their journey home that she finally realised she was no longer in love with Frederick. Admitting the truth to herself, she felt a strange sense of relief. However, she had the children to consider and she would never break up the marriage. She knew many couples who remained married publicly, but privately went their own way taking lovers and living separate lives, perhaps she should do the same...

When they reached London's Euston station, Rydell, who had by now introduced himself as an American Secret Service Agent, offered to accompany Frederick to Zurich to deliver the President's letter to the Baron. Frederick was delighted to have the extra security and readily agreed. Rosie did not see Rydell again.

Chapter Fourteen

May 1904

The winter of 1903 was very harsh, the cold and damp weather stretching into March 1904. Molly, Rosie's mother, had buried her sister Kate and much to their dismay, Alfred, one of her sister Nelly's boys, had been sent to prison. He had rather foolishly been stealing a load of bananas from Tilbury dock when he was caught by the police. Rosie had noticed that her mother did not seem to be her usual self and decided that she needed something big to cheer her up.

In the midst of so much bad news, Rosie was determined to give her mother a happy birthday and had organised a good old knees-up at the "Old Bull" public house in Stepney. Taking over the upstairs room she had invited her brothers, Billy and Freddie, her sister Alice and her cousins, Steffie and Sammy. Charlie's brothers Wellington and Nelson and his sisters Victoria and Elizabeth, together with their children, were also coming.

"All in all it should be a right grand do," said Rosie's sister Alice.

Molly hadn't seen such a gathering of her own and Jack's family since his funeral and it was good to catch up, despite the dubious background of some of their relatives. She knew her sister Nelly's girls were street walkers, but what could she do? She had got them both jobs at the match factory and also at the music hall in Shoreditch, Steffie selling cigarettes and Sammy as a hat check girl. Both had only lasted two weeks before getting up to their old habits and management had sacked them.

"Sorry Molly," said Frank Naylor, the manager, "but I can't have girls on the game in the hall. You know the police have been itching to raid me."

And now their brother Alfred had been sent down for stealing a load of bananas. The silly idiot, thought Rosie. Unfortunately, she knew that being 'light fingered' was something of a family trait. Her father Jack's two brothers, somewhat amusingly named Wellington and Nelson, worked the docks at St. Katherine's and both sailed close to the line, pilfering and working on the 'finder's, keepers' system. If any goods fell out of the large containers, or if something was conveniently broken, they would try to smuggle it out of the docks. As much of the dockyard lived on the odd bit of 'nicking', as they put it, a blind eye was generally turned. However, pinching pistols made in Belgium was quite a different matter. Rosie listened, half exasperated and half amused, as her uncles argued about their latest exploit.

"You're an idiot. The guns have been missed and now we've got bobbies and customs all over us like a rash."

Just a normal quiet family evening, thought Rosie, grinning despite herself. Her life had taken her on a very different path in recent years and she enjoyed a level of grandeur she could not have imagined as a child. However, she had found herself able to fit back into her former world with the same ease that had helped her to adapt to dealing with the upper echelons of society.

She turned to her brother Billy, wanting to talk to him about Molly's health. She had noticed that her mother didn't seem herself lately and had developed a persistent cough that Rosie did not like.

"I gave her the money to see Doc Randal but I know she hasn't been," said Rosie, shaking her head.

"Well, you know Mum, if she don't want to do somethin', she just won't," replied Billy.

Freddie joined them with a pint of dark ale in his hand.

"Cheers Sis, thanks for doin this."

Freddie was the oldest brother, but you wouldn't know it. When they had been having private school tuition, paid for unbeknown to them by Lord Berkeley, Freddie had skipped every lesson, preferring to sell fruit in the market or push around a fish barrow for old Mr Grime. Billy had made an effort and could read, write and was reasonably confident at maths. This had meant that the younger of the two brothers had risen to take over their father's union position. At the moment, he was gravely concerned about his uncles. There was a rumour that one of them had filched a score of new pistols from a crate which had split open in St K's dock.

Billy knew that the police wouldn't let it go lightly and were already all over St Katherine's with customs.

"Sooner or later someone will welch on them," he thought to himself, moving alongside Wellington. He liked his Dad's oldest brother

"Wells," he said in a low voice, calling him by the family version of his name. "Rumour has it you and Nels have been nickin' guns at St K's."

"What do you mean, boy?" His uncle turned towards him.

"Don't act on your high horse, I'm just warning you that if you are involved get rid now. The bobbies are at the docks as we talk and someone will grass you for a fiver."

Wellington nodded and moved off.

Rosie had hired a conjurer, who was showing tricks to the children, and as jellied eels were being consumed by everybody, Big John McCready, who ran the downstairs bar, rushed up to Billy.

"Bobbies downstairs looking for your Nelson," he said hurriedly.

Billy turned around to warn Nelson when the door crashed in and a dozen or more bobbies, all dressed in blue, poured in holding their truncheons.

Billy knew their Sergeant, a burly man, who he often slipped some contraband or a bottle of something.

"Welcome George I didn't know you knew Molly, my mother."

"Sorry Billy, didn't know your Mum was here. Just heard your Dad's brother Nelson was around."

"What you want him for George? He's family you know." Billy glared at the policeman who recognised the warning.

"Rumour has it, he nicked some guns from St K's," said the policemen.

"Well rumour's wrong George. Now I would be obliged if you would take your boys and have a drink on me downstairs, so my Mum can continue her party in peace."

The sergeant looked around him and nodded, disappearing back downstairs. Billy breathed a sigh of relief. Nelson was lucky; the inspector of police would not have been so easy. He liked his uncle but fancy nickin' guns. He would arrange for them to be found in the corner of the warehouse in St K's tomorrow, then the heat would be off.

Molly had watched the police activity with great interest. It wasn't the first time the police had interrupted a family 'do' and it probably wouldn't be the last. She felt tired and excused herself early, with Rosie and her sister Alice taking her home. Alice was concerned; she had been nursing for over five years now and had seen many cases of consumption. She had discovered her mother had started coughing up blood and had tried to convince her that she must see a doctor, but Molly could be a stubborn woman and had resisted her daughter's entreaties.

Alice took the opportunity to talk to Rosie about her fears and they agreed a little subterfuge was called for. The next day, on the pretext that she was visiting her grandson, Rosie sent a coach for Molly to bring her to Eaton Square. Waiting for her there was Lord Berkeley's personal physician. Molly argued, but it was no good, she'd been tricked. To Rosie's relief, she consented to an examination. The doctor did not hesitate in his diagnosis: Molly had tuberculosis and was sent immediately to a sanatorium in Kent.

Molly was forty seven when she died.

Many people said it was the biggest funeral procession anyone had ever seen in the East End. Every road in Stepney from St. Bedes Church to the graveside were two, sometimes three deep with people who wanted to pay their last respects. Afterwards at the wake, Billy said over two hundred people called and not for a free glass of something. All had something good to say about the "Angel from Islington". Molly had been an Islington girl and was Christened Angel. She used Molly as she found 'Angel' pretentious and, in any case, it insulted God. At the wake afterwards tears flowed and much beer was consumed. Lord Berkeley attended the funeral and laid a large wreath on her grave which read "Gone, but never forgotten, you are sleeping with the angels now, I will love you forever", simply signed "B".

It was Alice who forced Rosie to understand that it was not her fault. "The Holders are an independent lot," she said. "You gave Mum a row of houses where all the family lived, plenty of cash and she never went without anything and most of all the grandchildren. She loved your kids you know".

Rosie had tried to get her Mum to live with her many times but she just said, "My roots are in the East End luv. I can't be doin with rich houses and maids and the like".

Afterwards Father Dolan, who had conducted the service, told Rosie that Molly was the largest benefactor in the area. Hundreds of children had been helped by her generosity. Rosie knew it was the money she sent every week which her Mum doled out – but it didn't matter. Life was different somehow after Molly died. Rosie felt a great emptiness. Her mother had always been there for her and was like her rock – now who did she have?

Rosie first met Amy Rydell at a very heated meeting of the Women's League for Reform in May 1905. The League was a small splinter group who demanded more aggressive action in the fight for women's rights and particularly votes for women. Rosie had been invited to a closed "meeting" by Christabel Pankhurst, one of Emilee's daughters who also favoured, as she put it, a more hawk-like approach. Sometimes Rosie thought women involved in the movement were far too aggressive. She found gentle diplomacy more effective. Only last week, at a dinner party she had hosted for her Father, Lord Berkeley, to welcome the Italian Prime Minister, she had spent an interesting ten minutes discussing the subject of votes for women with Mr Lloyd George. Some of her arguments he was prepared to support but Mr Winston Churchill, on her left at the dinner party, was totally against the emancipation rights of women. This prompted a lively discussion; always with a twinkle in his eye, Winston provoked the debate. Lloyd George on the other hand did admit that it was inevitable that women would be given the vote and our society would change. Women were, he suggested, in a strong position in the boudoir and such attractive advocates were bound to bring concessions. But that's all he talked about – concessions. He conceded women should have more rights in the event of divorce. Whilst not going so far as was proposed by many of the more extreme views of some women for equal matrimonial rights, he agreed that assets of the partnership, as he called it, should be divided, but not equally. He and Churchill laughed at several of Rosie's suggestions that the women should have exclusive rights to keep the children after divorce. What would have happened to society, they suggested, if Rosie's proposal had been law. Children brought up by women. Or worse still, introduced to a home with other men who were not their father and able to influence them.

"No," Winston argued, "better to leave these things as they are." But losing many of the points of an argument, if you were a woman, was to be expected with most of the leading politicians having an entrenched and even old-fashioned view and from rather traditional English families, so Rosie just smiled.

Rosie liked Winston. He was a bold and almost reckless man, yet he had the ability to hold a group of people spellbound, even if they didn't agree with a word he said, which I'm afraid was frequently the case.

So there was, quietly working behind the scenes, a women's movement, not in the public domain, of women getting themselves arrested, throwing stones, knocking off policeman's hats or parading with placards, but nevertheless doing their bit to persuade politicians to consider votes for women.

The meeting today in Trafalgar Square had been called by Emilee Pankhurst and was attended by most of the more vocal, and from what Rosie could see, more anarchist women who advocated extreme action. Controlling these groups was a problem. Emilee, standing on her upturned soapbox, argued that at the moment public opinion was moving in their favour, however, they should refrain from violent actions which would result in a reversal and set back the cause, perhaps for ever. Some women, including Amy, who Rosie had met briefly, did not agree.

Given the passionate opinions it was perhaps inevitable that a break-away group of women would jostle, and that's all it was, with some policemen. When the first helmet went flying pandemonium broke loose. The police, who up until then had simply been standing by, moved into the group of women, one of which was Rosie. She found herself lifted up by a burly policeman and carted off to a police wagon. Dumped rather unceremoniously in the back of one of these "meat wagons", as these horse drawn vans were known, she found herself next to Amy who was rubbing a rather wicked bruise on her cheek. "Ah," Amy said, "diplomacy not working then Rosie?"

"Are you hurt?" Rosie replied

"One of the policemen didn't welcome having his helmet knocked off and hit me with his truncheon," said Amy.

"How could knocking off a helmet by a woman justify the heavy-handed response? Let me take a look?" she said. Then the door to the coach opened and two more women were dumped on their back on the floor of the van, which began to move. Amy and Rosie and the other women were taken to a cell in Bow Street Police Station. Rosie asked for some water and a young constable brought her a bowl and a piece of cloth that looked like it had seen better days. As she bathed Amy's cheek, which had swollen up considerably, Rosie realised that Amy was gazing into her eyes.

"What's up?" she asked

"Oh, nothing. You've just got such pretty eyes." Rosie stopped attending her face and looked at her, almost for the first time. Amy had short hair, not fashionable at that time, high cheekbones and wore no makeup, but had an attractive face, striking but perhaps not considered to be beautiful.

"You sound as though you're teasing me Amy Rydell" said Rosie. Suddenly Amy kissed her. Rosie was completely taken aback. She had never been kissed by a woman before and flushed.

"Don't tell me you didn't know I fancied you?"

"What, what do you mean?"

"You've seen me looking at you many times. Didn't you realise I fancied you?"

"No," Rosie stammered. "I'm sorry, I didn't"

"Oh, not to worry," and she changed the subject. Fortunately for Rosie Lord Berkeley received a telephone call from the nice young constable and dashed down to the police station. Not for the first time he arranged for Rosie to be released after her two hour stay, during which she found out much about Amy.

Amy had been brought up by her strict father after her mother died of typhoid. Her father had run a plantation in the Americas, but in 1895 he had returned to England when his wife died. She told me that he was a strict Presbyterian and sought a new wife in Wales. He found one, a woman who schemed for his affection. He didn't realise that was going on, of course, and when she became Mrs Rydell things changed for Amy. Amy had been schooled in America but the new Mrs Rydell decided she should attend Cheltenham Ladies College for some "refining", as she put it. Shipped off to a boarding school, Amy hardly saw her father after that. Still, boarding school was fun. She later told Rosie, "You've no idea what goes on when young girls are starved of male company," and laughed. At the time, Rosie had no idea what she had meant. Amy explained that her stepmother had created a distance between her father and herself. He had always been strict but loved his daughter and showed her affection. However, her stepmother was now in complete control but she hadn't reckoned with Amy's quick temper and one day after her stepmother had insulted her mother once too often, Amy lashed out slapping her around the face. That was the beginning of the end and her father had to choose. Amy was summoned and a day later told that she was being given a trust fund of a thousand pounds a year and that she was to leave Cheltenham College and go out to work in London. Her father made it pretty clear that he washed his hands of her. She didn't cry, thought Rosie when she was telling me this, just sat stone-faced showing no real emotion. Amy had told her that fortunately her real mother had a sister in London, Aunt Matilda, who lived in Knightsbridge and it was with Aunt Matilda that she went to live. A spinster of the Parish, Aunt Matilda was a fiery personality, but Amy discovered a hard shell with a soft centre. Aunt Matilda had loved her mother and argued bitterly with her father, Amy's grandfather, against the marriage of her mother and her father. She recognised a side of Amy's father only too evident as time went on, a bully and a religious fanatic. When Amy was born it transpired that he "upped sticks" as Aunt Matilda put it, and left for America to take his wife and baby as far away as possible. Aunt Matilda was not surprised he had remarried. "Such men have to have a constant house-keeper, they can control," although Amy doubted her father had chosen wisely this time! Amy explained to Rosie that she still lived with her frail aunt, who she clearly loved dearly and there was sadness in Amy's voice as she talked about the old lady.

Rosie found leaving Amy in the jail that day was not easy. In two hours Amy had formed an impression which stayed with you. She urged her father, Lord Berkeley, to use his influence to get her released and bless his heart, he did. A week later a note came from Amy inviting her to tea at her Aunt's house in Knightsbridge. Rosie sent back an acceptance and it was with some eagerness that she went for tea that day. She even found herself dressing very carefully and wearing one of her striking red dresses and a superb feather hat.

Amy greeted her at the front door like a long lost friend, kissing her French style on both cheeks. "So good of you to come." She looked at Rosie "And don't you look good enough to eat?" she laughed. Amy had an infectious laugh and Rosie giggled with her. She was expecting to meet Auntie but Amy told her that they had the house to themselves as Auntie had gone to Bath in Somerset to "test the waters" as she put it. Auntie's rheumatics and headaches were, it seemed, getting worse and she had heard that the waters in Bath might help her. Amy and Rosie chatted over tea like old friends talking about suffragettes, mutual acquaintances and the women's cause. Amy gazed silently when Rosie spoke about her children and Rosie found herself, for the first time in years, recounting the story of the kidnapping of her son. A tear ran down Rosie's cheek as she thought about her son and suddenly found herself in Amy's arms as she held her tightly. Gently she kissed her cheek, her lips and her head. She stroked her head and spoke words of comfort as Rosie sobbed her heart out. In hindsight, thought Rosie, it was probably Frederick's complete lack of affection for many years that led to her affair with Amy. Whereas Frederick never so much as held her hand, Amy drew her in, caressed her, stroked her and showed love. Amy was a proficient lover and that day and night they made love and for the first time for many months Rosie exploded with orgasms. For so long Rosie had waited for a lover to ignite her passions and Amy's gentle touch was perfect. Later Rosie would reflect that Amy always wore trousers and she laughed when she said to Rosie, "We are the first women to wear trousers you know."

Their affair lasted nearly a year until that fateful day. Auntie had died the previous winter, a blessed relief Amy said, although Rosie doubted she meant it. Rosie had been seeing Count Von Baston, the German Ambassador, for some time. Since her affair had started with Amy she had not had a male lover, but the Count – he was irresistible. In his forties, he was typically Germanic, but with a sense of humour not normally associated with that race. Tall, dark and very handsome. Rosie found herself falling into a pool when she looked into his black eyes. These things are sometimes inevitable, particularly if you are sharing an un-loving relationship, and when one day the Count and Rosie found themselves having to meet on business, it was a very short step to his Excellence's bedroom. To be loved by a man, Rosie had almost forgotten what it was like. The Count was a well built man whose physique was matched by his ardour. Passionate and gentle, he made love as though painting a picture, his brush strokes being one minute thrusting and next relaxed. Amy did not know of Rosie's affair with the Count and Rosie did not inform the Count about Amy. She chose to keep both her lovers in ignorance of each other until that fateful day. Rosie did not realise that Amy kept a record of such things. But one day she asked her when she last had the "curse" as she put it. Rosie replied that she didn't really know, but Amy did. "You're overdue," she said staring at her in a way she had never seen before.

"Oh my God," Rosie thought. She made an excuse and rushed away. She knew it would be foolish to jump to conclusions but Amy was right. It was two months since she last had a period. Rosie decided to consult a doctor, not the family doctor in Harley Street, but another doctor she had seen advertising in Wigmore Street. She had heard from other various ladies about Dr Marsh, a discreet man, who it seemed was also prepared to carry out a termination. Rosie's examination proved positive, "Hell's teeth," she thought, "she was pregnant. What to do, what to do?" The only person she thought to turn to was Amy. That was a big mistake. Amy's attitude to her had changed. She was cold, aloof and very angry. She told Rosie how she had hurt her and in the end there was a furious argument and Rosie had no choice but to leave. That was the last time Rosie saw her and as she tearfully left the Knightsbridge house her chauffeur, Hinds, gently asked "Is everything all right?" and Rosie was brought back down to earth with a thud.

"No, it is not all right," but she didn't elaborate.

Rosie struggled with her secret for two weeks, not knowing if she should terminate, but she knew time was running out. Frederick was in Zurich when she decided to go and talk to her father, Lord Berkeley. She knew if her mother was alive she would be furious and would not understand and certainly would never condone an abortion; it was to Lord Berkeley she turned.

Lord Berkeley was in a good mood that day. He had just attended a meeting at the Bank of England and it seemed interest rates were to be held, despite some reservations. People like Randolph Churchill were pressing for more money to be spent on armaments, but the country could ill afford such expenditure. In any case the country and the dominions were adequately controlled, even if Africa and India were a problem from time to time. Now he looked forward to his daughter coming for afternoon tea. Lord Berkeley pondered whether Rosie would bring her son, Frederick Junior, his grandson, as he was conscious that fairly shortly, as the Baron had intended, his grandson would be whisked away to a Swiss school.

He knew his daughter had something on her mind as soon as he saw her and rather anxiously he sat waiting for her to talk. She started slowly "Father Berkeley," she always called him that when they were alone. "I have a problem, a quite unexpected problem and I need your confidential advice."

"Of course, my dear," he leaned forward and took her hand. "What is it? A problem with Frederick?"

"No, why do you ask that?"

"No reason, what is it my dear, do tell me." Suddenly, she blurted it out.

"I am pregnant!" Lord Berkeley, momentarily taken aback, dropped her hand.

"What's that you say dear?"

"I am pregnant and Frederick is not the father." Lord Berkeley sat back taking in the news.

"Then who is the father?" Rosie slowly explained that she and Frederick had not shared the matrimonial bed for two years. She had not sought affection in the arms of another man, it just happened. Lord Berkeley listened. "Yes, but who is this man?"

"It is Count Von Baston, the German Ambassador." Lord Berkeley shut his eyes. Yes he knew the man, older than his daughter. She would have been a conquest he would have enjoyed.

"Does he know the child is his?"

"No, father I have not discussed this with anyone."

"Well what do you want to do?" he asked

"I don't know, I would love to have another baby but the scandal – the Baron – ." She didn't need to finish her sentence. "Yes, he will not welcome a new addition from the loins of the German Ambassador." Lord Berkeley sat thinking, while Rosie remained silent, something she struggled with, but had learnt when negotiating business matters or at board meetings.

"Wait here," said Lord Berkeley and got up and left the room. Minutes later he returned with an envelope in his hand. "Now I would not normally have shown you this dossier, but I feel that it is now important you know certain things about Frederick." He handed Rosie a large file he had taken from the envelope. "Read this, but don't react until you've finished it." As she read about her husband Rosie felt physically sick. The more she read the worse she felt. Finally she said, "Father I must go to the bathroom." He nodded, saddened that he had judged it necessary to present the daughter he loved with this awful document of deceit, lies and infidelity. Rosie came back, slightly pale, but composed and continued reading. Now and again gasping at the significance of some of the words as they hit her.

She put down the report, feeling as though her world was over, and cried, for only the second time since George had been taken. Lord Berkeley moved forward to comfort her. "Come now, I had to show you the document about Frederick. It may change the course of action you take. I should tell you that I did not undertake to find out these things lightly. It was when a boy approached me, as I stepped from my carriage and asked me for money to keep quiet about my son-in-law, that I knew something was wrong. Even then I collected this information discreetly and I hope you will agree I did not change in attitude or demeanour towards Frederick, your husband and father of your children." Rosie looked up and abruptly stopped crying.

"I should have realised something was amiss. He never spent five minutes with me in my bed since, well, over two years ago," she said, shaking her head as it all made sense.

"Do not reproach yourself. I am surprised you resisted the countless men, who I observe at all occasions trying to opportune you. Even the king, I saw make a discreet advance and yet you remained faithful. This situation is regrettable yet not a disaster." Lord Berkeley continued, "When is Frederick due back to London?"

"He is returning from Paris – and his lover," she added tersely, "this weekend, by boat train from Dover."

"Then the matter will wait until Sunday. This is what we will do – "

Frederick was not surprised to be lunching with Rosie and Lord Berkeley. His father-in-law lavished attention on Rosie and the children. Whereas his own father was more aloof and distant, Lord Berkeley was affectionate with the children who clearly adored him. They enjoyed an excellent duck and a fine claret from Lord Berkeley's cellar and after lunch retired to the library. Frederick was surprised when Lord Berkeley asked Rosie to join them; he had assumed they would be smoking cigars. Lord Berkeley offered him a Cuban cigar which he accepted, cut off the end and looked up as Rosie entered. "Don't think this is for you old girl," said Frederick.

"On the contrary," said Lord Berkeley, "I have asked Rosie to join us. Sit down my dear." Lord Berkeley got up, went to the bureau and brought back a file which he handed to Frederick.

"What's this?" asked Frederick somewhat taken aback.

"Read it," as Lord Berkeley handed Frederick the thick folder that Rosie had previously read, Frederick took the folder and somewhat gingerly opened it and began reading. Suddenly his face turned white and a twitch began flicking under his right eye. He gripped the report, his knuckles showing white and then threw it down.

"This is disgusting, none of this is true!" he spluttered moving to get up.

"Sit down Frederick!" barked Lord Berkeley. "I assumed you would deny a great deal of the content, that is why I have affidavits, sworn testimonials, photographs of you and various people in compromising positions and even your lover in New York, Dr Rees has signed a sworn statement."

"What! I don't believe you." Frederick was white faced and shaky.

"Let's not argue the facts Frederick, we wish to discuss with you the solution. Firstly though, I want you to read all the contents of this folder. I want you to realise we know everything, read it – now!" ordered Lord Berkeley. Lord Berkeley was a very commanding man and reluctant as Frederick was, he found himself picking up the report. It also gave him some time to think, what did they want? Divorce? He finished the report and felt sick. Lord Berkeley handed him a brandy and he gulped the first part down.

"Now," he paused, "that wasn't so bad, was it?" said Lord Berkeley. "You understand that all your activities – are known."

"I have something to tell you," said Rosie. Frederick had not looked at her until that moment. He felt ashamed and like a schoolboy caught with his fingers in the cookie jar.

"Frederick are you listening?" said Lord Berkeley. Frederick nodded.

"I am pregnant," Rosie announced matter of factly, "and I am proposing to keep the child." He looked at her blankly, not registering the information. "Frederick, did you hear me? I am pregnant and we know that the father is not you," said Rosie. Frederick gawped at her.

"You're pregnant? Who is the father?" he asked.

"All you need to know is that the man is of an aristocratic blood line," said Lord Berkeley.

"I don't see that you need to know," said Rosie

"Well what do you want?" He began to regain his composure. He was not his father's son for nothing as he realised that the situation had changed. Lord Berkeley watched the colour return to his cheeks and knew that his mind was calculating and assimilating the information and he was searching to turn it to his advantage. Frederick looked at Rosie. "You know the Baron will never accept a bastard child," he hissed feeling confident now. Rosie began to get angry; something she promised herself she would not do.

"Now see here Frederick," she said. "This is all your fault. Your fondness for boys and men and absence from our matrimonial bed, led me to fall for a real man," she paused, "however, I have a proposition for you."

"Go on," Frederick listened attentively; this could all work out well. His foibles out in the open, no more creeping around, no more fear of discovery by his wife and he could continue to meet his boyfriends.

Rosie continued: "You have a certain way of life that it is obvious you cannot change. I need love from a man that will care for me and I want to have this baby." Lord Berkeley sensed that she was beginning to struggle and he continued.

"Listen carefully Frederick. In return for continuing to look as though you have a normal marriage in public, Rosie will continue as your consort. She will act as your wife for all intent and purposes, except in the boudoir. She will act as your hostess and keep your secret life from all, including your father and as they grow up your children. In return," continued Lord

Berkeley, "you will not expose the unborn child as illegitimate and will in the public persona treat the child as your own. The child will bear your name and you will give your word that you will not divulge the truth – ever!"

"You can continue your lifestyle," Rosie continued as she looked at him disgustedly, as he looked away from her gaze, "but don't bring your lovers into my house or risk notoriety by being exposed, as surely you will go to prison, especially if you remain in England." The last thought had occurred to Frederick before. It was still a serious criminal offence to have sex with a man in England, punishable by a lengthy prison sentence, even though he knew of numerous judges, peers of the realm and even royalty who were inclined towards boys. He knew the court in England would jail him and his father's influence, even if he were to provide help, would be to no avail.

"Your father will remain blissfully ignorant," added Lord Berkeley, "so there you have it Frederick. The possibility of public notoriety, never being able to set foot inside England again, the risk of your father disinheriting you and casting you out and a painful public divorce for the de Courcy Bank. All that can be avoided if you sign this agreement." Frederick thought for a moment. Yes they had most of the cards, but he still had some.

"So," he looked this time directly at Rosie. "I can carry on my lifestyle – you will not interfere. I can live where I like and in return you have this bastard and I give it my name." Rosie was shocked by his stark summary of the situation but nodded slowly.

"Yes, and Frederick, I may or may not discretely take lovers. I do not intend to live a celibate life whilst you play around."

"And if my father finds out?" asked Frederick

"Why should he, unless you tell him? We certainly won't," replied Lord Berkeley. Frederick thought for a moment.

"Alright, what is it you want me to sign?" Frederick examined the document for a moment, then he signed the formal agreement, drawn up by Lord Berkeley's lawyers, accepting paternity for the child to be called Edward William de Courcy if a boy, or Elizabeth Mary de Courcy if a girl. In return the report attached to the agreement marked "Appendix A" would remain in a locked safe in Lord Berkeley's solicitor's office, only to be revealed to the world, should Frederick deny paternity of the yet unborn child. The housekeeper and butler witnessed Frederick, Rosie and Lord Berkeley's signatures. On reflection Frederick thought that all had turned out rather well. His father, the Baron, thought is was tremendous when another boy, they named Edward William, was born in September 1906. A big bouncy boy, born with a mop of black hair and jet black eyes. The Baron did think, momentarily, where those attributes had come from, but concluded Lord Berkeley's ancestors were responsible. The Baron was very pleased with Frederick and Rosie and gave them a gift of a painting by an artist called Picasso, who seemed to be coming into prominence in Europe. He couldn't stand the man's work himself but Rosie seemed pleased enough. He also immediately enrolled the boy into a Swiss school and to follow his father and brother to Paris and the Sorbonne.

Frederick found that he did miss the look of love in his wife's eyes, their occasional touch. He found her coldness particularly hard, especially early on after the agreement had been reached. They barely communicated anything now. If they were in the same house, or if she was required to host a dinner party, they would appear natural to the outside world, but inside both knew their terrible secret. They reluctantly, for the Baron's sake, attended Christmas at the villa beside the lake near Zurich and occasional holidays in the South of France or Italy, but never again was the intimacy present.

Through a friend of a friend, Rosie heard that Amy had sold the house after her aunt died and emigrated to America.

Chapter Sixteen

Alfred Horsfield (nee George de Courcy) 1907

The boy lurched toward him again. Three inches taller than Alfred, this opponent had the advantage of height and weight and he was two years older, but nothing takes account of good timing and a well presented upper cut to the stomach. His uncle Tyndall had taught him well. "Don't go into close quarters with the bigger man. Don't get caught with your back to the ropes and do land the first punch." The boy Johnson-Smith, his opponent that day, was a bully and terrorised the juniors at Brighton Metropolitan College. Being nine years of age Johnson-Smith had a better physique than Alfred and enjoyed pushing around the younger boys, but he had met his match. As Alfred's upper cut took the wind out of him he sunk to the ground and Alfred moved in. Johnson-Smith looked up and received a right hand full in the face and after that all he saw were stars. Alfred stood back; Uncle Tyndall had always said that know when a man is beat, no need to destroy him. What a man thought Alfred, Uncle Tyndall, ex- prize fighter and a champion of Southern England, as well as Royal Navy champion at light middleweight. At that moment, he couldn't thank him enough as all the boys crowded round patting him on the back. Suddenly he felt a pair of hands grabbing him by his collar and yanking him round. Mr Barclay-Warner, head of maths at Brighton Metropolitan, as he liked to title himself, was standing in front of him fuming.

"You despicable little urchin Horsfield," and catching hold of Alfred's ear he forced marched him to his office. "Right my lad, I'm going to teach you not to fight – trousers down." Alfred knew what was coming, the maths master, they called BW, was a cruel man who seemed to enjoy caning the boys. Hardly a lesson went by without one of the pupils receiving a stroke of the cane across his hand, or six of the best on his backside. Alfred gritted his teeth – this was going to hurt. Barclay-Warner was not a big man and he put a great deal of gusto into caning this lad. Several times he had given him a stroke across the palm of the hand, but it didn't seem to have any effect. Now he would break the spirit of this unruly boy. Working up a sweat, he dished out six strokes, making large red wheals across the bare cheeks of the boy in front of him. Alfred sobbed gently, determined not to let this man see him cry out loud.

"Right boy perhaps that will be a lesson to you. This school does not tolerate bullying or fighting. Now get dressed," he snapped. Alfred, with tears streaming his face, gingerly pulled up his trousers. "Get out of my sight!" shouted the master. Alfred limped away to see Matron, one of the only people he really liked at Brighton Metropolitan. Why his mother and aunt had insisted he go there, he would never understand. His best pal, Dickie Tagg, went to a local school and seemed to enjoy it. He hated every minute at the college, considered by his mother and aunt as his route to university. He knew the fees at Brighton Metropolitan must be high, as most of the boys came from a different background to him. Indeed he was one of the few "day boys", the sons of local traders, clerics or professional men. To say that he hated every minute wasn't quite true – he loved the sport and was already a promising batsman and had shown himself to be a fast scrum half during the previous winter. They also did pistol shooting, which he enjoyed and he often found himself top of the class with four bulls out of six shots. He knew he excelled at languages. He didn't know why, but he only needed to read or hear a phrase once, then he could remember it verbatim. When he got home that night, it didn't take long before his mother spotted how uncomfortably he sat at the dinner table. Finally she coaxed out of a tearful Alfred what had happened and as she heard what this man had done to her son, her temper began to boil. It was then that Uncle Tyndall came home for his supper. He was a fisherman now and went out looking for mackerel in a small trawler off Brighton beach during the day and searched for cod further out at night.

"Tyndall, take a look at what that "B"," she couldn't bring herself to say that word, "has done to my son." Alfred was made to drop his trousers. Tyndall saw the ugly stripes across the cheeks of his nephew's backside. The wounds were still weeping, despite the cream Matron and his mother had used when he had got home. Tyndall banged his great hand down on the table.

"My God I will do the man who has done this to you."

"Now Tyndall, remember the boy needs that education – calm down, calm down."

"But look what the bastard has done."

"Don't use that language at my table." Tyndall got up. "Where are you going?" asked his sister.

"Never you mind. I'll be back about 5 am after I've been out on the tide." Maggie sighed, she knew it was useless to argue with her brother – she never had won an argument yet.

Tyndall knew where to find the man who had marked his nephew. He did not have children of his own but loved Alfred like a son. He fumed as he approached the "Three Feathers", in London Road. He had seen the man they called BW in the pub on numerous occasions. He liked to flirt with a barmaid there, called Betty and that's where he found him laughing at his own jokes, slightly drunk, leaning against the bar in the "snug". "I want a word with you," he said to Barclay-Warner almost picking him up as he marched him outside. Barclay-Warner had seen this man before but he didn't have the faintest idea who he was.

"Now my man, unhand me or I shall call a bobby."

"Call who you like mate, but you and I are going to have words."

"But I don't know you. What do you want?"

"Well you may not know me, but you beat my nephew Alfred savagely today and now I'm going to beat you." Tyndall landed a fearsome blow in the master's guts. Barclay-Warner thought he had been poleaxed as he fought for air. Then he felt another blow and heard the crack as his nose broke. Taking punishment was not something a bully does well and Barclay-Warner was no exception. Whimpering on the floor he begged Tyndall to stop but the red mist had descended and Tyndall wouldn't stop until the bell went. Of course, it never did and when finally Betty came outside to see what had happened to the nice man from the college, she screamed as she saw Tyndall standing over the blood-splattered master. Betty's scream broke the spell and Tyndall looked at her and ran off – that saved the master's life, but he had to take compassionate leave for six months to repair three broken ribs, a broken cheek bone, a broken nose and most of all a broken spirit. The police were called, but Betty sensibly said she didn't know the man that ran off and only saw his back. Tyndall kept away from the London Road pub after that, but Maggie was furious. Joan, his other sister joined in the condemnation.

"What if you'd killed 'im? Are you a bigger idiot than we thought?" They packed him off to cousin Ira, in Cornwall, to fish down there for a while until the heat was off.

Alfred had heard about the maths master and the savage beating he had taken and thought it served him right. He didn't connect the events of that night, at the "Three Feathers", with his Uncle Tyndall gone fishing in Cornwall. "The stock of cod was apparently better in Cornwall at that time of the year," said his mother.

As the years went by, Alfred continued to excel at sport and represented the County at rugby. He was entered, by the school, in the under eleven's school boys, the all England pistol target shooting competition, at a place called Bisley. He finished a creditable third, with two boys just beating him. At thirteen, he was top dog at Brighton Metropolitan, even boys three or four or even five years older, respected him. Academically he was top of Latin, French and German but struggled with maths; he was adequate in English, History he loved and Geography. He got the cane a few more times, but no-one beat him again and for some reason BW steered well clear. Generally school life improved and he was being groomed to go to Oxford University – they wanted his sports skills and were prepared to accept him to study modern languages, when the war broke out. The boys had been excited for some time, as newspapers reported the breakdown of relationships between Germany and their European neighbours. All of them wanted to join up straight away. "It sounds a great caper," said Moxford, one of Alfred's rugby friends. Alfred had friends from his sporting prowess, he was, after all, captain of the rugby team and opening batsman in the cricket team and was the County rifle and pistol shooting champion. He had also been made a school prefect and many said, it was a certainty that he, even though he was a local boy, might end up being the head boy, and his family were not connected.

As the first world war continued, it became increasingly clear that it wasn't going to be over in five minutes, as the history master had predicted. The Germans were entrenched in Belgium and parts of France and the allies could not shift them. Basically, the history master explained, it was stalemate; neither side would give up their ground or talk peace. The boys in his class continued to look enviously at their brothers or cousins who were old enough to fight and they all longed for the day they could join up and had excited discussions about killing the Bosch. That was until, one day, young Moxford was summoned to the headmaster's study. Moxford's brother, Gerald, had been killed at the battle of The Somme, along with thousands of other allied soldiers. Moxford had been very close to his older brother, whom he had idolised and when his brother secretly left Oxford University and joined the Coldstream Guards, their late father's old regiment, he was extremely envious and proud of him. Now his brother was dead and his mother, who had doted on Gerald, was "terribly upset" which was why the master had explained she hadn't come down from Hertfordshire herself. Alfred tried to cheer up poor old Moxford, but to no avail and then one day he just disappeared. Alfred learned a week later, that he had lied about his age and joined up. Alfred nearly did the same but Uncle Tyndall virtually threatened to kill him if he followed that "idiot Moxford" who had been for tea several times at Alfred's house.

One by one, the deaths of old boys of Brighton Metropolitan were announced during assembly. The strain was beginning to show on the teachers and dear Matron, who had loved all her boys. This was no lark, Alfred thought, but it was still his duty. So on the 1st May 1916 he joined up. He left a note for mother, aunt and old Tyndall, but it was too late to stop him, he had signed the forms and was on his way for basic training. They sent him to a place called Catterick, from where he wrote to his mother. Alfred explained that they spent a great deal of time making sure they marched in time with each other and could carry heavy loads. But Alfred had impressed the instructors with his stamina and most of all his marksmanship. His skill with a rifle was attractive to the army and he was quickly fast-tracked to join the crack shots who became snipers....

Chapter Seventeen

The Birth of Sophie

February 10th 1911

Rosie screamed and let out a mouthful of mild swear words as the contraction forced her to push. The midwives were telling her not to push. Not to push, they must be joking! This baby wanted to be born and the contractions had got more frequent. Finally her cervix was ready for the baby to be born and thirty minutes later, after a relatively short period since her waters burst, Rosie gave birth to a girl. The midwife placed the bundle into Rosie's arms and she saw that the baby had a mop of black hair. The midwife left the room to inform his Lordship. Her father knocked on the door and then bounded into the room.

"I hear it's a girl, Rosie."

Rosie smiled at her father.

"Look father, she's lovely." Lord Berkeley looked down at the crib where the midwife had placed the newly born infant.

"She's got your eyes," and suddenly the baby cried, "and your lungs," they both laughed. "What are you going to call her, Rosie?" Lord Berkeley asked.

"I'm going to call her Sophie Anne."

"What lovely names. She looks like a Sophie Anne."

"Father."

"Yes dear."

"Will you send a message to Frederick and the Baron and go to Eton College to see Frederick Junior and Edward?"

"What about Anne?" asked Lord Berkeley. Her eldest daughter Anne was at Rodean boarding school, near Brighton.

"I have asked my sister to go and tell her and bring her home," Rosie replied.

"Good. I will arrange for her to be accompanied by my man Greig."

Rosie's sister Alice was waiting in the library. Alice was a nurse and had rushed to Eaton Square when the message had reached her. All of her family knew that Frederick and Rosie were estranged and Alice spent as much time with her sister as possible. Just then Rosie's brothers, Billy and Freddie arrived.

The whole family and Lord Berkeley crowded around the bed until Alice said, "Look I can see Rosie is looking tired. It is time we let her rest." Lord

Berkeley was the last to leave the bedroom kissing his daughter on the forehead.

"Father."

"Yes, what is it dear? Should I tell Frederick that I am prepared to divorce him on amicable terms?" Lord Berkeley thought for a few seconds.

"No, I don't think any decision should be made at the moment. Wait a few months and let's talk again." He kissed his daughter again and left.

Two days later, Rosie was up and making arrangements to go to the bank in Threadneedle Street. As she arrived at the Bank her father scolded her.

"I have a meeting with the German Ambassador, Count Von Baston."

"Oh, I see." Lord Berkeley knew that the Count was the father of his grandson Edward. "I am going to tell him that he has a son."

"Do you think that's wise? Don't be hasty. Consider how he might react."

Lord Berkeley accompanied her towards the Board Room.

"I've been thinking about it for some time," she replied, "a son deserves to know his father and even if I am to be shunned by society I am determined to tell the Count and later on, my son, the truth."

"Then let me stay when you tell him." Rosie kissed her father's cheek.

"No, I will do this myself." As they sat in the Boardroom, there was a sharp knock on the door. Lord Berkeley's secretary came in and announced that the Count had arrived.

"Bring him up to the Boardroom," said Lord Berkeley.

The Count sat on the rather sumptuous leather chair and wondered what he was doing here. He had received a short note from Cynthia, as he knew Rosie, and he was intrigued. Lord Berkeley's private secretary emerged and invited him to follow her. The Count was, as usual, immaculately dressed, but was slightly taken aback when he saw that Lord Berkeley was present in the room. After a few minutes of polite chit chat, Cynthia's father quickly left and he embraced her. The Count knew that Cynthia had just had another baby. "You look wonderful," he kissed her hand.

"Sit down Kurt." The Count sat and waited as Elizabeth, Lord Berkeley's secretary, brought in coffee.

"Now where were we?" he smiled that magical smile, which had enticed her the moment they had first met.

"I have something to tell you Kurt, but first you must tell me that you will keep calm." Rosie had seen the Count upend a braggart in Simpson's Restaurant who was boasting on another table how he alone could defeat the German army and she knew that he had a temper.

"What is it my dear?" he replied. Rosie sat back and pondering for a few seconds started hesitantly.

"Well, as you know, Frederick and I do not live together and have not done so for quite some time." He nodded, he knew all about Frederick. It was his job to know. Rosie had no idea that the man who had earlier been the German Ambassador was now head of the Abwer, the German Secret Service. She continued, "Well, my lovely daughter Sophie-Anne is not Frederick's child and neither is Edward his biological son." The Count was not surprised by this news, but nevertheless sat back in the chair with a quizzical look on his face. Where was all this going? He thought. Rosie paused, took a sip of coffee and then continued. "The reason I asked you to come to see me was that I have made a decision."

"A decision, my dear?" Rosie looked directly at him.

"Didn't you have the slightest curiosity when Edward was born? You knew I had been seeing you and," she added, "only you, for nearly a year." Suddenly the Count began to realise where this conversation was heading.

"What are you saying?" He looked at her somewhat more seriously.

"I'm saying, my dear Count, that Edward is your son." The almost playful attitude of the Count suddenly changed.

"My son, but are you sure?"

"Yes, absolutely certain." Rosie looked at him, how was he reacting?

"Donner en blitzen. Sorry but I am taken aback."

The Count was not an indecisive man but this news was not what he had expected when he had been invited to meet the lovely Cynthia again. He had been hoping that their affair would be rekindled, but this. "Why have you told me this news now?" Rosie looked at the man in front of her – typical, she thought that he should be looking for some sinister reason.

"The only reason I have told you, is that my marriage has irretrievably broken down and I feel Edward should be acquainted with his real father, even if, in the short term, that process may not be direct."

"I don't understand – you know I am married of course and you do realise that I cannot divorce, and even if I did, would you?"

"No, there is no question of divorces on either side," said Rosie.

"Then what is it you expect of me?"

"Nothing, absolutely nothing. But one day I will ask that you acknowledge your son and my hope is that you will." The Count sat perfectly motionless and considered the bombshell he had just received. He was not happily married, but his wife's and his own family had been closely connected for hundreds of years and he could not destroy the bond. Then there were his children, he had two girls.

"Where is my son now?"

"He is at Eton with his half brother." The Count thought for a few minutes and involuntarily rubbed the side of his face.

"Alright I will agree, that when the time is right I will acknowledge my son, but in the meantime I wish to become a part of his life, so we must devise a way I can see him. Perhaps his brother and he could can come and stay at my chateau in Bavaria?" Rosie stood up.

"I am sorry I never told you before Kurt but can I thank you with all my heart for how you have reacted." She kissed him on the forehead. The Count stood.

"Cynthia, you are an extraordinary woman and one day our son may wish to know he was conceived with love – you may tell him he was," and with that he stood, kissed her hand, clicked his heels and left. Lord Berkeley came back into the room and was shocked to find his daughter weeping quietly.

Kneeling in front of her he said, "What did he say dear? If he has upset you I will be very angry."

"No, father he has been a perfect gentleman. I am crying as I think of the life I could have had with the many different beaus I have met. Instead I live a sham with Frederick." There was no answer to that, so Lord Berkeley just pulled his daughter into his arms and let her cry.

Rosie settled down to her familiar role working for the two merchant banks and occasionally helping with some translation work for a government department. She was concentrating most of all on learning to drive. She had been given a Morris motor car by Lord Berkeley to celebrate the birth of her child and she had persuaded her father to lend her his chauffeur, Adam, to teach her to drive. Adam was an ex-guards Staff Sergeant and very serious. Lord Berkeley tried to employ as many of his old regiment when they retired and by doing so he had a fantastically loyal staff at home and at the bank. Adam was struggling with Mrs de Courcy and as he had explained to the Captain, one of Lord Berkeley's old adjutants, she cannot turn the wheel, it is too heavy for her, but she will persist. Finally after six months, meeting Adam every other day, Rosie drove to Guildford on her own. There wasn't much traffic, but you still had to watch out for horse drawn carriages, pony and traps as well as farm animals and single riders. She hadn't a clue why she had chosen to drive to Guildford, except that it appeared to be on main roads and that the distance was such that she could return in one day. Returning that day from Guildford she was ecstatic and the following evening she spent some time regaling a group of ladies she had invited to dinner, with her "maiden drive to Guildford" as she put it. Her dinner party was exclusively women only. It was one of the many Rosie held to help co-ordinate the fight for woman's rights. That evening Lady Astor attended, as did Charlotte Simmons, who had now been arrested six times and many others including Emmerline Pankhurst, Christabel Pankhurst, her daughter and Annie Kenney. They reflected on the progress being made since "the early days". In 1905 they had attended a meeting in London to hear Sir Edward Gray, a minister in the Government and had met Lady Constance Lytton. Years earlier Rosie had taken Lady Lytton on a tour of suffragettes locked up in Holloway Prison. The sight of these girls changed Lady Lytton's attitude and she joined the Woman's Political & Social Union and became an active member. It was not surprising when some of the women disagreed, sometimes quite violently. That night at dinner Lady Lytton was recounting her last tour of the country. She spent most of her time touring the country giving speeches, fighting the cause in Parliament, telling all her upper class friends about the cause to the point of boredom. She lost many friends that way, as not all women agreed with the views of the women that evening. Charlotte Simmons, for example, sat very quietly, towards the top of the dinner table, not really getting involved in the debate and it was difficult to tell whether she was a real activist or not. Lady Lytton had been imprisoned in Holloway again that year, for throwing rocks at an MP's car. She had hidden her identity and went on a hunger strike. Eventually she was force fed and suffered a heart attack. She was very lively and alert that night though. Christabel, Anne and Rosie laughed as they remembered the evening of Sir Edward Gray's speech. They had constantly interrupted shouting "Will the Liberal Government give votes to women?" The police were called and all three refused to leave. They were charged with assaulting a policeman, who insisted they had kicked and spat at him. Christabel, Anne and Rosie were found guilty of assault and fined five shillings each. After that Rosie had received an unusual visit from the Baron and Frederick. The Baron was adament she simply had to stop getting arrested. In the end, she was persuaded that her role was best suited to funding the cause and fighting behind the scenes. In some ways Rosie was pleased and she had agreed, as when the Baron said that Frederick would divorce her and take the children to Switzerland, she had no choice but to moderate her stance in public. She had always known the Baron was a ruthless man and didn't doubt he would do as he said. Later she told Lord Berkeley of the conversation and he was furious.

These were exciting times, but none of them realised that Charlotte Simmons had become a police spy. All the direct actions the women planned at Rosie's dinner party, were reported back to the Superintendent at Bow Police Station. Several years later Charlotte confessed to Christabel what she had done. The police had left a charge open against her son for stealing bread. The charge was false, but she had been blackmailed into spying for the police, and in return the charge would remain unactioned.

Life wasn't all intrigue and women's rights. Rosie was a regular in society and frequently Lord Berkeley asked her to be his Consul at important dinner parties. She was a favourite of Lloyd-George, the Chancellor of the Exchequer, who often squeezed her knee under the table and played footsie on every occasion they met. Rosie just smiled and occasionally kicked him, but this only seemed to inflame the man still more!

Meanwhile her daughter, Anne, was growing up and went to boarding school at Rodean, near Brighton. The school was ideal for girls of middle class families. They taught all the skills a young lady should develop but also, encouraged self-belief and concentrated on an all round education which was important to Rosie. Many of the girls' schools stopped short of actual detailed learning and certainly didn't encourage self-reliance, less it confuse a woman to believe that her place wasn't only in the home.

Rosie's son, Frederick Junior, was a thin boy who preferred visiting his grandfather in Switzerland to any other activity. Time and time again, Lord Berkeley tried to interest him in sport or visiting art galleries, museums or military gatherings, but to no avail. All he ever wanted to do during his holidays, was to go to Switzerland. Her son, Edward, on the other hand, despite being a quiet boy was very strong and a deep thinker. Virtually the opposite of Frederick Junior, he constantly craved the company of his Grandfather, Lord Berkeley, and they spent a great deal of time together. Lord Berkeley had involved himself in the upbringing of all of Rosie's children and he enjoyed himself immensely. He had obtained a place for Frederick Junior and Edward at Eton College and already they were both "down" to go to Cambridge, his old university, but the Baron would be an obstacle as he wanted both boys to go to the Sorbonne. But it was Edward who was frequently found sitting alongside his Grandfather, looking at books or studying exhibits in an art gallery or items Lord Berkeley had loaned from the British Museum. Who else could loan artefacts from the great museum, Edward wondered? Frederick Junior worried Rosie, he was far too serious for a boy of ten, yet what could she do? Her husband was never in attendance and only his grandfather brought any male attention to the boy.

Rosie was very careful and extremely choosy about her lovers, but from time to time, a man came along with charm and strength of character and who made her laugh. Yes, that was it, made her laugh. Frederick didn't care less and certainly they did not laugh together anymore. They hadn't shared a bed for more years than she cared to remember. The German Count Von Baston continued to intrigue her, but they met so infrequently nothing further developed. That year, June 1911, Rosie had been fortunate to sit in the fifth row at Westminster Abbey during the coronation of King George V and Queen Mary. At a dinner party later that week, Lady Astor had laughed when telling the story that the cleaning staff at the Abbey had discovered three ropes of pearls, twenty brooches, six bracelets, twenty golden balls dislodged from coronets and three quarters of a diamond necklace lying in the pews!

And so life continued ….

The summer of 1911 was very hot. People flooded to the seaside, especially fashionable Brighton, but the heat didn't help the tempers of the strikers. There was a great deal of workers' unrest. For the very poor or old, the high temperatures caused many deaths, rising to one hundred degrees Fahrenheit, the temperature was unusual. One such death was Rosie's cousin

Steffie. The family and Lord Berkeley, but no Frederick, had gathered for a simple service and funeral in Bethnal Green, when Billy announced his wife, Amy, was expecting their fifth child. Isn't it strange? Thought Rosie, a life passes on to the afterlife and a baby is born.

The year ended with extremely cold weather, snow in London and they all looked forward to 1912.

Chapter Eighteen

The Baron 1912

The Baron lounged back in the bath and picked up the report once again. His son was clearly in trouble again. The Baron knew all about his homosexual affairs, most of his rent boys and partners. He had never confronted his son with his sexuality, nor did he discuss it with anyone, including his partner of some ten years, the Countess. He had long suspected Cynthia, he could only think of his daughter-in-law as Cynthia, not the common name of Rosie, knew all about her husband. He was not a fool and knew Cynthia was a very beautiful and clever woman. She was more than an essential part of the Bank now and he would not like Frederick to be panicked and heaven forbid, if a divorce came about. The Baron knew he could not control Cynthia. She was headstrong and had the support of her father, Lord Berkeley. Formidable opponents indeed, but in any case he needed his granddaughter and grandsons to be nurtured and guided towards the de Courcy family. It was his intention that Frederick's male heirs follow in centuries of tradition and take an important role in the family Bank. A divorce would muddy the waters and surely result in a scandal affecting the Bank's reputation. No, it was unthinkable. Still, Frederick had clearly got a medical problem. Twice he had visited Wimpole Street and seen a Doctor Wilmsley–Scott or a Doctor Cooper. His detective had not been able to find out what the visits were about even though he had charmed the receptionist at the doctor's practice. All the detective had been able to report was that the Doctors specialised in rare and infectious diseases. Frederick, who had been oblivious to the Baron having had him followed for more than ten years, clearly had a problem. As he pondered his son's future, he reflected that he had nearly killed several rent boys and seemed to enjoy beating those urchins. He had no sympathy for the boys, nor did he now care about his son's activities, unless it affected the Bank. But, he needed to find out what the medical problem was and there was something he could do which might enable him to investigate further. His own physician, Doctor Grasson, in Zurich, had a brother who was working in London, in Harley Street. Professor Grasson was also on the General Medical Council and was one of the Royal family's physicians. If he could persuade his own doctor to ask his brother – he could find out that way what Frederick's problem was. He was prepared to pay a substantial fee to Professor Grasson towards research or anything else he wanted and he mostly found that money talks. The water began to get cold and as he stepped out of the bath to dry himself in front of the raging fire, he decided to contact Doctor Grasson, in Zurich, immediately. Dressing, he went down to dinner, planning his approach to his old friend the doctor.

Frederick was morose and increasingly anxious. The Doctor had said that he was in time, but that the secondary stage of the dreadful disease had commenced and he would get periods of depression. God – he could kill himself. How did he let himself catch this unspeakable disease. He knew about the risks. One of his acquaintances at the club had told him about Henry Riding, who had contracted Syphilis and died a terrible death, going mad in the end. How did this happen? He had always been careful to inspect the boys he used and he had many long term lovers who were without reproach – or so he thought. In fact, it was a chance affair with a Cavalry officer that had brought him to this. Curse that Captain Trowton, why did he ever meet the man.

The doctor in Wimpole Street had told him that the condition was not curable, but could be delayed. Frightened, he longed to tell Rosie. She was the only person he knew he could trust. But how would she react? How would she look at him? Would the knowledge that he had now caught this unspeakable disease prompt her to divorce him? He began to wonder if he was going mad now – the thoughts raced though his head and his palms became sweaty and painful. He took his clothes off and looked at the abrasions on his body again, my God they looked awful. Thank goodness Rosie did not see him naked these days. What about the children, would they hear about their father? He did not care about those bastards, Edward or Sophie but Anne and Frederick, what would they think of him? Rosie's lovers can take care of her bastards or her father, Lord Berkeley, if he was so inclined, but they would not get a penny of his inheritance, he had already seen to that. His father, The Baron, was in blissful ignorance about Edward or Sophie's true parentage but Frederick had made a will that would reveal all and made certain that Rosie's bastards were disinherited. As he pondered his condition, he felt slightly ashamed of his action that on his death he would publicly out Rosie, especially as he had signed an agreement, but he would be dead and owed it to his father to protect the lineage.

Frederick didn't think of Rosie much these days. From time to time she would be the perfect hostess, at a dinner party or at a function, but they spent hardly any time together. They had had separate bedrooms for nearly ten years and as he pictured Rosie he knew he was one of the most envied men in London, yet he didn't even share her bedroom. As he thought about his wife, he realised that she had blossomed into an outstanding beauty, who was intelligent, able to speak five languages fluently and negotiate with statesmen, bankers and businessmen alike. He congratulated himself, he had chosen well. When he had first noticed the strange "boil", as he thought, on the end of his penis, it had gone away after a few weeks and he took no further notice. Then he got a rash as well and decided to see his doctor. God how embarrassing that was, he thought. He reflected that the doctor told him that he thought he had a venereal disease and referred him to Doctor Wilmsley-Scott in Wimpole Street. With some trepidation he remembered the visit to Wimpole Street and the doctor who carried out the detailed examination, finding lots of faint rashes as well as rough reddish brown spots on the bottom of his feet. The doctor informed him that he had swollen glands and he confirmed that he had had a sore throat for quite some time and that his muscles ached and he felt tired. He remembered what the doctor said "The diagnosis is clear, you have caught Syphilis." The doctor explained to him that it was apparently in the early stages, but then he hit me with a bombshell – he could not cure me. This had not immediately sunk in, but now he realised how stupid he had been. This disease, it will get worse and worse. Doctor Wilmsley-Scott explained that he could delay the symptoms and he started that day. Frederick felt sick thinking about the revolting concoction, which the doctor had told him was mercury and a week later he had given him some arsenic, which Frederick swallowed with some trepidation. The trouble is, he thought, they don't seem to know if any of these revolting mixtures would work and the sores on my body are weeping and the number of places where sores are appearing is increasing. The doctor has told me that I have secondary Syphilis and that I should tell all my friends, as the doctor put it, to go for an immediate check up. Frederick reflected that, perversely, he nearly didn't tell Captain Trowton, but when he told him he was not shocked. Frederick suspected that he already knew and that just increased his anger. Doctor Wilmsley-Scott advised me to tell my wife or not have sexual relations, that was amusing, thought Frederick. As he sat thinking about his worsening condition, he reflected that he should tell Rosie but he certainly wasn't going to tell his father.

Chapter Nineteen

Rosie's Diaries Read In 1913

Shortly the start of a new year, 20th December 1913. Rosie was expecting her children any minute and knowing they would want her to read extracts from her diaries was studying various years. She often read her diaries now, so many memories, mostly good but some sad. Her thoughts turned to how she wrote through tearful eyes on occasions, but it was always after the event. Over ten years have past since I started writing my journals, she thought, and as I glanced through the pages, the notes force a memory to stir, sometimes good sometimes not so good.

She began to think about her beloved brother, Billy and she was trying to capture the moments spent with him. She turned to the entry 1st November 1913. *"My wonderful brother Billy has finally succumbed to pneumonia after a chest infection had struck him down last winter. What a wonderful man he was, a proud father of five children, an honest man, and a decent man, who followed in his own father's tradition and became a union leader on the docks.*

She paused and blinked away a tear and carried on.

The funeral was yesterday for Billy. The pavements were four or five deep with people. Many London Dockers showing their appreciation for a man who had always protected their interests and on occasions had kept them out of prison. Even the Pearly King had attended the church service at St Swithens in Bethnal Green. I don't understand life, Billy was only thirty three. Why did he die now? I miss him so much.

She thought of her mother, who had died some time ago and knew that Billy had joined her now and Dad Holder, as she thought of him. She wondered if her mother had ever fallen out of love with father Berkeley, who cared for her mother, of that there was no doubt.

She put the diary down and at random picked up another and flicked through the pages. She stopped at 7th June 1904. Gosh this was going back in time she thought.

Going to the Hurlingham Club today. Captain C has invited me to watch a match, between the Horseguards and the Hussars, for some trophy to be presented by the King himself. I can't say I am very keen on Polo but I am keen on Captain C!

Met Captain C, for appearances, at the Hurlingham Club. He was looking dashing in his uniform. Sat with the Countess of Warwick and Cybil Darling.

She smiled to herself as she turned the pages and leapt ahead stopping at 1st September 1904.

Met Captain C at Drury Lane theatre. Saw a play "Run of Luck". Enjoyed it but spent a lot of time listening to Captain C whispering sweet nothings in my ear. Went to his house on Pall Mall. What a lover, I had been waiting a long time for a man to take me in his arms. Caress me and love me.

Rosie turned the pages, put the journal down and thought "Can't read this one to the children" and picked up her 1905 diary. One entry on the 20th January caught her eye...

Went to the Hippodrome with Captain C. This is a beautiful theatre. You enter through a series of decorated foyers and the auditorium is magnificent. The decorations in the theatre are in the style of Flemish Renaissance and they give beauty and warmth. I love the colossal horse chariot on the roof of the entrance hall in Charing Cross Road. That afternoon, went with Captain C to Windsor to watch a dressage competition.

She saw the initials ML and she smiled to herself for she knew her code ML stood for made love. She had decided not to be explicit in her every day diary in those days. She turned the pages to February 14th, 1905:

Went to the Drury Lane theatre – the stage is the largest in Europe. Saw a play "Midsummer Madness" with Captain C – ML.

She thought of her childish codes and turned the pages again, to March 10th 1905. Gosh, she thought, I went to the theatre a lot. Again there was a visit to the Apollo Theatre, Shaftsbury Avenue; this time with father, Lord Berkeley. She had described the building as a magnificent building with a façade in the French Renaissance style and inside decorations of crimson, gold and white. She had noted that electric lighting was used throughout the theatre and saw that she and father Berkeley had seen a review of a new play, Shakespeare's "Julius Caesar". She skipped ahead to March 29th, 1905 ...

Went to the Alhambra, in Leicester Square. An oriental architecture with crescent domes. Saw a beautiful ballet "Swan Lake" with Count Von Baston.

She moved the diary forward to May and came to the page she was expecting to see, May 5th, 1905 ...

Met Amy. What a tempestuous girl! She is very interesting, but goodness me, she is extremely militant.

As she skipped through the diary that year, she saw that most of the next five months were about Amy, until she reached October 1st ...

Wilton's Restaurant. Met Count Von Baston. The finest St James's fish and game restaurant! Great food, fish, shellfish, game in season, meat dishes, great fun, and wine. The décor was interesting. Rich burgundy carpet, pale walls with large pictures of country scenes. Went back to the German Embassy.

Then she saw her initials ML.

October 10th. *Met Count Von Baston at Simpson's in the Strand.*

She saw the initials ML. October 17th...

Met Count Von Baston at the Russell Hotel, Guildford Street. Not been here before. There is a fine library, writing room, in oak, including some glorious paintings by Reynolds, Lawrence and Hayden. ML. November 10th. Went to see my sister who works in Southwick Bridge Road hospital. A privately supported hospital. We are very proud of Alice. November 20th. Went to the Garrick Club, an actor's club, on the south side of Garrick Street. Met Count Von Baston there. Many fine drawings and paintings of theatrical celebrities. It was great to see some of the actor's and actresses that I knew there to enjoy supper, I love this place; it is one of the most fascinating and entertaining places in town. Went back to the Embassy.

Terrible news the Count told me that he was returning to Germany – am I sad, I don't know? ML. November 25th, 1905 A great and royal day. The King invited father Berkeley and myself to the Marlborough Club in Pall Mall. This is a great privilege as the club numbers only a select eighty members and most of them are a small set of King Edward's special friends. I was surprised how plainly furnished the club was, but it is warm and well lit. Top class cuisine here and first class service. This was a privilege for me as normally women are not allowed in the card room or the billiard room, but I was still not allowed to play! December 1st. Went to Hurlingham Polo club and met Captain C. This was the annual dinner reflecting on the London season. It was interesting to watch all the carriages arriving. They travelled down the Fulham Road until they crossed Stamford Bridge. It's great fun here too. There are lots of games of polo and the weather has been quite fine; quite surprising for the middle of winter. There has also been a military band and we all sipped coffee and brandy whilst the men played polo. The weather is not quite good enough to walk around the lake, or the pretty gardens, but the club house, an old mansion, is quite adequate and they serve passable cuisine and the dinner rooms here have a lovely view of the grounds. Had dinner with Captain C. Went back to his flat ML.

She turned the page to December 2nd, 1905…

Went to Christie's Auction Gallery in Kings Street, St James's. Met father Berkeley who wanted to bid on a number of small miniatures he'd seen that were coming up in the sale. This place is a veritable treasure trove of rare items, including jewellery, works of art, silver and other collectable items. Father Berkeley had to keep stopping me putting my hand up, but in any case I bid for a cameo that sold in the sale for £9,400. Thank goodness I stopped bidding at £5,000!

Rosie remembered that year, as usual, they had travelled to Zurich and flicked through to December 16th, 1905…

Travelled to Zurich with the children. Had Christmas with the Baron and Frederick who deemed to join us! He is looking quite thin these days and I sometimes wonder if he is ill.

Rosie rang the bell by the mantelpiece and ordered a pot of tea and took out of her bureau the diary for 1906. The diary for 1905 was carefully placed back in one of the drawers in the bureau. She paused, because after all she knew the story…

Captain C has remained my lover for a year, now he has been posted to South Africa. He confounded me with the news that his wife was to travel with him and he felt that they should regard their relationship as a good memory.

Men, she remembered crying briefly, but they had had great fun and he was a proficient and energetic lover and after Frederick ignoring her for so long he had almost brought her back to life. She put the 1906 diary back in the bureau and picked up the diary for 1908. This was a red leather bound volume the Baron had given her. As she flicked through the pages, the first entry she read was May 18th 1908…

Frederick seems to be getting much worse he barely disguises his preference for young boys and I'm going to have to have a talk with the Baron about him again. I'm not prepared to be made a complete fool of.

She remembered that talk and looked up May 25th because she had travelled to Switzerland determined to resolve her problem with Frederick. On May 25th the entry read…

Travelled to Switzerland. Frederick is becoming a serious problem. He doesn't seem to be hiding his tendencies lately. Fortunately I know the Baron values the tradition and lineage of the Bank and is also concerned about Frederick. Together, we agreed that Frederick should be sent to America on a permanent basis. I met the Baron at the Lakeside Chateau and Frederick was summoned by the Baron from Zurich. He arrived the following day and was told, in no uncertain terms, that his latest behaviour in Switzerland and in Paris was unacceptable and that he was going to be sent to America. How extraordinary. I had never seen Frederick react to his father in such a violent way. He flatly refused to go.

She continued to look through the pages. She knew of course, that whilst they'd been living apart for some time, Frederick had a flat in Knightsbridge so that his dalliances could be as discrete as possible. It seemed that many people knew that they were separated. She had made a terse note in her diary…

Some of our good friends stopped inviting me to dinner or country visits or joining them in a box at the theatre, but I found out who my real friends were. Clearly the Baron had not expected Frederick's reaction to the meeting in Zurich.

Rosie continued to read her note in black ink…

I would have thought he should have expected some reaction, as Frederick had many boyfriends, amongst the various sets in Paris, London and Zurich and because he spent money like water, he had no trouble attracting new partners. He was so violently opposed to going, that his father agreed to leave him in Paris and London for the time being. That's very unfair on me. The trouble is that I know that the Baron had been unable to stop Frederick coming into his grandfather's legacy on his thirtieth birthday and unless he had spent the lot, he would be able to live independently and even leave the Bank altogether. The Baron knew that Frederick hardly went to the city any longer and that I was more an Ambassador for the Bank than he was. I have to spend more and more time at boardmeetings and travelling to other meetings to secure banking or loan arrangements. The Baron seems to regard me in a different light and father Berkeley told me that he now sees me as a tremendous asset and I quote "You are the beautiful daughter-in-law, fluent in virtually all the important European languages, who comfortably mixes in upper circles and knows the King." That's what father Berkeley told me anyway!

Rosie turned the pages, ah yes, did she want to read this again. Her heart turned cold, but she did … November 12th 1908…

Winston Churchill called unexpectedly. I haven't seen him for ages. He wanted me to go with him to a private hospital in Chelsea. Not one to take questions I'm afraid, I did however insist on some information. All he told me though was a tremendous shock. We were to visit Stafford? Winston must be teasing me. My old lover, my first lover, is dead. I can't take it in … what does this mean?

Rosie paused; did she want to hurt herself still more? But she read on…

Arriving at the hospital I didn't know what I would find. Stafford was alive? How could this be? I had attended his memorial service at Westminster Abbey. I rushed inside with Winston who was barely able to keep up. He led me to a private room on the first floor. I had noted what he'd said in that slow deliberate manner "You will find what is left of Stafford inside. It will be difficult, but try to understand why he has kept this from you. Turn to the love I know you have for him, and resurrect it for a while." We entered the dimly lit side room; a figure lay on the bed. I remember moving closer, but the figure hardly stirred as I approached the bed. "Is that you father?" He asked me. "No, it's Rosie," I replied. "Oh God, no, no. Rosie you mustn't see me like this." I have written this as it was so that I remember our final time together always. It was his voice, it was my Stafford. Stunned I approached the bed. "But I don't understand. You're dead."

It's silly to think I said that but I did, she thought as she continued to read the diary…

Stafford turned to look at me but turned away and coughed violently. I remember asking if I should get a nurse. "No," he replied. "I don't have long and you are due an explanation." He strained and coughed occasionally, as he told me the events of those dark times which I am recording here. It seems he had been captured. He described to me that the conditions in that dreadful place meant your best horses couldn't outrun the camels used by the Dervish, who also rode small powerful ponies. He had been commanding a patrol of Dragoons along the Nile and was ordered to scout an oasis near a place called Wadji. General Kitchener was travelling with the main force over land and had instructed Stafford to travel down the river. Stafford recounted that as he reached the oasis, they were attacked by tribesmen. They far out numbered his patrol and his troop was wiped out with the exception of him and two privates. He didn't know what happened to the privates, but he had received a head wound. A bullet had creased his scalp and he had passed out. He told me that when he awoke, he was in chains and bound across the back of a horse. After quite a long journey, where they took turns in hitting him and gave him hardly any water, they arrived in Khartoum. He was horrified to see that they still had Gordon's body strung up on the city battlements. I remember his voice lowered when he said to me, "They did unspeakable things to me, Rosie," and he sobbed and I cried too.

I remember moving forward and wrapping my arms around him, she thought as she continued reading…

"Oh Rosie don't look at me," he said. I did look at this man. The man I loved, still loved. I was shocked to see that he had no eyes – two empty sockets and long scars down his cheeks. "Rosie are you looking at me? Please don't look at me. I want you to remember me as I was." I remember thinking to myself, what a terrible thing they had done to him but I had started now and I had to go on. "What else did they do to you, my love?" I asked him. His voice quivered, this was obviously painful for him, as he remembered the treatment by those devilish people. "Firstly they pulled out my nails, my hands and feet," he whimpered. He regained his composure. "Then they cut me open from my neck to my abdomen and let rats run over my body until I screamed in agony as they ate my flesh in front of me."

Oh God, I remember, I nearly passed out and as I read my diary again I cried some more…

"Then they cut off my testicles and stuffed them into my mouth." I remember gasping and I gripped him tightly again. This does seem like a terrible nightmare, but here he was in front of me. He had the scars on his body which had been mutilated by those awful people. Stafford carried on. "And if all that wasn't bad enough, they used sharp sticks to blind me. I prayed and prayed to die quickly, Rosie, but that was not their intention. They cleaned up my wounds and sewed me up and later I discovered that they intended to exchange me for a Prince who had been captured a day ago by General Kitchener."

"And that's his story," Winston said. "He was shipped back to England after six months in a hospital in Cairo. The surgeons there could not believe the skill of the people who had sewn him up. By all accounts he should have died with the loss of blood. I remember Stafford said that he wished he was dead; day after day in darkness with constant nightmares and pain."

As I was reading these diaries, I shuddered again sharing his pain, with the tears rolling down my cheeks and I remember he said…

"I'm sorry you have seen me like this. Churchill promised he wouldn't tell you." Later I asked Churchill, "But why did you bring me after all this time?"

"He told me he's dying. Not of his wounds but of a parasite. They cannot determine what is eating away his insides. I suspect that those devils the Dervish left him with a final present. I knew he would like to hear your voice one more time."

Rosie shut her diary with a clump. Stafford only lived two further days and she remembered spending nearly every minute with him. She hoped that she had made his last few days a little more comfortable. The morphine helped, she remembered, but she knew he did not know who I was in the end. His mother and father were wonderful. It seems that they and Winston had known of our love for each other and had kept silent. I hope to keep them in my life … The pity of it all is I didn't marry Stafford but I sometimes dream that I did and we lived happily ever after; and there the following day she saw a single line in her diary…

Went around to father B's house to pour my heart out again.

Rosie turned to near the end of her diary and saw that again on 20th December 1908 they had travelled to Zurich, but this time father B came. How they'd enjoyed that Christmas altogether. Even Frederick seemed to pick up a little but he was continuing to look so ill.

It had been a very cold December day and Rosie was glad she had asked the butler to build up the fires. 'Still it will be 1914 soon,' she thought. As she sat pondering her diary extracts she idly wondered if she should dispose of her diaries before she died but then remembered when she had been given this handsome set.

She had been given a new set of red leather bound journals by her father, Lord Berkeley, at Christmas 1908 and she had started to continue to write her diary in January of 1909. As she sat, nearly five years later, reading the extracts, she realised that 1909 had been a momentous year for her, for more than one reason. She started to read…

January 16th 1909

I have been living the duel role of a director of father Berkeley's bank and acting as, in effect, a roving ambassador for the Baron's bank. Frederick had become Managing Director of the Swiss bank based in Zurich, despite father-in-law, the Baron's, efforts he refused to "up sticks" and live in Switzerland, he preferred Paris and in any case Frederick and I have had separate lives for a very long time now.

She continued…

January 17th, 1909

Father Berkeley is fifty three this year and intends to take us all and the grandchildren, to Cannes for a holiday in June.

Skipping forward she saw in June a note that she had made confirming that they had indeed travelled to the South of France and remembered the rumour that some members of the Royal family were intending to holiday in France that year. She hadn't seen the King or the Prince of Wales in June but later on in August…

Rosie jumped the pages in her diary, until she came to the entry…

I have received a personal invitation from the Palace, from the King himself, to join the Royal family at Cowes Regatta in August.

She knew she had written how excited she was as she had never been to Cowes before and she added why she knew the King had asked her…

He hadn't asked to seduce me, he has given that up a number of years ago, it was because I am was fluent in German and Russian and both his cousins, Kaiser William and Czar Nicholas, are expected to attend.

She smiled as she remembered her excitement which was indicated in a note that she had made…

This was so exciting, all the establishment and the whole of Queen Victoria's dynasty, in one place for the first time!

She moved on until she came to the day of the Regatta and continued to read…

I have dressed in a smart two piece suit, accompanied by my father, Lord Berkeley, and we moved effortlessly between members of the nobility, politicians and friends of the King. It was a glorious sunny day and King Edward was very excited, as his yacht "Nautilus" was racing in the blue ribboned event that day. One of the King's aides, a captain in the Grenadier Guards, introduced himself to us and after a few minutes of pleasantries he asked "Cynthia" (I do hate formalities!), "The King," always referred to me by my birth name, "wishes you to join his party talking to Kaiser William and Czar Nicholas." I was then taken by the captain and introduced. All three men stopped their discussion and all turned their royal gaze on me! The Kaiser seemed particularly taken with me. He didn't expect a translator looking quite like me! He didn't seem to want to let go of my hand, but after a few minutes or so, the conversation reverted, in a mixture of German, Russian and English, to the arms build up. The Tsar was adamant that his cousin Kaiser William's build up of military might, was a direct threat to mother Russia, as he put it. Kaiser William assured him it was not. I was having to translate from Russian to German and then to English, so that all three of them could understand each other fluently. Kind Edward saw the opportunity to suggest a slow down which Kaiser William said he would consider, but he pointed out that Britain ruled the waves, with a fleet twice the size of the German fleet. The conversation then turned to Belgium. The Kaiser seemed to me to be probing the intelligence that might be known to Edward. "How would Britain react if Germany were forced to defend their frontier by invading Belgium?" asked the Kaiser. Edward could not understand why William thought Belgium would be a threat. The Kaiser pointed out that the French were being particularly arrogant and aggressive. The three men laughed until, just at that moment, the Prince of Wales appeared. "Ah Georgie," the King said, "take this delightful young lady for a walk. She must be bored with us" and they all laughed. I identified this as my cue to leave and curtsied and left the three men, a memory I would cherish forever!

She saw that she had heavily underlined this sentence in her diary. The mood of the day continued, she had written…

George, who escorted me away, had always flirted with me and took me over to a croquette game on the grand lawn and invited me to partner him. We were a formidable pairing and very successful and after the game George admitted he had an idea I might be a good player. I told him I regularly played at Lord Berkeley's estate, at which the Duchess of Norfolk commented that she wished I'd mentioned that before the wager with the Prince of Wales!

The following day she read…

The Kaiser is an interesting man but I was amazed at how often he changed uniforms. He must have changed from one to another at least a dozen times and each one covered in medals! Today went quickly and was particularly exciting as the King's yacht did very well and finished second.

This Evening

That evening, I was introduced to two of the Princesses, the Czar's daughters, who both looked stunning in French silk gowns. I seemed to be attracting more than my share of admiring glances and father Berkeley beamed, as, I suppose, a father would, as he escorted me to dinner.

Rosie reflected on the dinner party that weekend and then, sadly, the events that followed as the King had died in May 1910. She turned the pages to May and read her journal…

The funeral of the King was a sombre yet lavish occasion. Heads of State, Crown Princes and nobility from all over the world attended. Theodore Roosevelt came from America and sent an invitation to me and father Berkeley for a private dinner at the United States Embassy, in Grosvenor Square. I had always been intrigued by politicians, as "they dart from leaf to leaf"; this was how father Berkeley described their hidden agendas. All too often, he said, the real reasons for dinners and meetings was to talk business.

She continued reading…

The American President tactfully enquired about the Cowes meeting. How had the three, Edward, Czar Nicholas and The Kaiser, got on? Was it true that the Kaiser didn't really like Edward? I heard a rumour that the Kaiser asked if they would react if he invaded Belgium? I didn't respond to his skilful probing and let my father field most of the questions, with neutral replies or simply astonishment at the question. After all he wasn't present during the translation. I was, of course, present at that meeting, but knew not to reveal what I knew, even though TR seemed to know exactly what was discussed!

The following day was another momentous day as I attended with father Berkeley, an unveiling of a stature of Queen Victoria by the Kaiser and King George.

Rosie carried on reading…

A day later the nobility and politicians left and life returned to normal …

Normal – that's an understatement, Rosie thought and carried on reading turning the pages quickly until she came to the 1st September, 1910…

I continued to receive, every year, a large trunk which comes from Tore, which I knew contained American Dollars. Once or twice a year, a message was delivered from America and I would travel to Liverpool by train to meet the boat. These days, I have an escort of four of the Baron's "security" people.

Rosie smiled as she read her description…

Tore is a charming man, a typical Italian, as Italian's always seemed to be!

Rosie's mind went back to the autumn of 1910; she remembered that she had waited in the foyer, of Liverpool's grandest hotel, for Tore to arrive and she looked up her diary entry, 15th October 1910…

Tore always liks to cross the Atlantic as quickly as possible and on this trip was on board one of the fastest ships of the line that had won the blue ribbon for the fastest crossing a few years ago. I went to the dock to enquire, as the ship was late docking. It seemed that there was fog in the Atlantic, which was hampering the great ship and it would be at least a day late in arriving. The weather was to prove very meaningful.

Rosie paused, had a sip of water and carried on reading…

On disembarking, Tore came over, followed by his two henchmen carrying the trunk (isn't it strange that you can bring money into this country without anyone asking to look in to the trunk?).

As Rosie thought about Tore she could see him in her mind's eye and she had written…

He was a very masculine man and powerfully built yet his soft brown eyes, ah, those brown eyes, and when he laughed his whole face lit up.

Thinking now, she had no problem agreeing with her description of him and when she thought back to the Grand Hotel in Liverpool, reading on…

The hotel has a number of private rooms and Tore had secured one. I am feeling fleetingly curious as to how, as the hotel was always so busy, that he managed to secure a private dining room? We enjoyed each other's company this evening and our laughter could be heard outside the dining room. Tore has many stories and the champagne flowed. I know he was trying to seduce me and I let it happen. After dinner, feeling a little merry, we went upstairs together. I don't know what came over me. We chose my room – he pointed out that if one of them had to leave quickly it had better be him! When he saw me, dressed in a white nearly transparent nightdress, he said he knew I was the woman of his dreams! These Italians! They certainly know how to treat a woman and slowly he caressed me, running his hands gently over my body and then he started kissing my neck and carried on down! His tender kisses and gentle fondling meant that we were soon locked together in a triumphant embrace. Searching, demanding and pouring out our love for each other, until the climax. I laughed, as he watched me lying on the pillow that night, with my hair spread out and for the first time vowed that he wanted to kill a man for no reason – Frederick. Silly me, I giggled. But I knew he would not. Tore was a great flirt and I am sure, had many women in America and I don't kid myself. We made love on another occasion before the morning, but when I woke in the morning, it was as though he had never been there; only his masculine smell remained on the pillow. What a man I thought, what a pity!

As Rosie thought about Tore, she realised she had seen him twice a year, for the past ten years, but still he didn't know about Sophie. Skipping her diary to mid March 1911 she noticed a slight stain on the corner of the page and remembered a tear had fallen. Looking down the page she read…

Calamity, Calamity I am pregnant again. It must have been that evening of madness with Tore. Shall I tell father Berkeley?

Rosie closed the diary and for a moment reflected. Yes it was a moment of madness but it had led to the birth of her beautiful girl, Sophie Anne. Tore still didn't know he was the father, as she had decided never to tell him. Italians can be so possessive, she thought.

Feeling tired, Rosie decided to put away her diary and retired for a rest before dinner. Several hours later, she was woken by her maid and bathed and dressed for dinner. It was nearly the start of a new year, shortly to be 1914 and the threat of war loomed. How quickly time passed. What would life hold for her family this year after Billy's death? She was preoccupied with her children; Sophie was such a sweet natured girl. Edward was at Eton with Frederick Junior who was showing he was academically gifted.

The balloon swayed, as a light breeze moved the huge construction. Alfie had joined the army in 1916, there weren't many questions as to his age and quickly his skill as a marksman had been identified. He was sent on a course to Bisley, in Surrey, to sharpen up his skills and when he returned to his unit, he was, without doubt, one of the best shots in the army. Snipers were used by both sides during the Great War and if you dared to stick your head above the trench, especially with a cigarette in your mouth, you were likely to be a dead man within ten seconds.

Today, Alfie was on static balloon duty. The observation balloon was cranked up 1000 feet in the air, for a member of the observer corp., in this case Teddy Ackland, to send messages by flag signal, to his mates down below, about how close the gunners were getting to their apparent targets. On a clear day, you could see for miles up there and with a pair of Zeiss binoculars, you could see the grey faces of the Germans, huddled in their trenches. Poor sods, he thought, they are as badly off as us, what the hell are we all doing here?

Alfie's thoughts wondered as he studied the air. His job today was not to kill the enemy, but to assist Teddy. He was the look out and what he did not want to see, was a German aeroplane heading in their direction. The Germans knew all about spotters operating from balloons and frequently sent one or more of their planes, to shoot them down. Teddy told him he hated it up there – for a start he couldn't stand heights and secondly he was "bleedin' scared!" Teddy knew several observers who had died when an enemy plane had swooped on the hapless balloon and machine gunned the occupant and set fire to the balloon. Nowadays, the observer had a gunner with him –

"Fat lot of good that will do," Teddy told him.

It was October 1916 and the war seemed to go on and on.

We made ground – they made ground. We attacked – they attacked. "It all seemed," he told Alfie, "a whole waste of time".

As he glanced across at his companion, Teddy saw a tall lad, funny thing; he noticed he had the top of two fingers missing. How could you be a good shooter when you had two fingers missing? Just as he was contemplating his companion's skills as a rifleman, a barrage started. Teddy picked up the binoculars; he had bought them a year ago from a private in the Grenadiers, who had taken them from a dead German officer – still seven shillings and six pence, wasn't a bad price. Teddy used his signal flags, to signal to the ground, that the shells were falling short of their intended target. Suddenly his companion gripped his arm and shouted.

"Signal to get us down fast, two German planes heading this way."

"Shit," thought Teddy and frantically waved the red flag. His mates below began the frantic winding up of the winch, which brought the balloon back to earth – but it was a very slow process.

Teddy began to panic, the German planes were closing and very soon the rear gunner would open fire, they were goners, unless a miracle occurred. As the balloon was slowly drawn to the ground it dawned on Teddy that they were getting too low to use their parachutes! Alfie sighted his Lee Enfield rifle and wiped his eye. Left handed, he rested the rifle on the top of the basket for support and waited. Licking his lips, he ignored the frantic waving of his observer and the tugging of his sleeve.

"You berk, stop pulling me, you stupid idiot," he said angrily, as Teddy pulled his arm and nearly sent his rifle over the top of the basket.

The German planes approached, Halberstadts, Alfie recognised them as twin seated and knew the machine gunner at the back was his target. The Germans had fitted a number of these planes with a machine gun. The gunner in the rear faced the other direction. The planes approached on a diagonal course to enable the gunner to swivel his machine gun and with the sun behind them, made it difficult for him to focus, but he waited. One thousand yards, eight hundred yards, suddenly the first plane started firing, the slow chatter of a machine gun breaking the silence. Teddy was lying on the floor, as tracers tore into the balloon. Alfie knew the bloody thing would not stay up if it was punctured too many times, or might catch fire and he had seen the gas in the balloon blow up before now. Taking careful aim he gently squeezed the trigger and fired – hit, the German gunner let go of his machine gun, but kept his finger on the trigger, which sprayed upwards in an arc, hitting and catching fire the fabric at the tail of the plane. The German plane started to nosedive immediately, the pilot fighting with the controls and the gunner dead, still in their cockpits. The second plane opened fire; tracers hit the balloon, which began to sag as it leaked gas. Alfie took aim, but this pilot was good, he changed direction and dived, just as he was about to fire. The soldiers on the ground fired at the German plane diving toward them, then the pilot changed direction again and turning once again, headed back toward the balloon. The men below frantically turned the winch, swapping over every few minutes, as their muscles ached.

Teddy had peed himself and was lying on the floor sobbing, "I don't want to die," as Alfie, once again, took aim. This time, the pilot was coming straight on and not from the west. He took aim and fired. The pilot wouldn't have known what had happened and would have died instantly, as the bullet penetrated his brain. The gunner was frantic, as the German plane lurched downwards, toward no man's land and then it was all over, in a ball of flame, as the plane hit the ground and exploded.

"Come on mate, get up it's all over," Alfie picked up Teddy. "Don't let your mates see you like this," he said.

Alfie looked up and realised that the rate the balloon was descending was not quick enough. Holed in several places, the balloon was rapidly deflating and was starting to burn; they would not reach the ground before it crumpled into a useless mess.

"Come on", he said, climbing over the basket, "we have got to climb down the rope, it's too low to parachute."

"I can't," said Teddy, "I'm scared." Alfie hesitated and then got back in the basket and slapped Teddy around the face.

"C'mon, you bugger, or you're a goner or will kill us both."

Half dragging Teddy he made him climb onto the basket edge and over the side and grab one of the ropes, holding the balloon to the ground.

"Go on climb down, hurry," he urged. Teddy did not move, his legs simply would not move. Alfie climbed to where he clung perilously to the ropes, trailing from the balloon to the ground. "You must go mate or we're dead," and he slapped him again.

Teddy began to descend with his eyes shut, with Alfie close behind him. The men below screamed encouragement, when suddenly Teddy seemed to miss his hold, cried out and fell. Alfie didn't look, just speeded up his descent. He was within thirty feet when he felt the balloon die. He had seconds to react, rushed down the rope ten feet, then jumped …

Alfie hit the ground with a thud and heard his ankle break. He rolled over just in time to see the observation balloon, or what was left of it, falling on him. He hated the dark and as he was enveloped by the balloon, he began to panic, shouting out for someone to pull it off him. Suddenly light appeared and two of the observers, who had been working the winch, pulled him out, from under the bullet-ridden balloon, now smouldering.

"You okay, Alfie?" Smithy one of the observer corps' newest recruits, who also hated balloons, pulled him clear.

"Tremendous shooting Horsfield," the voice came from Captain Stanton, the Corps Commanding Officer.

"I intend to report your heroism in despatches. It was a pity about Teddy, why didn't he just climb down?" At that the officer instructed Smith and the other private, Mooney, to help Alfie to the casualty field tent.

Alfie did not mind being fussed over by the pretty nurses, but his ankle hurt like hell. Eventually he was sent back to a field hospital, where his ankle was strapped. As they manipulated his foot, he cried out in pain; the young nurse had told him that that was the end of his war.

"You'll have to be sent back to Blighty, ain't you lucky?" Alfie remembered thinking she had a cheeky smile and gorgeous chestnut eyes, before he passed out.

The nurse was right though, Alfie was sent back to Calais and on a troop ship to Dover. Then he was transferred to a hospital in Maidstone, to check his broken ankle. Satisfied his ankle was bound tightly, they put it in a plaster cast and gave him a set of crutches and nine weeks' leave.

His mum, Aunt and dear old Uncle Tyndall were delighted he had returned, "more or less in one bit", as his Uncle put it. Still, nine weeks did not seem much of a break for Alfie. Most of the time he spent on crutches, but when the doctor at Brighton General Hospital took off the plaster cast on his ankle, he had to admit, he needed at least two weeks physiotherapy to regain the strength in his leg and his confidence.

The army caught up with him again and in the spring of 1917 he was sent to Catterick, training new recruits to use their rifles. Two months later he received fresh orders to join an Australian Unit going to the front for a big push. Alfie had been on many such "big pushes" before and had no illusions about a speedy end to this war. They joined up with a Canadian Brigade at Ypres and went to attack a place called Passchendaele. Alfie had been fighting Germans since 1916, but it was nothing like this. Alfie was required, with other snipers, to keep the Germans' heads down and kill any that were careless enough to show themselves. He gave up counting his victims after three months of the worse fighting he had ever seen. By God, he felt sorry for those Canadians and the British Fifth Army, who had to endure mud and now mustard gas. The mud was up to your knees and rats the size of cats were all over the place. As a sniper, Alfie was not required to charge across two hundred yards of no man's land, with tracers and shells likely to drop on you and shrapnel which would rip your body apart before you'd got fifty feet from the trenches. He reached Polygon Wood and lay up with two other snipers. He had to lie patiently waiting for a Boche to light a cigarette, or for the Germans to counter-attack – he'd usually get at least six before the whistle blew and they retreated back to their hell holes and trenches. Killing and more killing. Alfie was becoming immune to dropping another poor sod caught in his gun sights.

Then he had another piece of luck, a shell landed in the woods and a small piece of shrapnel hit him in the leg. With blood streaming down his leg, soaking his filthy fatigues, he was stretchered behind the lines. Later Alfie would reflect on that appalling place and the loss of life, on both sides – none of it made sense, for a few hundred yards, or a quarter of a mile, thousands of men were dying on both sides.

A stretcher bearer commandeered another soldier and they carried Alfie back to the field hospital. They sewed him up and shipped him back to

Blighty, for the last time. He considered he had been lucky. He had learnt early on not to make friends, because later that day, or in a week, they were likely to be dead – those were the memories that stayed with you, together with the mud, the rain and the cries of the wounded in no man's land.

Chapter Twenty One

June 28th 1918

Rosie had been staying at the house in Eaton Square for several months; working for the government's newly formed Secret Intelligent Service, which had taken her to France and Germany earlier during the Great War. She had been translating, at the Westminster HQ of the Secret Service, for the past month, not enjoying the office work. She was having dinner that evening, when a maid knocked on the dining room door.

"Sorry to interrupt Madam," Rosie looked up. "There is a Commander Langford waiting in the day room who would like to see you."

Rosie was used to her meals being interrupted, but not by the personal equerry to the King. What on earth could he want?

"I'm coming Sylvia." Rosie got up, checked her appearance in the mirror and joined the Commander. "Good evening Commander Langford."

Langford was a tall, gangly man who had lost his arm during an engagement at Scarpa Flo earlier in the war; consequently he shook hands with his left hand.

"Good evening Mrs de Courcy, I am sorry to disturb you at this late hour, but His Majesty would like to see you immediately at Buckingham Palace."

"I see, give me five minutes. Have you a driver?"

"Yes, he will drive you and bring you back."

London was glorious in June, thought Rosie, as she made the short drive from Eaton Square to the Palace. Entering by the West Gate, the Commander showed his pass and they were allowed to park inside the Palace gates. Hurrying along Rosie had a job keeping up with Langford's pace. He had hardly said a word since they started their journey. Rosie, in her turn, had sat in deep thought. George V had been chasing her for some time. He had been much more persistent a few years ago, but even now he often whispered suggested meetings to her at functions they both attended. Rosie thought he loved the chase, but knew that's all it was and had never taken him as a lover.

Shown into the King's private chambers, Rosie was surprised to see Sir Mansfield Cumming sitting in front of a superb leather topped desk.

"Sir Mansfield."

"Cynthia." Mansfield always called Rosie, by her more formal name.

"Are we to see the King?" asked Rosie.

"Yes, but I will let His Royal Highness explain."

Sir Mansfield Cumming was the long standing head of the Secret Intelligence Service. Established as the Foreign Section of the Secret Service, Cumming had been running the organisation since it was established in 1909. The Secret Service Bureau was abbreviated to "Secret Service" with Mansfield signing himself "C" in green ink. Cumming had achieved a degree of autonomy, but the war office, between 1914 to 1918, had managed to exercise virtual control over his actions, integrating intelligence gathering with the Foreign Section of the Military Intelligence Directorate. For much of the war, Cumming's organisation was known as MII and it was this section Rosie had worked for on a number of occasions during the war, but mostly she translated documents at the Westminster HQ, when called upon to do so.

The door opened and in scurried Commander Langford, followed by a man dressed smartly in a two piece grey suit. The man introduced himself as James Horsley-Smythe, private secretary to the King.

"The King is awfully sorry he has been delayed, would you like some tea?"

Cumming muttered, but said "Yes, tea would be lovely."

After a considerable wait, King George arrived, dressed in a blue suit and sporting a cravat, one of the new modern dress styles. Introductions followed, but King George made it clear he wanted no formalities and started the meeting, coughing slightly.

"Hm, now Cynthia and gentlemen, to business." The room went silent. "As you know, my dear cousin Tsar Nicholas and his family have been imprisoned by the Bolsheviks, since last November. Well thanks to Cumming here," he nodded toward Sir Mansfield, "we have discovered where the red devils have taken them. Cumming please continue." Cumming cleared his throat.

"Since late last year, we have been endeavouring to discover the whereabouts of the Tsar and his family through," and he paused, "various methods. We now know that they are all held at a house in Siberia, near a major city called Ekaterinburg," he pronounced the name in pieces. "Eka-terin-burg." King George interrupted.

"Now, we are not going to sit idly by as my cousin is imprisoned, or worse; tell them Cumming." Rosie could see that Sir Mansfield was getting faintly irritated by the interruptions, but he continued.

"Yes, as His Majesty has said, we intend to stage a rescue," he then opened a large map which had been folded on the table. "This is the Russian's most desolate area, Siberia. Here is Eka-terin-burg," he pointed, "and here is Moscow. The plan is to spirit away the Tsar and his family, with the help of the loyal Russian soldiers they call "The White Russians" and flee, firstly to the border with Mongolia and then hide until the family can be smuggled across the border, into Mongolia and onward into China. It will be a very arduous journey, but it is the easiest way to get out a large family, travelling by coach and horseback and possibly by train."

"A bold plan indeed," said the King. Rosie, who had been to Russia on several occasions, kept her own council, but thought them all mad. Woman, children, no worse still, Royal women and children, travelling thousands of miles by coach, what were they thinking?

"Now Cynthia," said King George, "I know of some of your exploits, which are frankly astounding, but we need you, as you are the only person, at short notice, we can summon up with any, how shall I say, field skills, who speaks fluent Russian. I must say, Cumming here speaks highly of you, but this is a wretched job for a woman – so feel free to say no."

Rosie thought for a moment. "Of course I will help Your Majesty."

"That's the spirit old girl," said the King beaming. "Now Cumming I will leave it with you. Do your best everybody." He looked at them all, nodded and left the room, followed by his secretary.

"Well, that's it then," said Cumming. "We will reconvene at Westminster, to discuss the plan in greater detail and as time is of a premium, I suggest we go there now." Gathering up papers, Cumming led the party back to the car waiting at the West entrance of Buckingham Palace. During the short journey to Victoria Street in Westminster, Cumming or "C" as he had become known, remained silent and only Commander Langford made smalltalk, which Rosie suspected was for her benefit.

Arriving at the headquarters of the Secret Service, Cumming led the way to his third floor office. Commander Langford and Rosie were then introduced to a man waiting there, called Steven Alley. Not sure what he was doing there, Rosie kept quiet.

"C" went behind the rather tatty desk and unlocked a drawer, withdrawing a manila file, stamped "Utmost Secret". Opening the file he extracted three A4 typed sheets also marked "Utmost Secret" and passed them to Rosie, Commander Langford and the man Steven.

"Now, before you read your instructions let me introduce each of you and explain why you have been picked for this mission," said "C". "First of all Cynthia," he looked up at Rosie, as a headmaster would, checking she was paying attention. "Cynthia de Courcy has worked for us on a number of occasions. She was very active in the war and went behind enemy lines on many occasions. Cynthia speaks Russian, like a native of Moscow and here is our trump card, she holds a Swiss diplomatic passport and is a director of two banks, one, the de Courcy Merchant Bank in Switzerland, the other based in London. Cynthia, is a crack pistol shot and so as you need have no doubt, has killed before," he paused as the information he had provided, sank in. Certainly the two other men were regarding this beautiful middle-aged woman in a somewhat different manner. Cumming continued his introductions.

"Alley here, is a Secret Service agent, who has worked successfully for me many times and speaks a little Russian, better German and French." He continued. "Commander Langford is a Royal Navy officer, who was seconded to this bureau by the War Office in 1916, particularly to develop a strategy against the German U-boats, who were attacking the allied shipping. So, introductions complete please turn over and read your briefing note," There was a pause whilst they studied their notes. Then opening a large map of Europe "C" urged them to stand and study the map.

"We've a number of ways to get into Russia," he cleared his throat, "but we have to consider a cover story and how you are going to get the family out."

The two men and Rosie remained silent, looking down at the map. "Well Langford, what is the easiest way, by ship?" "C" asked.

Commander Langford studied the map for a few more seconds and then said, "The closest we could get, would be to embark here," he pointed to Kaliningrad, "in the Baltic Sea, north of Gdansk. The trouble is the Bolsheviks have had a bit of local trouble with the Poles and security is likely to be very tight. The Reds may have taken power, but everyone is very nervous, so the Charges d'Affair at the Russian Embassy, tells me. So, my preferred route is, we sail for Helsinki in Finland." He pointed to the map. "Then catch a train to Moscow, changing here." He pointed to a town at the top of the Gulf of Finland. "Having reached Moscow, security will be tight."

Rosie interrupted. "I was in Moscow last year on another matter and have a perfect excuse to travel there. I went by train through Poland". The men looked up again, rather surprised.

"What is the security situation in Moscow?" said the stocky man, Steven.

"They are very nervous; the Poles, prompted by the Russian White Army, caused general uproar, by attacking Russia. I was visiting the Finance Minister, Pyotr Bark and was subject to considerable scrutiny and escorted all the time," replied Rosie.

"That's not good," said Steven.

"What did you mean, you have a good excuse?" asked "C".

"Well", Rosie paused to collect her thoughts, what could she tell these men, it was, after all confidential banking business, involving her directorship of the Swiss bank. "Suffice to say, that the Finance Minister and the head of the Russian Bank are expecting me to contact them on a delicate matter, I cannot discuss further."

"Come now," said "C" abruptly, "this is of national importance. What is this delicate matter?"

"I am sorry, but my duty as a director of de Courcy's bank in Switzerland, prevents me from answering your question," Rosie said firmly. "C" spluttered and seemed about to explode, his face turning red.

"Okay, well, does this good excuse enable us to go into Russia?" asked Steven.

"Yes," replied Rosie.

"Then we will use it, but the reason we can travel will only be known to you."

"How's that going to work?" asked the Commander.

"Well, Rosie would be expected to travel accompanied. I shall be her personal assistant, with forged Swiss papers. I speak passable German and French; in any case, I doubt they would check into my credentials too deeply."

"H'm, that is very plausible," said "C".

"What say you Cynthia?" asked Steven. Rosie thought for a moment.

"Yes, I think that is the way in, but with a variation." Looking down at the map she pointed. "Here is where we should embark."

She pointed to Odessa on the Black Sea. "Then we catch a train to Moscow, via Kiev and Tula. We get off the train at Moscow and meet the Finance Minster. We explain, during the conversation with him, that we have a meeting with the Japanese and are intending to catch a train to Vladivostak, where we are meeting a boat, to take us to Tokyo. In fact, we will sail from Vladivostak, but, south of Japan into the East China Sea, out into the Pacific, away from Chinese territorial waters and then sail home."

There was a silence, as the men absorbed what Rosie had outlined. It was "C" who broke the silence. "Good plan Cynthia. Can you meet the party at Vladivostak, Commander, after dropping them off at Odessa?"

"I will need to steam back through the Black Sea, through the Bosporus and dock at the entrance of the proposed Suez Canal, Port Said and then journey by road and pick up one of His Majesty's ships at the apex of the Red Sea. Then steam toward Singapore, where we will attract least attention. There, I propose to hire a coastal trader, hopefully a steamship and proceed to Vladivostak, with a cargo of fruit or something applicable, to meet up with the fleeing party. We will then reverse the journey, meeting a ship of the line, at Singapore. However, it would be nice to arranged for a Greek or Turkish ship to take the party on the first leg, from Istanbul to Odessa – one of His Majesty's ships would attract far too much attention."

"Capital, capital," said "C".

"There are problems, Sir," interrupted Steven. "C" looked irritated.

"Well, what is it Steven?"

"As I understand it, the Bolsheviks have taken all the Romanov family, there must be at least ten, and if they insist on bringing servants, we can probably double that number." There was a silence. He continued. "With all the best will, I don't see how Cynthia and I can arrange sufficient transport from their prison to the station, at Ekaterinburg. If we don't travel fast, they will cut us off and be waiting."

"What about a diversion, indicating you are heading north?" said the Commander.

"But who would believe anyone in their right mind would head deeper into Siberia?" Asked Steven.

"No, you are quite right," replied "C". "I have a contact in Moscow, who will arrange coaches and will be your liaison person. He is a sympathiser and a white Russian."

"Sorry, Sir, coaches really won't do." "C" looked up from the map.

"Why not Steven?"

"Well, consider the terrain, there are not likely to be any good roads between where they are being held and the station at Ekaterinburg and, let's face it, we are going to have to travel fast."

"That settles it." "C" moved back behind the desk and sat silently for a few seconds. "Sit down everybody," "C" said and continued. "It is becoming increasingly clear, that we cannot save all The Romonov's. I have, therefore, decided that your principal task will be to kidnap the Tsar, Czarina, the Prince and any of the older Princesses you judge able to ride swiftly. The maximum number of people will be five. We will provide identities and passports for the Tsar, his wife and look alike identities, which could be used for two of the Princesses and the Prince. The Romanov's can speak passable French, so they will all, like you, hold Swiss passports." He held up his hand, "If you can transport the haemophiliac Prince, do. Furthermore, your other cover story will be that you are on a trade mission to Russia and Japan. Any of the younger members of the Romanov family will be older children who are accompanying their parents for the experience."

"Sir," Steven interrupted. "C" looked at Steven, who choosing his words carefully said, "These Romanov's are not used to taking orders and I suspect will not want to leave all their family."

"I agree the plan has difficulties, Steven. If they won't come easily, you must kidnap them." A buzz broke out around the table.

"May I say something?" Rosie interjected. "We have no choice but to limit the numbers. Ideally only the Tsar should be spirited away. Any more than one person joining us increases the risk of us being questioned at every major station and town on the way. We also have to move fast. The Bolsheviks will be hunting us and surely head for the station at Ekaterinburg."

"I agree," said Steven. "Let's concentrate on bringing the Tsar and perhaps Czarina." There was a momentary hush as "C" made the decision.

"Alright, your orders will be to bring out the Tsar. If you can also bring out the Czarina and up to one further member of the Royal Family, then do so." At that they all left Westminster to make arrangements to leave tomorrow.

For Rosie it was easy enough. Anne and Sophie were at Rodean Boarding School and Edward was at Eton, with Frederick. Meeting Lord Berkeley, Rosie explained the task ahead; she was not concerned about National Security, as her father probably would be briefed by the King anyway. Her father was very agitated. Approaching his seventieth year, he was suffering from arthritis and high blood pressure and was afraid for his daughter. He knew she had carried out many daredevil missions in the war, but this was different. The Bolsheviks were an unknown entity. How would they regard Swiss neutrality? He knew her story to enter Moscow was factual, but just in case there was a problem getting a boat out of Istanbul, he told Rosie that he would send a telegraph to a Greek shipping magnate he knew and ask him to send a ship. A message would be sent to Commander Langford at Portsmouth, before sailing tomorrow, with further details.

Sailing out of Portsmouth harbour, on HMS Sheffield, Rosie and Steven had been asked to keep below and reluctantly obeyed their instructions. The Commander was keen that no-one should know they were on board.

Making 20 knots, the destroyer reached their first stop, a port near Athens, Greece, after a day and a half. There, they boarded a Greek steamer, "The Athenia", carrying a load of fruit, oranges, lemons and grapes to Odessa, via Istanbul. Once again, Steven and Rosie had to keep out of sight as they passed Istanbul, through the Bosporus, into the Black Sea. Half way across the Black Sea they had gone up on deck. It was a glorious summer day and Rosie leaned on the rail of the aged Greek steamer. Black smoke trailed into the Azure blue sky, the sun sparkled on a low swell and the ship made good time.

"Beautiful day." Steven joined her leaning on the rail. They had become friends; Rosie knew Steven would like to be more than friends, but kept him slightly at arm's length.

"How long before we reach Odessa?" asked Rosie.

"About four hours, I guess," Steven replied.

Disembarking from the freighter, they walked toward the railway station.

An old train timetable they had seen in London suggested that a steam train left Odessa for Moscow at 10 am, which meant another overnight stop somewhere. However, Rosie and Steven did not expect the train would be running on time and had allowed a wait of up to 12 hours in Odessa. Intelligence received when they docked in Athens led them to believe that Odessa was stable, but as soon as they docked, they realised things were not that straightforward. Walking through the streets there was an undercurrent and twice they were stopped and questioned. When they reached the railway station, a train was waiting in the station, but, on enquiry, it had been waiting to leave for a day. It was then that a group of armed men challenged them. Rosie tried to explain that they were Swiss diplomats, but despite her protestations, they were hauled away and locked in separate cells in the police station. Their possessions, including passports, had been taken and for the first time in a long time, Rosie felt alone.

The door of her cell opened and a policeman entered and motioned for Rosie to follow him. Outside the door, another policeman, a younger man, joined them. They led her to an office and on entering, Rosie saw a bearded man in a green uniform, sitting behind a desk. That was the only furniture in the room and there was an odour in the air Rosie identified as urine. The man looked up saying nothing. The guard behind her, a sullen man, pushed her from behind. She stumbled into the room. The bearded man looked up. "Your name?" he asked in Russian. Rosie met his gaze despite a slight tremble in her leg. Fortunately she understood his Russian.

"Cynthia de Courcy, I am a Swiss national with a diplomatic passport. You have no right to imprison me!" The bearded man flicked through her passport. She saw that her suitcase had been emptied on the floor and the contents of her handbag was on the table top.

"Why have you a letter addressed to the Russian Finance Minister?"

"I am a Swiss Diplomat, I am not obliged to discuss diplomatic business with you," Rosie replied in her impeccable Russian.

"Undress," the bearded man barked. Rosie looked at him. "I said undress," he barked. Rosie went pale but held his gaze.

"I will not. You cannot be in charge. Who is your Commander in Odessa? I wish to speak to him." The man sneered and moved around the table menacingly.

"Undress, take off your clothes." Rosie moved backwards, but suddenly felt a sharp blow in her back, she fell to the ground. "Get up and undress or shall we do it for you?" Rosie slowly got to her feet and began to unbutton her blouse, pulling it out from her knee length skirt. Dropping the blouse on the floor, she loosened her skirt and it fell to the ground. She stopped. "All of it!" Barked the bearded man, licking his lips. Rosie pulled her petticoat over her arms and it dropped to the floor, revealing a pair of lace cami-knickers and a white wired bra. Her bosom heaved and her nipples protruded through the flimsy material. The guard behind her moved to the front, presumably to get a better view! The bearded man made his move. He grabbed at her. Rosie easily avoided his attempt to grab her and pushed straight fingers into his eyes. As he cried out, she hit him across the exposed neck, with the side of her hand. Immediately he was gasping for air. She turned her attention to the surly guard, who raised his rifle.

"It is not easy to kill someone," Rosie said looking him straight in the eye. Rosie moved forward.

"Stay where you are. I will shoot you."

"I don't think so; you've never killed a woman before have you? Why don't you put the gun down?" She moved to unclip her brassiere and let it drop. "I didn't like him, but you," she smiled and held out her arms. Rosie was a beautiful woman with firm round breasts. The soldier dropped his rifle and moved toward her. Rosie, who was still wearing shoes, kicked him catching his knee cap, and he shrieked in pain. She turned sideways and struck him with the side of her hand, across the side of the neck. He dropped to the ground struggling for breath. Then she felt an arm around her neck. The bearded man. She shifted her weight and threw him over her shoulder. He clattered heavily to the ground. Stepping backwards, she picked up the rifle and was surprised when the door opened and another man, followed by two soldiers, appeared in the doorway.

"Ah, a stand off I see," said the man looking Rosie up and down. "You seem to have the better of these fools; why not put down the gun, get dressed and we will talk?" he smiled.

Rosie thought for a second, dropped the gun on the floor and picked up her clothes. "Take out those idiots," the man instructed the man behind him. He watched as she dressed, clearly enjoying the sight before him. "My name is Petr Skoroposky. I have the dubious honour of being the Commander, here in Odessa and the northern approach. We are the army of Free Ukraine "the Central Rada". He pronounced the name "Tsentral 'na rada". Rosie had dressed as he spoke. He went around the desk and brought her the chair. "Please sit. I must apologise for those idiots, they exceed their authority. Tell me who are you?" he asked. Rosie looked at this man, as he sat on the edge of the desk, looking down at her, clean shaven, deep blue eyes, an open friendly face, but a firm chin and the look of a man in authority.

"My name is Cynthia de Courcy. I am a Swiss diplomat, on my way to Moscow to meet the Finance Minister, Pyotr Bark."

"And what do you intend to discuss with this man?"

Rosie hesitated for a moment. "I am instructed, by interested parties, to negotiate for a cash sum, the freedom of the Tsar and his family." The man, Petr, got up and walked around the desk. He picked up the passport and examined it, then looked through the items, which had been dumped on the desk from Rosie's handbag.

"Is this a letter of introduction?" He had picked up the letter embossed with the Swiss flag, discreetly on the flap.

"Yes." He slid his finger along the sealed edge and opened the letter, reading the content, he turned to Rosie.

"You seriously expect the Bolsheviks to give up the Tsar?"

"Most people at least think, when offered a great deal of money, and we think Russia is in need of money."

Rosie shrugged. "How much are you offering?"

"I am sure you understand that I am bound by confidentiality, suffice to say, it is a massive amount of money." The man Petr sat motionless.

"And who is your companion?"

"His name is Marcelle Gineroux (Rosie used Steven's cover name); he is my assistant and bodyguard." Petr laughed.

"You don't need a bodyguard," but then more seriously said, "Unfortunately your companion has not been treated well, I will take you to him, but first, how were you to travel to Moscow?"

"We intended to catch a train; is Marcelle hurt?"

"Superficially, yes, but he will be okay." At that he got up. "Come we will see him."

Walking at a brisk pace, followed by an armed guard, they went back to the cells. Unlocking a door the guard entered, followed by Rosie and the Commander, Petr Skoroposky. Steven, alias Marcelle, was lying motionless on a dirty mattress on the floor of the cell. Rosie knelt down to look at him and he opened his eyes, moving simultaneously to grab her.

"It's okay Marcelle, it's me Cynthia," she said in French. He sat up and looked at her.

"It looks worse than it is," he grimaced as he felt his nose, which was caked in dried blood.

"Bring water and a cloth," said Commander Skoroposky to one of the guards. "Sit up Mr?" he said, speaking passable French.

"Gineroux, Marcelle Gineroux." He looked at this newcomer.

"Allow me to introduce myself, my name is Commander Petr Skoroposky. I have the dubious honour to be in charge of this region, for the Central Rada." The guard returned with a bowl. "Perhaps you would like to help your companion?" the Commander said, with a lilt in his voice. Rosie cleaned up Steven's face. He had taken quite a beating, his nose was probably broken, he had a cut lip and a black eye was developing. Steven winced as Rosie dabbed his cheek, which was swollen. "Now you are cleaned up, can you come with me please," said the Commander.

They followed the Ukraine Commander to another office, this time there were two chairs facing the desk. Skoroposky sat behind the desk and invited them to sit. A soldier knocked and came in with a coffee pot. "Coffee?" offered the Commander. He poured three cups of thick black coffee and passed them around. He looked at them both. "We are not animals. The Ukrainian people have declared independence from Russia and the Bolsheviks. Naturally, it will not be easy to achieve our freedom and we have many men who are, how I shall say, peasants we have armed. We would like to see the Tsar released from captivity, but we are not able to directly interfere, otherwise the Bolsheviks will have even more of an excuse to attack us. There is a train in the station, it has been held up there for two weeks. I will instruct the driver and stoker to fire up the train and take you to Kiev." He held up his hand as Rosie went to speak. "I cannot guarantee your safety once out of the Ukraine. I will accompany you to the border, then you are on your own."

"How do you recommend we proceed to Moscow from Kiev?" asked Rosie.

"I think the only way would be by horse, to Gomel and then hope the train is running, otherwise you will have a very long ride," he chuckled.

The following morning, it was an early start at 7 am, the train, with only three carriages and one of them was a flat top, with machine guns, a small cannon bolted on and manned by soldiers, left the station. Rosie, Steven and Skoroposky sat uncomfortably on the hard seats. The Commander was an affable man, who delighted in explaining how Ukrainian leaders in Kiev had organised the Central Rada, headed up by Mykhaclo Hrushevsk. They had, he explained, sought the approval of the Russian Provisional Government, in Petrograd, but were rebuffed. Apparently the Central Rada were a mish-mash of Ukrainians, Russians, soldiers and elements of the Russian Army and last November, after the Bolshevik coup in Petrograd, they declared a Ukrainian People's Republic in Kiev. They favoured a federation with Russia, but the Russian Bolsheviks insisted on an all-Russian Union. They then renamed themselves, the All-Ukrainian Congress of Workers', Soldiers' and Peasants' Soviets and declared a Bolshevik government of the Ukraine. But, alas, he said, relationships soured with the Russian Bolsheviks and they now had mobilised for open war. "We control much of the Ukraine," declared Skoroposky, puffing out his chest.

The train laboured along a hilly track, stopping for water and topping up coal at Uman. Arriving in Kiev at 11.30 am, Skoroposky suggested they remain in the carriage, until he had spoken to the local Commander, a man called Vilebsky. Returning shortly before 1 pm, he asked them to accompany him to a meeting in the Town Hall.

The Town Hall in Kiev had seen better days. There were shell holes in the wall and signs of fierce fighting. Skoroposky explained that the Soviet Bolsheviks had briefly held Kiev, before they drove them north. They entered the Town Hall and headed down a wide passage before going upstairs. Knocking and entering they saw a group of men looking over a map on the table.

"Ah, Skoroposky, are these our guests?" asked a short man with a trim moustache.

Skoroposky introduced the local Commander, Ivan Vilebsky, who smiled and shook hands with Rosie and Steven. "These two men, Vladimir and Aleksandr, will accompany you to the border," he made a space for Steven, who grinned. Rosie was used to Russian men, they considered women should serve in the Army, but not as leaders. "Your name is Marcelle?" he asked in Russian. Rosie translated immediately, as Vilebsky had spoken quickly with a Ukrainian dialect. "You speak Russian?" Vilebsky addressed his question toward Rosie.

"Yes," she replied. He nodded, appreciating this woman's skills and she was also very attractive.

"Come look," he said to Rosie. Pointing at the Ukrainian and Russian border, he indicated a route they would have to take to Gomel. "There is a possible train here," he said in English.

Rosie, speaking in Russian said, "Would you prefer I speak in English, I am fluent?"

He looked at her and smiled. "No. If there is no train you will have a very uncomfortable ride," he laughed. Shaking hands they left the Town Hall. A rickety old car, Rosie had no idea of the manufacturer, pulled up and all five got in. Rosie judged they were heading north. Skoroposky held a conversation, broken up with raucous laughter, about various bars in Kiev, with the two guides until they reached a barracks. Driving in, they were greeted by a uniformed officer who seemed to be expecting them, who led them to the stables where four horses were tied up. They parted company with Commander Skoroposky, who gave Rosie a kiss on each cheek, holding her close, albeit briefly.

"Good luck Cynthia de Courcy, it would be my great fortune to meet you again one day." Rosie smiled at the Russian, was given a leg up and mounted a chestnut horse who immediately attempted to buck. Luckily she was expecting a reception and reined the horse in tightly. The Russian men laughed.

Riding north they soon left the outskirts of Kiev and passed through a checkpoint. A light shower soaked the riders but their guides set a fast pace. Suddenly the man in the lead, Vladimir, held up his hand and indicated the party should leave the road. Rosie saw why a few minutes later as a patrol of soldiers appeared on the road. Vladimir smiled. "It's okay they are ours," but from then on Rosie realised that Russian Bolshevik soldiers might also be in the vicinity. They rode without a break for six hours, but then reaching a disused farm their two Russian guides decided they would rest for the night. Eating cold meat was not Rosie's idea of good eating but it was sustaining and it was washed down with rather strong vodka. Steven, or Marcelle as they thought, tried to talk to them but it was difficult. Rosie decided to sleep as it was likely to be a long day tomorrow and felt rather sore after the day's riding.

Breakfast was more of the dried meat - Rosie didn't ask what it was, preferring not to know - and a cup of thick black coffee. Thank goodness it had stopped raining. In fact it was a beautiful day with a cloudless blue sky. "How far?" Rosie had earlier enquired. This was met by a shrug of the shoulders and so they mounted up and went on.

For three days they rode north, occasionally sighting other riders and once hiding in a forest whilst a group of men, apparently Bolsheviks, rode past them. It had rained intermittently all day. Light showers, which Rosie found refreshing a sentiment her companions all seemed to share. They crossed a river and approached the outskirts of Gomel, one of their Russian guides had told Rosie that he would ride on ahead and ascertain if the train to Moscow was running. Now deep inside Bolshevik territory, they hid out in a forest and were told by the other guide they were some five miles from Gomel. They waited two hours before the other man returned. He cheerfully told them that there was no train at Gomel as the track had been blown up.

After some debate between their guides, it was decided to ride east, to Bryansk, bi-passing Gomel, which was apparently the local headquarters of the Bolsheviks. Rosie knew her two guides were pushing along at a fast pace, especially the further north they rode. They, after all, had to ride back through enemy territory. They had grown to like Vladimir and Alek, as he liked to be called and talking in French, Rosie and Steven decided that if there was no train at Bryansk, they would go on alone. Tired of dried meat and black coffee interspersed with vodka in the evening, Rosie was desperate for a change of dry clothes and some liniment for her sore posterior. Riding in wet clothes had aggravated sores and the thought of a hot bath – heaven. Riding mostly off the beaten track and through forest and across fields, it took a further two days to reach the outskirts of Bryansk. Again, Alek, the guide, went ahead into the town. This time he retuned delighted to tell them the trains were running. He also handed Rosie a package. "I have purchased dry clothes for you both. The Commander said that you will need to buy more clothes when you reach Moscow." They rode silently to the southern outskirts of Bryansk, leaving their horses in a quiet road which Alek said was 10 minutes from the station. They had agreed that their story was a simple and to some extent true one, that they had not been able to continue their train journey to Moscow from Kiev or Gomel due to "rebel" activity, hence they had to ride to Bryansk. However, there was no military sign as they bought tickets, thanked their guides and parted company. Rosie hoped the two young men rode undetected on their return to Kiev and gave them both, much against their protestations, two hundred roubles to buy their family a gift, as she put it.

Rosie and Steven had found out that they had a two hour wait and had decided to find a café. Not entirely trusting the stationmaster's time estimation they walked quickly. It was then that they were challenged. Two men approached them.

"Why are you rushing?" said the first man, a tall bearded man.

Calmly Rosie replied, "We are hurrying because we have been told that the train leaves shortly. We are visitors passing through to go to Moscow." The bearded man was carrying a pistol, the other stood slightly away with his hand inside his pocket.

"Papers," said the bearded man. Rosie handed over the letter from the Swiss Consulate, addressed to Pyotr Bark the Finance Minister, together with her passport. Steven did the same.

The man, Rosie doubted he could read very well, grunted and gave them back their documents as Rosie asked, "We were rushing to find a café, is there one nearby?"

"Yes," the bearded fellow pointed down a side road, where some horses were tethered and an old vehicle was parked. Approaching the café, Rosie started to think that possibly this wasn't a good idea, as lounging outside were a half a dozen men with red sashes and sporting rifles and pistols. It was too late to turn back, so they boldly walked up the narrow street and passed the men entering the café. Inside were several tables and chairs with a corner table occupied by four men, who looking irritated, and watched them go to the counter. The café owner, a short, bald headed man, looked concerned as they ordered coffee and asked if he had any bread and cheese. He nodded but then leant forward.

"You are visitors?" he said

"Yes," replied Steven.

He leaned forward. "Don't wait once you get the coffee, drink and leave with your bread and cheese". The four men continued to stare at them and one sliding back his chair noisily, got up and approached.

"You are not from around here?" He glared staring at Steven.

"No," Rosie said. Rosie and Steven passed their passports and the, by now well thumbed letter for the Finance Minister. The man laughed. "Is there a problem?" asked Rosie

"Well for you maybe," he thumbed through their passports. "Swiss, yes?"

"Yes, we are," replied Rosie.

"When did you last see Pyotr Bark?" the man asked.

"Last year in Petrograd," she replied.

"Well, you won't see him again, he is no longer the Finance Minister," he smiled.

"Is Ivan Shipov still governor of the State Bank?" Steven asked. The man thought for a moment, then shouted out to his companions, who had sat watching his interrogation. One of them said that he had heard the name.

"It seems he is," said the man. Rosie and Steven finished their coffee and paid the café owner who had looked on pensively. The man handed them back their passports muttering "Swiss" to his companions and quickly Rosie and Steven left the café. Stared at, once again, by the men outside, they walked at a pace, but resisted the temptation to run back to Bryansk station. They sat on an old wooden bench, eating the bread and cheese they had purchased. Suddenly Steven stopped talking, they were discussing the events of the past, in French

"Listen," he said. Suddenly there was the sound of a steam train approaching from the north and wisps of white smoke appeared in the distance. The train slowly approached the station with a few people standing near doors. Stopping with a blast of the whistle, the doors were opened by a few people, who got out. Rosie and Steven got on the train, there were no empty seats and only three carriages. A flat top, at the rear of the train, had a mounted machine gun, with three or four men in attendance. The train was uncoupled and slowly shunted down to a siding. The points were changed by the stationmaster and the train reversed, moving slowly up the platform on the other side of the carriages and then waited for the stationmaster to catch up. He then reversed the points at the end of the connecting track and the train went forward, crossing the points and then reversed back onto the carriages with a bump. The flat top was now next to the train's coal tender; "pretty useless" thought Rosie. Once the train was secured, the driver and his fireman got down. Rosie loved trains and was intrigued by the aging monster that was hopefully about to take them to Moscow. Steven nudged her, "Don't look now, but our friends from the café have just got on."

Once the social graces had been completed between the driver, his engineer and the stationmaster, they boarded the train, stoked up the boiler, let out a blast of steam and slowly the train moved forward.

The journey to Moscow was uneventful, other than that they stopped six times and the train got more and more crowded. The good thing was, the inquisitors at the café in Bryansk were nowhere to be seen. Reaching Moscow, after a tiring 7 hours on the train, they left bundled along in a throng of people. Talking French, Steven alerted Rosie to the security check at the end of the station. Once again they showed their Swiss passports, this time Rosie kept the Finance Minister's letter in her bag. "Where are you going?" said a tall, thin man. He was wearing a fading dark suit and looked a most unpleasant individual. Just then the four men they had been interrogated by in Bryansk caught up. There was an exchange between the men before the unpleasant looking man said, "You have a letter for Pyotr Bark?" Holding out his hand. Rosie reluctantly handed over the letter, which he read. Rosie decided to take the bull by the horns.

"I understand," she said, "that Pyotr Bark is no longer Finance Minister; our business will be with his replacement and the Governor of the State Bank.

"You will come with me," the man nodded to another man.

"Where are we going?" asked Steven.

"Just come with me," said the grim faced man. They had no choice and were escorted to a battered car, standing in the station forecourt. The drive from the station, as far as Rosie could tell, was toward the centre of Moscow. The grim faced man sat in the front, his colleague at the back. Rosie spoke briefly to Steven in French.

"Hopefully they are taking us to someone in authority."

Rosie recognised the Finance Ministry and breathed a sigh of relief, as the car stopped and they were escorted inside. They waited outside a large double door, with one remaining guard, as the grim faced man went inside. He returned and they were ushered inside. A man sat at an enormous desk smoking a cigarette. The office was austere, but the pictures that were originally on the walls, had been removed, leaving ghostly outlines. The grim faced man introduced them and they heard the name Mikhailov, who barely nodded at them. Still standing, he studied their passports and the letter for Pyotr Bark. There was a knock at the door and in came the

Governor of the State Bank, Ivan Shipov, who Rosie had met before. He clicks his heels and shook hands with Rosie and was introduced to Steven.

"You know these people, Shipov?" asks Mikhailov indicating they should sit down.

"Yes, Finance Minister, well that is to say I know this woman, she is a director of the de Courcy Bank in Zurich and a Swiss diplomat. The man I do not know."

"Good," replied Mikhailov. "Now, why have you returned to Moscow?" Rosie made a swift decision, it was risky but she could not discuss bank business in front of Steven.

"Sir, with respect, my colleague is my escort in these troubled times and cannot be party to our discussion." Steven looked at her with surprise, but got up and left the room. When the door had closed Rosie continued. "As you know," she assumed this man Mikhailov had been briefed, "the last Finance Minister, whom I met last year in Petrograd, sought from our bank details of an account held by the Tsar, in the name of the Romanov family." Mikhailov sat bolt upright.

"You have an account in your bank for the Romanovs?" Rosie realised that this man had not been briefed on her previous visit.

"Yes," she replied. "We were asked to provide details and access to the funds in the account, on behalf of the Moscow Soviet."

"How much is in the account?" asked Mikhailov. Rosie thought carefully, she was not empowered to disclose sums of money, indeed her father-in-law had not told her the exact sum involved.

"I am unable to furnish those details," replied Rosie. Mikhailov banged the table with his fist.

"This is our money, stolen by the Romanovs, we demand you co-operate."

"We have a banking code, which is known throughout the world and no amount of pressure will make us reveal information on private accounts."

"You say that now, but one day in the Yaroslavskiy prison will loosen your tongue," he snarled.

"Minister Mikhailov, may I say something? asked Shipov. The Minister nodded.

"Cynthia, may I call you Cynthia? We only wish to access our own funds that have been removed by the treacherous Tsar Nicholas illegally," he said.

"Mr Shipov, you understand the banking code of practice. Unless the Romanovs and all their legal beneficiaries are no more, we cannot accede to your request." Mikhailov looked menacingly again as Shipov continued.

"But you do at least confirm there is an account?"

"Yes, I do," she replied.

"So, if the Romanovs signed the account over to the state, this would satisfy your "banking code?" smirked Mikhailov.

"Well, subject to scrutiny by our Directors in Zurich, yes, I believe you would have access to the funds," Rosie replied in accordance to her father-in-law's briefing. He wanted to politically remain in a banking relationship with, as he put it "the new Soviet government" and had instructed Rosie on precisely what to say. Rosie had argued with him that his action could result in the Tsar being forced to sign such a form, how would the bank know if it was genuine? The Baron had shrugged and said "We must look out principally for the banks' interests."

"Very well," said Mikhailov, "we will do as you require." At that it was clear the meeting was over and Shipov accompanied Rosie to the door. He dismissed the guards.

"I will escort our guests to their Embassy." Outside the building an even older battered black car stood. "Allow me," he held the door and Rosie and Steven got in. "The Swiss Embassy," Shipov ordered. As they reached the Embassy, Shipov slipped Rosie a piece of paper, on the pretext of shaking hands. They thanked Shipov and went inside the Embassy.

The Swiss Ambassador, Francois Thermieux, was a friend of the Baron's and was well aware of the reason, so he thought, for the visit. Rosie was glad of a hot bath and a change of clothes and later that evening, at dinner with the Ambassador and his wife, a charming woman called Yvette, they discussed their awful journey. The Ambassador recommended they return home to Zurich through Hungary and Austria, but there was a considerable debate. "Europe is in turmoil and no country was safe or easy to cross," he said shaking his head.

Rosie and Steven met later in her room to discuss the events of the day. The Russian Shipov had given her a note which read "Much has changed. Meet me in the Cathedral at the centre of Moscow at 11 am tomorrow."

"I wonder what he wants?" asked Steven

"Well, there is only one way to find out." Despite Steven's attentions Rosie managed to limit him to a kiss on her hand. She looked at her naked body in the mirror and wondered why younger men continued to be attracted to her. Dressing in a nightie, kindly loaned by Yvette, she thought of Steven as she lay there – but no, it would be foolish.

The following morning there was a sharp knock on her door and she left for breakfast in the sumptuous dining room. A superb French impressionist painting was hanging over the fireplace. As Rosie looked, she realised it was a Monet.

"Do you like that period?" The Ambassador had come into the room.

"Very much, I have several impressionist paintings," she replied.

"We are going out this morning for a meeting. Can the Embassy chauffeur take us and wait?" Steven asked.

"Why yes, of course," the Ambassador looked puzzled. "When are you leaving for Zurich?" he asked.

"This afternoon we will take a train, if the schedule permits," Rosie replied.

After breakfast, Steven and Rosie left for the cathedral. Not for the first time, as Rosie approached the cathedral she admired the magnificent building built in Gothic style. Approaching 11 am, they entered by the main entrance. Rosie went first; Steven shadowed her keeping a watchful eye. Rosie sat in a pew near the front. Suddenly a voice spoke from behind. "Do not look around, I may be followed. You are in danger, leave Moscow. It would not surprise me if Mikhailov picks you up to hold you in prison until your bank accedes to his request. He desperately needs money to arm the Bolshevik army. Take the train to Ekaterinburg, get off and a man will meet you in the café outside the station. Good luck."

So Shipov was the contact "C" had spoken about in London. Rosie waited a few minutes then without turning got up and left. Steven joined her at the door. "Was the man who prayed behind you our contact?" he asked.

"Yes."

"What did he say?"

"We are in danger. He thinks Mikhailov will pick us up. We are to take the train to Ekaterinburg, where a man will meet us in a café outside the station today." They quickly found the Embassy car and hurried back to the safety of the Swiss Embassy. Rosie asked for a meeting with the Ambassador and explained to him that they were leaving immediately and needed his security guards to guarantee they boarded the train. She explained that they had other business now and were going to Akademgorodok, which was an important Soviet town. The Ambassador did not ask the purpose of the meeting. Escorted to the station, to board the train for Akademgorodok, which also stopped at Ekaterinburg, they had to wait for over an hour before the train departed. Rosie was sorry to see the two burly Swiss guards leave; she knew they were in great danger but shaking off her fears they secured seats watching the station for anyone following.

It took the best part of six hours to reach Ekaterinburg, but there was no sign of any tail. The Ambassador had given them a pack of cold meat and cheese and a bottle of water each. Steven recommended they eat frugally and save some food for later.

They arrived at Ekaterinburg at 6.45 pm. It was a clear, bright evening but there was a nip in the air. Once again, Rosie was grateful for the overcoat, supplied by Yvette and the Ambassador. Steven went ahead and entered the café outside the station. The café was full of travellers and starting to bulge at the seams as passengers from the train joined the throng. Then a table became available near the door, Steven sat down and minutes later Rosie joined him. The waiter, a dark haired young man, asked them for their order. They ordered coffee and cake. Rosie had found out that they had some homemade cake, but as she spoke the young man gazed around and she doubted he had heard her. He seemed polite though and asked if they were Swiss. As they were finishing their coffee, the waiter approached them and began clearing the plates. Then quietly he whispered "Go to the toilet" to Steven. After ten seconds Steven went to the toilet. He stood washing his hands, when the waiter came in.

"A black car will be outside the front of the café in 10 minutes. It will take you to meet Nicholas, who will help you. Goodbye."

Peter came out of the toilet and whispered to Rosie the instructions. They waited a few seconds, then paid the bill and left. Just as the waiter had said, there stood an old battered black car. Steven knocked on the window and the driver gestured for them to get in. "Who are you?" asked Rosie

"I am Nicholas, we must go quickly from here, Bolsheviks often stop and check cars." They drove in silence for twenty minutes, heading eventually out of town onto a bumpy road, signposted for Moscow. Turning down a dirt road the car bounced, as the suspension was tested to the full, until finally they reached a farmhouse. Parking the car in a barn, the man Nicholas asked them to follow him. The farmhouse was in a very poor state of repair. The roof had a huge hole, and in the rafters there were signs of where birds had made up their nests. The door was not locked and they went inside. As they entered the darkened room, a voice said.

"Would you raise your hands? No, don't turn round," as Rosie went to look around. They did as they were told. Someone frisked them both, not stopping to differentiate between searching Steven or Rosie.

"Okay, Nicholas they are not armed. Please sit down," said the man behind them. "Now tell me, and your life may depend on your answers, what are you doing here?"

Rosie, speaking fluent Russian, decided to minimally describe their instructions to help the Tsar escape and that they had been told to meet someone who could help at the café. Nicholas picked up Rosie's handbag and passed it to the other man.

"Can I see your passport?" he said to Steven. There appeared to be only two men, but Rosie could not be sure if any attempt to gain the upper hand would be disastrous, so she let events proceed. "Who told you to come to the café?" the man behind them asked.

"I am not prepared to tell you that."

"Why should we trust you?" he asked.

"What else are we doing here, risking our lives, if not trying to save the Tsar?" asked Rosie.

The man muttered so quickly, that Rosie couldn't catch all he said. Then a man appeared in front of them.

"My apologies Madam de Courcy, we have to be very careful. Come, please sit down and I will introduce myself." Rosie and Steven sat on the two rickety chairs. "My name is Count Dimitry Kuriev, this is Nicholas and

Yuliy." So, thought Rosie, there were three men. Just then the door opened and a further man entered.

"No one is following," he said.

Count Dimitry nodded and continued. "You are very brave to come here, it is very dangerous. Because the Tsar and his family are held nearby, there are hundreds of Bolsheviks around."

"Can we see where he is held?" asked Steven.

"Yes, in good time. We must wait until dusk before approaching the buildings." He went on to describe that all the Romanov family were held in a compound surrounded by a high brick wall. "They are well guarded and the guards patrol the area around the house."

"How many guards?" asked Steven.

"We counted at least twelve," replied Count Dimitry.

"How many men have you?" asked Steven

"We have ten, all Cossacks, so numbers will not be a problem to break in and release the prisoners – but getting them away," he stopped in mid sentence.

Rosie nodded. "We feel that it is very difficult to take them all and had planned to rescue the Tsar and up to two of his children. Regrettably we would have to leave the Zsarina and the rest of the family," she said quietly.

"What you say about escaping with them all is true, but we are duty bound to try, even if we die in the process," said the Count.

"Then how do you propose to transport them?" asked Steven.

"By horseback, all are proficient riders. We have a barn outside with plenty of spare horses. Look, let me show you a rough plan." Using the dirt floor, he marked out where they were and approximately where the house and compound was, where the Romanovs were held. "There is forest here and here, he marked. We can approach unseen at night by leaving the horses here. Then we scale the wall and eight men go inside to rescue the family. The shots will attract other guards. We will be waiting here and here," he pointed to two points close to the outer gate of the walled compound. "And we will have heavy machine guns, we rescued from the Bolsheviks," he laughed. "Once we have control of the immediate area, we will take the family back to the farm here on foot. We will then ride east all night, toward some friends and stay for several days. Then head down south to our sympathisers in the Ukraine."

Rosie sat back thinking carefully. A simple plan which just might work, but so many Romanovs – that worried her.

That night they crept close to the walled compound and helped up onto the wall Steven surveyed the house as best as possible. It was a cloudy night and all he could really see was that there was very little natural cover around the house. If the guards in the house caught them in the open, it would be slaughter. They went back to the house and prepared for their raid. There was no sense waiting another day, so they planned to leave at 1 am.

As they approached the walled compound, for the second time, Steven told Rosie to stay outside. Rosie tried to disagree, but Count Dimitry also insisted. "You must guard our back," he said. Rosie held an old carbine and a pistol in her pocket. The Count had armed Steven with a rifle. They climbed the wall, one man acting as a "back" whilst others clamoured over. The two perimeter guards outside the wall had both been dealt with. These Cossacks certainly are fearless thought Rosie. Suddenly a machine gun opened up and a hail of bullets followed, as pandemonium broke loose. The shooting lasted five more minutes, then an eerie silence. Someone was coming over the flint wall and dropped down next to her, then another figure. It was Steven and a woman. "Come we must go, it went wrong, there were more guards than they thought." A machine gun started in front of the gate, then another, as the Count's men at the front of the gate opened fire. Steven said more urgently, "Come let's go." They ran with the woman in between them. Reaching the horses, guarded by young Nicholas, Steven quickly explained that there had been too many Bolsheviks. "Many were killed," he said, "but still they had more men."

"What happened to the Count and the Tsar?" asked Nicholas.

"The Count was killed as we reached the basement area. We fought our way into the basement killing the guards. We tried to lead out the Tsar and the family and went upstairs, but there were too many. More guards arrived. We reached the front room upstairs and we were cut off. I had no choice but to climb out of a window, down a drainpipe and much to my surprise, this lady followed me. We ran across the open compound and bullets whizzed around us. Luckily the rope was still on the wall and I helped this lady up and climbed up after her. I don't think anyone followed me." Just then, a scuffle and another man appeared.

"Come, ride, all is lost," he said.

They mounted and rode through the forest, following a cart track. As it was difficult to see in the forest at night, they had decided to follow cart tracks taking them south. For hours they rode, until the horses began to tire, then they came to a farm. "Wait here," said the other man, who had been introduced by Nicholas as Eduad Timshin. He rode into the farm, which appeared deserted and five minutes later returned. "It is okay, no-one here," he said.

The old house had been visited before by someone, as it was a wreck. Steven saw evidence of gun fire and dark patches, of what looked like blood.

"How safe will we be here?" he asked Eduad.

"I don't know, we stay until just before first light, to give the horses a rest," Eduad replied. Pulling old moth eaten curtains, Rosie found some oil in a lamp and lit it. The room bathed in an eerie light actually had some rather old and poignant pictures on the walls, of bearded men and their women. They decided to light a fire to make coffee and ate the provisions of cold meat, cheese and bread. The woman sat silently, she had not said one word. Rosie decided to try and talk to her, who was she? Sitting next to her, Rosie began chatting in Russian.

"I am sorry we could not rescue the Tsar and Zsarina," the woman looked at her.

"Who are you?" she asked.

"Friends of the Tsar," Rosie replied.

"I heard you speak French, you are French?"

"No, Marcelle," she pointed, "and I, are travelling on Swiss passports," she continued. "Your countrymen here, are loyal to the Tsar."

"I am worried about my mother and father."

"What is your name?" Rosie asked, but the young woman remained silent. Eduad kept guard as they all slept. Then Steven relieved him at 2 am. They had decided that the sixteen year old, Nicholas, Rosie hadn't realised he was so young, should guard the horses, their only lifeline out. Discussing their plan of action with Eduad, they had decided to ride to Bryansk and catch a train to Gomel and then south, if the train line had been repaired. If Eduad knew the identity of the women he did not let on. Silently they rode, fearing that the Bolsheviks must be close on their heels, until Eduad told them that a rumour had been spread amongst the men who tried to rescue the Tsar, that they would catch the train to Vladivostok. He suggested someone would talk and their pursuers would be chasing shadows in the wrong direction.

The journey was a difficult one and they had to find somewhere to stay overnight and rest the horses as they travelled south. Rosie continued to find the young woman quiet and unwilling to talk, but one night as they lay, trying to sleep in a leaking disused barn, she heard her sobbing. Getting up, she went to the lonely figure lying on her side crying. She put her arm around the girl and lay there. "It's okay, it will be fine," she said.

"No, it won't," the girl spoke through her sobbing. "What will happen to Alexai and Jemmy?" Rosie thought that she meant Alexai, the Tsar's son, but who was Jemmy? Rosie cuddled up and the girl settled down, but before she slept she said "I don't know who you are, but my family will be very concerned and I wonder if I should go back." She then fell into a fitful sleep. Rosie thought about the girl. No older than her daughter Anne, spoke in almost a childish Russian, but could speak fluent French. Dressed well, lovely top coat – made a note to ask her how come she was dressed for the outside? Then fell asleep herself.

At first light, the small group set off again. Eduad said that they would have one more full day's riding and would then reach Bryansk. They travelled anxiously, but had seen no-one until, suddenly Eduad, who had ridden on ahead, urged them into the forest from the cart track they had been riding down. Suddenly a group of riders came galloping by, heading north. Ten to fifteen men thought Rosie, if they had been caught out in the open, they would have stood no chance. Eduad thought they were Bolsheviks and they rode the rest of the day very nervous and with either Eduad or Nicholas out of sight, at the front of the small group. Stopping outside a small village, Eduad managed to barter and they had a hot meal of eggs and ham with a rye type bread, which tasted slightly bitter,. Rosie sat next to the young woman who had started to talk to her last night.

"I am curious," said Rosie. "You followed Marcelle out of the window and were obviously dressed for the outside," pointing at her top coat. "Why did you have your coat on?" The young woman looked at her.

"And why should I answer any of your questions?" she said firmly.

"Because I am your friend and curious," replied Rosie. The young woman looked at her and seemed to make up her mind.

"I had just come in. Gregor, one of the guards, allowed me to walk my dog, Jemmy, in the grounds. He followed me, of course, and when we came in, I went into what they laughingly called the library, to get a drink of water. As the sound of gunshots reached us, he turned and I hit him over the head with a shovel they used to put logs on the fire. I picked up Jemmy, she didn't like those people and I was about to leave, when that man," she pointed to Steven, "came in. He didn't see me as I was behind the door, but when he opened the window and climbed out I don't know why Jemmy and I followed him."

"Jemmy was your dog then?"

"Yes," she replied.

"What happened to Jemmy?"

"Just as we reached the outer wall, she wriggled out of my pocket and ran back to the house. I went to follow her, but the man grabbed me and I found myself climbing over the wall. There were lots of guns firing."

"And Alexai is your brother?" Rosie gently asked. The young woman nodded. "What is your name?" The young woman looked at her with a look of incredulity on her face.

"You don't know me?"

"No, remember I am not Russian." The young woman seemed to make up her mind.

"My name is Anastasia. I am the youngest of the Tsar's daughters." Rosie pondered on this information for a second.

"I think you were wise to come with us," she said. The break was over and they rode on reaching the outskirts of Bryansk, as the sky darkened with heavy rain.

"Shelter," Eduad had found an old wooden mill. "The horses around the back, I will come back as soon as I can." Two hours passed. Steven and Rosie were becoming concerned. Nicholas had been chatting to Anastasia, so Rosie told Steven the story. They had rescued one of the family.

In the distance they heard riders approaching. Steven unslung his rifle and went to the top floor of the mill and crouched down. It was Eduad and another man. They rode around the back and tied up their horses. Coming into the mill, Rosie, Steven, Anastasia and Nicholas looked at them enquiringly. "This is Ivan." They all nodded. "We cannot go to the station in Bryansk, it is crawling with Bolsheviks. A train is going to Nezhin, carrying Bolsheviks to attack Kiev. It would be dangerous to board the train. However, this man will guide us to Kursk, where he thinks there is a train going to Zaporozh'ye near the coast and then we take a small boat to Odessa."

Peter and Steven discussed the plan in French. They could tell Anastasia understood every word as she listened intently. "Where are you taking me?" she asked.

"To see one of your father's friends," replied Eduad. "Count Skoroposky is the Commander of the Ukrainian army in Odessa," said Eduad, "You remember him?" Clearly this appeased Anastasia who said nothing further.

"How far to ride to Kursk?" asked Steven.

"At least a day and a half," Eduad replied.

"Well, we better get going," Steven looked at Rosie who nodded.

Riding nearly a day in wet clothes made Rosie's saddle sores even worse and she imagined Anastasia was suffering as she noticed the girl switching her position a few times. But they made good time and stopped at a farm owned by a cousin of Ivan's. They were made welcome by a robust man, with a full greying beard and his family. His wife, Ivana, was a big, weather beaten woman with huge hands who clearly helped around the farm. The ten children, with ages ranging from a baby in arms to 14, Rosie guessed, were very disciplined and each had a job. Dinner that night was the most delicious meal Rosie had eaten for over a week. A stew washed down with a light red wine, and then the stories started. Ivan's cousin, Sergei, had been a corporal in the Russian army. Rosie thought he had probably deserted but didn't say anything as he told of terrible hardships and poor conditions. "At one time," he said, "we ate the horses. We had no choice, as there was no other food." Sergei told story after story of terrible famine, poorly armed soldiers, often with no bullets in their rifles and some with no rifle at all. In the end, he said that morale was very bad with only the Tsar's elite cavalry holding their discipline. "Many men died," he muttered sadly. Rosie changed this rather sombre subject, to talk about the farm and Sergei delighted in explaining that they eked out a living, based on a dozen cows, chickens and by growing wheat. He also traded horses and already Ivan had done a deal by swapping the tired horses for fresh animals and a handful of American dollars which Rosie produced. Rosie knew he could change the American dollars in most towns and many preferred doing business in gold or dollars rather than Roubles. Anastasia had been silent until she suddenly asked, "Have you any news of my family?"

Ivan and Sergei looked at each other but said, "No."

Having left the relative comfort of the farm, they journeyed for another day before reaching the outskirts of a small town. "Kursk," said Eduad. "Ivan and I will go into the town and check if there is a train. I don't think there will be Bolsheviks this far south." Thirty minutes later they returned. "We are in luck, a train leaves for the south in twenty minutes."

They reached the station without incident and bought tickets for Anastasia, Steven, Rosie, Eduad and Nicholas. The stationmaster also sold the tickets, but didn't bother to check passports or seek identity papers. Sadly, they parted from Ivan, who had guided them and left him with their horses as a token of their appreciation – he seemed very pleased with his new found wealth, especially when Rosie gave him some dollars, which at first he refused.

The train only had wooden benches, which jarred every muscle that ached in Rosie's back and backside. In the end she chose to stand most of the way,. Thank goodness she had changed to dry clothes the Swiss Ambassador's wife had given her at the farm. Whilst Sergei's daughter, Katrina, was apparently only 14, her clothes fitted Anastasia! Slowing down, a blast of the train whistle announced their arrival at Zaporozh'ye. At least Rosie presumed that's where they were, as the sign was in Russian and had long since deteriorated. Eduad led the party toward the river. He and Rosie then went ahead to talk to a fisherman, whose boat was tied at a wooden pier. Yes he would take them to Odessa, but he knew how to drive a hard bargain and Rosie used up all the rest of her dollars. The next four hours were uneventful, all of them tried to relax on the deck, but it wasn't easy. The boat smelt of fish and there was no accommodation on board. The owner of the fishing boat steered a well practiced route and three hours later they reached the harbour at Odessa. Eduad jumped onto the jetty – tied up the boat and headed off with Nicholas to find Count Skoroposky. Rosie, Steven and Anastasia, thought it best to stay on board until the Count arrived, but Steven stood on the quay watching. He and Rosie still had pistols from the aborted raid on the house, which they kept out of sight. The Count arrived with a dozen other men, Nicholas and Eduad amongst them. He enthusiastically greeted Rosie and Steven and then turned to Anastasia.

"My dear girl, you must be exhausted," and kissed both cheeks. "Come let us go to my house, where you can rest and change." He looked at Rosie's garb and smiled. The Count had a large villa in the centre of Odessa. A handsome square building, with pretty blue flowers growing up the front elevation. They entered and were introduced to Alexandra, the Count's wife, who took charge of arranging baths and fresh clothes. As she talked, Rosie looked at her body in a rather old mirror which had dark patches, where the mirror was deteriorating. She sighed, there were red wheals all over her backside and her back was red from riding in wet clothes and she felt very sore. A maid knocked and entered and gave her a liniment and a set of dry clothes. Trousers western style and a plain white shirt. Rosie had hung her underwear out across the window frame to dry and looked at the jar of goo she had been given. "Oh, well," she thought and applied the thick cream. It was as though a miracle had occurred, the soreness stopped and she began to feel human again. They had arranged to come down to dinner in two hours, but Rosie left her room shortly before. She didn't get far. The Count had stationed two men along the passageway and they would not let her pass. Steven came out of his room, but still the men refused to let them pass. Conferring in French, they decide to do as their host required for now and returned to Rosie's room. Thirty minutes later, there was a knock on the door, Nicholas had come to escort them to dinner. It was at that moment that Rosie realised the striking resemblance Nicholas had to the Count. She asked him.

"Are you a relative of the Count?"

"Yes," he replied, "I am his nephew." Rosie smiled and they went into a large room, with a long rectangular table laid out for dinner. Anastasia came into the room, accompanied by Alexandra. Anastasia was wearing a white dress, with a string of pearls and her long hair cascaded down over her shoulders. She looked much more relaxed and greeted Rosie and Steven. You would not have guessed that the Count's guests had hard ridden for three days, enduring wet weather and mostly cold rations, in drafty barns, as they gave a good account of themselves. Rosie was able to amuse the table, telling them tales of dinner parties and her acquaintances with the good and the great. Steven kept quiet, he seemed to be observing the guards, which patrolled the outside. A very adequate meal, of beef, in a delicious sauce Rosie did not recognise, was washed down with copious quantities of red wine. Anastasia did not drink, but seemed happier than Rosie had seen her since they had started the hazardous journey south. Candles were lit, as dusk began to descend. The Count apologised, explaining that there was no electricity at the moment. Retiring for the night, they agreed to discuss the next stage of their journey the following morning, but Rosie was not sure the Count intended Anastasia to leave with them. It was something he had said when she talked of England. "Well Anastasia must be delighted to hear about her cousin's, she may see them sometime in the future," he'd said.

At breakfast the atmosphere had changed. The guards were everywhere and Rosie and Steven exchanged glances, as they realised something had happened. The Count came in, looking grave. "Sit please," he said. "His Imperial Highness, the Tsar of all the Russians and his entire family have been executed, murdered yesterday," Rosie was stunned, even Steven sat back shocked hearing the news.

"When did this news arrive?" Steven asked.

"This morning, the Bolsheviks killed them all, murdered them, even the children and their servants. The news was brought to me by a trusted confident, he does not know what they have done with the bodies, but saw them being loaded on a cart. He looked mournful as he said that day, "The 17th July 1918, will long be remembered for this barbaric act."

They sat briefly in silence, then he said. "This news changes everything. The Bolsheviks know Anastasia lives, they will hunt for her." He held up his hand stopping Rosie saying something. "She was going to stay here with us until the Bolsheviks were defeated by the White Army, the British and the Japanese, but it is too dangerous now. Even in our stronghold, there are sympathisers working for the Bolsheviks, we must get Anastasia away from here." He looked at Steven. "Have you a plan?"

"Yes," replied Steven and outlined how they intended to buy a passage to the Bosphorus, then board a British warship, which they would arrange to come and collect them. Steven explained that they would wait at the Swiss Embassy, in Istanbul, until the British ship arrived.

"Tell me the truth," the Count said. "You are not Swiss, are you?" Rosie and Steven glanced at each other, Rosie nodded.

"No," said Steven. "We are working for the British Government."

"Ah, I thought so. Well Anastasia is a cousin of your King. I take it you were trying to rescue the Tsar?"

"Yes, we were and feel devastated that we failed," replied Steven.

The Count shrugged. "My wife and I will tell Anastasia of her loss shortly. We are letting her sleep peacefully at the moment. Then after breakfast, we will make the arrangements for your journey to Turkey." He left the room and shortly after, Rosie and Steven did likewise, to rest before the next leg of their journey home.

Rosie heard the scream from her room and went to leave the room, but there were guards in the hall and she had no choice but to return and sit on the bed. Ten minutes later Nicholas knocked on the door. "My uncle asks if you are ready to leave."

"Yes," replied Rosie.

She joined Steven and the Count and Countess downstairs in the hall. The Countess then went to fetch Anastasia. She had obviously been crying, but maintained a bearing, just nodding at Rosie. Kissing her on each cheek, the Countess's eyes filled with tears and as she said goodbye to Anastasia, they spilled down her cheeks. Accompanied, by an even bigger contingent of the Count's men, they reached the harbour. The Count had already arranged with a Turkish Captain, with whom he clearly had other business dealings, to take three passengers to Istanbul. The Count clicked his heels at Steven, kissed Anastasia and Rosie and they boarded the vessel. There was no cheerful waving goodbye. Anastasia stood looking into the distance, but not seeing anything. Rosie and Steven stood close by. The journey would take hours the Turkish Captain had said. The ship was probably able to get up to speeds of 10-15 knots, Steven had advised Rosie.

After the first day, Anastasia seemed to settle down, less tearful but nonetheless very morose. She hardly ate any food and attempts by Rosie and Steven to talk to her were ignored. That morning, Rosie was wakened by a door closing. She shared a cabin with Anastasia and looked down at her bunk, Rosie had felt she should sleep on the top bunk and looking down saw that the bunk was empty. Throwing on her clothes, Rosie hurried upstairs to the deck. There was no sign of Anastasia. Steven joined her on deck, Rosie had knocked on his door on her way to the deck.

"Where is she?" he asked.

"I don't know," replied Rosie.

"You go aft and I will go forward," said Steven. Moving quickly Rosie went to the rear of the ship. Suddenly she saw Anastasia. She was straddling the rail on the side of the ship.

"Anastasia, what are you doing?" Rosie shouted and ran toward her. The girl looked around at her, briefly raised a hand and without a word, jumped overboard. Rosie rushed to the rail and looking down thought that in the half light she saw Anastasia floating. Steven came running along the deck toward Rosie. "Did you see her, she just jumped?" said Rosie.

"We must turn the boat around," said Steven and ran to raise the alarm. The ship took an hour to turn, in a lazy circle and return to roughly – the Captain was uncertain that it was the precise spot and conducted a search. There was no sign of Anastasia. After three hours of zigzag searching with the crew, Rosie and Steven scouring the calm sea, the Captain called off the search.

"The girl has drowned, we must go on or run out of fuel." Rosie cried for the first time in many years. Steven held her tight as all the pressure and stress of the past two weeks came out.

Docking in Istanbul, the Captain asked them to wait, until eventually he found a battered taxi, with dents on most of the bodywork. They were taken, in silence, to the Swiss Embassy. Rosie showed the guard, at the entrance, her passport and asked to see the Ambassador, who was expecting her. Five minutes later, they were recounting their sad story to the Ambassador. They stayed two days at the Embassy, before a boat was arranged to take them to Cyprus, where Commander Langford and HMS Sheffield were waiting to take them back to Portsmouth. The three day sea journey and then by train to London went slowly and for Rosie it did nothing to ease the sadness she felt. Arriving at the Victoria Street HQ, they reported to "C". He sat silently listening to their report and then, without comment or sympathy, excused Rosie, as he motioned for Steven to stay behind to talk further to the Head of British Intelligence.

Rosie was not up to a Secret Service life after the loss of Anastasia and a week later tendered her resignation. There was no comment from "C" and she never saw Steven again. Six month's later, she met King George at a dinner, in Mansion House, who was polite, but didn't say a word about the daring rescue attempt or the death of his cousin, the Tsar. Commander Langford came to see her shortly after and said the King was very sorry he had not said how much he appreciated her efforts to save his cousin. He explained, that the new protocol the government were trying to establish with the Russian Government, meant the King had to refrain from comments on the murders and he gave her a gift from the King – a beautiful small portrait of the Tsar and he had attached a note. "My warmest appreciation to a brave and resourceful woman." Commander Langford told her that possibly Anastasia had survived. No body had ever been found and there was a rumour circulating that a fishing boat had picked up a women that morning swimming in the vicinity of the area where Anastasia had jumped overboard.

"Perhaps she is safe, Rosie, I do hope so," he said.

Chapter Twenty Two

Alfie Horsfield (nee George de Courcy) 1919 – 1924

Returning from the war for the second time, Alfie found a great deal of change. Peace was celebrated with school holidays, street parties and dancing in the streets and Brighton was no different. Alfie had read in "The Daily Express" that the Kaiser had been allowed to go to Holland – he thought he should have been hanged, a popular opinion at that time.

The victory peace procession through London was witnessed by Alfie who had travelled up on the train in February 1919 to meet a few old comrades who had survived. Roses were thrown in the path of General Haig and of Marshall Foch; thousands lined the streets to salute our brave boys. That's a laugh thought Alfie, most of "our brave boys" are dead. He had read the front page of "The Times", a man had been reading the paper sitting opposite him on the train, "More than two million wounded and 900,000 dead" was the headline. Alfie saw the faces of some of them when he shut his eyes.

But life goes on and Alfie noticed the girls had got more daring and forward. One even asked him if he ever went dancing! It was very hot in 1919, the grass was burned yellow and it was just as well, as many returning men found work hard to come by and many had to sleep in the open.

The Germans continued in the news, even eight months after the surrender, by scuttling their fleet at Scapa Flow. Forty eight ships sunk when German sailors on the orders of Admiral Von Reuter opened the sea-cocks. For Alfie the biggest story of 1919 was Captain Alcock and Lieutenant Brown flying the Atlantic for the first time. A picture in "The Daily Express" showed Mr Churchill presenting both of the intrepid men with a cheque for £10,000. Alfie was very envious, what he could do with that much money.

Alfie had tried to settle since returning from the war, but despite Uncle Tyndall inviting him to help him on the trawler he was bored and yearned for a different life. Due to his wound he had a slight limp where the muscle had been torn. His old sergeant major visited him late in 1919 and they enjoyed a few pints of beer in "The King's Head". "Why don't you rejoin Alfie boy?" Sergeant Curtis asked him. "I am going to Ireland next week to shoot a few of the Irish." Alfie had read that a movement called "Sinn Fein" had been organised during the war, to separate Ireland from British rule and there was a bitter rebellion, organised murder, as one paper put it and arson around the towns and countryside. But he was not tempted, he had served with many brave Irish boys in the last one who wouldn't be going home, and reminded the Sarge of Christy and Seamus, who had save his life in the summer of 1916.

"I know," said the Sergeant, "but it's all I know is soldiering. What else would I do?"

When the Sergeant had left, Alfie reached a monumental decision, but it was how he was going to tell his mother, aunt and uncle.

He got his opportunity the following Sunday. Uncle Tyndall had acquired some rabbits and they were having a rabbit stew for lunch. Suddenly Alfie said, "I don't want to upset you all, you know that, but I must leave." There was a stony silence.

"Go on," said Uncle Tyndall.

"I have booked my passage to Australia, from Southampton, in four days time." His mother, who had been serving a bread pudding, wobbled and sat down. His aunt looked flabbergasted at this bombshell, their little Alfie leaving. Suddenly, they all realised they would probably never see him again and firstly his mother, then his Aunt, began to cry.

"Now then, now then, you women, this is difficult enough for the lad without all this," Uncle Tyndall tried to diffuse the emotions, but it took two days before his mother could stop breaking down in tears every time the thought of her Alfie crossed her mind.

Then came the fateful day. Alfie was to travel by train to Southampton station and then on to the docks, where he was to board "SS Minneh" to Melbourne, Australia. His mother and Aunt could barely talk, but just before he left his mother gave him an envelope. "You'll be needing some help when you get there Alfie. No!" As he went to open the envelope. "Don't look now." They hugged and kissed, Alfie didn't look back he was afraid his resolve would break.

His Uncle Tyndall had wanted to accompany him to the station, but he said no. They shook hands , then hugged and Uncle Tyndall passed him his pocket watch.

"Here lad, I don't need this, but every time in that Australia you look at the time, think of us sometimes," and he turned and left, his shoulders shaking. Alfie shed a tear, quickly dried his eyes and went to meet an old army pal, Malcolm Markham, for a farewell drink. Malcolm said they should go on the pier for the last time …

Boarding the large steamship, the officer directed the men to the lower cabins. He found he was sharing with two others, who hadn't yet arrived. He chose the top bunk and threw his army kitbag, all he brought with him, up top and went back to the rail side, for a last look at Blighty. He had left England once before but he thought this would be the last time.

The band played "It's a long way to Tipperary" and a number of the passengers struck up the song, including a lovely girl, the man noticed, leaning on the rail 50 yards away. Perhaps the journey wouldn't be too bad after all, he thought.

As the ship steamed lazily though the Suez Canal, he gazed into the distance, deep in thought. It was May and a hot day. "Penny for them?" He looked up to see a scruffy looking ginger haired young man, about his age, standing next to him.

"H'm sorry what did you say?"

"I said, penny for 'em, you were miles away," said the young ginger haired man.

"Yes, I am sorry, I was rather gazing into the distance."

"This is amazing, this canal isn't it? Reduces the time to sail to Australia, thank goodness," the ginger haired lad turned toward him. They watched as the ship went slowly through the canal and waved back as local people lined the bank waving. "Drink?" The ginger haired lad passed Alfie a bottle.

"What is it?" he asked.

"Oh, only plain water, I can't afford any of the hard stuff. I'm saving all me money for the new life. My name's Eustace, Eustace Cummings. People call me Ginger." He turned and looked at the young man.

"I'm Alfie, Alfie Horsfield. Thanks, clean water tastes really good after those bloody trenches, did you go?"

"Yes, I was lucky though, I was in the catering corps – never fired a gun in anger me. What about you?" asked Ginger.

"I was there," Alfie's eyes went hard and distant.

"Sorry mate, I didn't mean to bring it all back."

"What? Oh, don't worry. Fancy a stroll around the deck?"

"Yeah, there's a great looking girl I've seen once or twice and I'm trying to pluck the courage to chat to her," said the ginger haired young man.

"Come on then. Let's see if we can find her," said Alfie and they set off around the deck. But they didn't bump into the girl. Strange how a chance encounter, at the rail of a ship bound for Australia, would lead to a friendship with Ginger, the nickname Alfie used for Eustace Cummings.

Alfie lay back on his bunk and drifted into a fitful sleep. He didn't sleep well and hadn't done since he had returned from the war. He guessed that it was the constant tension and the need to be alert that had changed him to sleep light and wake instantly. Finally he drifted into sleep.

"Wake up mate, you're dreaming." Sweat ran down his body and he looked at the ginger haired man shaking him. "Bad dream," said Ginger.

"Yes," said Alfie and swung out of the bunk.

"Do you want to talk?" The ship swayed alarmingly.

"No, it's only old stuff, I'd rather not think about."

"Alright mate, sweet dreams," and Ginger settled into his own bunk, to see out the night, bad weather didn't worry him, he just went to sleep. Alfie lay for several hours contemplating that dream. It would be vivid – it had happened.

He had hit the ground with a thud and heard the crack as he broke his leg – he grimaced. In fact the doctor said he had been bloody lucky, he could have done irreparable damage, instead the leg would knit and they told him he would be as good as new. They shipped him back to Blighty, but there was no one to make a fuss of him and he had to rejoin his unit nine months later. Meanwhile, they had sent him a letter, telling him he had been awarded a Military Medal for "Conspicuous Bravery", whatever that was, he thought. I just did my job and went over the top, like everyone else.

Fully awake now it was daylight, Alfie got up to take an early morning run around the deck. He liked to keep fit. Sprinting down the port side, he picked up speed to take the corner, when suddenly he collided with a figure, knocking the person and himself over. Gingerly getting up, he looked across at the prostrate woman lying on the deck. He rolled her over and looked down on the most beautiful girl he had ever seen, with flowing auburn hair but she lay unconscious on the deck. He swept her up in his arms, about to carry her to the doctor's cabin, when she awoke.

"Put me down immediately, you brute." He place the now irate girl on the deck and caught her arm as she swayed. "Don't touch me," she glared at him.

"Are you alright?"

"I am, no thanks to you," she said.

"My name is Alfred, Alfie to my friends, I am so very sorry. I didn't see you as I came running around the corner."

"I gathered that," she looked at him, her expression softening. "My name is Georgina Hole," she said. There was no doubt ,this was the most beautiful girl he had ever seen and just for a second he was tongue tied and stuttered.

"Can, can I escort you to your cabin?" She gripped his arm and gingerly they went through a door and down to the cabins.

"I am in cabin 25," she said. "I share with three other women, so you cannot come in."

"Can I meet you later, to see how you are?" said Alfie. She looked at him, then smiled and her whole face lit up.

"Alright, I will be on the deck where you hit me at Midday."

Alfie was delighted and did a little skip as he returned to the top deck to continue his exercise, things were working out well. Over the next few days, he sought out the lovely Georgina as much as possible, but then so did every other young man on board, including Ginger. Alfie had found out that she was alone, her mother had died recently and that's why she left London - her father had been killed in the war. She had decided on a new life, the old one had been awful. Her father had been a baker, with a shop in Cheapside. Alfie vaguely remembered seeing her board, but had lost her in the melee. They chatted, leaning against the rail of the ship. Alfie used every opportunity to steady her and held her arm as the boat rocked. Ginger found out after the first day and whilst he was initially very peeved, he quickly changed when

Georgie, as they all called her, introduced him to Polly, another girl from London, who shared the cabin with her.

"We've landed on our feet here Alfie," said Ginger.

"Have you kissed yours yet?" Alfie had to admit he had not. There never seemed to be the right moment.

Then they reached Melbourne, sailing up the River Yarra and docking. There was much hustle and bustle and Alfie panicked, he had lost her in the crowd. "It's alright mate." Alfie looked around to see Ginger coming along the quay with both girls. "I've got the cargo mate." They all laughed. Alfie took Georgina to one side.

"You know I told you I haven't much money, but I intend to travel inland and buy some land to farm and rear livestock," he paused, "Look I know we haven't known each other long but … Georgie will you come with me as my wife?" Well that's it, I've said it, he thought. Georgie looked at him and broke into a smile that lit up her face.

"Of course, I will Alfred Horsfield. It's taken you long enough to ask." They fell into each others arms with Ginger and Polly laughing and slapping them on the back.

They found a church, St Stephens, in Melbourne and rushed through the formalities. Ginger was best man and Polly the only bridesmaid; both were their witnesses. Georgie looked radiant wearing her mother's wedding dress and had had no trouble persuading a Scotsman, Mr McIntosh, who ran the hotel where they stayed, in separate rooms, to give her away. Alfie was to learn that anyone would do anything for Georgie.

Then came the time to decide where to go and Mr McIntosh again came to the rescue. "Go to the Yarra Valley," he said, "my cousin farms near there and take him my letter of introduction."

The journey by horse and carriage, Alfie had to buy both, using up some of his cash, turned out to be for four. Ginger and Polly came with them. Ginger took a bit of persuading, as he had little money, but together Georgie, who no one seemed able to refuse, persuaded him and he talked Polly into coming, on the basis he would make "a proper wife out of her" when they settled.

They reached the Yarra Valley after a day's hard travel. The roads were not very good in Australia in 1920 but they found a hotel nearby in Healesville and then set out to find Mr McIntosh's cousin. He was a brusque, Scottish farmer, who had emigrated ten years earlier, but he was hospitable and read the letter, muttering incohesive Scottish words. "Well you won't find much land not taken round her laddie," he said. He stroked his moustache, then beamed. "I'll tell you where to go though," and he outlined a plan of action to them.

The advice turned out to be good. Mrs Dunwoody was a widow, her husband Jed had been killed at Gallipoli and rumour had it she was thinking of selling up her farm and one hundred acres. She was struggling to control her farm and admitted it was no life for a single woman. She would go to her sister in Sydney who ran a haberdashers shop and start again. Alfie had to use every penny of the money he brought with him and thanked his lucky stars he had taken the money. Then they had a farm. Luckily, Ginger had worked on a farm before the war, otherwise I don't know what they would have done. Georgie and Polly, set about growing vegetables and acquiring from everyone they came into contact with, seeds, plants, fruit trees and of all things, grapevines.

"Why on earth grow grapes?" said Alfie.

"You wait and see," said Georgie. "I've got a hunch." That year they built Polly and Ginger a house nearby and were delighted when they married in a Presbyterian church in Healesville.

Then Georgie was pregnant. A shock to Alfie, he somehow had not expected to become a father, but when the local doctor declared he thought Georgie was having twins, he actually got drunk, a very rare thing indeed, with Ginger carrying him to bed that night. The winter was difficult, but not as bad as the summer that followed, it simply didn't rain. Ginger had sunk wells and finally struck "gold" or it seemed like gold, a well filling with water which they screened from the never ending sun and they survived. Ginger had commented when Alfie brought the farm, how lucky he was to have a small lake on the land – little did he realise, that would disappear after three months of intense heat. All the vegetables except the spinach and cabbage died and they had to net the entire vegetable patch with fine muslin to stop the insects and kangaroos eating everything. The grapevines survived and Georgie surprised them all by producing a dozen bottles of drinkable wine. Cultivating the root stock and being humoured by Alfie, Georgie extended the vines until she had cultivated an acre. Next year this produced four dozen bottles – then she pinched, as Alfie put it, another two acres, until two years later, they were supplying several hotels with good wine.

But then came the great crash in 1923. Farmers going bust and many people gave up. Alfie bought land, borrowing money against his own farm. Ginger was concerned, they seemed very stretched to him, but he left all the financial matters to Alfie. It was very difficult, Georgie had given birth to twins, a boy and a girl, two years ago and Polly to a boy and a year later a girl. They managed, some thanks being to old Mr McIntosh, who frequently called with some unusual foodstuffs his cousin had sent from Melbourne.

Georgie and Ginger sat on the veranda watching the bright sun ball slip out of the sky and watched as the kangaroos appeared to eat in the twilight. Ginger reflected how good it was to have a supply of fresh meat, even if it was kangaroo, it had kept them going on more than one occasion. Then a car was seen coming up the driveway, towards their house, a trail of dust marking its path. You don't see many cars thought Ginger, I wonder who this was calling …

Frederick lay looking out of the window. He picked up the hand mirror and gazed at the face of a stranger, his face was grey and eyes sunken. He had some nasty looking open contusions, on his chest, legs and forehead and his face was very thin. He wheezed, as he breathed, but lay reflecting the first time he had met Rosie. Even then, he knew he preferred the company of men to women. He had already had sexual encounters with young men at school and at the Sorbonne. But, the vision of this beautiful girl. Ah, and yet she turned out to be intelligent, loved the arts and poetry, could recite Keats, Tennyson and extracts from Shakespeare plays. As soon as he first saw her, he knew she epitomised all his father was seeking as a daughter-in-law. The only problem was, she came from a humble background, father would not accept that. He remembered the trips with Rosie, to galleries and walking along the Seine, taking her to ballet or the opera. She loved it all and in his own way he loved her. He reflected that the stumbling block was his father. Suddenly however, his father's attitude changed and he approved a marriage. He coughed and brought up some vile muck, mixed with blood. What happened after that? He found his memory very sporadic, one minute it was clear, the next he was lost in mist. He rang the bell by the side of his bed. A young woman came in. He couldn't remember any of their names, anyway what was the point, he knew he was dying.

"Can you give me more pillows, I want to sit up?"

The nurse left the room and returned with several extra pillows. Cautiously, she placed them behind him and another male nurse came in to the room to help lift him higher up the bed. The nurse knew he was no longer a physical danger to her, he was very weak, but when he had first come into the Klinik, he was violent and had erratic mood swings. He gripped her arm.

"The pain in my head is bad; can I have something to help?" he asked. The nurses looked at each other and the older male nurse told her to go and see the doctor.

Doctor Kliebber was Austrian, but spoke perfect French and English. He felt Frederick's head and took his pulse, it was intermittent and fading.

"So, not feeling good Frederick?" He took out a hypodermic and jabbed him in the arm with morphine. They were keeping Frederick alive, because the Baron was paying them handsomely. Any other patient, with the final stages of Syphilis, would be allowed to die. Frederick was forced to eat, mostly soup and drink water. They were permanently on watch, as he had tried to commit suicide twice. But now his anger had abated, his eyes closed and he slept.

The doctor hurried downstairs. There was no point in keeping a rich benefactor waiting. The Klinik Mirshof was situated on Lake Geneva, with grounds that ran down to the lakeside. The doctor only saw very ill, usually mentally ill patients, of rich benefactors. Some lived years in the tranquil surroundings, others died swiftly, but always they were well paid. Such people liked to hide their misfits, or embarrassments. Frederick de Courcy was no exception. Admitted a year ago, he had reached the stage in his illness of terrible periods of blackness, even insanity. His father had brought him one night in a straightjacket. He remembered, he had one of the new Daimler cars, perhaps he should increase his charges, he thought. He entered the exquisite downstairs room. They deliberately spent a great deal of money on the appearance of the Klinik. Rich people liked to consider the opulence of all their surroundings, even when they were incarcerating a relative.

"Good evening Herr Baron and Mrs de Courcy," the doctor bowed, surprised to see Frederick's wife.

"Ah, Kliebber, we had arranged to visit Frederick, but now I understand we cannot," said the Baron abruptly.

"Well, that is not strictly true, you are welcome to see him, but he sleeps," said the doctor.

"I would still like to see him, Baron," said Rosie. This place upset her. She had seen through slightly open doors and heard the cries of anguish, from other patients. She had once been to a place in London, called "Bedlam" and it seemed the same to her. One of her cousins had been sent there, gone mad, the judge had said and all because he had danced naked in the street in Bethnal Green one lovely summer's day. The cries in "Bedlam" were the same as she heard here and she did not like it. But Frederick was her husband and father to three children; she had a duty …

Entering the room, she pulled back the heavy drapes on the windows. Frederick lay there, sleeping fitfully. Now and again he cried out – presumably some terrible nightmare. Rosie knew she had no part in Frederick's demise, but she still felt terribly sad. She remembered the handsome young man, not the pox faced, grey and emancipated man who lay before her. His hair had turned grey and was dropping out in large patches. What other indignities awaited the poor man, she thought and gripped his hand. Frederick stirred and opened his eyes.

"Ah mother, I'll get up shortly," he said. Rosie smiled.

"That's all right dear, you rest." She was used to his rambling. He rarely recognised her, or the Baron.

The doctor accompanied the Baron into the room. He had taken him to one side, to explain that Frederick was not long for this world. The Baron looked at his son and felt nothing. Long ago, he realised the activities of his son repulsed him. He could not bear to touch him. How could a de Courcy sink into such a world? "Thank goodness," he thought, he had managed to sire male children, the dynasty would go on. Already, young Frederick Junior was proving an able pupil. He hadn't wanted his grandson to go to Eton, but his daughter-in-law, backed up by Lord Berkeley, were strong adversaries, so he had to let them win. In return, Frederick and Edward came to Zurich three times each year and he spent all the time he could with them. He took them to battlefields where the de Courcy's military prowess had won the day; he took them to bank meetings and afterwards explained tactics and the principles of banking. Frederick was particularly interested, as the Baron had explained to him privately, one day when he was 11 years old, that he would inherit most of the bank and it was his responsibility to pass it on to the next generation of de Courcy's. He didn't discuss his own son of course – no one did. The boys and their sister Anne knew their father was ill, all except the youngest Sophie who was still only a child. In any case, you did not explain these things to a female and Anne had only recently been acquainted with the truth.

"He looks better, Cynthia," the Baron stood at the end of the bed but didn't approach his son.

"I think not, Baron," replied Rosie tersely. She was appalled by the Baron's behaviour toward his son. Never once did he talk to him, or hold his hand, no warmth, or love was passed on.

Rosie knew they did not tell her any information about Frederick's true condition, but she knew he had syphilis, her father told her, stressing she was not to have even the slightest sexual relationship with Frederick. Rosie sighed, they stood looking at Frederick as he thrashed about the bed, a terrible journey in his head.

"Can you help him with these nightmares, Doctor?" said Rosie

"No Madam, I regret not, he is sedated, but we cannot control his dreams."

They left at 6pm to drive to the Baron's home in daylight. Silence, nothing remained to be said, just thoughts. Rosie thought that it would be a merciful release, if Frederick died soon. The Baron was calculating who would take charge in Paris. Frederick had long since ceased to be of any use to him, but the Manager of their luxurious office in Paris was being promoted to Zurich and he needed to consider a replacement. Rosie still did odd jobs for the Baron, mostly in London, although her linguistic skills had been used in Germany and France on many occasions. The road back to Zurich was bumpy and it was three hours before they reached the house in Bahnhofqual. The first thing Rosie did was go to St Peters Church to say a prayer for

Frederick. The Baron ordered dinner for 10 pm and asked his servants to prepare his bath. The tin bath had been replaced by a room, many people called the bathroom, with the principle furniture in the room a large enamel bath.

Soaking in the bath, the Baron was irritated by a persistent knocking on the door. Wrapping himself in a large gown, he opened the door – his butler, Jeeves, an Englishman, stood there.

"I do beg your pardon Baron but there is a man from the Klinik Mirshof downstairs, he says he has an urgent message." The Baron, these days quite a portly man, decided to dress rather than give all the servants something to titter about.

"I will be down shortly, Jeeves."

Ten minutes later, just as Rosie came in the front door, he was descending the stairs.

"Cynthia, there is a man here from the Klinik; I fear it is about Frederick. You had better come as well." Rosie took a deep breath, she had known for some time that Frederick was dying, but it was hard to deal with. They went into the library, where an elderly man sat. He got up immediately.

"No, sit down man, you look exhausted," said Rosie. The man, a steward at the Klinik, explained that he had followed them to Zurich by coach, preferring it to the slow car they had. He went quiet and then said.

"Here is a message from Doctor Kliebber," handing the Baron a note. The Baron slit open the envelope with his gold knife and read the letter. He passed it to Rosie and went across to the brandy decanter, pouring out two glasses. Rosie sobbed as she reached the second paragraph.

"I am sorry to say that your son, Frederick died at 7 pm this day, in his sleep. His last words were father, mother forgive me." The Baron handed Rosie the crystal brandy goblet and turned to the messenger.

"Thank you good fellow, tell Kliebber arrangements will be made to collect the body shortly and no post mortem is required." The doctor had offered to arrange a post mortem to determine the cause of death. He rather thought his heart had given out, but it could have been a blood clot to the brain.

"If you would like to rest, before returning to the Klinik, one of the servants will show you to a room," said Rosie recovering her composure.

"No thank you, madam I will rest in the coach," he bowed and left. The Baron and Rosie remained silent deep in their own thoughts, until the Baron, forever the practical, broke the silence.

"I will send a note to the Archbishop of St Peters; I think we should aim to hold the funeral in seven days."

"But the children," Rosie protested.

"The oldest can easily travel here in six days, I will send a telegraph message to London today," and at that, he left the room.

What a cold, ruthless man he was, thought Rosie as she went across to the decanter and poured another brandy. She then sat at the writing desk and composed letters for a number of Frederick's banking associates and friends, in London and America. They would not be able to travel here in time, but at least they would receive the news before it was published in "The Times". Then she composed several telegrams; the first was to Pierre, now a ballet choreographer in Paris. She had known that Frederick and Pierre were lovers, but more than that, they were in love. It was a difficult message. The second to Countess de Blois. Rosie knew the Baron would not inform her immediately of his loss. Finally a telegraph message to her father. Her hand shook as she thought what to say, until deciding that the message to her daughter and sons should be:

"Your father, after a long illness has peacefully died in his sleep. God is looking after him now, your loving mother."

The funeral was a sombre affair. The Baron had invited all Zurich's rich and influential, with dozens of politicians, bankers and ambassadors filling up the pews of St Peters. The Baron read a eulogy about Frederick, which made Rosie squirm, as she had long realised the Baron disliked his son. Then Frederick Junior read the 23rd psalm and Anne talked about her father's contribution to help the disaffected, in Paris and London. This had largely been talk on Frederick's part, but he did make some handsome donations to churches and charities, working with the poor. The burial took place in the exclusive plot owned by the de Courcy family in the grounds of St Peters church.

Rosie had been most concerned about her children. In the tradition of the de Courcy family, the coffin had been left open until the last minute. The Baron had insisted that Anne and the boys follow him and Rosie, to say a final farewell. Rosie had been dreading this, what would he look like? But the Baron had arranged for discreet theatrical make up to be applied to Frederick's face and he was fully dressed, in a blue suit with polished black shoes and a blue tie. He looked serene and at peace, Rosie was greatly relieved.

Rosie had spotted a man she did not know earlier at the graveside and when he approached she turned toward him. He was medium height, very slim and had jet black hair. Handsome, in a boy like way, he looked embarrassed as he spoke.

"Mrs de Courcy, my name is Pierre. You wrote to me," there were tears in his eyes. Rosie embraced him and for the first time her resolve broke down. She burst into a flood of tears. Holding each other for a few seconds, it was as though they had been lovers, but their connection was unique and both needed to talk.

"Let's meet in Paris," Rosie said, "it is not easy to talk here," and so Pierre threw a single flower into the grave of his lover and left.

"Who was that, Cynthia dear?" asked the Countess de Blois.

"Oh, just a friend of Frederick's," and Rosie turned to comfort her daughter Anne who was crying. Anne had been close to Frederick, at least as close as anyone had been, for the past 10 years. When the children walked past the coffin, only Anne stopped and touched her father's head. Edward was completely impassive, but that was hardly surprising - of all the children, Edward had been the one virtually ignored by Frederick and after a while, he did not try to seek out his father, or expect him to attend prize giving or award ceremonies. Frederick Junior looked at his father's body and felt his eyes well up – but stiff upper lip, he controlled himself and walked on.

Three weeks later, the family had one more shock and it happened at the reading of Frederick's will. The immediate family and close friends, such as Countess de Blois and several of the bank's directors, attended the office of Ericcson et Poute solicitors offices, at Basteiplatz, in the centre of Zurich, for the reading of the will. The proceedings started ordinarily enough, with Monsieur Ericcson reading out a number of bequests, notably 100,000 Swiss Francs to Pierre. Then the solicitor paused. "I am now required by the terms of the will to read a letter to you." He slit open a small embossed envelope, sealed with the de Courcy seal, read the contents and then looked up. "Very well," his expression neutral, he said, "Here is the letter I am required to read." Rosie frowned and looked at the Baron, but from his reaction, she knew he did not know what was to follow either.

"To my family," the solicitor read, "if my solicitor is reading this letter, I have passed away. Do not be sad for me, it is a merciful release. I met and married a lovely woman, who bore me three children." The gathered ensemble looked at each other, what did he mean? The solicitor continued. "Yes, only three of my children, are from my loins and I am sorry to say that Edward and Sophie are not." A stunned silence followed as Lord Berkeley stood and roared.

"That is enough, stop immediately." The Baron moved around the table where the solicitor stood.

"Let me see this letter," he said. Not wishing to argue with his most important client, Ericcson gave the letter to the Baron. The general hubbub quietened down as he read.

"Alright, Monsieur Ericcson must finish," he held up his hands. The solicitor took the letter back and continued reading.

"I have no wish, after my death, to cause recriminations. Indeed, Rosie is the one true friend I have always had. Never critical, never anything but supportive, a fine wife and mother. But I, Frederick, was cursed. Cursed with the love of others and after a while Rosie also had to turn to others for love and comfort. Let me make this quite clear, Rosie did not commit adultery, I did. Rosie did not do anything that in any way reflects on her or Edward and Sophie. But I must protect the lineage of the de Courcy's and it is for this reason and this reason alone, that I have disinherited Edward and Sophie." Frederick Junior looked at his brother and smiled.

Edward was crestfallen and went to get up, until a firm hand held his shoulder.

"Now Edward, stay where you are, you must hear the rest," Edward looked up to see Lord Berkeley. The solicitor continued.

"Edward is not my son, nor is Sophie my daughter, but both are the fruit of my dear wife Rosie. I have, therefore, left in my will, provision for both children. I hope one day, they will forgive me and Rosie; I am so very sorry ... signed Frederick de Courcy. Witnessed by a solicitor in London and the Swiss solicitors Erriccson and Bute on receipt."

Edward only had one thought, to escape this moment; he went to get up, his world had been turned upside down. His sister Anne, sitting next to him, put her arms around her brother, who was weeping openly. Rosie moved from her chair toward her son, who brushed aside his sister as he got up angrily, and stormed out of the room. Frederick Junior turned to his sister and said, "Oh, don't bother with him. I always knew he wasn't one of us." Rosie heard her son and reaching him, slapped him around the face.

"Don't you ever say such a thing again." Frederick Junior was knocked back with the force of the slap. Rosie headed toward the door, but Lord Berkeley was ahead of her.

Catching up the boy with some difficulty he shouted, "Edward for God's sake stop. I am older than you, I cannot catch you up." Edward turned, he loved his grandfather and waited. "Come with me Edward," Lord Berkeley put an arm around the boy and led him into an empty office. Rosie saw them disappearing into the office and followed.

As she came into the room, Lord Berkeley was holding the boy in his arms – she nearly wept, seeing her father with her distraught son. "Now Edward," said Lord Berkeley, "listen to me." He saw Rosie enter and signalled her to wait, he continued. "This news is a great shock to you, but there are a number of things you must, and I mean must, take in." Edward stopped sobbing and saw his mother, who immediately swept him into her arms. "Let me talk to the boy, Rosie," Lord Berkeley said.

"Very well, listen to grandfather Edward, then listen to me."

"Well Edward, this news is a great shock – but you must look at the whole of a picture. You are still Rosie's son and my grandson. You have half sisters and a half brother. You also have a father." He paused as the news reached the confused Edward's brain. "Rosie it's up to you now."

Just at that moment Anne came into the room. Looking up, Rosie said, "Come in, this concerns you as well." As she composed herself: "I did not wish to tell you some of the events, I now find I must," and she went on to explain how, after an initial happy time, Frederick found love elsewhere. She did not explain Frederick's homosexuality, it would have been too much for poor Edward to hear. "After several years of your father being unfaithful I was wretched. I could not divorce, it is against all I have ever believed and yet I had no loving man and my life was awful." Rosie became emotional and with her voice breaking said, "Then I met a kind, fine gentleman and we fell in love. When you get older," Anne looked at her mother as much as to say, I am older, "You will understand that, when bathed with love, it is the best thing in the world. The result was you, Edward, and a more wonderful outcome of my love I could not have asked for. Of course, your father Frederick," she added, "knew that Edward and later Sophie were not his children, he had not after all, shared a matrimonial bed with me for years. He was indifferent, I could have had 50 children and he would not have cared. But you must understand, I love you Edward and Sophie and so does grandfather, your uncles in England and so I might say, does your real father."

Edward looked up, he had been staring at the ground. "But who is my real father?" He asked looking directly at his mother.

"A wonderful, distinguished man, who I will arrange for you to meet quite soon."

"But who is he?" Edward persisted.

"Edward, you have had enough news for one day, you will find out and hopefully, realise that your life is much the same, except your father is alive." Lord Berkeley gently had the boys head in his hands. "And remember you are dear to us all, we love you and always will." Now Anne began weeping and all four hugged each other, until the spell was broken as the door opened. Countess de Blois, who had always had a soft spot for Edward, entered the room.

"I hope I am not interrupting, but the solicitor wishes to read the will."

"Are you coming back in Edward? asked Rosie.

"No mother, it does not concern me."

"Very well, I will sit with Edward," said Lord Berkeley.

They entered the solicitor's chambers and took their seats. Rosie did not look at Frederick Junior, she had been disgusted by his outburst and realised the mistake that she had made, letting the Baron spend so much time with him. He had turned him into a son she did not know.

The solicitor cleared his throat and began reading the will. "In summary, the will leaves a trust fund of 500,000 Swiss Francs for Anne and in the event that "dear George" is ever found, a trust fund for him, but Frederick's shares in the Swiss bank, he had inherited 30% on his thirtieth birthday, were to pass, in trust, to Frederick Junior. My beloved wife Rosie is left the house in Eaton Square, all our goods and chattels and an annuity of 100,000 pounds sterling per annum, payable until she remarries, if ever." Rosie immediately reaised that it wasn't fair, Anne had the trust fund, but Frederick Junior had shares, worth over one thousand times the size of the fund. Rosie didn't care about the money for herself, she lived comfortably on the director's salary her father paid her, but she did resent Frederick's uneven distribution. What if George was found? He is the oldest. Frederick had made no provision for this, other than a trust fund of half a million Swiss Francs, which would revert to his brother Frederick Junior when he was thirty if, of course, George had not claimed it. It was all unsavoury and unpleasant.

The Baron meanwhile had taken all in his stride. He had long suspected Edward and was certain Sophie were not of the true blood line. Thank goodness Frederick had retained sufficient sense to reveal the bastards. Now he would change his will, leaving all to the boy Frederick Junior and an income to Anne. His daughter-in-law had done rather handsomely already and of course, she had her father's estate, assuming the old bugger left it to her. He went across to his grandson Frederick Junior.

"Frederick, you and I will meet soon and if ever you want to come to Zurich just send a message and I will make the arrangements." Frederick Junior smiled for the first time since his mother had slapped him. She had looked so angry, he had never seen her look so angry. He couldn't help it, Edward was not his own father's son and that has certainly changed things. No longer would he have to watch what he said to his brother, indeed he may never speak to him again. When he had been at Eton, he had rarely sought the company of his brother, unless he was being bullied, then Edward, much the younger boy, but the stronger of the two boys, always weighed in. But still, he would not tell his old cronies at Eton, no need to besmirch the family name, would Edward though, that's the question?

The following day, Rosie rounded up her children and together, with Lord Berkeley and Countess de Blois, who accompanied them as far as Paris, as she wanted to visit the fashion shops, left Zurich by train to Paris.

The steam train whistled as they passed under a viaduct entering Paris Gare du Nord station. Lord Berkeley, had already cabled for several cars to meet them. Thinking about the children and to break the journey, Lord Berkeley had decided they should stay overnight at the St George Hotel, near the station. A charming old hotel, with huge chandeliers in each room. Frederick wanted to go back to college and had arranged a cab, to take him to the Sorbonne. He had been studying there for 6 months, Economics and History and welcomed the opportunity to get away. The journey for him had been very difficult, he loved his mother, but had always been jealous of the attention Edward got from Lord Berkeley and his sister. He hadn't realised, of course, that the Baron pandered to his every need and virtually ignored Edward – in any case, that was not the point. He was the oldest male, he would be in line to inherit both banks, his grandfather, the Baron, had told him. Now he knew why he hated Edward, he wasn't his true brother. He had attempted a conversation with Anne, but she continued to show she was very annoyed with him. Why, he couldn't understand, after all he was her real brother, not a half brother like Edward, or a half sister like

Sophie. Journeying toward the Sorbonne he was relieved. Mother had surprised him when she slapped him, but he loved her dearly. That's not to say he apologised or attempted to repair a bridge with Edward. He kissed his mother's cheek, shook hands with Lord Berkeley, must keep a relationship with the old boy, and ignored his brother and sister. Determined to return to his relaxed life in Paris, he would seek out Maximillian, the Jewish friend who was the son of one of the directors of the de Courcy Bank. The two boys had resumed their friendship six months ago and were now close friends. They had visited their first bordello together a few months ago, not as though either had performed very well. The ladies of the night had made an easy 50 Francs that evening, as both the young men got very excited and spilled their seed very quickly. Still, they had been back several times since, to enjoy the company of Mimi and Antoinette, two painted fifteen year old girls, who belied their age. What do I care about the family in England, thought Frederick, after all, I am going to solely inherit the de Courcy Bank, as he knocked on his friend's door.

The following day Rosie continued the journey to London with Lord Berkeley and the children.

Frederick's relationship with his sisters and brother, the subject of Rosie's thoughts, were interrupted as the train whistle signalled a sleepy level crossing on the route to Calais from Paris. Startled, she looked around the first class carriage. Sophie was asleep in the arms of Anne, who smiled at her. Lord Berkeley and Edward had gone to the refreshment car on the train. Thank goodness her father had been at the reading of the will. Edward had been badly hurt by the public announcement of his true lineage. As for Frederick – well she realised now that she had let the Baron spend far too much time with her son. She didn't recognise the look of hatred on his face, when he leered at his brother – did he truly hate his half brother? The train jolted as it eased forward across the level crossing, waking Sophie. Anne loved her half sister and it mattered not, who her father was and gave her a kiss as she stirred.

Chapter Twenty Four

Anne October 1920

Anne de Courcy had a number of attributes, all of which blossomed under the careful tutorage at Roedean College near Brighton. Roedean was a girl's school of some repute, for they strove to educate young women towards the future, not the endless domesticity or subservient role young women had played in the 19th century. Young ladies were encouraged to think. Not only were they taught to manage a household together with deportment and refinery, but they were also taught to explore their skills, as well as enjoy competitive sport. This suited Anne, who had been a spirited girl since she could first walk. So it was not surprising, that choosing from a number of first class establishments for young ladies, Rosie elected for Roedean to educate her daughter. It was, of course, very near London and that helped the decision.

Anne did, indeed, excel and when she left Roedean at 18 she was an athletic girl who was extremely bright. Lord Berkeley had been working behind the scenes at Oxford and Cambridge for some time, trying to get his granddaughter accepted. But in the end, it was probably the move towards votes for women and newly elected female members of Parliament that forced the issue and Anne was selected for Cambridge. She was not the only woman selected, but it was an exclusive club and naturally the male undergraduates welcomed the new students enthusiastically. So much so, that a group of final year students bet with each other as to who would breach the women's sexual defences first. Anne was like her mother, very beautiful, with flowing brown hair and blue/green eyes. Pursued relentlessly by the male undergraduates, she tired of their stupid behaviour and decided to stop the competition she knew, a charming professor had alerted her, was taking place by declaring her love for one student. The trouble was which one.

William Henry Kirk was president of the student's union, like his father and his father's father had been. Destined to join the family solicitors, Kirk, Kirk and Wilberforce, in Cheapside, London, his life was already planned out. The first time he saw Anne, after she had enrolled at Cambridge, he hadn't thought much of the other first year female students, until this vision, in a blue suit, walked by his table at the Freshers' Fair. Since then, like most of the male students at the university, he had been pursuing her. By fair and foul means, he was determined to have her and he had hatched what he thought was a clever plan. He had purloined a piece of Professor Hardwick's personal writing paper and together with the toady Hamilton, his creepy friend, they had written an invitation. Reading it again, he thought it was a masterpiece, who would be able to resist?

When Anne received the letter she was surprised, but certainly not suspicious. "Will the honourable Miss Anne de Courcy come to the University boathouse on the River Cam at 6.30 pm for a trial rowing for the University." Asking around, it was indeed Professor Hardwick who presided over the University Rowing club and yes, trials were being undertaken this week. The boathouse on the river was out of the way and dusk was descending on a cloudy October evening. This should, of course, have alerted Anne. How could you have trials in the dark? Anne walked around the front of the boathouse which appeared deserted. Firmly knocking on the front door, she found it open and entered. It was dark inside but she had brought a lantern. Searching for the electric light switch, slowly she edged forward. "Hello, Professor Hardwick, is anyone there?"

She had gone ten yards inside the boathouse, when she heard a scraping and the door shut behind her. Wheeling around, she became concerned. Suddenly, a hand clamped her mouth, as somebody grabbed her from behind, she struggled and tried to bite the hand, but whoever it was, had her clamped tightly. Then another figure appeared in front of her, with a black hood with eyes cut out. Now, she was really scared. The two men, she realised they were men, half dragged her, half carried her toward the office at the rear. Forcing her through the door, one of them let out a whoop and forced a piece of cloth over her eyes. He was tying the cloth, when she brought her knee up, firmly catching him in the groin.

"You're a spirited little thing." the one from behind said. Then they began to rip at her skirt and blouse tearing the linen. They forced her onto the ground, the larger of the two men, who had failed to blindfold her, began to rip her undergarment, tearing her pantaloons. He began to fumble for his trousers, when suddenly, as she later described it, the man on the top of her let out a cry of anguish and rolled off her. The other man cried out and she heard a crunch and something being broken. The man on the floor moaned and suddenly a third man came into view, he kicked the figure on the floor viciously, who cried out in pain. Then she saw her saviour's face and recognised him. Asmail Issam was Lebanese by birth; his father was General Issam, the head of his country's armed forces. Luckily for Anne, he was a keen rower and that evening, together with Charles Harding, they were going to get a skull out and practise fast strokes in the moonlight. The idea was not to alert the entire rowing club and to catch their rivals by surprise in the trials. Asmail had seen the girl go into the boathouse and then heard a stifled scream. Quietly he entered. It was dark. When his eyes accustomed to the dark, he could make out two figures, holding the girl in the office at the rear. Picking up an oar, he moved slowly toward the unsuspecting figures. By God, Asmail was a Christian and knew he should not even think disrespectfully toward the Lord God, but they were trying to rape the girl. Stealthily, he approached. One of the men was on top of the girl, who was kicking and screaming, but the other held her arms – she stood no chance. Choosing to strike the man on top first, he crashed down the oar, on the man's back. The other man, he noticed for the first time they were wearing masks, started to make for the door, but Asmial was too quick and hit the fleeing figure, who screamed and crashed into the door frame. He walked over and looked at the man on the ground, who cursed him, so he kicked him hard in the stomach. Asmail had trained in self defence since he was three years of age and didn't need a weapon, but as his father said "If in doubt, try and even up the odds." He turned his attention to the girl.

"By all that's holy, it's that beautiful girl Anne!" he thought.

"Come," he said helping her to her feet. "The university security will be here soon. Are you okay to walk?" He held out his arms and helped her up. Her skirt and blouse were torn and she tried to tidy herself.

"Who are you?" she asked knowing fully well.

"Ah yes, my name is Asmail Issam, you were fortunate I am trying to win the single skulls and came to practice." Just at that moment, a number of men arrived. Charles Harding burst in, with a lantern, followed by security men.

"Are you okay?" said Charles to Asmail and looking at Anne.

"Yes, I am fine," replied Anne. "But our friends in the back room aren't so fortunate, Mr Smith," who was the head of security, "would you please detain the two men in the office, they were trying to rape this woman?" said Asmail

The three security guards went to apprehend the perpetrators, when suddenly Smith pulling off the hood stepped back in surprise.

"Strooth, it's William Kirk!" The security guard was astonished and moved across to the inert figure in the corner. Hamilton was moaning as the security guard pulled off his black hood. "And who do we have here?" He looked at the face closely, which had blood trickling from the nose. "Ah yes, Hamilton. Come on then, you two, it's up before the Vice-Chancellor for you."

Meredith had been a security guard at Cambridge for 28 years. Other than his war service, when he had been wounded on the Somme, he had, like his father, worked at the university. William Kirk began to take stock of the situation, this was not good, think now, he urged his brain, despite pain across his back and a terrible pain in his stomach.

"What do you mean, Smith?" He sounded as brash and irritable as he could.

"Now young sir, you know what goes on here," Smith had always said that allowing young women into college was a big mistake. "Men get urges," he told his wife.

"Oh come now, Smith, this was a prank that has gone wrong."

"Prank, is it sir? Let's see what the Vice-Chancellor makes of it?" Realising his trousers were undone, William Kirk did himself up, then took the offensive.

"If you are making any allegation against me Smithy, you had better take care," he snarled. "My father is the college solicitor and one of the Governors is my godfather. Do you really want to risk your job?"

Smith stopped in his tracks. He had half a mind to belt the young man himself; he had seen the state of the young lady. "Don't go worrying yourself on my account, Mr Kirk." Kirk, realising he could not defuse the situation here, kept quiet. Hamilton was shaking, but saying nothing, just as well thought Kirk. They were marched up to the administration office by the three security guards, but unfortunately, neither the Vice-Chancellor nor the Head of Year, were available.

"Gone to some do," the front gate porter told them. There was nothing for it than to let the two students go to their rooms, but Smith left them knowing, in no uncertain terms, that they were going to be on the carpet tomorrow. Bribing the front lodge porter, Kirk slipped out heading towards the White Hart, in the town centre. He knew the girl on reception and wanted to use their telephone.

Anne meanwhile had recovered her composure and was drinking tea in the Girton College refectory with Asmail, Charles Harding and her friend Helen, another of the elite group of women who had been selected.

"God, Anne how awful," said Helen, "and it was show off Kirk and the beastly Hamilton?"

"Yes, and they wore black masks with holes to look through."

"It's unbelievable," said Charles.

"Well, thanks to Asmail," said Helen, "you were saved, because I think they intended to rape you." Asmail sat very still, watching this beautiful girl. Even though she had been attacked, she was very calm and it was only when discussing her assailants, that she got very angry. Smith, the security guard came into the refectory.

"Just to let you know Miss, that I will be reporting this matter to the Vice-Chancellor tomorrow. Meanwhile the two culprits have been confined to their rooms." Anne smiled her thanks.

"I feel very tired," she said, "I think I will retire to my room." At that, the group escorted Anne to the room she shared with Helen and another friend.

"Are you sure you wouldn't like to see matron?" Asmail and Charles asked, but she declined and they left.

Anne could not sleep – mainly because she kept picturing her rescuer,

Asmail and smiling to herself, and it must have been 3 am before she finally dropped off.

The following day, Kirk was up early. Knocking on Hamilton's door he went in. "Now listen Ham," his nickname was Ham for want of nothing better. "I have spoken to my father and explained how our prank went seriously wrong. Father has already spoken to the Proctor and Sir John Blakeney, my godfather. All you have to do is remember what happened. Stupidly, you persuaded me to send a letter to the girl to meet her in the boathouse, on the pretext of having a trial for the rowing club. Got it so far?"

"Yes," Hamilton said subserviently.

"The girl arrived and what started as a prank to scare her, got a little out of hand. But then this lout arrived, a first year, I think. He assaulted both of us, seriously injuring my ribs and by the look of it, breaking your nose." Hamilton winced as he went to look in the mirror. "Now, if you stick to this story, it's their word against ours and I have already spoken to father. Now don't mess this up Ham." He glared at the spindly figure of Hamilton, who was gently prodding his nose.

At 10 am, the head porter, a man often bribed by Kirk to let him come in late or bring young ladies to his room, knocked at his door. "Mr Kirk Sir, the Vice-Chancellor would like to see you in his office, now." He also knocked on Hamilton's door, who came to the door looking white and bleary eyed, from a lack of sleep. "Come on both of you young gentlemen, you can't keep the Vice-Chancellor waiting."

Anne had also been summoned, but at 9.30 am, to give her account of events of the previous night. The college Matron was present when she, with great resolve, described how the letter from Professor Hardwick lured her to the boathouse. She showed the Vice-Chancellor the letter, who mumbled something incomprehensible. "Yes, my dear take your time," his words seemed warm and comforting. She told him how she went into the dark boathouse. The Vice-Chancellor interrupted her, "Tell me, weren't you a little concerned – there were no lights, or sign of anybody?"

"Well yes, I was, but I didn't go in very far, before someone grabbed me around the mouth from behind." Matron sat upright, as Anne described how her attackers tore at the young lady's clothing and then forced her to the ground. Matron knew very well that the two young men intended to rape the girl, but kept her own council. Anne finished, a tear falling down her face, which she quickly dabbed away. As she left the room, she saw Kirk and Hamilton sitting waiting. Kirk looked smug and smiled at her, but Hamilton was as white as a sheet. Anne ignored them and walked out.

Kirk's explanation of events was not very believable, unless your father is the college solicitor and your godfather is Sir John, a Governor for over 10 years. Both had been on the telephone late last night, explaining how concerned they were that a security guard had apprehended William after what was obviously a prank gone wrong. "The man, Smith, is out of order," Sir John had said. Sir Edmund Kirk had been even more vociferous about the lack of supervision of women, who led men on, particularly when the catch was his son William and how outrageous it was that louts could assault his son, when all he was doing was responding to a temptress.

They interviewed Hamilton, who shook the entire time from head to toe, but his story tallied with William Kirk. Then they briefly saw Asmail, Charles Harding and the head of security, Smith.

In the circumstances the young men should have been sent down for certain, but the good name of the University and the connections came to the rescue and after a short deliberation, the Vice-Chancellor declared that both of the young men would be suspended for one month and made to send a written apology to the girl, Anne.

Anne, whilst shook up by the attack, didn't tell her mother about the incident. It had been difficult enough to persuade her to let her go to Cambridge, after Lord Berkeley had been instrumental in getting her a place.

Kirk and the toady Hamilton, kept out of her way, largely, she suspected, because she spent all her time with Asmail. The news of her attack and the disgraceful way her attackers had avoided being sent down shocked the women at Cambridge, but as Anne said "We must not give in to any sort of intimidation or the cause for women is lost."

Anne and Asmail began seeing each other regularly. Walking by the River, visiting churches, working on their studies together.

Anne fell in love with the kind man from the Lebanon. He was so attentive and brave. Look how he had single-handedly seen off her attackers and how handsome and those black eyes …

Four months later, 27th February 1921, Anne secretly married Asmail. His friend Jackson, an American, was best man and Anne was given away by the publican at the "George and Dragon", in Whitstable. Sadly, Anne kept the wedding a secret from her family and it wasn't the childhood fantasy dream of a white wedding in a church. Instead, they went to the registry office at Whitstable Town Hall and sad though Anne was that her mother, grandmother, grandfathers and uncles were not present, she thought discretion was the most important factor. She was four months pregnant and now had a growing bump and didn't want the complications of explaining matters. Putting off her mother coming to see her at Cambridge had been difficult, especially as summer approached and she knew if they were to avoid family ramifications and some difficulty with the Baron, they should marry quietly and not inform the family. Asmail had totally understood and agreed. He knew his father General Issam would object to the marriage, after all he had arranged for Asmail to marry Sonata, the daughter of a prominent businessman and politician in Beirut. After the registry office ceremony, they went back to the "George and Dragon" for the wedding breakfast, accompanied by Anne's maid of honour, Charlotte, a friend from Cambridge, Jackson and Henry Mortimer, a policeman and his wife Carol, who had agreed to be witnesses. The weather that weekend was fabulous. Anne and Asmail spent the weekend walking hand in hand, along the stony beach at Whitstable and around the town. They planned their lives. What would they call the baby? When would they tell their families? Where would they live? Asmail insisted they would have to live in Beirut and Anne reluctantly agreed, but couldn't help but wonder how she was going to explain all this to her mother.

"Your mother, brothers and grandfathers could visit and stay as long as they liked," said Asmail. It all seemed idyllic on a sunny day in Whitstable.

Now looking very pregnant Anne returned to university. It was two weeks before Anne plucked up the courage to telephone her mother. Her mother was out so she telephoned her grandfather. "Could mother come to Cambridge this weekend grandfather? Anne thought it was a good idea if Grandfather Berkeley was with her mother; he was such a wise grandfather, he would surely understand.

Rosie had sensed that there was a problem almost immediately, but was persuaded by her father, Lord Berkeley, to travel on Saturday, by train, from London. Rosie knew Anne was seeing a boy in Cambridge, but little else was known, perhaps the relationship was serious and at long last Anne proposed to introduce them.

Anne was waiting at the station, as the steam engine whistled, and it slowed down approaching the platform. She watched as her mother and grandfather, accompanied by Lansdowne, a driver on Lord Berkeley's estate in Norfolk, walked slowly along the platform. Lord Berkeley was 71 now, still sprightly, but suffered from gout – too much port he told Anne. Anne stood at the exit and for the first time in her life, felt apprehensive. She hugged her mother and grandfather, noticing her mother look at her quizzically. They exchanged pleasantries about Cambridge and the train journey and still Anne felt her mother staring at her. Reaching the Hotel Ely, in Cambridge, Anne had booked them in for one night; Anne arranged to wait in the tea room. She said "A friend will be joining us for tea mother," Rosie just nodded, not at all sure what was going on, but something was.

Hot scones and jam, were the speciality of the Hotel Ely's tea room, with muffins, if you preferred a more traditional fare. Grandfather Berkeley had the muffins and Anne, Rosie and a charming young man called Asmail, had scones. As they were sipping the first cup of tea Anne suddenly said.

"Mother, Grandfather, I have," she paused, "we have, something to tell you." Rosie and Lord Berkeley stopped eating, put down the tea cups and waited. "Ah, I don't know where to start," Asmail held her hand, Rosie noticed the bump.

"Come darling, start at the beginning," said Rosie. And so Anne did, telling them about the louts that lured her to the rowing club and how Asmail had saved her. Then she explained they had begun to see each other and she looked at Asmail.

"We fell in love." Rosie was not altogether surprised by the announcement.

Lord Berkeley just muttered. "It's to be expected."

Anne continued slowly. "But there is more," she stopped and looked at Asmail, gallantly he took over.

"Anne and I got married two weeks ago, at a registry office in Whitstable." There was a stunned silence. Rosie had been expecting the worst, but this news took her completely by surprise.

"What. Married you say?" said Lord Berkeley.

"But why didn't you tell us, tell the family?" Rosie was having trouble not showing how inwardly seething she was. Her daughter married in a registry office, no family at the ceremony.

"Because mother, I am pregnant."

Rosie felt her pulse quicken, she leaned forward. "You are pregnant, how long?"

"Four and a half months, according to the university doctor."

Rosie looked at Asmail. "And you, young man, are the father?"

"Mother, of course he is," replied Anne looking crossly at her mother. Asmail looked at the stricken mother of his wife and her grandfather and thought he perceived exactly what they were thinking.

"I love Anne and also have failed to tell my family that I have married and god willing, will soon be a father."

"On another day young man." Lord Berkeley stopped midstream. Rosie recovered her composure.

"Well, at least the child will have a father," she looked at Asmail properly, for the first time. Tall, light brown skin, black eyes, a very good looking young man, with an honest face and a strong chin. She leaned over and took his hand. "Welcome to our family Asmail."

"Oh mother, thank you for understanding," said Anne. She left her chair and embraced her mother. Lord Berkeley signalled to the waitress to pour out another cup of tea, as conversation turned to their plans for the future.

"I will have the baby in London, can we stay with you mother?"

"Of course," replied Rosie.

"Then we will wait a suitable period and travel to Lebanon, to meet Asmail's father." They explained his mother had died two years ago.

Rosie had suggested that they write to Asmail's father in the meantime, but Asmail felt it would be better to wait until a grandfather could see his offspring, before announcing the marriage and childbirth.

A plan was discussed. At the end of June, Anne and Asmail would travel to London to stay at Eaton Square. Asmail would return to Cambridge in October, but Anne would not. After the baby was born, they would wait six months, until March next year, to travel to Lebanon, taking a ship to Cyprus and then on to Beirut. That way, Asmail could continue his degree, missing very little of his course. Not as though he wouldn't have sacrificed all the remaining time, but Anne had insisted that he must complete his studies. She would reluctantly leave Cambridge now to stop the idle chatter that accompanied her everywhere. She went and lived with her mother at Eaton Square.

Dr Morney visited Anne again that morning. She hadn't been feeling well for a week or more. Rosie blamed the silly girl for going out in the rain, she had caught a chill. The doctor seemed unconcerned, although he told Rosie her blood pressure was a little on the high side – still nothing to worry about. That night, Anne felt awful, she felt flushed with fever, shaking with cold and then sweating. Rosie had been sitting by her bedside for five hours, when Dr Morney came again. He took Anne's temperature, felt her pulse, listened to her chest and finally gave her an internal examination. He asked Rosie if he could "have a word privately."

"Your daughter has a high temperature and I think the babies will be coming soon. Please send for the midwives, meanwhile we must try to bring down her temperature."

Rosie looked at him "Babies." What do you mean babies?"

"I can detect a second heartbeat; I think Anne is having twins."

"Oh my God, why wasn't this detected earlier?"

"Sometimes one twin is masked behind the other and a gynaecologist only detects one heartbeat," he replied

Lord Berkeley arrived; Rosie hurried downstairs to update him. "Right, I will send for McIntosh," he meant Sir Philip McIntosh, the eminent surgeon and President of the British Medical Association. "For a second opinion, you understand."

Dr Mornay remained at Anne's bedside, until Sir Philip arrived. They consulted and Sir Philip examined Anne. "How long has she had the temperature?" he asked Dr Mornay

"It started yesterday," the other doctor replied, "and reached 102° this morning."

"I think we must operate to remove the babies."

"You concur that she is carrying twins?"

"Yes, I believe she is." The doctors scrubbed up in the first floor bathroom and were assisted by two midwives who had arrived.

Asmail had been summoned from Cambridge yesterday and arrived extremely agitated at 10 pm.

"How is she?" he asked anxiously. Rosie and Lord Berkeley explained as best they could and that Anne was expecting twins. He was struck dumb at the thought of twins and that they were at risk and the doctors intended operating. Asmail asked about the risk to Anne and Rosie answered.

"She has a high temperature, we must pray to God for the safe delivery of the babies and Anne." They all sat in the drawing room but time seemed to stand still, the relentless beat of the mantle clock and the chimes of the grandfather clock in the hall, told them it was midnight and still no news.

Suddenly they heard the cry of a baby. Simultaneously, they rushed toward the stairs, Asmail being the younger beat them and taking two steps at a time reached Anne's bedroom. At that second the door opened and Sir Philip emerged. He held up his hands.

"The babies have been delivered, a boy and a girl."

"And Anne?" asked an anxious Rosie.

"She is sleeping fitfully, Mornay has sewn her up, but she lost a lot of blood," he said.

"Does she still have a temperature?" asked Lord Berkeley.

"Yes," replied Dr Mornay. "The next 12 hours are crucial."

Lord Berkeley left the room as Rosie bathed her daughter's head with a cold towel. The twins had been taken to the nursery by the two nannies hired by Lord Berkeley and Rosie.

Rosie had sat all night on the chair by Anne's bed, with Asmail on the other side. Lord Berkeley had also spent the night, in a winged leather chair, brought into the bedroom, as he insisted on staying close to his granddaughter. Dr Mornay remained in attendance, as did two of the servants, who took turns in providing tea.

Just after 4 am, Anne woke, looked at her mother and said "How is my baby?"

Rosie, looked at her daughter and squeezed her hand, smiling in relief at her daughter, she replied. "You have healthy twins, who need you to summon up all your strength and will to survive." Anne closed her eyes. It was to be the last words she ever spoke, she died at 6 am.

The doctor said that the loss of blood, coupled with pneumonia and the childbirth, had all been too much for her. Rosie wept uncontrollably. Asmail sat shocked at the side of the bed, holding Anne's hand and Lord Berkeley blew his nose repeatedly, as he arranged for the now crying servants to leave the room.

Sophie and Edward, wakened by the sounds coming from their sister's bedroom, came into the room. "I am not sure you should be here," said Lord Berkeley.

"No, father, let them come in and say goodbye to their sister." When the implication of what their mother had said to the two children, sunk in, Sophie burst into tears and ran to her mother. Edward stood for a moment and then rushed out of the bedroom.

"Shall I go after him?" asked Lord Berkeley.

"No, leave him for a few minutes. He adored Anne and will need to cry for a few minutes," Rosie replied hugging Sophie tightly.

The funeral took place at Hexham, Lord Berkeley's ancestral home, in the family chapel. Only the immediate family were invited. Rosie's brothers mourned the loss of Anne deeply. It turned out, that Anne had often, unknown to Rosie, visited her grandmother and uncles during her pre-university days, wanting to know all about her heritage, her grandfather Holder and the Holder family. Secretive perhaps, but typically Anne, always went with a gift for Rosie's nephews and nieces. There wasn't a dry eye in the house, as Frederick Junior spoke about his sister. Frederick loved Anne too. Anne had always been the one person Frederick could rely on. If the boys at school were treating him badly, Anne would come to a school play, or sports day and almost parade herself on Frederick's arm. Frederick became extremely popular with the older boys, as his sister was a stunning girl. She taught him Latin, laughed with him, had late night feasts with him and Frederick, like everyone else, adored Anne. The Baron was, as usual, a stony faced man. He had no great place for women and it was fortunate he didn't express his view, that at least another de Courcy male heir had been born. After staying the night at Hexham the family journeyed in a convoy of motor cars back to East London and Eaton Square.

The Baron and Frederick Junior chose the occasion to visit some colleagues and returned to London to stay at the Dorchester Hotel. Rosie was disappointed Frederick Junior didn't intend to stay with her at Eaton Place and it was probably then that she realised that she had virtually lost her son to the Baron's influence. Lord Berkeley was furious and told Rosie he was going to drag the young man round to be with his mother, but Rosie persuaded him to take no action and so he did nothing except mutter.

Edward remained withdrawn for weeks, barely eating. He hadn't been sent back to school, as he was so morose, Rosie wanted to keep him close to her. Lord Berkeley came to the rescue again. One day he called and on finding Edward had not come down for breakfast, went up to his room. No one knows what he said to Edward, but it did the trick. Edward returned to school to see out the term.

Sophie cuddled with her mother at every opportunity and kept asking her mother if she would see Anne again as she hadn't kissed her goodbye. Rosie just kept the family together, loved them all and thanked God for her father, Lord Berkeley, who was a tower of strength. That didn't mean she didn't cry for her Anne's passing. It took a month before the tears stopped appearing every time she thought of her.

Asmail had reacted badly to Anne's death. He had fled back to Cambridge unable to deal with his grief and his new fatherhood, leaving his babies with Rosie. Rosie had to find and employ a wet nurse and two nannies, all of whom lived in. The wet nurse, Sylvia, was indeed a find.

Sylvia had lost her baby son to consumption one week previous, when she was brought to the house by one of the maids, Diane. Diane begged the madam's pardon, she was talking to Rosie, but her cousin Sylvia had lost her baby boy recently and was still producing milk. Was this any use for the twins? Rosie had interviewed the girl Sylvia and found a lovely girl, with brown eyes, who desperately missed her son. It was worth a try, she thought, and with some reluctance, Rosie introduced the babies to Sylvia. The next is history, both babies suckled contently and Sylvia loved her new charges.

They did not hear anything from Asmail until one day in December, he came to the house unexpectedly. He was, as always, the polite young man, apologised, saying that he had to talk to Rosie. Rosie had wondered when he would approach the subject of his children and had expected a visit. Asmail was still racked with pain, just looking at him you could see that. Once again Rosie found herself having to bear her own grief and comfort another. Asmail told Rosie he was going home to Lebanon. He couldn't bear to be anywhere where Anne and he had been, it was much too painful. As for the babies he said, "I cannot be a father right now, I know it's a lot to ask but would you look after them?"

Rosie had secretly hoped he would leave the babies with her and jumped at the suggestion. No time limit or discussion about the length of time the babies would remain with Rosie took place. Asmail went into the nursery, picked up each child in turn, kissed them and then turned, tears streaming down his face. He rushed out of the house without even a proper goodbye – but Rosie understood. Would she hear from him again? Rosie wondered.

In fact, it was Christmas 1922, nearly a year later, when having heard nothing since he left, a letter was received. Asmail had returned home, which had not been a popular decision. He explained in the letter that his father General Issam had been very angry that he had not finished his degree. He explained in the letter that the family means everything in Lebanon and how he felt he had let down his children by running away. He also went on, "I have followed in my father's footsteps and joined the army. I am a Captain and spend a great deal of my time commanding a unit on the Syrian border. I have been a coward in so many ways and here I can redeem myself in the army. I think of you all and my children often, but do not feel the time is right to return, my heart still aches. I hope you will understand, if I leave the children in your care for a little longer."

Rosie sat thinking about the content of the letter; for a little longer, what does that mean, three months, six months, a year, how long? Rosie knew she was going to find it very difficult if Asmail came and wanted to take the children away. Life had changed with two babies in the house. But for all of them and Edward and Sophie, the two babies had helped them over the loss of their beloved sister, Anne.

Rosie had to make decisions about the babies very early on. She arranged the christening in Westminster Abbey. Frederick Junior and Edward were godfathers and Sophie and Countess de Blois godmothers. Frederick Junior spent very little time in England. Based in Switzerland he rarely saw his family. Not that he regarded Edward and Sophie as his family, because he made it quite clear that he didn't. But he had loved Anne and adored her twin babies. The Baron had also explained to Frederick Junior how important another male in the de Courcy line was to the well being of the bank.

A certain amount of wrangling had taken place. Once again the Baron subtly tried to manipulate. He wanted his grandson christened Henry William Frederick, but Rosie remained firm and chose William Edmund after her father, Lord Berkeley. The Baron wanted to arrange schooling in Switzerland and university at the Sorbonne, as he had tried to with Frederick Junior. Rosie refused to be persuaded and put down her grandson's name for Eton. The baby girl was christened Louise Elizabeth Anne and a place arranged for her at Roedean, her mother's old school and where Sophie went now.

All the excitement at Eaton Square centred around the twins. Even Lord Berkeley found himself engrossed with the two contrasting children, Sophie and Edward and spoiled them terribly. Baby William could do no wrong in their eyes and Louise was adorable.

The babies grew alarmingly quickly. William, was a typical boy and it wasn't long before they were having to move ornaments and watch his every move, as he explored the house. Louise was a quiet baby and slow in developing. Happy enough, but seemingly content to let her twin occupy all the nannies with his activities.

Chapter Twenty Five

Rosie 1924

The two children rushed into the drawing room and hurtled into the arms of their grandmother, Rosie. The twins were aged three and quite a handful. Following hot on their heels was Nanny McKenzie, who had come from Edinburgh ten years ago and recruited by Rosie two years ago. Rosie's children Sophie and Edward entered the room. "Can we have a story Grannie?" William jumped up and down, on his grandmother's lap and gave her a kiss.

"Yes, please Grannie," said Louise.

"Can we have the diaries, Grannie?"

"Calm down William, or we won't have anything," Rosie put a restraining hand on his shoulder.

"The diaries would be good, mother," said Sophie.

Rosie's diaries were all her children's and grandchildren's favourite stories and they had sat for hours, whilst she read extracts from her earlier life. Naturally Rosie had to skip some parts; she just smiled to herself or changed events slightly to suit their young ears.

"Can I bring you tea, madam?" said Mrs McKenzie.

"Yes please Nanny and bring a cup for yourself." Rosie was not a snob and often took tea with her servants; a practise much frowned upon by the aging Baron. Lord Berkeley, on the other hand, had taken it all in his stride and was even known to make the tea! A revolution was occurring in the role of male and female since the vote had been given to women. Women were no longer considered mere assets, playthings, or worse still, just breeding mares!

"Can we start with the war mother?" said Edward. He liked the stories of derring-do and the part his mother had played during the great war of 1914-18. Her daughter, Sophie, who was a quiet little girl said, "Go on mother, tell them." She loved her niece and nephew and was very protective toward both.

"Very well." Rosie deposited her grandchildren on the chaise longue, as she went to a locked bureau, used her key and removed two huge piles of diaries. Selecting the diary marked "1914-1918" she went back to her seat in the huge armchair. Both her grandchildren scampered back and sat by each side of her Edward her son and Sophie, sat at her feet. They waited for Rosie to start.

"Well let's see," she said. "Yes, this is a good place to start. The date is the

15th January 1918 and things have been going badly for the Germans. You must understand children, that this war was not the case of the victors in battle always winning. Frequently gains made by the Allies were taken back a week later. Our soldiers lived in a muddy trench, with rats for company, constantly fearing attack by shell or gas. Snipers made it very difficult to move about in the trenches, as often the British and their allies were within shooting distance of the German front line, about 500 yards away. The Germans had made a number of, as it turned out, desperate attempts to sweep through the lines and had failed. "Not as though the Tommy's in the trenches knew it, but we were winning," she told her young audience. "The Germans were being ground down, their morale," Rosie explained to William and Louise what that word meant, "was very low. So I'll tell you what happened on that dark Monday evening."

"At midnight, I left the British trenches, accompanied by a second lieutenant, Morgan was his name, and, also a private, a Welshman they called Taffy. We had chosen to go as the moon disappeared behind a cloud, taking a risk because it was a reasonable night with only intermittent cloud cover. I remember thinking "perhaps we should have waited?" when suddenly machine guns opened fire to our left. We knew this was the Germans getting spooked, as no other soldiers were due to go over the top that night. I and my escort were to have a clear run. Earlier that day, I had been summoned to General Haig's command post. I knew the General from various other assignments and also socially, he had been to Sandhurst with your grandfather. I cannot say I liked the man. He was a born leader, but was sometimes short tempered and gruff – you had to listen to every word he said, or you might miss the important part. The General instructed me on what he wanted me to do and I shivered. Not for the first time, I was asked to cross the lines between the British and German trenches and take a note to Count Von Basten, the German head of combined forces. No mention was made of the content and I didn't ask," she paused. "What, might you ask," she looked at her grandchildren, "was your grandmother doing acting as a messenger between the two Generals, orchestrating this terrible war?"

"Why did they choose you mother?" asked her son Edward. Rosie thought for one moment.

"Well, it was simple really. I am fluent in German and I had met Count Von Basten and most of the German High Command a number of times during peace time. I was accepted by the Kaiser himself and had met him several times socially. And I had been recruited into the British Secret Service early in 1914.

Edward grinned proudly. All the children looked at Rosie with adoration, but her granddaughter sat impassively not understanding what was so good about being acquainted with the Kaiser himself or Count Von Basten.

"Go on Grannie," William was, as usual, getting impatient.

"Now, where was I?" said Rosie.

"You had started to cross no man's land mother," said Edward. Rosie dropped her voice – the consummate story teller as always.

"Ah yes. It was a dark night with a light drizzle and it suited my purpose. The lieutenant and private were to accompany me half way across no man's land and then leave me. We reached the half way point, about 200 yards from our trenches, as best as we could, then a tap on the shoulder indicated to me that they were turning back. I raised my hand in acknowledgement. Dressed all in black, hopefully the German line would not easily spot me. My face was blackened up with boot polish and as long as the moon was behind the cloud, there was a good chance I would reach the designated point at the German trenches before long.

Then suddenly the moon broke out of the cloud and the whole field was bathed in the light of a full moon. I hit the floor, any movement seen now by the Germans would result in a barrage of bullets. Slowly and silently, I inched forward." She glanced down and couldn't resist a smile at the incredulous expressions. William snuggled up to his grandmother; he didn't really like this bit, but had to pretend to his older uncle that he did.

"Go on mother," urged Edward again.

"Suddenly a powerful searchlight illuminated the area and I froze. Had they seen me? I heard the rat tat tat of several machine guns before I saw the tracer streaking out toward me. I tried to bury myself in the ground and lay completely still. The Germans were sweeping the area adjacent to me with machine gun fire. Then the light went off and the firing stopped. But I knew better than to move, that's how the Germans had captured me six months ago."

"You were captured mother?" questioned Edward.

"Well, yes that's another story," teased Rosie.

"Oh, do tell mother," said Edward.

"Oh, just briefly then. Well suffice to say, that I was carrying out a mission to deliver a message to the Kaiser himself, from our King George. It was at the end of summer, on a dark August night, when the soldier who was accompanying me trod in a hole, fell and woke up the entire German line. Tracer and bullets poured from the German lines, the private was hit, but I luckily survived as he fell on me and acted as a shield. I was wounded in the shoulder," Rosie absent mindedly felt her left shoulder.

"What happened then?" said Sophie absolutely riveted as the twins snuggled up.

"The Germans sent out scouts, they wanted to determine the strength of the supposed assault. I stayed as still as I could, but suddenly the body of the private, who had saved my life, was pulled off me and several pairs of hands grabbed me."

"You were lucky mother, they didn't kill you," said Edward who acted as though he knew all about these things.

"Well remember, it was normal to take prisoners, to try and get information on the opposition's strength, numbers, morale and whether the person knew any decent information. Dragged back, I was taken to a dug out in the German trenches. What a sight I must have looked, as they sent for a doctor to tend my wounds. In fact, I only had a minor wound, luckily the bullet had grazed my shoulder and the rest of the blood was from the poor dead private whose body had protected me."

"Did you ever find out who he was mother?" asked Sophie.

"Yes, he was a private Caplan. I visited his family at the end of the war, to give them the military cross he had been posthumously awarded for his bravery."

"So, they had you mother," Edward said.

"Yes, but fortunately the German doctor recognised a woman when he saw one." She smiled remembering his shock, "and he realised after I showed him the sealed letter that I had to be taken to the Kaiser immediately. Knowing a language fluently boys, can be extremely useful." Rosie's arm was going dead under her grandson's weight, so she shifted her position and continued. "I was escorted to the German High Command headquarters, where I was somewhat rudely questioned by a Colonel Von Hindenburg when Count Von Basten came into the tent. I had already met Von Basten." Rosie didn't elaborate but Sophie picked up on it.

"You knew Count Von Basten?" Sophie said wide eyed, whilst Edward remained silent.

"Well yes, but only fleetingly," Rosie moved on again, moving slightly to change the weight on her arm, her grandson was putting on weight, she thought. "After I explained that I had crossed no man's land to deliver a personal letter from the King to the Kaiser, the Count escorted me to a building several miles behind the German lines. After speaking to an Adjutant, I was shown into a large room to meet the Kaiser himself. Goodness me, he had aged since I had met him in the summer of 1909 at the Cowes Regatta. He looked drawn and tired, but looking up from the leather topped desk, he smiled, recognising me. He came around the table and clicking his heels, kissed my hand. I remember he said, "How nice to see you Frauline, you are very brave. You have a letter from my cousin?" I handed the Kaiser the brown envelope and as he repositioned his monocle, he tore the seal. He read the letter silently and when he finished, put it back in the envelope and sat for a moment and then said, "I know it is asking a great deal, but would you take a letter back to George?" The Kaiser opened a draw in the desk and passed Rosie a small envelope embossed with his seal.

"Yes, of course," I replied in German.

I was ushered into another room but before he left he said, "You are a formidable woman Cynthia de Courcy," he spoke in English, demonstrating his own linguistic skills. "I do hope we may meet again in more pleasant circumstances," he said, as he came around the desk, took my hand and kissed it, clicked his heels and left. His Adjutant hurried into the room.

"Pardon me Frauline. Come, we will have to hurry." I was not sure why I had to hurry, but all would become clear," said Rosie to her enthralled young audience.

"Well, what happened next?" William was becoming impatient again.

"The Germans took me back to their front line positions and I was introduced to the Captain, who would escort me half way across the lines. Count Von Basten was waiting for me and drew me to one side. "We are about to start a bombardment, so you should go now." Rosie thought for a second - what he really said was, "Take care my love I hope we both survive this foolish war to meet again."

"The Captain led me through the maze of trenches; the Germans were amazingly adapt at zigzagging trenches nothing was in a straight line."

"Why did they dig zigzag trenches mother?" asked Sophie.

"Oh, that's simple," blurted out Edward, "to stop any enemy soldier getting into their lines and seeing a straight trench, being able to shoot a long distance," Edward said looking pleased with himself.

"Yes, that's right," said Rosie beaming at her son.

"The Germans had started a bombardment several hours before and on a signal from the Count, we started up the ladder and over the top, into no man's land. The British had been keeping their heads down, but as soon as the big guns stopped firing, I knew they would man their trenches, expecting a German attack."

"How did the British soldiers know it was you, grandmother?" asked William.

"Good question, William," Rosie beamed at the boy in the crook of her left arm. "I was given a special code word, which, when I got near the trenches I could shout out."

"The Captain, I don't remember his name, and a young Austrian corporal, accompanied me across no man's land. Shells screamed through the air and battered the British lines, 500 yards away. Very often a star flare illuminated the sky and the area below, as the British kept a look out for movement."

"Can I have a drink of water grandmother?" asked Louise.

"Yes dear, of course. Edward get Louise a drink."

"Oh please hurry mother, can't you all stop interrupting," Edward, considered as the oldest, that he should dictate the speed of the story and frowned upon his young niece and nephew and his sister for their constant interruptions. Edward returned with Louise's drink and they settled again. "Now please don't interrupt any more," requested Edward looking at his sister and Louise. His mother looked at him and winked. He did not smile.

"Now where was I, Oh yes, the German Captain zigzagged across no man's land, keeping very low and dropping into every shell hole. Suddenly a number of machine guns opened up from the British trenches and a barrage started from the allied side. Shrapnel and bullets whizzed about our ears, we ducked into a deep shell hole and stayed there. The shell hole was half full of water and a dead horse was decomposing in the corner." Rosie shivered, but knew better than to hide the story from her children and grandchildren and expected the question.

"What was a dead horse doing in the shell hole grandmother?" William obliged.

"Sometimes horses escaped from their enclosure behind the lines and then panicking, gallop into no man's land, sometimes they survived, other times they were hit by shrapnel, or shot."

"Gosh," Edward's eyes had widened, he liked shooting on his grandfather's estate at Hexham and had already brought down several rabbits.

Rosie continued. "It was cold, half sitting, half lying in water and as time went on, I knew I would have to move on soon, as I had to get across to the British lines by midnight."

"Why midnight?" asked Edward.

"Remember, I told you that each time a patrol, or in my case a person on a mission, went into no man's land, they had a special word to shout out as they approached the British line, this was to warn the soldiers in the trenches that you were friendly and not a German. My word was "Hercules" and it only lasted as a code word until midnight that day. The German Captain crawled beside me.

"It is time," he said. "I think, to move on, I am afraid we must go back." As the moon disappeared behind a cloud, we all went our opposite directions. A star flare burst in the sky 100 yards down the line and a machine gun opened up. Suddenly I heard the whine of a bullet, so close I began crawling, zigzagging all the time. Then another bullet thudded into the ground next to me. Someone was shooting at me from the British line." Rosie looked at her two children, my, how handsome they were – both totally different. Edward was heavily built and always tried to be the older brother. Sophie was dark and beauty was emerging.

"Is that the end of the story grandmother?" asked William.

"No, not quite. I had less than 30 minutes to reach the British lines. I had to keep going and still every twenty seconds or so a single marksman tried to shoot me. Suddenly I felt a tremendous jolt, which knocked me over. Stunned for a second, I looked down, I had not been hit, but the leather pouch I carried around my neck had. My life was saved by the thick leather satchel and the Kaiser's letters had cushioned the bullet.

"God, you were lucky," said Edward.

"Yes, I was and when I finally got to the line and gave the password, I clambered over with a sticky feeling around my chest. Quickly I was escorted to the front line command post and a Captain, who realised who I was, arranged for me to be driven to the Command Centre.

When I reached the Command Centre I gave General Haig a letter and requested an immediate transport to Calais to cross the channel, as I had a letter for the King. After Haig read the letter from the Kaiser, he nodded and my journey continued.

Once I reached Calais, a boat was commandeered for my journey. I ate what I could, but it was not until I reached London and Buckingham Palace that I relaxed. I passed over the Kaiser's letter, which had a hole straight through it, sat down on a chair and fell asleep. I awoke in the most sumptuous bedroom, in a four poster bed, and as I aroused, I realised I had been undressed." Edward and Sophie glanced at each other. "After a meal of bacon and eggs, I felt human again, bathed and I was given some clean clothes. It seems I was to meet the King." Neither Sophie or Edward looked the slighted surprised, as they knew that their mother had met the King on a number of occasions.

Rosie completed the story by telling them that the King greeted her warmly and presented her with a bullet. It had penetrated the satchel, gone through all the papers and whilst it had made a hole in the back, had spent itself and lay in the satchel. The feeling of something sticky that I felt when I was waiting for General Haig was blood – the bullet had parted the skin just above my heart. She didn't tell the boys that it had been the bone in her brassiere that had finally stopped the bullet's progress, knocking it backwards into the satchel.

"Great story mother," Edward got up, kissed his mother's head and patted William and kissed Louise. "I am going to get ready now." Rosie knew he was going to his grandfather's house.

"Edward are you going out tonight?"

"Yes, I am meeting grandfather, we are going to the Reform Club." Rosie smiled, how her son loved Lord Berkeley, he even went with his grandfather to his favourite club, when he could be out with his friends swooning after young ladies.

Nanny McKenzie and Rosie accompanied Louise and William to bed and Rosie sat reading them a passage from Mr Kipling's wonderful "The Jungle Book" and then finally the house was quiet. Rosie thought to herself that they had forgotten the other story she had started to tell them, still it was just as well, as she thought once again, of Count Von Basten, her lover from those halycian days, and Edwards's father.

Chapter Twenty Six

The Journey

It was April 1924 and the American economy, which had been fragile for some time, hung precariously. Banks in America were in real trouble. Fortunately, neither Lord Berkeley's merchant bank, or the de Courcy Swiss bank, were overly exposed, but both had granted loans to American companies. Particularly Mr Ford and Mr Gillette. Both banks had also lent the American government considerable sums. The collapse, when it came, was terrible. Associates in America, bankers of repute, committed suicide, established businesses collapsed. The world had not witnessed such economic disaster before and it was a while before confidence began to return to the banking sector.

Then, in early May that year, Rosie had a visitor. The day had started like most others. Rosie had checked on the twins, organised their lunch together and left them with the two nannies. She sat having a leisurely breakfast in the extended breakfast room of Eaton Square – last year they had employed the eminent architect, Sir Andrew Browne, to design and oversee the extension of the rear of the house in Eaton Square. Sir Andrew had become more than a friend to Rosie and had been pursuing her relentlessly for over a year. But she knew she would not marry again even for the flamboyant and debonair Sir Andrew. Reading "The Times" that morning, there was a knock at the door and the butler, Robinson, entered the breakfast room.

"Excuse me madam," Rosie looked up from the paper. "There is a priest to see you."

"A Priest," repeated Rosie, looking most surprised. "Show him into the drawing room." It was 8 am, what did a priest want so early? Collecting for charity perhaps, Rosie was a well known philanthropist. She went into the drawing room. "Hello, I am Rosie de Courcy."

"Thank you for seeing me, my name is Father O'Malley." Standing before her was a small, slightly built man, with a bald head, aged in his late 60's. "I came to see you as quickly as I could," he explained.

"Thank you Father, but what did you come to see me about? Please sit down."

"Yes, of course, I will explain. As I said my name is Father O'Malley. I am the parish priest at St Stephen's church, Tenterden, Kent. I was called yesterday to attend a dying woman, at Benenden Hospital. You may know the tuberculosis unit at Benenden Hospital, a lot of the poor souls, who contract that terrible disease, go to Benenden to recuperate or die."

Rosie said "Father, do forgive me, Would you like some tea?"

"Well yes, thank you, it's been a tiring journey." Rosie rang the bell and ordered tea to be brought.

"Please continue," she said, as the maid brought in a tray from the breakfast room.

"Well," he paused, collecting his thoughts. "As I said, I went to Benenden Hospital. I had been summoned by a sister there, to read the last rites to a poor woman who was dying of tuberculosis and exposure, I think she had been living rough for some time." Rosie nodded wishing he would get to the point. "Well," he repeated. "It was late last night and I sat by the bedside of this poor soul. Suddenly she woke, looked at me and extremely lucidly told me a story," he paused to sip his tea and take out of his bible a tatty old newspaper clipping. He continued. "Well apparently she had lived in London, with an actor named, Peter." Rosie sat up immediately as he continued. "This man was a bad sort, he beat her," the priest looked at Rosie, "and worse, he kidnapped a baby boy." He opened up the cutting and handed it to Rosie. "The woman told me that she had escaped the man's clutches and run off with the baby, as she thought he intended to kill the child. She said she was very scared and got the first train at London Bridge station, which was, by chance, going to Brighton. On arriving at Brighton, it was getting dark. She had little money, but booked into a bed and breakfast establishment, near Brighton station, something to do with Nelson. I am afraid I didn't understand what she was saying."

Rosie began unfolding the crumpled newspaper cutting her hands trembling slightly. "Please continue," said Rosie.

"At this point, she did not know, it seems, what to do. Scared that this man Peter might find her or the baby, she left the baby at the bed and breakfast and ran away." Rosie read the newspaper cutting "Prominent Banker has twin baby kidnapped" was the heading. The article, which had been in the Daily Sketch, still showed the newspaper's title and the date. Rosie began to shake.

"What is it dear?" said Father O'Malley.

"I am sorry father, give me a minute." Rosie collected herself. "Then what did she say Father?" She looked at him,

"Nothing much more, I am afraid, except she asked me to find the mother of the baby and ask her for forgiveness and tell her that when she left, the baby was alive." Rosie sat silently, looking at the crumpled newspaper cutting. "I made some enquires with the Bishop of London yesterday evening and found out the address of the house where the baby was stolen – it was from here, was it your baby?"

Rosie nodded, not trusting herself to speak, this had brought back all the pain of the loss of her son and just for a minute, her normal, clear head, was failing her. Suddenly, with a hugh force of will, she snapped out of it. "Father, will you come with me to Lord Berkeley's house, my father, and repeat the story you have just told me?"

"Yes, of course, my child." He finished drinking his tea, whilst Rosie arranged for her chauffeur, Charles, to bring around the Bentley. Rosie owned a Mews house in Chelsea with a garage. The chauffeur and his family had use of the house and Rosie's pride and joy, a Bentley was kept there.

An hour later and they were on their way to Lord Berkeley's house, on Park Lane. It was only a short drive, but Rosie sat silently with the priest, in the back of the car.

Arriving at 15 Park Lane Rosie, who had phoned ahead, thank goodness for Alexander Bell, she thought, was greeted by her father.

"Come inside, is this Father O'Malley?" Lord Berkeley shook hands with the priest and stepped aside as his daughter entered. Comfortably sat in the library, Lord Berkeley had summoned his butler to serve tea. "Now Father," Lord Berkeley looked at the priest. "Would you be so kind as to repeat the story you told my daughter?"

The Priest put down his tea cup and repeated the account of the demise of the poor woman in Benenden Hospital. Lord Berkeley sat for a moment. "So what you are saying is, this woman, we don't know her name, told you the name of the braggart, who stole my grandson, was Peter."

"Yes, that's right, Peter," replied the Priest.

"And this woman travelled from London Bridge to Brighton station, you say?" The Priest nodded. "No clue as to the road where she stayed with the child?" asked Lord Berkeley.

"Just down from the station, was how she described the road Sir," the Priest replied, "and she talked, or rather mumbled something about Nelson."

"Do you have anything, anything at all you can add Father?" asked Rosie. The priest thought for a moment. "Well only," he paused.

"Yes, what is it?" asked Rosie.

"She did say, the women who owned the house had a brother, a fisherman. I am afraid she then passed away."

The Priest seemed content to enjoy the warmth of the hospitality at Lord Berkeley's house, but eventually, they obtained his address in Tenterden, in case they needed to see him again and then, after presenting him with two fifty pound notes for his church funds, Lord Berkeley rang for his butler to arrange a cab to take the priest back to Victoria Station.

Rosie and her father sat pondering this turn of events. Finally, they decided to go that day by train to Brighton and try and find the house where the woman lodged and left her baby, George.

It took them two hours to travel from London Victoria station to Brighton station. They travelled with Lord Berkeley's chauffeur and when they reached their destination, he went off on a recce, whilst Lord Berkeley and

Rosie rested at the station. Twenty minutes later he returned, very excited. "I went out of the station and first turned right, walking around I came to a pub. I asked if there was a pub called "Lord Nelson" nearby. The reply," he turned to Rosie excitedly, "was, yes in Trafalgar Street on the opposite side of the station." Lord Berkeley looked at them. "Trafalgar Street – Nelson, maybe she couldn't remember the name of the road, but knew it was something connected to Nelson."

"I think you may be right, let's go and look," said Rosie. Trafalgar Street was a few minutes from the station and as they turned into it, Rosie felt apprehensive. They walked up and down the road twice – no sign of a bed and breakfast. "Let's split up and knock on the doors," suggested Lord Berkeley. "Tell the occupant you are looking for a woman who has a brother who is a fisherman, who did bed and breakfast in 1901." It was a long shot but after knocking on numerous doors, Rosie found a woman who knew a Mrs Horsfield at number 27 whose brother used to be a fisherman. Rosie found her father and Lord Berkeley's chauffeur.

Taking a deep breath, unsure of what lay ahead, Rosie knocked on the door of 27 Trafalgar Street. After a few minutes, an elderly woman, with steel grey hair, answered the door. "Can I help you?" Lord Berkeley took the lead.

"My name is Lord Berkeley, this is my daughter and chauffeur." The woman looked at the strange trio in front of her.

"Nice to meet you, can I help?"

"Are you Mrs Horsfield?" The woman nodded. "Do you have a brother who is or was a fisherman?" She looked at them, nodding slowly a confused expression on her face.

"Yes I do, how do you know that?"

"May we come inside, it's difficult to talk on the doorstep?" The woman looked at them again, seemingly making up her mind hesitantly.

"Yes, come in." They went into the terraced house and were shown into the front room. Rosie looked around the neat room. "Please sit down. Would you like a cup of tea?" The woman asked.

"That would be very nice," replied Lord Berkeley. The woman left the room as Rosie got up walked to the fireplace and picked up a photograph. It wasn't a very good photograph, taken during the war, but showed a young man in battle dress, but the smile, the smile, this was George, she was convinced. Rosie passed the photograph to her father. The door opened and the woman entered carrying a tray.

"That's my son, Alfred."

"I see," replied Lord Berkeley. As the tea was served in dainty cups, with flowers on, they waited for the moment to talk.

"I do enjoy a bit of company," she said, "but what brings you here, is it my brother?"

"Mrs Horsfield," Lord Berkeley took centre stage. "Twenty four years ago, a young woman came to your house. It would be late at night. She knocked on your door and you found a woman with a small baby." He held his hand up as she went to speak – she had actually spilled her tea as she put the cup down. "Then, I believe, a day later, this woman left leaving the baby with you." Mrs Horsfield began to tremble – this was the moment she had feared for over twenty years. "Is that not so?" Lord Berkeley was a very commanding man. Mrs Horsfield was not used to dealing with aristocracy, but it was Rosie who broke the silence.

"Look Mrs Horsfield, we haven't come as the police or authorities. I need to tell you something. Twenty four years ago, my twin babies were being walked in a perambulator, in the square in London where I live. One of my twins, a boy, George, was snatched, by an unscrupulous crook and a female accomplice. This man tried to blackmail us into paying a large ransom." Mrs Horsfield sat motionless, her hand shaking. Rosie, swallowing back tears, continued. "We tried to pay the ransom and catch the criminal, but unfortunately he was fatally injured, but not before he told us where to find my baby. We went to the address he gave us, but his accomplice, a young woman, had gone – with my baby." Rosie stopped and looked at the woman. "Mrs Horsfield, I don't doubt you have loved that baby, who has now become a man, but tell me you didn't have a knock on the door and that a young woman stood on your doorstep one night, with a baby and we will go away."

Mrs Horsfield shaking all over, took out a grubby handkerchief from her pinafore and dabbed her eyes, then blew her nose.

"Mrs Horsfield, nothing is going to happen, as long as you tell us the truth. We can find out you know," said Lord Berkeley. Mrs Horsfield started to talk very quietly, Lord Berkeley had to lean forward to hear.

"You are right in what you say. She left the baby, we did not know what to do. I contacted my sister who had lost her own baby to pneumonia a few months earlier. We thought God had given us another baby," she began to cry.

"Mrs Horsfield," Rosie took her hand. "Don't upset yourself, all I want to know is where my son is?"

She looked at Rosie. "He's gone," she began to cry again.

"Gone," said Lord Berkeley. "Gone where?" Rosie shook her head. Oh God he wasn't dead. Between sobs, Mrs Horsfield explained how Alfie had come back from the war. A change had occurred, he couldn't settle down, he had nightmares. He decided he had to go away.

"But where did he go?" asked Rosie. Mrs Horsfield looked at Rosie.

"He went to Australia, over four years ago," she sobbed.

"Australia!" said Lord Berkeley incredulously. Rosie sat back flabbergasted. A stunned silence, which was interrupted, as the front door was shut. The door opened and another elderly woman came into the front room. Seeing the people gathered around the room, her eyes lighted on her sister, who was crying.

"What is it? What's happened – is it Alfie?" Mrs Horsfield looked at her sister, who owned the house, and had let her and the baby stay, knowing she loved Alfie as much as she did.

"No, well yes, it's about Alfie, but don't worry, nothing has happened, as far as we know," she went on and told her sister who they were.

Rosie pulled out several cuttings from "The Times" and "The Daily Mirror" and a copy of the advertisement she had published for two years after the kidnapping failed. She handed these to the women. Having read the articles and looked at Rosie's advertisement, Mrs Horsfield turned to them. "But how do we know for certain, Alfie is your baby?"

"That's easy enough, Mrs Horsfield. The evil man who kidnapped my son, cut off the tip of two of his fingers and sent them to me."

Mrs Horsfield shrieked, "God how could he, I am so sorry dear."

"Did the boy you call Alfie have two fingers with part missing?" asked Lord Berkeley.

The women looked at each other. "Tell them."

"Yes he did. When he was left with us, his poor hand was bound up with a dirty rag and when I looked at his hand, I was shocked, but I did not for a moment suspect someone had deliberately cut the little lad."

"Had the fingers been cut from one or both hands?" asked Lord Berkeley as Rosie shut her eyes.

"One hand, the two middle fingers of the left hand," replied Mrs Horsfield.

"The woman who kidnapped our child had distinctive hair, what colour was the hair of the woman who left the child with you?"

They thought for a moment then they both said "Ginger, she had long ginger hair."

"That settles it, Rosie," said Lord Berkeley. "Now tell us about the man you called Alfred."

The women sipped a fresh cup of tea, as one after another they told Rosie and Lord Berkeley about the upbringing of Rosie's son. They explained how he acted, without consulting them, when he joined up. "They," meaning the army, "sent him on special training, he wouldn't talk about what he did." Said Mrs Horsfield. "He came back once, having broken his ankle. Then just before the end of the war, they sent him home, he had been hit by shrapnel."

Rosie's hand involuntarily went to her face as she gasped.

"Oh, don't worry dear, it was a minor wound and totally healed. He did have a bit of a limp though," added Mrs Horsfield.

"Did he give any idea, where in Australia he was going?" asked Rosie.

"No, except he was sailing to Melbourne from Southampton."

"And you haven't heard from him since he left?" asked Lord Berkeley.

"No, we have been very worried, it's not like Alfie. Sorry did you say he was called George?"

Before they left that day, they had a complete history of Alfred Horsfield, Rosie's son George. They heard about Uncle Tyndel, who had taught "Alfie" to box and taken him out on his fishing boat. Tyndel had died last year, leaving Alfie £200 and his fishing boat, which had been hauled up on the beach at Brighton.

Eventually, they left the tiny terraced house and walked back to the station. Rosie felt exhausted and a little deflated, she had really hoped that she was going to be reunited with her son. Lord Berkeley, ever philosophical, said to her "Don't worry darling, he sounds a tough nut, we will find him." And sure enough he began to plan their trip to Australia.

September 1924

As the car pulled off the road into a driveway marked "Horsfield Farm", there was an arrow painted onto a piece of wood, Rosie felt a lump in her throat and clutched her father, Lord Berkeley's hand. Thank God her father was there with her.

The journey had been long and dusty. The Model T Ford they had collected in Melbourne was a new model, only just shipped to Australia. They had left most of their luggage at the Grand Hotel in Melbourne and hired the automobile and driver to take them to Healesville, a few hours drive. The road from Melbourne to Healesville changed dramatically once you left the outskirts of the city. They had decided to travel by automobile, but on reflection, Rosie saw the sense of the Hotel Manager in Melbourne, who had told them that roads were bumpy and dusty and that a horse drawn coach, or riding themselves, would have been a better choice. However, Rosie thinking of her father, had opted for the automobile, but after an hour of bumping up and down on the hard dirt tracks, the springs on the Model T took a battering, she had regretted their decision. Reaching Healesville, a small town consisting of three shops and a loosely termed "hotel", which doubled as a bar and general store, they stopped to make enquiries. Sure enough, the barman, a jovial character - "Call me Kanga, everyone does" - directed them to the Tarrawarra Road. "Go about ten miles toward Yarra Glen and you will find the Horsfield Farm," he said. Their journey to the farm took another hour, Rosie, Edward and Lord Berkeley stepped out of the automobile, just as the front door opened. There, silhouetted in the doorway, was a man in working clothes. Could this be her son, Rosie wondered? Lord Berkeley was the first to address the man.

"Tell me young man, am I speaking to Alfred Horsfield, late of Brighton, England?"

The man looked at the group now gathered on the veranda. Who were they? What did they want? "And who is it, wants to know?" he replied suspiciously.

"Ah yes. This is Mrs Cynthia de Courcy and her son Edward and my name is Lord Berkeley – and you sir?"

The man paused and seemed to make up his mind. "I'm Ginger, Alfie is out on the farm, he won't be back 'til late."

"Who is it, Ginger?" a woman's voice asked. Just then, a young woman, dressed in a pale blue dress joined them at the front door.

"This lady, her son and this man, Lord Berkeley," he paused, almost congratulating himself for remembering his name, "want to see Alfie, they're from England."

The woman looked at them closely, firstly at Rosie, then Lord Berkeley and Edward. "Well you had better come in then." At that she moved aside form the doorway.

Inside the single storey house was a huge room, which you went into straight from the front door.. A number of young children were running around and the woman shouted out, "Calm down all of you and Jess go and put the kettle on." A young aborigine woman went to the kitchen. "Please sit down," she pointed toward a threadbare Chesterfield and two leather armchairs, which had seen better days. "I'm Georgina, Alfie's wife. You have met our business partner, Ginger, and these," she pointed at three children, who were staring at them, "are our children, Alice, Mary, John and our Jess. The oldest is an aborigine we adopted, who has gone to make a cup of tea."

Rosie smiled at the children and that seemed to break the ice. "Is that the new automobile, miss?" asked the boy John, who appeared to be about three years old. Rosie looked at this boy and a lump appeared in her throat – he was the spitting image of George or how she imagined George would have looked at three years of age.

"Yes," she replied. "It is a Ford Model T, would you like to sit inside?" The children all jumped up together.

"Yes please."

"Edward, take the children to the automobile and let them have a look." Edward smiled at the children. "Come on then," he said. Lord Berkeley had been sitting quietly taking in the scene and resting from the bumpy journey.

"Tell me, madam," he asked. "Have you farmed long?" Turning to look at Lord Berkeley, Rosie saw that Georgina was a very attractive woman, with dark hair, trimmed in the style of the fashion houses of the 20's.

"We came here in 1920 from England." The woman Georgina seemed reluctant to give them too much information, but was hospitable scurrying off to check how the tea was coming along.

Ginger just sat staring, first at Rosie, then Lord Berkeley, before he said. "Are you really a Lord then?"

"Yes I am," replied Lord Berkeley. "We have come from England to see Alfred." He decided not to elaborate.

To avoid periods of silence, first Rosie and then Lord Berkeley, asked Georgina and Ginger about life farming in Australia. Rosie was intrigued to hear that Georgina had planted grapevines, which were beginning to establish. The children played around them with Edward, who seemed to be thoroughly enjoying playing with home made toys. They certainly were a happy family, thought Rosie and that oldest boy looks like George, she felt her pulse quicken.

"Ah, here's Alfie now," said Georgina, as a group of riders pulled up outside. Ginger hurried outside, presumably to forewarn Alfie that they had visitors from England. He returned, followed by a tall dark haired man, with fine strong features. His face was very sunburnt which showed the outdoor life he was living. Rosie looked closely at him, her heart was pounding, but it was her father who stood up and moved toward the young man. Rosie hadn't immediately noticed that he was carrying a rifle over his shoulder and as Lord Berkeley moved toward him, he let the rifle slip so that he held it facing her father.

"Now, just who are you people and what do you want?" he asked rather aggressively.

"You look as though you are pointing that rifle at me, young man," said Lord Berkeley. Rosie slipped her hand into the handbag on her lap.

"Just precautionary mate, now who are you?"

"I never answer questions facing a gun barrel, learned that in the war in Africa, how about you?" Georgina moved towards her husband.

"Now come on Alfie, these English people mean no harm, I can tell." Alfie, it seemed to Rosie, reluctantly lowered his rifle, but she noticed he kept hold of it.

"All right, we get nervous in these parts, lots of thieves and braggarts."

"Do we look like thieves?" said Lord Berkeley showing a trace of anger in his voice.

Suddenly Lord Berkeley caught everyone by surprise, producing a pistol; he placed it against the temple of the man, Alfie. "Now drop your rifle, Sir! Kick it over towards my daughter," Rosie had been taken by surprise, but moved swiftly to pick up the weapon and also trained her small Derringer on the other man, Ginger, who stood open mouthed.

Georgina screamed. "What is this, you are welcomed into my home and now you rob us, an old man, a boy and a woman."

"Rob you, no my dear, you have got the wrong end of the stick. I am simply taking precautions. Now let's all sit down shall we?" The three men and Georgina sat down, with Rosie and Lord Berkeley the last to sit, on the two hard seats, brought from the dining table earlier.

"What's this all about?" asked the man, Alfie.

"We will come to the point shortly," replied Lord Berkeley, who looked at the man disdainfully. "Now," he said. "Tell me who you are."

"What do you mean?"

"What's your name and where do you come from?" Rosie noticed her father had only lowered the pistol; he still had it pointing admittedly downward, but in the direction of the man. Alfie looked at the old man in front of him and was clearly contemplating his choices of overpowering this elderly gentleman, then he looked at his wife and the children, who she had clustered around her protectively and he seemingly decided to talk.

Rubbing his arm he said, "My name is Alfred, Alfie Horsfield, I am from Brighton."

"Now sir, don't tell me lies, I may look old, but I am not senile."

"What do you mean?" said Ginger. The first time he had spoken.

"I said this man, is not the Alfred Horsfield we have been expecting to meet," replied Lord Berkeley.

Suddenly the man, Alfie made a lunge for the pistol of Lord Berkeley. Despite his Lordship's age he kept himself fit and neatly sidestepped, the lunging Alfie. "Well," said Lord Berkeley. "You have just confirmed it now, unless you tell us exactly who you are, I intend to tie you and take you to the police authorities, in Melbourne. And before you think you can overpower us, my daughter is an expert shot and has served with bravery in the world war and our driver is also armed." The man Alfie looked up with a sinister look on his face.

"For God's sake Alfie, you are scaring the children, what do these people mean, you are not Alfred Horsfield?" The man calling himself Alfred Horsfield hauled himself to his feet. Rosie raised her Derringer pistol, but he simply sat back on the moth eaten sofa.

"All right, all right I am not Alfred Horsfield."

"You had better tell us who you are," said Lord Berkeley. The man glanced toward his wife, who was looking at him incredulously.

"My name is Malcolm Markham, I am from Cornwall."

"Good that's a start, but why have you taken Alfred Horsfield's identity?" Lord Berkeley's voice seemed to change to anger.

"He insisted."

"What do you mean?" Rosie had left Lord Berkeley to question this man up until now, but she couldn't stop herself. The man calling himself Alfred turned towards her.

"Just as I said, he insisted," he smirked.

"Tell us now, or its Melbourne and jail for you my man," barked Lord Berkeley.

"Well, it was on the ship that we concocted the plan. I wanted to go to Australia to start a new life, but I couldn't."

"Why not?" asked Rosie. The man pretending to be Alfred Horsfield looked at her and then his wife.

"Because I had a criminal record," his wife Georgina gasped. "Hold on,

313

hold on," he said. "It wasn't anything too bad, just thieving and house breaking."

"So," said Lord Berkeley, "you're saying Alfred Horsfield agreed to swap identities? Why would the real Alfred Horsfield agree to do that, what did he stand to gain?"

The man smiled. "He was a bit loopy if you ask me, kept going on about 216 men he had killed, no chance. He said he saw their faces in his sleep and on and on like that. Then he suddenly said to me, perhaps if I change identity with you, I can change my dreams and make a fresh start."

Lord Berkeley sighed and looked at Rosie. It was just what the man was waiting for, he charged at Lord Berkeley, knocking him down onto the floor. The younger man easily overcame her father and reached for the pistol. Suddenly there was a shot. Georgina screamed. The man calling himself Alfred Horsfield looked at Rosie in amazement and then at his shoulder. Blood had started to trickle though a small neat hole in his stained shirt. "Get off my father," she commanded pointing the pistol. "Now you listen. I don't believe a word of your lies, my son would have more to him than that, you have exactly ten seconds to tell me the truth, or I am going to kill you."

His wife screamed out, "For God's sake tell the truth Alfie, or whatever your name is. Do you want your children to see any more violence?"

Holding his wounded arm the man sat up. "All right, let me sit," he got slowly up and fell onto the sofa.

"Now tell," said Rosie moving closer. "I can't miss from here." She raised her small pistol again. Holding his hand over his wounded shoulder, he looked at Rosie.

"It's true I met Alfred Horsfield on the troop ship coming home. I had known him in the trenches, except he was a sniper and I was an ordinary soldier."

"Go on man," Lord Berkeley had now recovered his pistol and was standing out of his reach.

"Well, when we returned to Blighty, I saw a bit of him. He worked with his uncle as a fisherman, off the beach at Brighton. I met him in a pub, called the "Three Feathers," in London Road, Brighton. Often people used to say how alike we looked, almost as though we were brothers. Then one day he told me he was going to Australia. He had got his passport and entry forms and had been accepted for emigration from England. That part of my story was true, I had tried to go myself, but had been rejected on account of nothing, two minor offences and they stopped me going."

"So what happened?" Lord Berkeley was becoming impatient with this man.

"The, real Alfred Horsfield was due to join his ship at Southampton. He had said his goodbyes, but agreed to meet me for a farewell drink, before catching a train from Hove station. We met at a fancy bar on the seafront near the pier; you know the big pier half way along, not the one nearest the town."

"Yes, yes, go on," barked Lord Berkeley.

"Well, we had a couple of tankards of beer and I suggested he go onto the pier and say a last farewell to the sea he had been fishing for the past six months. We went to the end of the pier," he stopped.

"My patience is running thin, I will kill you," said Rosie taking a stance aiming her pistol at the man calling himself Alfred. The man moaned.

"Look I need a doctor."

"Later, what happened on the pier?"

"Yes," said Ginger. "What happened on the pier?"

"I made the mistake of telling Alfie my idea, I was going to pay him with some jewellery I had stolen, but he got angry, told me to bugger off and started to walk away."

"Then, go on, what happened?" said Rosie.

"I hit him over the head, I had a cosh." Rosie flinched; she was a hairs breadth from killing this man.

"Rosie, let him finish," her father had seen the look on her face.

"Well," he paused, "I took the identity papers, the entry certificate, his passport and some money in a packet."

"Then, what did you do?"

"Nothing, I left him. I stuffed my identity card in his pocket."

"What, you didn't know whether he was dead or alive?"

"Somebody was coming, I had to go around the back of some seats, they would have found him."

"You piece of scum," said Lord Berkeley. "You didn't know if he was dead or alive."

Georgina let out a scream, moved across to the sofa and slapped the man impersonating Alfred Horsfield around the face. She looked at Rosie and Lord Berkeley. "I seem to have married a rotten apple."

"Now come on Georgie, we have had a good life."

"Don't talk to me," said his wife, as she cradled her children.

"Come Rosie, we are leaving," said Lord Berkeley. Rosie looked at the man called Ginger on the other side of the room.

"You say this man is your partner?" The man nodded. "Well I suggest you look after this woman," she pointed her Derringer toward the impersonator, and find yourself a new partner."

She went to fire, but her father knocked her hand and the bullet passed harmlessly by the impersonator's shoulder. "No Rosie, no point," Lord Berkeley trained his pistol and said, "You sir, are a lucky man, but I will be informing the authorities in Melbourne of your subterfuge, don't try and follow us or I will kill you, he was my daughter's son, the man you hit in the

315

cowardly way you did, and my grandson. Come Edward," his grandson walked in front of them ashen faced.

In the car Edward said, "Why did you stop mother killing that man Grandfather, he killed my brother."

"Firstly Edward, we don't know George is dead, secondly his punishment should be by the appropriate authorities. In any case he has lost his new life, his wife, his children, he is finished – did you see the look on her face?"

"I see, Grandfather," replied Edward. "When I grow up, I think I will find that man." Lord Berkeley looked at his grandson from a new perspective; he was indeed Count Von Basten's son.

They reached Melbourne without incident, driving into the outskirts as it got dark. "Tomorrow we will go to the police," said Lord Berkeley.

"But he will be gone," said Rosie.

"Yes, I expect he will, but he will be a wanted man and I don't expect his wife will want him to stay around – he will lose everything."

"Come Edward," said Rosie. "There has been enough excitement for one day, sleep now." Reluctantly Edward obeyed his mother.

"And you as well Rosie," said her father. "We have to travel back to England and I think a boat leaves tomorrow."

The following day, Lord Berkeley telephoned the British Ambassador and asked him to pave the way for a visit to the Melbourne Police. His meeting with an inspector of police enabled him to swiftly explain the circumstances of their visit to the impersonator of Alfred Horsfield, a man called Malcolm Markham, now wanted for theft and attempted murder in England. Leaving the police station that day, Lord Berkeley, for the first time, felt his age. When he had thought their search would bring a happy reunion with his grandson George, he had plenty to look forward to, now he ached and felt very tired. Returning to the Melbourne Grand Hotel, Rosie and Edward had packed their trunks. Lord Berkeley had all of their luggage taken to the docks, as they prepared to embark and return to England. As the great ship was manoeuvred along the Yarra River and out into the ocean, they all stood on the upper deck leaning on the rail. "Well we didn't get to see much of Australia," Lord Berkeley looked tired.

"Why don't you go and rest father?" Rosie was concerned her father was looking grey and tired.

"Yes, I think you are right. I will meet you later for dinner."

Rosie kissed her father on the cheek and Edward said "See you at dinner grandfather. Can I walk with you to your cabin?"

"Yes, my boy, delighted to have the company. Reaching his cabin, Lord Berkeley felt very tired and had been glad of the boy's arm. "Don't worry about me Edward, I will rest and see you at dinner."

As dinner approached, Rosie knocked on Edward's door. "Grandfather has not called for us. Come Edward we will knock on his cabin door." They couldn't get an answer and Edward went to find the cabin steward. The steward used his pass key and they entered the cabin. The curtain over the porthole was closed and the room was dark. The steward pulled the curtain and they saw Lord Berkeley in the bed. Rosie gasped and moved to her father's side. "Father, father." Then she felt his hand, he was stone cold and she realised her father had passed away. A tear ran down her face. "Oh, father, there was so much I still wanted to share with you," she cried then. Realising Edward had approached his grandfather, Rosie said, "Grandfather has passed away Edward." Her son looked at his beloved grandfather, then wheeled and rushed out of the cabin. Rosie turned to the steward – "Call a doctor and then the Captain. I will be in my son's cabin."

Edward was crying into his pillow on the bed. Rosie sat by him and let him weep, barely restraining her own tears. Placing her arm around him, she said "Grandfather loved you very much and will always be with you."

Edward turned and through his sobs said "Why do all the people I love have to die mother?"

"I don't know the answer Edward." She hugged her son and began to cry herself. Lord Berkeley's body was moved to the chapel on the ship and then to a cold storage. When they reached Cape Town, a message was sent to the bank and to the household. Rosie knew Middleton who had transferred to the London bank would take over all the arrangements and sure enough, when the ship docked at Southampton, a hearse was waiting to take Lord Berkeley's body to the station. Rosie and Edward met Middleton and they accompanied Lord Berkeley's body to the train and on to London.

A memorial service took place, on the 15th November 1924, at Westminster Abbey. The Prime Minister, James Ramsay Macdonald, did the eulogy and HRH King George V and Queen Mary joined a "whose who" of British aristocracy, actors, actresses, Ambassadors from a dozen countries, the heads of the armed forces and many ordinary people, who paid their last respects, to this much loved and well liked man.

Rosie, her sister Anne, brother Freddie, his wife and their children, sat alongside Edward, Frederick and Lord Berkeley's beloved Sophie, who cried throughout the funeral. The Baron sat with Frederick and was inwardly pleased that the boy showed no emotion. Edward, his son Frederick's bastard and the other child Sophie, cried through the service. Strength, thought The Baron, important in a man. The Countess de Blois was actually quite angry with the Baron and she had told him so, when he had discussed with Frederick the possibility of merging the two great Banks, now Lord Berkeley was dead. As the choir sang part of Bach's requiem, the King and Queen had led the mourners down the aisle, followed by various Lords and Ladies, then close family and the Prime Minister and all of the cabinet, including opposition leaders and other members of parliament.

Rosie and Middleton held a wake at Lord Berkeley's home in Belgrave

Square. The King and Queen attended for a brief period. The King saying to Rosie "England has lost a great man. He was one of the finest men I have ever known." Rosie curtsied and a tear ran down her cheek. The Baron seemed to hold court with most of the Ambassadors and many of the bankers present, but Rosie didn't mind, that's how he was. Edward found himself despising his brother Frederick, all he could talk about was the succession, confident he would shortly inherit the title of Lord Berkeley. The funeral itself was a private family affair. The following day the body of Rosie's father was transported to his estate at Hexham for burial in the private chapel in the grounds. Only immediate family, faithful servants, close friends and employees of the Berkeley Merchant Bank were allowed to attend. His old guards regiment escorted his body to the family graveyard and were resplendent, in red, carrying the coffin. A 42 gun salute was fired in the grounds, the guards had arranged for four field guns to be brought to the estate from a barracks at Colchester. Lillie Langtry, now in her 71st year, made the congregation packed into the chapel, laugh. She told how, on one occasion, Lord Berkeley had had to play Malvolio, the straight laced steward, one of the characters in Twelfth Night, as the actor playing the part had fallen ill at the last minute and his Lordship was the only man around, at the time, who knew the part! When Rosie did her eulogy she spoke of the love for her second father, who she only found when she was in her twenties, but how for thirty years he had been her rock. Sophie and Edward read from the scriptures, tears unashamedly running down both their faces. Private moments were relived of the life of a truly great and well loved man.

Two weeks later, two Bentleys pulled up at the chambers of Stewart, Lander and MacCambie, solicitors in Cheapside, London. The firm were acting for the Executors for Lord Berkeley's estate and had called a meeting. Out stepped Rosie, Edward and Sophie from the first vehicle and Frederick Junior, The Baron and Countess de Blois alighted from the second automobile. Frederick Junior was very excited. Was this the moment he would be declared a Baron "The Right Honourable The Lord Berkeley of Hexham", he day dreamed as the automobiles pulled up in Cheapside.

The Baron, his grandfather, was apprehensive. His solicitor in London had told him that the system of passing hereditary peerages in England, meant that Cynthia, Lord Berkeley's daughter, would receive the title and estates. He already knew that Cynthia was to inherit, in trust, the majority shareholding of the Berkeley's Merchant Bank. This did not concern him, as he knew she was a valuable director of de Courcy's and he needed her connections, linguistic skills and charm, to continue to further the growth of de Courcy's Bank in London and Zurich. In any case, there was still the possibility of a great merger between the English Berkeley Merchant Bank and de Courcy's Bank. The group were ushered into the board room, by Sir

318

Joshua Lander, grandson of one of the founders of the firm of solicitors. The other partners Sir James Stewart and Alistair MacCambie were introduced as they all sat around the huge oak table.

The formalities out of the way, Sir Joshua cleared his throat and then began to read. "This meeting on the 29th November in the year 1924, has been called to read the last will and testament of the Right Honourable The Lord Berkeley of Hexham, who died on the 2nd November 1924." He began to read the will which, on the face of it, looked to be a lengthy document. Rosie sat passively holding Sophie's hand. Sophie had found the death of her grandfather extremely hard. Rosie knew her father had created a bond with her children, even Frederick Junior had been fond of his grandfather, but Sophie and Edward had loved Lord Berkeley as both a father and grandfather, so their intense grief was not a surprise.

Rosie's thoughts had wandered, so she concentrated on the events at hand. Sir Joshua completed the preliminaries, reaching the start of the formal will. "In accordance with the laws of succession, the title will pass to my daughter, Cynthia de Courcy." Sir Joshua paused, Frederick Junior banged his pen on the table, Edward smiled, "who from this day forth shall be known as The Baroness Berkeley of Hexham." He paused ... "The estate at Hexham will pass in trust to my daughter, Cynthia de Courcy, including all the lands and the buildings. The houses at ...." A long list of properties were then read out, all passing to Cynthia de Courcy.

Rosie let slip her façade for one second, as a tear rolled down her cheek. Her father, who had watched over her, loved her and had loved her mother, had made sure after his death that everyone would have no doubt that he regarded her as his legitimate daughter. "All my goods and chattels shall pass to my daughter Cynthia de Courcy." So far, every part of the estate had passed to Rosie. "Concerning my cash assets, stocks and shares and government bonds, these shall pass to my daughter Cynthia de Courcy, except," and there was a pause, "the following amounts I bequeath to my grandsons, Frederick Junior and Edward, I leave in trust the sum of £500,000. To my granddaughter Sophie, I leave the sum of £550,000 in trust. The additional sum is to secure her a fine education, as I have already arranged for her to be accepted at Cambridge, to follow in the footsteps of my beloved granddaughter, Anne. To my great grandchildren, William and Louise, I leave the sum of £250,000 in trust, in equal proportion. I am confident that my grandson George is not dead. I have therefore, left in trust, in his favour the sum of £500,000, which will revert to my grandchildren Frederick Junior, Edward and Sophie and in equal proportion to my great grandchildren, all to receive 25% of the Trust Fund, if my grandson George is not proven alive by the year 1990."

The implication of the wording stunned Rosie. Her father had made certain that the sum of money left in trust for George would not be able to be accessed until George would have been 89 years of age. In effect, he had blocked any attempt to access this money, by any of the other descendants. How clever he was, she thought. "The balance of estate, some £2,000,000, shall pass to my daughter, Cynthia de Courcy outright and not in trust." The solicitor continued. "The trusts in favour of my grandchildren and great grandchildren will prevent access to the capital until they reach thirty years of age, but income may be taken, by agreement of the trustees. The trustees will be Mrs Cynthia de Courcy, now Baroness Berkeley of Hexham, and the firm of solicitors Stewart, Lander and MacCambie and Countess de Blois." The Countess did not look surprised. "Concerning the shares in the Berkeley Merchant Bank," silence enveloped the room. "Ninety percent of the shares, will pass to my daughter Mrs Cynthia de Courcy. Two percent of the shares will pass in trust, to each of my grandchildren Frederick Junior, Edward and Sophie and to my great grandchildren, one each. Two percent of the shares will pass in trust, to my grandson George, when discovered."

The will went on to determine, once again, that the shares in trust, for George would revert to the estate of Cynthia de Courcy in 1990, if he had not been discovered. A considerable number of bequests followed, ranging from household servants, to his old regiment and an endowment for Cambridge University and Eton College of £100,000 each. Sir Joshua concluded the reading of the will.

Frederick Junior wanted to ask some questions, but the Baron had briefed him not to do so at the reading of the will. He was very disappointed. Not only did he not succeed his grandfather's title and lands but the sum, which admittedly was substantial, was held in trust, until he was thirty! He would still have to rely on the paltry salary his grandfather, the Baron, paid him in Swiss Francs – God how would he manage, he owed various money lenders a considerable sum now …

Edward, on the other hand, was delighted. Since the reading of Frederick de Courcy's will, declaring him a bastard child, he had hated the reaction of his half brother. The income from the inheritance from his beloved grandfather, Lord Berkeley, would enable him to chose his career. He rather favoured the military – but now was not the time to talk to his mother.

Rosie got up from the table relieved that her son Frederick Junior had not inherited the title and properties. She knew he loved her, but he had a side to him that was not pleasant. To live with his arrogant behaviour would not have suited her. What would he have done about Edward, Sophie and Anne's dear children? As always her dear father had worked out ideal solutions and had forgotten no-one. How she missed his wise counsel and his love.

Chapter Twenty Seven

Finally

After the excitement of the will, Rosie remained in mourning for her father. He had written a letter shortly before he died which the solicitor, Sir Joshua, had passed to her

'You will be reading this letter as I have died. I am sorry if there is unfinished business, particularly if we haven't found George yet. Yes, I believe George is alive. I write this note knowing we are travelling to Australia and by now we may have found George, I hope so. If not, keep searching, he is the grandson of two aristocratic families, he will be resourceful and strong. Since I came formally into your life, you have allowed me to share your family. I cannot tell you what pleasure and love this has given me.

Just a word now about blood. As much as it grieves me to write this, there is bad blood between Frederick Junior and Edward. Keep a close eye on the situation, because Edward is the stronger and may not always tolerate his brother's attitude toward him.

My dear, I know the reasons you have chosen not to divulge their true father to Edward and Sophie, but I urge you to think again. I know myself how important the love we found, albeit belated, has meant to me and I hope to you. Don't deny a father's love to his child, think again.

The twins may prove to be the cause of heartbreak. I have checked with my lawyers and I am afraid Asmail can return at any time and claim them, taking them to Lebanon or wherever.

I wish I could have lived a little longer to help you through some of these difficult times, but rest assured I shall be there with you in spirit,

I have loved you always, you loving father, Edmund.'

Rosie cried, until she realised her tears were dropping on the letter whilst her father would have wanted her to mourn his passing, most of all he would have wanted her to find George.

She had retained her father's servants at all the houses, including the chauffeur. Sending a message to the mews house where he kept the automobiles, she instructed him to be ready tomorrow to travel to Brighton.

This time the journey to Brighton was full of apprehension. Gone was the steady optimism of her father and his steadfast approach to any situation. But Rosie travelled with a firm resolve – she would find her son.

Reaching 27 Trafalgar Street again, she knocked and was greeted by Mrs Horsfield. Somehow she looked much older, or perhaps she hadn't noticed her grey hair before. It seemed to take her a few seconds to realise who she was and then she was invited inside. Rosie hadn't gone back since returning, unsuccessfully, from Australia. Now she felt guilty. These two women had loved her son, fed him and nurtured him – she owed them a great deal more than words can say.

Both women were home so she briefly recounted the trip to Australia. The disappointing discovery of the impersonator of George (Alfie to them), the despicable Malcolm Markham. There was no point leaving out the incident when George was coshed on Brighton Pier, in fact the women may be able to use their local connections to find out what happened after that.

Finally, as she left the women she told them about the death of her father. Mrs Horsfield, looking at her mysteriously, said. "Don't worry dear, he is still with you."

After her visit to Mrs Horsfield, Rosie decided to go to the local hospital – Brighton General Hospital. A rather brash receptionist didn't seem to want to help hunt through records of people brought into the hospital four years ago, so Rosie asked to see the Matron. Matron was more receptive to meeting Baroness Berkeley of Hexham. A brusque and businesslike woman she readily agreed to arrange for the records to be scrutinised – could The Baroness come back at 10 am tomorrow?

Then Rosie went to Brighton Police Station. Once again her card gained her a meeting with the senior officer. The superintendent in charge listened silently to Rosie's account of the events in 1919 that had changed the life of her son. He examined the letter from the Australian police. Just as well her father had insisted that his conversation with the Chief of Police in Melbourne had been recorded. The Superintendent nodded, calling to a sergeant in his outer office, he instructed him to search police records for any information on an incident on the West Pier and also for details of a certain 'Malcolm Markham'. Rosie was asked to return tomorrow.

Rosie had booked into 'The Grand Hotel' on Brighton seafront. The Grand Hotel was a splendid hotel and if you had a front bedroom, you could see the sea. It was lavishly decorated, with impressive glass chandeliers hanging from the high ceiling. Rosie had a light meal before retiring but her thoughts had turned to Edward as she remembered the words of wisdom her father, Lord Berkeley had written. She must ask the Count to come to England, so she could formally tell Edward, who had been pressing her for some time, who his real father was. Likewise, the American, Tore is due with his usual deposit for the de Courcy bank in a few months, she would ask him to come to London and introduce him to Sophie. None of this would be easy she thought. The risk was one or other of her children would blame her for not telling them about their father earlier. It was easier to do nothing, but then the words her father had written kept coming back to her and she resolved to tell both her children.

The Grand Hotel was aptly named, thought Rosie. She had enjoyed her kippers for breakfast and now her chauffeur drove her to Brighton General

Hospital, for her meeting with Matron. The sky was grey, a typical December day, promising showers or even heavy rain. Luckily, Rosie had instructed her chauffeur that they would travel to Brighton in the Model T Ford. Slower than the Bentley Coupé, but at least they wouldn't have to dress in waterproof clothing in the open top Bentley.

Matron was waiting for Rosie at the reception and after the initial courtesies, showed her into an office on the ground floor. Tea was brought and after serving, Matron took out a green folder from the desk drawer. She put on a pair of spectacles and began reading.

"Ah yes," she looked up at Rosie. "We have found a man called Malcolm Markham," she paused. "He was brought in by the police suffering from concussion – it seems he had a head wound and was found by a man walking his dog on the West Pier. We kept him in for three days," she turned a page. "U'm he seemed to have amnesia. He couldn't remember his name or what he had been doing on the West Pier. He was a fit young man in his twenties, he had been treated for a gunshot wound or shrapnel wound to his side. Other than his apparent amnesia, he was perfectly healthy."

"What happened then, you say he was discharged after three days."

"Yes, our records show that when he dressed he was arrested by the police."

"What!" Rosie was taken aback by this answer.

"That's all the file shows I am afraid." Seeing Rosie looking disappointed Matron then said, "But I have found a nurse who was on duty when he was brought in and during his period with us." She got up went to the door. "Charge Nurse Coulton please come in."

A tall, thin woman, in her mid to late 30's came in and was invited to sit. She was introduced to The Baroness and they shook hands. The nurse seemed unsure of what she was doing here, but Matron, looking down over her spectacles, got straight to the point.

"Nurse you remember, I discussed with you a young man who was brought here in November 1919, a Mr Malcolm Markham?"

"Yes, I remember him," the nurse replied. "He had the tips missing from the top of two fingers and I was curious as to how that had happened."

"Did he tell you?" asked Matron.

"No, he didn't seem to remember anything."

"So what treatment did he receive?" asked Rosie.

"One of our psychiatrists, Dr Mornay, saw him several times," replied Matron looking at the file notes.

"And his conclusion?" asked Rosie.

"Dr Mornay thought he genuinely had lost his memory and it would come back to him, given time," replied Matron.

"But you discharged him," said Rosie. The nurse looked at Matron for her comment.

"Yes, we were desperate for the beds, more and more soldiers were being transferred from Army Hospitals back to their local hospital, we simply had no room," replied Matron.

"Do you remember the police arriving to take him away?" Rosie looked at the nurse.

"No, I wasn't on duty that morning, but I did talk to Gladys Lupton, who was on duty and she told me that two policemen had come and arrested him, she didn't know what for, The poor man seemed totally confused," said the nurse.

"Did he say anything, anything at all?" asked Rosie.

The nurse thought for a moment. "Well he was such a good looking man that we, us nurses, did spend time with him," she blushed.

"Go on," said Matron rather sternly.

"It's just," she paused. "He talked in his sleep."

"What did he say?" asked Rosie.

"Well mostly it was incoherent, but he did have terrible nightmares, about shooting someone."

"That's all?"

"Yes, oh and the name, what was it?" She sat trying to remember. "I'm sorry, I can't remember – it was a strange sounding name but … I am sorry."

"Not to worry, Nurse Coulton, you have been most helpful." Rosie got up from her seat and the nurse left. "Well thank you Matron for all your help, I am arranging for my secretary to send the hospital a small donation, please use it as you think fit."

Matron gushed as she thanked Rosie and showed her to her car. "If anything else comes to mind I will contact you," said Matron and at that Rosie walked to her car and instructed her chauffeur to take her to Brighton Police station.

Rosie had telephoned, from The Grand Hotel, the Chief Constable of the Sussex Constabulary and asked him to contact the local station and, sure enough, the Sergeant on the front desk, clearly was expecting her. "Come this way Lady Berkeley." He led Rosie to an office on the first floor, knocked and introduced her. "Chief Inspector Hulme, Baroness Berkeley of Hexham."

Rosie smiled to herself, she still wasn't used to the grand title and found different reactions from people. This Chief Inspector was a dour man, in his fifties, not inclined to 'cow tow'. Rosie remembered her mother's expression which suited the occasion perfectly.

"Please sit down Lady Berkeley," then he asked rather abruptly. "Would you like tea?"

"No thank you," replied Rosie. She unzipped her leather carrying case. "Has the Superintendent had any success?" Rosie referred to her meeting yesterday with the other officer.

"Yes, he is sorry he has had to go on an urgent matter," the Chief

Inspector looked somewhat doubtful, as he explained the absence of his superior officer. "Let's see now," he looked at a sheet of white paper on the desk in front of him. "Yes, a man, Malcolm Markham was arrested at 9 am on Thursday the 9th November 1919 and was charged with possession of stolen property."

Rosie sat back, taking in what he had just said. "What stolen property Inspector?" She deliberately dropped his rank. She didn't like this man whose finger nails were bitten down to the quick. He looked at a file.

"A diamond and ruby ring, mam." He continued reading. "The officer who attended an incident on the West Pier, Brighton on the 5th November 1919, searched a man for identity papers and discovered, secreted on his person, the said gold, diamond ring. He was suspicious how this man had obtained the ring and following enquiries at the station, discovered such a ring had been stolen from Ambury House, the house of Sir Reginald and Lady Alton in Hove." He read on. "Ah yes, here we are. That evening, Lady Alton was shown the gold, diamond ring and identified it as a ring her mother had passed to her shortly before her death; the ring was valued, for probate, at £500." The Chief Inspector took a sip of tea. "Now then, let's see … Yes the man was identified from an army pay book in his pocket, as Malcolm Markham, with an address in Bognor Regis," he carried on. "On checking the said Malcolm Markham to see if he had a criminal record, we found he had served six months at Lewes Prison in 1912, his date of birth was 7th October 1894, dark hair, blue eyes and there was the photograph." He paused. "We therefore charged Malcolm Markham on the 9th November 1919, with possession of stolen property. He was bound over in custody, for trial at Lewes Crown Court. His trial took place on the 1st December that year – he was found guilty and received a sentence of one year in Lewes prison."

"Was there any suggestion that the man might be suffering from amnesia?" asked Rosie. He looked at the file and read the interrogating officers notes.

"Yes, he claimed he couldn't remember his name or what he was doing on the West pier. Clearly the jury did not believe him."

"Did someone represent him?" again he looked through his file.

"Yes, he was appointed Lewis Rawlins & Shephard, a Lewes solicitor."

Rosie thought she had obtained all the information she could, but suddenly thought. "Obviously this man was released four years ago. Have you any record of him since?"

"No, checked that, he has been clean since," he replied.

Rosie stood up, thanked the Chief Inspector for his help and left.

As they drove away, back to the Grand Hotel, Rosie was already deciding to visit the solicitor in Lewes and the prison. Reaching 'The Grand' she asked her chauffeur to bring the car back at 2 pm and walked through the elaborate swing door at the front of the hotel. Using the hotel's telephone,

Rosie then began a series of telephone calls. She had earlier arranged for the Chief Inspector to get her an appointment tomorrow at the prison. Now she obtained the telephone number of the solicitor in Lewes, from the hotel receptionist and telephoning made an appointment to call before her visit to at the prison. There was nothing more she could do today and looking out of the window decided to take the air.

Walking along the promenade, at Brighton beach, Rosie was blown by a blustery wind and showers, but enjoyed the fresh air – it gave her time to think. Poor George had clearly suffered – she must find him.

The following morning the Model T Ford, much admired by the doorman at the Grand Hotel, headed toward Lewes. "About nine miles," said the Concierge when she had earlier enquired for directions to the prison.

Thirty minutes later, arriving at Lewes Prison, Rosie saw the prison was a typical old Victorian Prison, with high imposing walls, with that grey look she had seen at Pentonville and Holloway. Passing through the outer gate and showing her card, she was escorted to the governor's office. The Governor, Mr Pinson was a portly man, dressed in a smart dark blue suit, who offered her tea, which she accepted. "Now, how can I help, Lady Berkeley?" The Chief Constable had also telephoned Pinson, the prison governor, as he was a fastidious man who liked everything 'official'.

"The Chief Constable has briefed you that I am looking for information about a man you knew as Malcolm Markham". The governor nodded and produced the customary manila folder. He read the first page which he seemed to read twice before he said.

"Malcolm Markham served one year, no parole, for receiving stolen property. He was released on the 1st December 1920. He did his sentence with little trouble, although he was reputed to have knocked a man out on E Wing, but no internal charges were laid against him".

"Do you know where he went when he left prison?"

"He was given five shilling by the Salvation Army, who seemed to believe the story he had maintained, since he was convicted."

"Sorry, what story?"

"Well – he maintained he was not Malcolm Markham, but another man whose name he couldn't remember. We thought he was a little ...." He pointed his finger towards his head.

Seeing no further information was likely to be forthcoming, Rosie excused herself and went to Lewes High Street to meet Mr Barry Shephard, the senior partner of Lewis, Rawkins and Shephard, solicitors.

Mr Shephard, a dapper man in his sixties, put on his spectacles, as he examined the file in front of him. "Markham – Malcolm, yes an interesting case. The police relied on the evidence of a ring discovered on his person and the jury convicted. Due to his past transgression, he was given a one year sentence at Lewes Prison."

"Yes, thank you I have been to the prison and seen the governor. Tell me who represented him at the trial?"

Barry Shephard looked through the pages. "Ah, here it is – Miss Susan Murchison, a barrister from chambers in Brighton."

"That's interesting, she must have been one of the very few women practising."

"Yes, I believe, at that time, she was a recent graduate of Oxford University."

"Where can I find her?"

The elderly man left the room and returned with a sheet of white headed notepaper. Rosie thanked him and left. Reaching 'The Old Steyne, Brighton', Rosie alighted from the automobile and went up the short flight of steps. Entering the foyer of the offices, in this regency building, a young woman asked if she could help. Rosie introduced herself and quickly ascertained that Susan Murchison was indeed in chambers at the moment and went off to announce Rosie's presence. Moments later an attractive young woman, with dark hair in a bun, approached.

"Lady Berkeley, my name is Susan Murchison, would you come this way please." They went into a large room, with dark oak panelling on four walls. In the centre of the room was a large oak board room table which smelled of wax polish and was surrounded by leather chairs.

"Please sit down, Lady Berkeley." Tea was offered but declined by Rosie.

"How can I help you?" The young lady looked quizzically at Rosie. Rosie recounted the story of how a young man was found on the West Pier, searched by police, found to have stolen goods and after a short hospital stay, was held on remand and then tried and convicted. "And you defended that young man, Miss Murchison. His name was supposed to be Malcolm Markham, but in fact he was really at that time Alfred Horsfield." The young girl went pale. "Are you alright, dear?" asked Rosie

"Yes, yes I am fine. The information you have just told me accounts for a great deal. Let me explain. I remember this trial, it was my first case. The man was apparently suffering from amnesia, but no one believed him. I brought the doctor from the hospital as a witness. He thought the amnesia was genuine. Unfortunately, the police had discovered stolen property on him and this was damming. The jury found him guilty of receiving stolen property and he was sentenced to one year in Lewes Prison."

"Did you have any contact with him after he was incarcerated?" The young woman thought for a moment and then made up her mind.

"Yes, as a matter of fact I did. I felt sorry for him. I believe he had lost his memory, so I visited him."

"Did he regain his memory?"

"No, and after twelve months, he was released, having served his sentence."

Rosie looked at this young woman and sensed there was more than she had told her. "Where did he go when he left prison, do you know?"

Miss Murchison looked at Rosie. "Look don't mind me asking, but why all these questions?"

Rosie took out several cuttings from her handbag and passed them across the desk. Miss Murchison began reading and then put them down on the table.

"What are you telling me?"

Rosie told her the story and filled in the gaps about how Lord Berkeley and herself had traced her lost son to Brighton, twenty years after his kidnapping. She explained how they had journeyed to Australia, hoping to find George, her son, but had discovered an impostor who had stolen the identity of Alfred Horsfield. Rosie stopped to let the story sink in, before continuing.

"Unfortunately my father, Lord Berkeley, died on the return journey, but I have been pursuing what happened to the man called Alfred Horsfield and now I know – he was wrongly imprisoned as the thief, Malcolm Markham."

"This is incredible," said Miss Murchison. "My brother is due to meet me for lunch shortly; will you wait a few minutes, as there is more we can tell you?"

Rosie was shown to a more comfortable chair in a nearby room and brought tea. Ten minutes later, Miss Murchison came back accompanied by a tall young man with ginger hair.

"This is my brother Matthew." The young barrister told her brother the story the Baroness had explained in its shocking detail.

"Well I always knew he was a good sort," said Matthew.

"Tell the Baroness where he is now Matthew."

He looked at her, reticent to add more bad news. "He's gone I am afraid."

"Matthew explain." He looked at his sister appealingly.

"When the man we knew as Malcolm left Lewes Prison, my sister tried to help him. She found him lodgings in the village where I work at Lindfield, some ten miles north of here. I found him a job as an agricultural labourer. We got to know him very well over the next two years and he settled into village life. Then one day he was riding out to oversee the movement of some cattle, when he was thrown by his horse."

"Go on Matthew, get to the point," urged his sister.

"He hit his head on a fence post, was found unconscious and taken to the cottage. They sent for me, I am the local doctor you see. As I came into the bedroom he stirred, opened his eyes and said something, I thought very strange at the time."

"What did he say?"

"He said, I am not Markham, I know who I am." I settled him down, as best I could and left for the night, when I was satisfied he was recovering."

"You left him alone?"

"Well no, my sister had arrived, she stayed with him."

"You stayed with him?" Rosie looked at this girl, who looked sheepish.

"Yes I did. I had formed," she paused, "an attachment for Malcolm, sorry George, and when I heard from my brother, he telephoned me from the Rose and Crown and told me he had been injured, I got the train to Lindfield that evening."

"Please continue, Miss Murchison."

"Well, I arrived as my brother had decided his patient was sleeping and was going for some food at the Rose and Crown. I went upstairs and sat with him," she continued. "He slept fitfully, talking about the war and an uncle, it sounded like Tyndall, and then he woke up, as daylight streamed on through the window."

"You had sat with him all night?"

"Yes."

"What did he say when he woke up?"

"He said he was hungry. I went downstairs and found no food in the larder. This was not unusual, as he took most of his meals at the Rose and Crown. I went to the pub to get some bread and eggs. When I returned, much to my horror, he was gone."

"Gone – gone where?"

"I rushed out looking for him but to no avail. We have," she looked toward her brother, "been looking for him for two days."

Rosie got up from her chair. "You say he mentioned Tyndall and seemed lucid at the time?"

"Yes," the girl replied.

"Right, that's my first stop then. Trafalgar Street, where the family who brought him up live – he had an Uncle Tyndall, you see."

"Can I come with you?" Miss Murchison asked.

Rosie looked at this young woman. "Yes, I would welcome the company."

Rosie, accompanied by Susan Murchison, knocked on the door in Trafalgar Street. There was a shuffle of feet and Mrs Horsfield opened the door.

"Ah, Mrs de Courcy." She seemed quite lucid this time and Rosie didn't bother to correct her on her new title. "Come in. I have been expecting you."

Rosie and Susan entered the small terraced house and were shown into 'the front room', which was how Mrs Horsfield described her best room.

"Would you like tea?"

Both women declined, preferring to quickly find out if Alfred (now George to both Rosie and Susan) had been to see her.

"I knew you would come to see me. Thank you for your note explaining what a ghastly trick had been carried out by that rogue …," Mrs Horsfield paused to remember his name. Rosie hadn't sent a note explaining why she hadn't come to see her after arriving back in England but had visited a few days ago – it seemed Mrs Horsfield was losing her memory. "My condolences for the loss of your father," Mrs Horsfield continued. Rosie nodded and waited patiently. "Yes, Alfred, oh I am sorry, I shouldn't keep calling him that."

"That's fine Mrs Horsfield. I understand and please continue. You were saying he came back and were about to tell us something?"

Mrs Horsfield seemed to be searching her memory.

"Yes, Alfred came back the day before my sister's birthday, let me see that would be two days ago." She looked at them both. "But he's gone again."

Rosie could see that she had to coax the information out of Mrs Horsfield and asked. "Did he say where he was going?"

"Yes, something about tracking down a man called," she paused "Markham and taking his name back. I must admit he explained things to me but I didn't really follow and I forgot to tell him about you."

Mrs Horsfield had clearly deteriorated considerably since Rosie had last seen her and it was clear she was having trouble remembering things.

"Did he, by any chance, mention how he was going to trace Markham?" asked Susan.

Mrs Horsfield looked at her, "And who did you say you were, dear?"

Rosie interrupted. "Mrs Horsfield, did Alfred tell you exactly where he was going?"

She thought for a second and then nodded. "Southampton, he was going to London to get a passport and then to Southampton."

Both women instantly knew that George had put two and two together and had realised Markham had sailed to Australia on his ticket. Excusing themselves they went back to the car.

"What do you intend doing?" asked Susan.

"I am going to Southampton to try and find him, before he boards a ship, as I suspect he will go to Australia."

"May I come? I know what he looks like now."

Rosie thought for a moment, yes it would be useful, she nodded.

The car dropped them at Hove Station and as they walked along the platform, Susan told Rosie about the two years since George had left prison. He had fitted perfectly into an agricultural life and old Farmer Simmons apparently found him indispensable now. Rosie was beginning to like this girl. They decided the quickest way to Southampton was by train and made enquiries at Brighton Station. There was a London to Southampton train, stopping at Hove station, in forty five minutes – plenty of time. Rosie had already instructed her chauffeur to return to London, and the two women waited for the train.

Just over two hours later they were at Southampton station. A horse drawn cab then took them to the docks. Rosie's new status and her card got them into the harbourmaster's office, where enquiries confirmed that SS Athena was leaving for Australia, via Cape Town in three hours and no, there had not been any other sailing in the past three days to Australia. Checking the passenger list Susan found Mr A Horsfield.

"He's here," she said excitedly.

"Come then, there's no time to waste!"

The women left the office, escorted by a clerk and were shown to the docks, where a large liner was loading and passengers were still milling around. The clerk explained to the officer on the bottom of the gangplank, that they were looking for a passenger, Mr A Horsfield. The officer, a young man with bushy sideburns, examined the passenger list.

"Yes, he has boarded – he is in second class, cabin 72."

They asked a seaman on the deck where cabin 72 was in second class. He offered to show them the way and minutes later, with trepidation, Rosie knocked on the cabin door – no answer.

"He must be up on deck," said Susan and they returned to the upper deck.

"You go that way and I will go this," said Rosie pointing aft. "I'll find you if you're talking to him." The women separated and Rosie started walking around the upper deck. A few minutes later, she spotted Susan coming from the opposite direction.

"Nothing, he's not on this deck," said Susan.

A cabin steward was showing some passengers to their cabins, when Rosie said, "Excuse me, is there another deck, we are looking for someone who is probably leaning on the rail, but he is not on this level?"

The man looked curiously. "Yes, go up those stairs," he pointed to a metal staircase. "There is an upper observation area, he might be up there."

They climbed the metal stairway and reached a semi-circular observation area, just below the bridge. There were a number of couples up there and one solitary figure, gazing into the distance. Immediately Susan said. "There he is." George heard Susan's voice and turned. Rosie nearly fainted, the likeness to her father, Lord Berkeley was uncanny.

Susan ran toward George and he smiled.

"I know you realise you are not Malcolm Markham, but there is another, even bigger surprise for you – can I introduce Baroness de Courcy."

George turned toward the middle aged woman, who stood before him with tears streaming down her face.

"Madam what is it?" He pulled out a handkerchief and passed it to her. Rosie looked at him, dabbed her eyes and replied.

"I have a great deal I must tell you and quickly, as the ship sails in under two hours. Let us go to a lounge to talk."

The next hour was spent convincing George he was not Alfred Horsfield and dealing with his shock. Rosie told him about Australia, even about shooting the impostor, he looked at her in a new light after that. Carefully, Rosie explained what had happened, not denigrating The Horsfields, who after all had cared for him and loved him.

George sat shocked by these revelations, but it was Susan who said. "Please don't go looking for this man, George. He has already paid the price and is a wanted man." He looked at her and it was clear to Rosie, George loved this woman. He held her hand.

"How can I go now – there is so much to find out, so many people to meet," he looked at his mother, "and I need to spend time with my family and also see my …," he stopped in mid sentence. "I am sorry it will take a while to get used to my mother not being a Horsfield."

"Don't worry George," replied Rosie. "We have all the time in the world."

Acknowledgements and Notes.

Marie York and Sarah Cheeseman who edited my book and Fran who typed my manuscript.

Information on the period was found on the internet and by reading a number of interesting and informative books including, "The Womens Century" by Mary Turner," England –A century of Change" by R. J. Unstead, "The Edwardian Country House" by Juliet Gardiner, "Between The Wars 1919-1938" first published by the Daily Express author not known ,"Britain, Then And Now" by Philip Ziegler.

Forgive my literary license as the first woman Barrister to practise in England was in 1922 – Legal Pioneer Helena Normanton (1882–1957).

Also – before October 1920 women were not allowed to matriculate (i.e to become members of a University) or to graduate. From the late 1870's women had attended lectures, taken examinations, and had gained honours in those examinations. They were however, unable to receive the degree for which they studied, which had they been men, their examination would have entitled them. (Oxford University Archives)

In 1900 the Olympic Games in Paris were the first that women were allowed to compete.

Ted York's Next Novel:
Death is a Certainty

A ruthless team of ex-KGB agents, led by the Russian Katya, are murdering British citizens - why?

Until one of the Russians targeted James Harriman it had been all too easy to kill these elderly people.

Colonel James Harriman is a retired SAS officer, now running his own security consultancy and he didn't appreciate the attempt on his life! Why was someone trying to kill him? Was the past catching up?

Colonel Harriman enlists the help of his friends in the security services and discovers a sinister hit squad.

The Prime Minister wants the deaths kept secret but when several of Harriman's men are killed there will be no easy way out.

What is the connection between the deaths of so many elderly people?

Who's next?

Go to Ted's website - www.tedyork.co.uk